The Things We Bring To The Table

The Things We Bring To The TABLE

A NOVEL

ROD PALMER

Black Wren Press
Columbia, SC

BLACK WREN PRESS LLC

LIBRARY OF CONGRESS CATALOGING-IN-PUBLICATION DATA

Names: Palmer, Rod, author.
Title: THE THINGS WE BRING TO THE TABLE/ Rod Palmer
Description: [South Carolina] : Black Wren Press [2022]
Identifiers: ISBN(Trade Paperback) 979-8-9864282-0-8
ISBN (ebook) 979-8-9864282-1-5
LC record available at https://lccn.loc.gov/
LC ebook record available at https://lccn.loc.gov/

International edition

Printed in the United States of America

This is a work of fiction. All characters, organizations, and events portrayed in this novel are either products of the author's imagination or are used fictitiously.

The foreignness of what you no longer are
or no longer possess lies in wait for you in
foreign, unpossessed places.
—Italo Calvino, *Invisible Cities.*

The ability of writers to imagine what is not
the self, to familiarize the strange and mys-
tify the familiar, is the test of their power.
—Toni Morrison.

Chapter 1

The Backstory

The resemblance is uncanny. Filth and grassy hair aside, the woman emerging on the doorcam video is the feature vocalist of The V.V.S. Band, Lucretia Hughes, better known by her stage name, Lulu McQueen. There's a scratch by her sideburn from which dried blood-tracks contour over her cheeks as if she'd been lying face down for quite some time.

Lulu hurries nimbly up the porch steps, overwhelmed, like a castaway's dirt-caked astonishment of finding civilization – of finding herself now on the brink of rescue from a death she once thought imminent. Her blood-dyed palm abuses the doorbell, leaving DNA to match against the hairbrush sample her mother would deliver to the precinct.

She comes right up on the doorcam, unaware she's being filmed, glancing back over each shoulder. Her brow wrinkles. Something's off: the residents taking too long; the house too quiet. Lulu puts an ear to the door and holds her breath to mute the sound of her own breathing. There's no stirring inside, just the TV left on, in what's probably an empty house.

Hope of someone answering the door is costing precious time. Hope is the proverbial limb Lulu must gnaw away and leave in the snare if she intends to hobble on and survive the night. She chokes down that one hard gulp that precedes plunging face first into the unknown, but the instant Lulu twitches to run, she freezes mid-action, blurred by the butterfly effect of the paused video.

The remote-control lowers on the arm of Detective Ryan, who appears to have stepped out of a television detective series from the eighties, with his clean-shaven cleft chin and thick mustache. He sits across from the prime suspect, Charlene Hamilton, the mayor's daughter, who sits upright in truculent southern piety. Detective Ryan says, "I get it – how you must feel about Miss Lulu Hughes, for effectively running off with your groom. Still, I figured that, on some basic human level, you might find this video disturbing," he says. "Seems you enjoyed it."

Charlene, gazing at the paused video, submits, "Gotta hand it to her. That performance… Oscar-worthy."

"Performance? You didn't see her bleeding from the face? Do you really think she'd put her mother and twelve-year-old daughter through a scare like this?"

Charlene tires already of the questions. She's here merely as a show of humility, to purport that she is not, in fact, above the law. She is without legal counsel, to lend the perception that she has nothing to hide. Charlene waves a lazy backhand. "Mark my word: it's a stunt, coming after Russ put an end to their little whatever, and came crawling back to me. Either that, or she just wants publicity for her little concert."

Ryan's brow lifts in delightful confusion; mockery posing as fascination. "Russ came back crawling, to you?"

"If he told you any different, he's a damn lie."

Detective Ryan clears his throat. "I'll just say that your fiancé has this funny way of saying by not saying. You see, the things he didn't say makes me think, maybe you were the chess move, so that Russ could, by way of marriage, stand to inherit two empires." Detective Ryan, over a gentle palm, offers, "The affair was your doorway out – unless you prefer being just a wax seal on a social contract between two wealthy men: your father,

Wade Hamilton, entrusting the care of his legacy to Russ Rutledge."

Charlene looks away as if the detective's cynicism is a hot oven, but her eyes cut back to him, emblazoned with this warning: "I'm here to answer questions – not to sit here and be insulted. Do keep in mind, detective, that I can make one phone call from the parking lot, and by the time I reach my doorstep at home, you'll be cleaning out your desk."

Detective Ryan smirks at the find, because beneath every threat lay the insecurity he could use to break a suspect. "Be that as it may, I'd much rather be the one serving such a dish, than be the one having to eat it." Ryan huffs. "One phone call, you say? You're not as impressive as you think. You could've followed your father into politics – would've made the old man proud, but no. You want the easy route, to be a kept woman, your appointment calendar scribbled with spa days, shopping, brunch and sangrias with Fran Haulsey and them." Ryan dips to keep eye contact with Charlene, who looks down in shame. Ryan adds, "Russ doesn't have to say it... It takes only a man to see that, in marrying a woman like you, love is the casualty – a casualty Russ thought he could stomach, until about a month ago when he finally happened to run into Lulu, his old flame – his ex-wife, in fact–"

"–A cokehead and unfit mother," Charlene boasts. "What can a woman like her possibly bring to the table?"

"No man ever fell in love with a table, Miss Hamilton. He doesn't even look at that table if his heart is full," Ryan says, with the conviction of a man who has walked away from a full table himself. He says, "You've been Russ's girlfriend – more off than on – for a decade, for good reason, Miss Hamilton. This wedding was out of obligation, but Lulu made him forget y'alls title of love and remember the feeling of love... the passion... like hot sauce in his veins."

Charlene leans under a fresh new perspective. "So, this is what you do? Pound away at a person's insecurities, send them reeling to explain themselves right smack into the bombshell confession? Sorry to disappoint you, Ryan. I can't confess to something I didn't do." She crosses her legs. Eyeing the cigarette pack in Ryan's shirt pocket, she says, "Spare me one, will ya, if that's allowed in here." The detective taps one out of the pack for Charlene, lights it, then whips the chrome lighter back to his pocket.

Charlene takes a long draw and then deflates in a cloud of smoke. "You've got a whole grown-assed man in custody, right now. Found him near the scene, shirt ripped half off his body and you're wasting time in here chatting with me."

"I'm not trying to hem you up, miss, I swear. I'm offering you the advantage of being first." Ryan, observing Charlene's irreverent disbelief, shrinks between two earnest palms. "Seriously, I've seen it – I don't know how many times. The one who talks first gets to control the narrative. You go second, and everything you say seems retaliatory, which is especially bad for you, being that the only known person with a motive – and a damn good one – is you. Osman has no reason to harm a hair on Lulu's head, but for that cloud of debt hanging over his. Word is that he's got bank debt, family debt, street debt, and even casino debt; ungodly amounts. Had to be one hell of a slick talker to borry that kinda money, but now he won't talk at all – can't talk, it seems."

Confusion and humor mixes in Charlene's face. "So, you think I'm paying his debt for him to kidnap Lulu? Well, if you all got the sense to put together such a theory, then tell me how is it that you all lack the sense to figure maybe he was near the scene because he was helping Lulu. Maybe she's paying him?"

"Paying him with what? Lulu's 'bout broke as a joke."

"Broke? There is no such a thing to a woman." Charlene peeps the detective's confusion, and rolls her eyes at it. She elaborates by slapping both palms on the desk, lifting herself out of her chair, and leaning over the support of locked elbows. "A woman, Detective Ryan, is never without means," she says, with a surly underbite.

Facing Charlene's perfumed cleavage, the logic erects in his mind.

Charlene smooths her dress under her, quite ladylike, as she lowers into her seat. "Lulu was hell-bent on stopping my wedding. I have texts of Lulu threatening to harm herself. Said if she can't have Russ in this life, she'll 'have him in the next.'" Charlene gathers her hands on the tabletop in rest, along with her case.

Ryan turns an ear to her. "All this time, and you're just now mentioning texts? Lemme see 'em, for God sakes."

Charlene is bashful, suddenly. "Well, now, the thing is... That string of texts is from a broader conversation – personal matters that I will not have go down in a statement and end up in the papers. You know Charleston is to gossip, as a hog is to slop... My lawyer will turn over the messages once she can protect my personal business as much as the law will allow." Detective Ryan tries responding, but Charlene cuts him off. "I've said too much already, and I won't say another word more, absent of legal counsel." She's pulls her purse strap over her shoulder.

Detective Ryan raises a hand to halt her. "Miss Hamilton. You act as if there idn't a life at stake. I'm not asking you to submit the texts into evidence or nothing. Just let me see, just in case—"

The room door bursts open. Without even a glance, Ryan yells, "I'm busy!" After a half-beat of not hearing the door close, Ryan turns.

A young, wide-eyed cop says, "Mr. Osman's finally talking, but he's talking crazy – saying he's an angel."

Charlene produces a smile, to which Detective Ryan points a finger. "Oh, believe me, you won't be smiling for long."

Charlene blows a plume of smoke in Ryan's face. "Thanks for the cigarette, detective."

Ryan, shaking his head, enters the hallway to go question Mr. Osman.

Chapter 2

Mrs. Rutledge

In this life, Lucretia Hughes-Rutledge, better known as Cree, has everything a woman would want. She has wealth, purpose, the admiration of her community, and to top it off, she has her hot husband – Mr. July on the fund-raising calendar she published a while back: Russ Rutledge.

Her abundance is on full display. There's a ribbon cutting ceremony for her charitable foundation's new building. Cree only wishes her mother were still alive to see her taking the stage as the woman of the hour. Her mother is present both in spirit, and etched in the face of Cree's beautiful twelve-year-old daughter, Meryl, who sits in the audience between her grandparents on Russ's side of the family.

Cree approaches the podium before an audience of who's-who onlookers, each one flush with either admiration or envy. Mayor Childress adjusts the microphone for Cree and then steps aside.

Throughout the speech, Russ is her biggest supporter. Her speech is short but, as always, poignant; circling the landing in themes of family and community, but not without asking her wealthy peers to go into their wallets. "In the brochures we've handed out, you'll find an envelope for donations. When you write the check, I ask you to think about the future of this non-profit organization – not the past, when we were a school supply drive, operating from a trucking container," she smiles nostalgically. "Don't even think about this new office for which we're cutting the ribbon. I ask you to, instead, consider our *future* vision, wherein lie the audacity to believe we could grow into a self-sustaining trust, to subsidize teacher pay – so we're not doomed to losing our best teachers to industries that can afford to pay them what our state-funded education system cannot."

When it's ribbon cutting time, she calls Russ up the steps to share in the victory. Like Cree, his presence draws admiration and envy. It's almost fictional to be as wealthy, yet as charming; as tall yet as graceful, or to be as young yet as wise. As Mayor Childress once said, if Charleston were Gotham City, Russ Rutledge II would be its Bruce Wayne.

In front of the audience, Russ takes his wife into his arms where the couple gazes in apparent unabashed affection. They peck for show, but repeat the gesture in slow motion. Russ cradles her face, nearly escalating to the level of make-out, but Cree taps his arm as a reminder that they're in full view of an audience. Cree turns to them, feigning embarrassment, but a pearly smile breaks through and exposes her; she loves the display. Together, Cree and Russ is the power couple to which power couples aspire.

During the hour of mingling, they're together arm in arm. Russ gets this way when Cree proves how vital a role she plays for Rutledge Enterprises. She's taken what was once only a tax haven and made it into one of the most recognizable charitable foundations in the city, which adds credibility to the Rutledge name and brand. So, Cree is well aware of the source of Russ's affection, however, she's been so deprived, it wins her over regardless.

Cree only wishes it were real, or maybe if the public performance can carry over to the bedroom tonight. If tomorrow they go back to sleeping in separate wings of the mansion, it's still worth coming together for one night – even in a contrived and fleeting passion. It would be enough to reset Cree's psychological clock, ticking down to insanity, from the slow torture of being invisible in her own home. Russ shares her hope for this evening, it seems, from all the affection and the energy behind his support.

They separate only once, and the watchdog reporter Hal Sweeney pounces. He makes a b-line for Cree. Russ nearly knocks over a catering tray in his effort to intercept, but Russ arrives just after Hal gets off his on-camera question. "Is it true, Cree, that the mayor fit the bill for this office with tax payer money which you, in turn, convert to your personal gain by contracting your husband's construction company to build it?"

Russ tries to protect his wife by ushering her along without dignifying Hal with a response, but Cree digs in her heel. Her head side-cocks at the nerve of this reporter with the mismatching toupee calling her to task. With a confident smile, Cree responds. "You make it sound so underhanded, Hal. It's the private sector receiving a city grant to facilitate a public service that the city is unprepared to facilitate itself. And I find it funny how you omit that every dollar was donated back to the foundation where the phase two manifesto outlines how the money will supply its own set of grants right back into the community." Hal tries to interrupt, but Cree overtalks him. "Charleston politics may dictate that I run with wolves, but do not mistake me for actually being one, mm-kay?" Her hand pops open inches from Hal's face and hangs there as she shoulders by, denying Hal the chance to point out that they're getting a tax write-off from the sleight of hand donation made with public funds.

Cree's around-the-way-girl attitude was part of Russ's initial attraction to her, but once Cree began representing the family name in higher circles and in the press, it became a point of contention and embarrassment for Russ. This time, however, she's on camera giving a veteran reporter the talk-to-the-hand gesture and Russ is tickled; his wife could do no wrong now that reconciliation is on the horizon.

They aim to take their momentum home straightaway after the event, but the mayor and his wife extend a dinner invitation, which Russ and Cree accepts, fearing that declining might bear insult, considering how far Mayor Childress had extended himself to make the new building a reality.

When they arrive at the tapas bar, a jazz band sets up at the back of the room. Cree orders a bottle of Russ's favorite wine in hopes to keep his spirits up, but that's when the Russ Rutledge show begins; his poker-faced disposition while pitching his next grand idea to Mayor Childress, which only adds tension to an evening meant for winding down.

The maître d' personally fills the glasses, since this table includes the mayor, but Russ is so involved in selling a dream to the mayor, he doesn't notice the maître d'. Cree tries not to cut her eye at Russ when she slides his glass closer, "It's Abbey Creek, hon." Cree realizes she's lost him for the rest of the evening when Russ reaches over the white-clothed table and set his hand down on its five fingertips.

"What I'm trying to tell you, Ted," says Russ. "Is that I have more than just some vague notion. I've got a complete vision for highway forty-one."

What both men need not have explained is that Mt. Pleasant, a city just over the Charleston Bridge is the third fastest growing city in America, with its influx of northern retiree settlers spreading gentrification like wildfire, running off the natives and their Gullah Geechie heritage and now breathing down the neck of the little community down highway forty-one where Russ's kin (on his mother's side) had acquired their land a hundred years ago, back when blacks were largely illiterate, thus, without written wills – ergo the donning of heirs property laws to exploit the lack of wills with probate court mandates to divide sale proceeds evenly to all living descendants. With the estate sliced often forty times or more, no one's cut enables them to purchase new property that is on par with the land that imminent domain forces them to sell, so they're left with no choice but to migrate from the land they call home, to depressed rural areas or inner-city ghettos, in systemic segregation from middle class white communities.

Russ proposes, "I've got a completed neighborhood master plan for luxury builds. I'm talking tile roofs, granite floors, three to four thousand square foot a piece... a golf course... But for the families forced off of land they owned for nearly a century, we'll pass on a portion of the Home Owners Association fee back to them, in perpetuity, so they can eventually relocate to areas with halfway decent schools."

Hearing enough, the mayor says, "Very noble indeed, Russ. But keep in mind, I've been mayor for only five years – not forty years like my predecessor. I can't move and shake to a level you've all become accustomed to, and I *sure* as hell don't have the gall to step in the way of free enterprise." The mayor's head shakes no, bashfully, but he offers, "This is between you, the banks, and your people. You've got roots there; they'll trust you. Get out to the residents before imminent domain does."

Still, the men calmly go back and forth, ideologies locking horns while they politely nod and smile through the painstaking clarifications.

Their wives try to set an example of how the evening should go. Cree Rutledge and Linda Childress take in the atmosphere, grading it in conversation, of how refined the decorum, how eclectic the wine selection, and when the food arrives, how excellent the roasted lamb and the seared swordfish. The women laugh loud in attempt to break the trance the men are under, but to no avail.

Cree, having given up on Russ, now gives herself over to the rhythm, her shoulders grooving so much that Linda is compelled to comment. "Really enjoying this piece, are you?"

"It's *all* jazz for me – and Neo Soul. I swear I'd be a singer in another life," Cree says, with a nudge to Russ. He only gives a brief smirk before returning to his discussion with Ted.

Cree, desperate to revive their vibe from the ceremony, decides on one last-ditch effort to pull Russ up from the table to dance, but first he'll need a song that'll move him, something husky with bass. Cree takes a napkin from her purse. On it, she writes *Window Seat*, walks over and lays the napkin at the foot of the stage like a prayer on an altar, but when she turns to go back to her table, she bumps into a woman with a nose ring and a raspberry beret, who pushes a microphone to Cree. Apparently, it's open mic, with Cree as the evening's only taker, but Cree waves her hands in refusal. "I was submitting a *request*," she says, but when Cree checks across the room and finds Russ looking in disapproval, when earlier he wouldn't look to her for conversation, Cree changes her mind. She kindly takes the microphone to the stage.

Band members queue each other with nods. The feisty drummer tumbles on the snare. On the keyboards, the Nubian woman with locks falling away from the shaved side of her head, lays the intro like butter on toast. The bass player, in just five plucked chords, claims the lead.

Cree holsters the mic. She lay her head back as if standing under a relaxing shower. Although the entire dining room looks directly at Cree, she stuns them with her whistle-clean pitch.

So, presently, I'm standing
Here, right now, you're so demanding
Tell me what you want from me

From the very first frame, the audience knows they're in for a treat, how Cree delivers *you're so demanding*, with the back of her hand to her forehead in feigned exasperation. On the long note, when Cree leans away, stretching herself as she stretches the word *me*, she is everything that twenty-years of at-home broomstick concerts have been waiting for.

By the time the piece reaches its abrupt end, where drumsticks pop the snare and a closed hi-hat, Cree has made witnesses of them all. Those exiting patrons that had doubled back at the sound of her voice, now stand by the bar, clapping with keys in hand and purses on their shoulders, satisfied with their decision to stay.

Cree bows under the weight of validation. Her brow settles on Russ as she walks off the stage through the standing ovation, misty-eyed but invincible, as if she'd just pulled Excalibur out of stone.

Cree is out-of-body for the remainder of dinner, lost in the world-building of the life she could've had as a singer had she followed her passion: the fail-safe for happiness, even if love goes bust.

As much as she'd like to make Russ the villain, Cree concedes that Russ was always somewhat supportive of her singing, but infinitely more supportive of her role in his family's corporation.

As exiting patrons pass by Cree's table, they pat her shoulders or bow next to her chair to share their glowing reviews.

Russ calls for the check, which prompts Ted to get to his main reason for proposing this dinner date: "You know what," says Ted. "I almost forgot about Antron."

"Who?"

"Antron Manigault, your architect. Wife's in hospice."

"I know that, but how do *you* know Ant," says Russ.

"His mother, Mavis, helped raised our children. She was a long-time nanny for us. She and Linda still talk on the phone from time to time. Seems Antron's been suffering in silence. Medical bills and the loss of his wife's income has got him fixin' to lose the house. Please, look out for him in any way that you can." Childress raises a finger. "Do *that* and I'll see what help I can give on this plan of yours."

"I'm on it," Russ promises. "I'll have Cree take care of it tomorrow morning, in fact."

THE car ride home starts off in silence, and seems set to remain that way, until Cree notices Russ driving enroute to his parents, which forces Cree to say, "I asked them to keep Meryl overnight." Cree gazes out the passenger window. "I should've known not to get my hopes up."

Russ sighs. "You're not the only one who had their hopes up." He uses past tense, seeing how earlier she'd snubbed his attempt to hold her hand on the way to the car.

"Then why give all your energy to the mayor and not me?"

Russ frowns. "Someone needs to hold his feet to the fire. They exalt him for the symbolic gesture of supporting the removal of that confederate statue, but what does it matter if he won't do anything to stop the actual oppression?"

"Sorry I asked." Cree's hands plop in her lap. "I'm done."

Russ examines her. "What do you mean done?" It's been bad long enough for any adjective of finality to hint at divorce. They go quiet for a while, afraid of inflicting more harm, afraid of dashing all hope that tonight might still be salvageable.

When they enter their home and the time comes to part ways down separate halls, Cree gives in. She spins around in front of Russ. "What happened to us," is all she can manage to say.

The question requires no answer; it's merely an olive branch, but taken literally it offends Russ. "You don't know? For starters, I refused to keep walking on eggshells; *that's* what happened to us."

Cree sighs. "So, is clapping for me considered walking on eggshells, then? I get a standing ovation and my husband stuffs his hands in his pockets?"

Russ offers no visible sign of contrition. "You spent our whole marriage trying to prove to me – or maybe to yourself – that you don't need me, while I've spent our whole marriage trying to reassure you that I *do* need you, and it seems to have cost me my right to ask anything of you in this relationship."

"Are you really trying to justify not extending your wife the same courtesy of a room full of strangers?" Cree seems to collapse internally from emotional fatigue. "I gave up my dream for the sake of Rutledge Enterprises. Maybe our marriage won't get out of this funk until I go ahead and follow my dream, so I'm not holding any underlying resentment towards you."

Russ swirls a finger at her. "You see that?"

"What?"

"How you try to pass off something you want, as a solution for us?"

Cree slaps the back of one hand to the palm of the other. "I'm expressing my truth and here you go, finding a way pull a threat out of it – like a rabbit out of a hat!" Cree stares at Russ through the blur of tears. "I just refuse to believe that you've become this poisoned against me."

"Tears now?" His hands toss in despair. "When all else fails, huh…"

"Momma always told me…" Cree sighs, as if it's a final sigh before dying. "…ya know it's over when he'll minimize the things that builds you up, but shine a spotlight the things that tear you down." Cree turns and heads for the bedroom.

Russ, unable to let the conversation end with dirt on him, returns fire, "You *would* be one to take the advice of a clown." Russ regrets it the moment it leaves his mouth.

Cree stops, for the insult against her dead mother. She doesn't turn, yet Russ knows the tears are falling fast. Cree starts walking again.

Russ takes two steps and stops in shame. Instead of himself, he sends his voice after her. "You know I'm not speaking ill of your mother, Cree. You can't hold that against me."

Cree slams the bedroom door behind her. She lay in a ball in the center of the bed and cries until her eyes are puffy.

Russ wanders off to the bar in the den, pours a shot, but leaves the glass and walks away with the bottle. The other hand grips his tie and rips it down. In the same manner, Russ rips his shirt loose; buttons trickle on the floor.

He sits on the floor outside the bedroom door where Cree has retired. Russ drinks himself into a stupor. With each tremoring return to self-awareness, he materializes sitting in a different position, the bourbon level vanished by inches.

Russ shakes his head at himself, this foolish cycle, where these skirmishes crops up, he holds his ground, believing he's reclaiming his power, but out of that posture, he ends up saying something that further divides them. He now sits on the hard floor, robbed of the power to pick himself up and knock on the bedroom door, nor fix his mouth to apologize from outside.

Chapter 3

Collision Course

By feel, Lulu can count the bones in her feet; they're inflamed from the long journey. Lulu treks inside the forest, unseen, parallel to the highway. The canopy of trees blots out the sky, save the scattered flecks glittering through the stencil of branches. The eggy smell of sulfur is but a memory. A saltwater scent, alone, rides the breeze, meaning the tide has risen to cover the banks on the other side of the highway.

She goes to the edge of the trees to assess her whereabouts and finds herself standing across the painted street from destiny: that one opening where the creek bends close to the highway, and where entry isn't a death drop. Lulu looks right. Left. Red brake lights shine in the steamy distance.

Fidgeting like a doe, Lulu springs for it, in a stumbly run on tired legs and aching feet. On the other side, she goes down the embankment, quickly but carefully, grasping fistfuls of marsh for balance. The bog grabs her; she fights for her right leg back. She goes further in, cool water climbing up her ankles, knees, then crotch.

The moment draws nigh. Lulu's belly stirs as if it's home to a school of fish. She spots a cattail bobbing from the landing of a dragonfly. Downstream, a long-mouthed pelican dips its beak into the water, and then throws its head back, making a chute of its leathery throat. Paradise is upon her. She wholeheartedly believes Nathaniel who said there is a mansion already prepared for her.

Lulu takes one last look into the distance, watching how light and shadow smear along creek's surface, shimmering into the accumulation of fog, into which Lulu peers deeper, suddenly, because she thinks she sees something.

In the looming, shape-shifting mist, a canoe eases into view with the silhouette of two men aboard. A mounted drum-sized fog-light swivels directly at Lulu. They wave and yell. They dip their oars in the water and paddle hurriedly.

Lulu prefers no witnesses, but there's neither time nor opportunity for preference; she can't come this far and not go through with it.

Standing waist deep in the middle of the creek, in the fog-scattered spotlight, Lulu looks like a ghost. The men call her by name. Lulu does not react, as if she does not hear them.

Lulu looks down into her murky reflection wavering in the waist level water. The twin stones on the ring that Nathaniel had given her lights up like fireflies. She reaches forward so the relic breaks the water's surface first as she folds from the waist, collapsing into her reflection.

The volunteer rescuer in a frog-suit keels backward over the side of the boat and swims underwater. He makes many passes, skimming the murky bottom with an underwater flashlight. There is no sign of Lulu; she is gone without a trace.

CREE

Cree wakes up and chooses violence. She prepares in the vanity mirror, in the candescent glow of track lighting where, with two fingers she applies concealer to the T of her face like war paint. This morning she has awakened with the clarity of a new paradigm from which all their marital woes stem: an incident from years ago where something supposedly *didn't* happen between Russ and Charlene Hamilton.

Cree goes to her room-sized closet, throws the double doors open and scans from the doorway, like it's an arsenal from which to choose her weapons. She arms herself with stilettos and a satin wrap dress with a thigh-teasing split. Cree marches out of the bedroom with her curves on blast, certain that the man trying to go cold-turkey of his desire for her shall suffer a relapse.

Had Cree known that Russ spent half the night outside her bedroom door wallowing in regret, she would've had a different approach. She sees Russ snoring on the couch. The echoing click of her heels across the Italian marble floor doesn't wake him; he's hung over.

Cree clamps a hand over his nose and mouth. Russ comes up flailing from the rude awakening, his wide eyes stretching wider from the closeup of a glossy thigh peeking through the satin split.

Eerily, Russ asks, "Why are you dressed like that?" Flaunting his loss as she walks out on him, he fears.

Cree folds her arms. "We need to talk."

"Babe..." Russ, gathering his whereabouts, looks around and blinks hard. "Talking is precisely our problem. We can't get through to each other because we're holding too much against one another."

Russ thinks his assessment is spot on, but Cree quickly destroys it. "If you never own your own shit, you hold *everything* against the other person. Did you have sex with Charlene? Because I'm thinking you must have, and you're holding it against me, under some belief that I drove you to it. But you can't come out and say *that*, so you're forced to reach, which is why you don't even make sense to me."

Russ stands, only so he could look down on her theory. "We dealt with this *how* long ago? You know I didn't."

"You never come out with a straight answer. Why do I always have to put your back against it?" Her arms unfold and flop at her sides.

Russ's glare intensifies. "Is an answer what you really want? Or are you just looking to take the discussion to a place where you feel power swings to you? And you're mad because I won't hand you the strap to beat me with."

Cree bites down and closes her eyes. "I am seeking clarity, Russ. This is *not* some power struggle. This is *not* one of your business deals. I'm your wife–" Cree stops. She smiles at how foolish she is to argue with a brick wall. "You know what..." She pivots and marches for the door.

Russ yells, "Cree! Get back here. Now!"

Cree spins and marches back with a pointed finger leading her like a joust. "Who do you think you're talking to!"

Ignoring her words, Russ puts a hand on her waist. Cree swats it. Russ puts the hand on her waist again, firmer this time. He studies her, licking his lips. "Come here, girl." He pulls her into his body.

Cree folds her arms again; her only act of defiance.

Russ says, "You ain't answered *my* question yet. What's the first thing I said to you?"

Cree responds, "You asked, why I'm dressed like this."

Russ peers down at her, bites his lip, and slowly lets it pull from under his teeth. "See, you take me for somebody to play with." His hand moves from the waist to her buttocks and he squeezes.

Cree allows it, even moments after being unable to stand the sight of him. Her husband is dripping with dominant, flirtatious energy; she doesn't let on that she's somewhat intrigued to see where this is going, but before it could possibly go any further, Cree has but one contingency. "You said some ugly things last night, Russ."

"It was ugly how you accused me of cheating with Charlene just now," Russ says, as if they're even.

His response kills the suspense. Cree cranes back to examine him. "So, you think you can just lick your lips, squeeze my tush, and you get to pin my legs back? Think you can pound away the hurt from what you said about my mother?"

The memory falls out of the cloud of hangover, and it crushes him, that even in anger, he would say such a thing. Cree is marching for the door and all Russ can think to say is, "Where do you think you're going dressed like that?"

ANTRON'S home itself seems rather indistinct, but it is at the center of a landscape design that has all the lines and symmetry of an architect. From the moment Antron answers the door, Cree notices how the party dress and stilettos throws the man for a loop, with his delayed speech and his forgetting, initially, to welcome in the woman who'll pay off his mortgage. Once inside, she's unsure if it's her own self-consciousness or if she senses the effort that it takes Tron to *not* look, how his glances ricochet off of her. This transaction would've been less awkward at the office, but a prideful Tron didn't want his financial woes known in the workplace, where it could inspire colleagues to go above and beyond their current gestures of flowers to his wife's hospice room.

They're in the kitchen at opposite sides of the island counter, Cree poised to write out the check. A small dog barks from his crate in the other room. Tron stares at his phone on speaker, awaiting the representative's return to the line with the payoff amount. The all-treble orchestra hold-music is the classical score to Tron's soliloquy, "As Tia dies, a part of me dies too, ya know? Each day a little bit of perseverance dies, a little bit of my faith dies. My dreams..." He bites down. "My dream was *her*, growing old with my bestie... giving our kids the world. So, with all these things dying inside of me, how can *I* truly live?"

Cree allows a few beats of reflection then adds, "I remember when the company was more tight-knit and we used to have the outings and the holiday parties and the annual conference. Tia never sat one out; she was always your and-one. And you two were always at the center of all the fun." Cree sighs deeply. "She was always the most important person in the room to you." With this, Cree recalls last night where she was the least important person in the room to Russ. The thought of Tron – by no fault of his own – losing everything that she and Russ are foolish enough to squander, makes Cree seize up feverish with emotion. Cree fans her face, saying, "Sorry. Don't mind me, I just…" She touches Tron's hand, a gesture permitting him to stay where he is; she doesn't need consoling.

Tron misreads Cree's touch of his hand; he sees it as a subtle trespass of boundaries. Ever since his wife fell ill, Tron has had to endure the overreaches of kindness coming exclusively from women, even at church. He doesn't stand out among most men, this rather tall Kevin Hart, but one thing this experience has taught him about women is that, for them, the most attractive thing about a man is the glow that he gives his lover. The love that he and Tia had, truly radiated from her.

Chapter 4

The Fabrication

The representative returns with the payoff amount. Cree, hearing over speakerphone, transcribes the amount onto the check in splendid cursive handwriting. Tron says, "I'll never be able to express how grateful I am for this. How can I ever repay you and Mr. Russell?"

Cree withholds the check for some words of her own. "By taking care of yourself... taking as much time as you need to heal. Your job at Rutledge Enterprises will always be waiting for you." Cree, being quite the orator, hears how formal her words sound, so she adlibs, placing a hand on his shoulder, but not quite looking into his eyes. "And I wish you restoration of faith and perseverance and zest of life. Earlier when you posed the question, are you really living? I felt that statement more than you can ever know." A tear escapes her. "I don't have a dying spouse, but... in a dying marriage, parts of you die the same. Like you, the future I'd always envisioned–" Cree becomes aware of herself, pouring out her emotions, along with she and Russ's private affairs, to an employee. "I'm sorry," she says. I don't know what made me say that, I..." She can't talk her way out of the emotions taking hold of her. Cree leans forward into Tron's chest only to hide her crying face from him.

The man with the dying wife consoles the woman whose spouse is still healthy and quick. "It's gone be alright Mrs. Cree. You and Mr. Russ gone work it out."

Cree closes her eyes. Being in Tron's arms makes her re-member being in Russ's arms just minutes earlier. It was the first time being in Russ's arms in quite some time, and it will likely be quite some again before the next. She shouldn't have pressed him for an apology, Cree thinks. The pull of regret is so strong, she's completely rapt in the embrace she yearns to have back, that it changes the character of the embrace she's in. Her fingers knead Tron's back; she nestles firmer into the grooves of him.

Tron, feeling Cree's breath heating the side of his throat, he turns to give Cree a kissing angle – if it's what she requires to release the check.

Cree rears upward, eyes still closed, but the press of lips tells her it's not Russ. Cree opens her eyes and jumps back. "What just happened?" She can't believe she'd suffered such a pro-found lapse in time and place.

Tron beats her to the apology. "I'm sorry," he says. "But I just can't. If that's what it takes to get you to hand that check over…" His head tremors no in silence.

Cree, realizing she'd withheld the check, tosses it like a hot potato. "Take it!" She starts backing away, eyes wide with terror. She smooths her hair back as she takes it all in.

Tron explains, "I can't go sit at the bedside of my dying wife with guilt all over me, understand?"

Cree feels her face. The touch is real. What just happened, was real. "Tron… I promise you; that was an accident."

Tron looks her over. "Dressed like that by accident too, huh?" Tron swipes the check off the counter and holds it up. "All I ask, is that you *please* do not put a stop on this check."

"No… No, Tron. That's the least of your worries–"

"–Are you sure? Does Russ even know about this check?"

"Does he *know* about it? It was his idea."

"I don't trust it," says Tron, who slides the check across the counter."

"Deposit the check, Tron. Russ, needs for you to cash this check or Childress won't–" Cree's hand traps her mouth; she'd said too much.

Tron turns an ear to her. "Come again? Y'all using my dying wife, and our money problems as leverage with the mayor? Hell to-the naw!"

"That came out wrong," Cree says, fretfully.

Tron rubs his chin. "Trust, I'm not coming out of my mouth wrong when I say this: you write me another check – a hundred thousand dollars, or I will show Russ what you did." Tron points. "You see, I got doggy cameras all through the house, which angle you want, huh? How about that one!"

Cree's face swings to the mark. She stares at the camera while a slow, cold death creeps over her. "Tron. Please! I couldn't explain another check for that amount of money."

"Make it cash! Pay in installments. Do what you gotta do."

"You got this all wrong Tron. You should know me better!"

An unfazed Tron replies, "I'll give you a week to come to your senses, and if I don't have a hundred bands by then, I'll sell the video to the media – to Hal Sweeny to be more precise, and you know he has it out for Russ. They may not pay me much for it, but in the long run, it'll cost you a lot more than the hundred thousand dollars I'm asking for."

Cree runs out of the house, horror movie style – all zigzag and stumble, looking back in terror. If her car were not keyless, Cree surely would've struggled with the ignition. Cree races homeward. She's suffering a nervous breakdown in the worst place: behind the wheel.

Fortunately, the morning traffic has dissipated. The winding backroad is clear, except for a pedestrian walking the highway shoulder in cargo pants, a blouse tied around her waist, and a crop top like Cree herself used to wear in order to show off her flat tummy.

Cree is almost convinced that she's not seeing another person, but an aberration or mental projection of herself, so vivid though, so earthbound, she thinks.

The woman checks over her shoulder. As Cree drives by, their eyes meet; their heads rotating, in passing, like orbiting planets. The resemblance is uncanny.

Cree feels as if she's looking upon another self, unbound my mirrors – a phenomenon that gives Cree an existential glitch, a lapse for merely two seconds – but a crucial two seconds. By the time Cree regains focus, she's unprepared for the next bend in the highway, which flies at her like a curveball.

The car gallops off road, fishtailing down a grassy slope. She tries to steady the steering wheel, but it muscles against her, nearly spraining her wrists. The car slides, as if on skates, closing in on a troupe of wild geese and a wall of trees. Cree could do nothing but scream and watch the scatter of geese and then the blizzard of feathers, clearing from the windshield just in time for a glimpse of the stout palmetto tree that makes everything go black.

Chapter 5

Out Cold

Lulu sprints down the grassy valley along the muddy tire scars that disappear into the trees, some fifty yards clear of the highway. Lulu is the only witness. Closing in on the pretzeled car, Lulu's run breaks to a trot and then to a brisk walk, high stepping in tall grass with a revolver drawn.

There's an engine hiss and a metallic crackle. Lulu looks in. Beyond her opaque reflection in the driver's side window, she looks upon the wealthy, married version of herself, motionless behind the blown airbag. Judging by the loud bang of the crash, and the condition of the crushed car, Lulu is quick to believe that Cree is dead, and quick to feel what immeasurable relief it brings, for not having to use the gun. That one sin would trump thirty-three years of sins amassed in her parallel world.

The driver door is stuck. She hurries around to the passenger side. It takes her planting a foot on the body of the car to heave the door open. She works fast. They're down in a small valley; hidden from the cars on the road, but still...

Once inside, Lulu collapses the air bag and unfastens the seatbelt in a frenzy, but reality stops her with a chest punch: it is truly herself, lying motionless with a bleeding head in this twisted metal tomb of finely stitched leather interior. Lulu is overcome with sadness; a living witness to her own death like one of those staged funeral interventions.

Lulu doesn't know when their worlds diverged, but since Meryl exists in both worlds, she knows it was after Meryl's birth but before the divorce because, in this world, Cree and Russ are still married. According to Nathaniel, this woman takes herself so seriously that no one dare calls her Lulu. It's Lucretia or Cree, always, with no respect of persons. Lulu wonders how the same person manifests so differently in a matter of only a decade?

As Lulu positions herself to drag the body out of the car, her eyes fall to the wedding ring, it's mass, it's sparkle and aura. She takes it. She slips it on her finger. She relaxes in the passenger seat while examining the back of her hand, in awe of how the large diamond churns out spectral light like a kaleidoscope, which lulls her into a daydream, imagining herself in the hospital bed, thrilled as nurses refer to her as Mrs. Rutledge. Her very own Mr. Russ Rutledge storms in, worried sick, and promptly whisks her home to their mansion, which is already prepared with pictures of their three-member family, a wine cellar, a master bath that is her own little plot of heaven, and to top it off, there is a wardrobe to die for. It doesn't really sink in until they're in bed, Lulu on top, reveling in her most prized possession, kissing a trail from his lips down to his bare black chest. Lulu moans in such delight she sounds outside of her own body, as if her moaning comes from someone else – because it does. Cree in the driver's seat, moans as she comes to.

Lulu's daydream vanishes. She's still sitting in the passenger seat of the wrecked car, gazing at the wedding ring she'd just taken from Cree. Lulu aims the gun at Cree's head. She can mop up the blood with her own clothing and change into Cree's, she thinks – but the thought is merely calculative. The aiming hand lowers under the gravity of murder. She should've brought some coke, she thinks. She doesn't regret deciding to leave her cocaine habit in the world she left behind, but wishes she'd brought the equivalent of four lines; enough to cancel her conscience, because plan B has a low chance of success. Lulu stashes the pistol under the seat and waits for her twin to rouse.

A groggy Cree keeps adjusting in her seat, struggling to manage the weight of her head, which finally lops over, facing the passenger side. That's when she sees. "No... No," Cree sees herself and thinks it's her grim reaper. She's terrified, but she's also loopy, as if she's upright in the dentist's chair, coming down off the gas. Cree peers through a hard squint.

Lulu calmly says, "You're not dreaming. I'm you. You're me."

A sobering Cree says, "How am I still feeling pain if I'm dead?"

"You're not dead." Lulu says, but notices something awfully peculiar in her twin's reaction, showing the same manner in which disappointment registers on her own face – the slight scowl, the heaviness that sets in the bottom lip, as if she's disappointed that she's not dead. Nathaniel was right; there is a good chance that Mrs. Rutledge, might be game to swap lives. Lulu asks, "You were driving like that because you were trying to kill yourself?"

Cree's head waves no but it's like the inadvertent head-waving no of a fish, merely a consequence of the action of its tail. Cree's no comes from a deeper place, a rejection not of the question but of the questioner, a carbon copy of herself, which defies all reality.

Lulu believes that Cree's silent *no* is heavy with disappointment. Like being stood up at the altar yields a wedding with no marriage to show for it. Cree seems disappointed to have this whole car wreck gone to waste with no death to show for it.

"This can't be," Cree frets.

"Skepticism. Really?" Lulu folds her ear forward, revealing a scar. "Curling iron, freshman year. Hurt like hell, didn't it?" Lulu thinks of one better. "I got one for ya: how about the recurring dream where I'm a child again, at the historic Angel Oak tree. I guess I somehow wandered off from momma and daddy because they're nowhere in sight. I'm small – small and alone, sobbing. And suddenly, those massive, mossy branches start closing around me. It's so real, isn't it – how those branches crackle and whine as they collapse around you like a hand closing to a fist..."

Cree stares in space for a few beats. "I don't remember ever sharing that with anyone, so… What are you – some ghost of Christmas past? How am I the Scrooge in this? I run a non-profit organization; I'm an excellent mother; an excellent–" She cuts out with a sigh to escape lying.

"Not excellent wife? What, Russ left you? That's why you was trying to kill y'self?"

"No," Cree frowns, irritated. "And no, Russ isn't going any-where." Cree pulls out her phone and unlocks the screen. "Are you gonna dial 911, or me? I'm bleeding here."

Lulu stops short of snatching the phone. "Call 911 for a band-aid? It's just a little scratch from like, flying glass or some-thing–"

"–*I'll* call, then," Cree brings up the dialer on her phone.

"Before you do…" Lulu, doing her best not to resort to the gun, says, "One question: you say you run a non-profit – that's what you led with – not singer?"

Cree looks away, unable to bear the judgement from eyes that are her own. "No… I… you know… Life kinda got in the way."

Lulu touches her hand. "You have a gift, beloved. I assumed every version of us would be compelled to embrace that gift."

"Every version of us," Cree frowns.

Lulu's eyes blaze with the obvious. "Parallel universe."

"No." Cree tremors. "I'm at home in my damn bed. This is a dream."

"Gone pinch y'self, then," says Lulu. "At some point we were one, but everything branches off like every five and a half years. In the beginning, when the universe was much smaller, a new universe branched off every nanosecond…"

Cree stares at Lulu in facetious wide-eyed suspense, eager to see how much more *un*convincing Lulu could be. "Girl, if you don't get out of my car!"

Lulu gulps and starts again, which is precisely what her listener does not want. "Ok, now I'm no quantum physicist, but it was explained to me something like this." She takes a deep breath before the dive. "Okay, it's like, the universe is expanding so fast, that, like – you know how waves crash the shore and fold back into the ocean, the expanding universe crashes against the cosmic horizon and folds back onto itself and this wave comes back carding through the holographic universe..." Seeing how Cree looks at her like she's crazy, Lulu tries a different approach. "Le'me put it this way: think of a notebook of drawings, when you cascade the pages and the drawings come to life. We only see the animation. We'll never truly grasp it until we have the technology to look beyond the animation of the universe and see the actual cascade of pages." Silence hangs. Lulu looks at her disenchanted listener, and adds, "I know I butchered the explanation, but hey... even science has it wrong."

"I'm familiar with multiverse theory, through Meryl. She's at the age where she's fascinated by the stuff."

"*Your* Meryl." Lulu looks off in mach shame.

"So, who are you consulting with, that's smarter than all the scientists of the world?"

"He says he's not an angel but... I don't know what else to call him."

"An angel." Cree both smirks and frowns, as if to some vulgar punchline. "And what's an angel doing shooting the breeze with you?"

"I saved his life. He's in human form, in the body of a man named Malik Osman, but *his* name is Nathaniel. Some bad people had him tied up, fixing to kill him over some debt."

"So, basically a genie grants you one wish and you use it this foolishly? Why are you here?"

"Angels ain't God. They don't grant wishes. They don't have powers; they have relics that have power–"

"–*Why*, I said!" Cree yells. "Of all things, why come for this version of me?"

"It's about daddy." Lulu presses back in her seat as if ashamed. "Have *you* reached out to him – built a relationship with him like I have?"

Cree rolls her eyes. "You reached out to daddy? We *can't* be the same person. I would never."

Lulu says, "He didn't do it. There was a deathbed confession. A lady named Henrietta Jameson, right before she died, told her sister that her late husband was the one who beat that lady to death. The evidence that would exonerate daddy was hid in their attic. But that house burned to the ground four years ago–"

"–So, in *this* world the house is still standing?"

"Right!" Lulu blasts. "Now, this doesn't change the fact of daddy being an addict and that's what put him in that predicament in the first place, but... He's been wrongly imprisoned, which denied him the chance to ever make things right with me, or with momma. So, *there's* the reason; *that's* why I'm here. So, what's up with you? You say you weren't trying to kill y'self, so why were you driving like a bat out of hell?"

Cree peers into a memory from her past. "Give me a minute... I'm just... Sitting here, next to myself, talking to me about daddy... So much is coming back to me, and... As a child, I remember always being on-edge that daddy would do something crazy. Sell the TV; go missing for days; that day he left me sitting in the parked car for hours when he was passed out in that crack house–"

"–I've forgiven him for everything but that."

"You know what..." Cree says as she gazes into eternity. "It just hit me: I've transposed my distrust for daddy onto my husband – not that I'm going through his phone or keeping tabs, but it seems I constantly require reassurance from him, as if our twelve years of marriage doesn't already speak for itself. He sees it as being controlling, emasculating–"

"–As he should," Lulu says, clapping the syllables.

"I have to talk to him, now. I gotta call Russ, I may have messed up, but I think I now know we can fix it."

"Messed up? What do you mean?"

It takes Cree a few moments to bring herself to even say it. "I kissed another man. It just happened."

Lulu looks her over, seeing the dress, the heels. "Are you sure *all* you did was kiss?"

"Only barely. We instantly pulled back."

Lulu's head shakes. "So that's the mess up? And you're thinking about calling Russ to tell him *that?* You are me, right? So how do you *not* know that men can dish it out but can't take it?"

"But if I don't tell him, Antron will, unless I pay him a hundred thousand dollars. He's got us on video – said he'll even sell the footage to the media."

"Pay the man. And take that straight to your death bed like Henrietta did. End of story," Lulu says, with a searing glare, but then a smirk cracks. "The name's Antron, though? Went and got you a thug, huh?"

"No, I didn't, *Miss* Cree—"

As if the name Cree offends her, "It's Lulu, all day every day."

Cree's head shakes. "No one's called me Lulu, in *years*. Anyway, Lulu, for your information, Antron isn't a thug. He's an architect for Rutledge Enterprises. What makes this thing even worse is that his wife is dying in hospice with probably days left to live."

Lulu looks at the wealthy version of herself like she's turned grotesque. "I would never do no shit like that."

Cree says, "Well, you did. We *are* the same person, right?"

Lulu rolls her eyes and says, "Anyway, back to what I was saying. We only need to trade places for about four days, so I can—"

"—Trade places!"

"I promised Nathaniel. We can't risk being found in the same world at the same time. Our fingerprints, our DNA is all the same."

"So!"

"*So?* Girl, you wanna bring on the rapture before time?" The expression on the face of Lulu's twin says she wants no parts of that. "Well, that's what can happen. If both of us are found in the same world, we give man evidence of things God doesn't want him to know!"

"Regardless, we're not trading places. Tell *me* where the house is. I'*ll* bring you the evidence myself. Trust me."

Lulu's patience burns; her eyes redden. "How could I trust you to do anything, when some guy's blackmailing you over a kiss, and you're up here trying to kill ya damn self over a video that would be more damaging to him if his dying wife were to see it? Besides, a sista like me... I know guys I could pay to make that video disappear." Lulu tilts her head and frowns. "What happened to you, huh? You can't do for yourself no more? You been coddled by a man so long, you forgot how to stand on your own two feet? I don't have a husband to hide behind. I'm a single mother out here doin' it by myself, gettin' it out the mud."

"Being a single mother is nothing to pound your chest about – not that it's anything to be ashamed of either..."

Lulu turns to her, wide-eyed, a finger pointing into her own chest. "I know I'd much rather be a single mother than a wife who's not doing the very thing she's been set on this earth to do. I'd rather be a single mother who didn't sell away her life's dream just so she could call herself a wife!"

"Life's dream." Cree cuts an eye. "So, you sing at church? Bar gigs? Weddings?"

Lulu pops her imaginary collar. "I have a Grammy nomination to my name, 2012. Admittedly, the last ten years I've been living off of the success off of that one record. I have a concert at the North Charleston Coliseum in just a few days, and it's sold out already."

Cree's eyes wow; she doesn't need to say the word.

Modestly, Lulu swats at the reaction. "Sold out because it's the hometown, of course, but... You'll have just three days. I've got recordings of all my concerts in the DVD player, and the written lyrics in a file on my laptop so you can use those to prepare. You'll see. Once you experience the crowd at a packed concert, you'll know that you were born for this. And as far as Russ goes... I'll bet your husband Russ can't hold a light to my boyfriend Russ."

A suspect grin grows on Cree's face. "Me and Russ, together in two totally different worlds? *Dating?*"

Lulu hands over some items waterproofed in a Ziplock bag. "We just recently rekindled, so the relationship is new. In other words, we haven't had sex yet, so if you can help it, don't sleep with my man, okay? But if you do, you better put it on him as good as I would."

They laugh together but quickly periscope to each other, Lulu speaking for both, when she says, "Ew, *that's* how my laugh sounds?"

Cree inspects the Ziplock bag where there is a cell phone and notebook papers with instructions. Cree is ready to accept, but she has one condition. "If I'm going to do this, you have to solve that problem for me. You say you know someone you can pay to get rid of the video?" Cree sets her purse on the console. "Bank cards, check book, it's all in there for you to use at your disposal."

They get out of the car to set the plan in motion. As they disrobe, they bring each other up to speed on the lives they'll be substituting in for the next few days. Cree changes into Lulu's cargo pants and sports bra, and ties the blouse around her waist. Lulu leaves the dress and heels dry in the car; she's naked while ushering Russ's wife out into the creek. Cree is reluctant at first. "This water looks so filthy up close," she says, but she goes in anyway.

The pair give their last-second reminders while waist-deep in the moving tide. Lulu positions herself behind Mrs. Rutledge and reminds her, "Don't forget to go down the contact list on that phone and call Fly Guy, my manager. Tell him that it's still a go, as far as the concert. I've been missing since Monday, so they think something's happened to me."

"Will do." Cree takes a deep breath to ready for the plunge, but then she remembers. "Funny thing: I just recently per-formed live. I thought it came about by accident, but now I know it was God preparing me for this moment."

Lulu says, "On the written instructions in that plastic bag, it has the time and place for us to meet up again. Be on time, okay? No excuses."

Before plunging into her murky, brown creek reflection, Cree halts for one crucial thing. "One second." She remembers to hand over her wedding ring, but it's gone. In the creek's murky reflection, she spots the ring on Lulu's hand, which rests on her shoulder. Cree looks back with leery eyes. "Lulu? Did you take my ring while I was unconscious?" Lulu clamps the back of Cree's neck and forces her underwater face down.

Face up, Cree breaks the surface, shedding water. There's no more Lulu. In the distance, there's no car balled up against a palmetto tree. She's in another woman's drenched clothing, feeling like the biggest fool in two whole-wide worlds, standing waist high in a shit-colored creek.

LULU had felt Cree sift through the grasp of her fingers like salt rinsed away with the tide. It is done. Everything Lulu ever wanted is hers. Hurriedly, she runs, splashing through the moving creek, screaming in elation. She runs for the car, changes into the dress sitting dry on the front seat; Lulu is now Mrs. Rutledge.

The 911 operator nearly blows off the call as a prank. Never had they heard anyone sound so giddy about totaling a hundred-thousand-dollar car.

When the police and EMTs arrive, neither do they know how to take Mrs. Rutledge's reaction. She seems convincing one moment and the next, she's looking down and away in mischief, hiding a smile. When they strap her on the gurney and snap on the emergency neck brace, to where she can no longer turn to hide her face, the ambulance double doors close on a hospital-bound woman, smiling with a gate of teeth clear across her face.

Just like Lulu had daydreamed, the nurses refer to her as Mrs. Rutledge and it thrills her. One nurse quietly signals another when she catches Mrs. Rutledge refreshing her makeup in her clamshell mirror as if she's going dancing right after having her car balled up against a tree. When Russ arrives, Lulu's smile drops. Lulu, in tears, throws her arms around Russ's neck, tip-toeing in his embrace and very methodically plants her lipstick all over his face – cheek to lips to chin to forehead to eyes, as slow tears roll down Lulu's face. She may have had to leap one life for the next, but with a long, tearful kiss, her happily ever after is sealed.

Chapter 6

Wonderland

Cree hears the call of a fisherman; she turns. The man runs along the marsh in knee-high mud boots, headphones down around his neck, a hand waving above his head. He has thick black eyebrows and he's so tanned he could pass for Serbian, until he speaks with that thick southern drawl. "You a'ight, there, mam?"

"I'm alright," Cree confirms.

He twitches with the curiosity of a pup. "You that missing singer, Lala or Lulu or…"

"Lulu."

"Yeah Lulu," he says, squinting, as he helps Cree up the boggy banks. "Can't say that I follow your music much, but…" He stops, distracted by confusion. Scratching his head, the man asks, "Where in the heck did you come from, anyway? How're you coming out of the water when I been out here a good hour – ain't you or nobody went in."

"But I did, actually, just a minute ago," says Cree. "Over there."

He gives a deadface appraisal of the apparent lie. His head dips, horse-like. "Now, I ain't callin' nobody no liar. I'm just appealing to common sense. If that was the case, I would've seen you, mam. I'm settin' right over there got my head on a swivel for game warden. Lest you come from out that bend there yonder – but ain't no man I know, can hold their breath underwater like'at. Even a dang porpoise'll have to bring his blowhole to the surface."

Cree shrugs. "I don't know what else to tell you, sir–"

"–Tom. They call me Tom-Cat, for short." He waves her along. "Come this-away let me get you some help."

Cree waits as the man gathers his rod and bucket, then follows him through the high grass toward the highway where there's a pickup truck parked on the grassy shoulder.

"I'm 'on be straight with ya. Umma call the law, but I can't hang around till they git here. Man, I got unpaid tickets, suspended license, no insurance, you name it."

They stand on the grassy shoulder in the same spot where Cree ran off the road in the other world. While Tom wraps up his call with 911, six, seven cars may have passed before one, and then another, pulls over. Tom, spooked by the attention, hops in the truck and drives off with a wave. "Take care, now."

A dog walker also closes in on the scene, pointing and calling her by her stage name. Lulu McQueen, it seems, is far more recognizable in this world than Cree Rutledge in her own world, where she's duchess of the Rutledge empire.

As good Samaritans close in around Cree, she learns that since Monday, Lulu had not only been missing to her band and manager, but that Lulu failed to mention that she was missing to everyone, and thought to be dead, her disappearance headlining the news. Cree is rushed to the E.R. by screaming ambulance – as a precaution, EMTs say.

In a blur, she's at the hospital, upright in the bed, having lights shined in her pupils; a stethoscope moving along her back as she inhales. When the blood pressure sleeve deflates, she feels the upward surge of blood coursing back into her deadened bicep, a sign of mortality that makes it all real to her.

These smiling nurses disguise their discovery questions with small talk, as if they'd like to be friends. All the mandated examinations, they conduct under the guise of personal concern, *I just want to make sure you're alright* – they say, as if they're not milking the visit for every billable exam allowable while playing kind and devoted, like missionaries to this depraved refugee, until they move on to the next emergency, leaving Cree alone with a blanket and a juice box.

Cree has a moment to breathe uninterrupted – without having her tongue prodded with a popsicle stick, nor her knee tapped with a rubber mallet. Cree is allowed but one relaxing sigh, and then Detective Ryan comes in with a grim mood change, eyeing her blanket and juice box as if resentful of the comforts given to her.

He questions her like an immigration officer, prodding for excuses to send her back over the border. "Where have you been… Who was holding you hostage…? What were you doing standing in the middle of the goddamned creek?"

Oblivious to questions only Lulu can answer, Cree pieces together intel from their conversation. Lulu said she saved the life of an angel who was being held hostage, so Cree figures it's safe to confirm, "I was kidnapped."

"So, you *were* kidnapped," says the detective. He then follows up with questions about the kidnappers, their location, and the details of her escape.

Cree trumps all his questions with, "I don't remember."

Detective Ryan bites down and says, "I was really hoping you'd at least remember the canoe incident – you going underwater to escape your own rescue; disappearing into thin air. Any recollection of that, by chance?"

"Disappearing into thin air," Cree says with a scowl, as if it is the detective who has some explaining to do.

"You're killin' me," says Detective Ryan. "You being who you are and the attention you bring, I got people breathing down my neck for answers."

"Don't I have a right to some answers, myself, since this investigation is about me, after all?"

"Shoot."

"Like… who are the suspects? Who, in the world, would have any reason whatsoever to kidnap me," Cree asks, just as a nurse returns with a halved turkey sandwich and fruit cocktail, but the nurse doesn't leave; she observes the conversation.

Ryan gazes in disbelief. "Are you pulling my chain, Lulu? When you say, 'you don't remember'–"

"–Any of it. The doctor says I have a concussion," Cree says and then looks out the window, finishing her sentence in thought, *from a car accident in another world.*

"Miss Hughes," calls Detective Ryan. The woman who's been Mrs. Rutledge for the last decade, figures he's calling the nurse by name. "Miss Hughes?"

"I'm sorry, um… yeah…" The gaff raises Cree's insecurity, which Ryan detects like a shark to blood in water.

Detective Ryan pinches the bone between his eyes. "I'm starting to wonder if you and what's-his-name was abducted by aliens and had your memories wiped. Like you, he seems to can't even remember his own name."

Showing off some level of competence, Cree offers, "You mean Nathaniel?"

Detective Ryan's eyes bulge. "Now, who the hell is Nathaniel?"

Only now, Cree remembers Lulu telling her that Nathaniel is in the body of another man. "Malik, I meant to say."

"If he goes by Nathaniel, maybe that explains why he forgets to answer to Malik."

The nurse, having seen enough, speaks up. "Memory loss with a concussion isn't rare. You should probably interview Miss Hughes in another five days."

Cree says, "I'm sure my drinking didn't help my memory much, either."

Detective Ryan, tilts toward her. "Drinking and what else?"

The nurse interjects, "Should we be doing a urinalysis?"

Cree beams at the same nurse who'd treated her like family earlier, but now so easily sides with the state.

"We don't anticipate any criminal charges, so I can't request a urinalysis," Ryan says, a sly smirk growing. "But I assumed maybe you'd have some medically necessary reason for it, due to the—"

"—Nice try, detective," the nurse says, wryly, as she slips out.

With no one else to look at, the faces of both Detective Ryan and Cree swing to each other. Ryan says, "Lemme just ask, straight out: did you fake your disappearance to disrupt Charlene and Russ's wedding?"

Cree nearly catches a stroke. "Charlene and Russ's *wedding!*" Cree squints to examine Lulu's apparent lie. She couldn't have been dating Russ if he has plans to marry the same woman with whom Cree suspects Russ of having had an extramarital affair years ago.

Ryan, eyeing Cree's frown, says, "All coming back to ya now?"

"Me, fake my disappearance? That's laughable."

The detective doesn't laugh. "Many think you were desperate to stop the wedding and it worked. Apparently, it's being rescheduled. Russ couldn't go through with it with your possible death weighing on his conscience, after that cryptic message you sent."

"Cryptic message?"

Detective Ryan unfolds a sheet of paper and hands it to Cree saying, "Charlene's lawyer gave us a transcript. It doesn't contain all of the messages, but even taken out of context, there's no chance for misunderstanding." Russ points. "See here, where Russ says it was a mistake reconnecting with you? Now here's where you send a message to Charlene's phone, saying, if you can't have Russ in this life, you'd have him in the next."

Those words hit like a hammer. Lulu, with whom Cree traded places, does in fact have Russ in the next world. Cree's eyes fall closed, pressing tears through her lashes. Cree exhales, as if all hope hangs on this question: "What about my father's case?"

Detective Ryan slowly repeats, "Your father's case…"

"It was reopened, right? Because of the deathbed confession?"

Ryan says, "I talked to him yesterday, actually. That was my last-ditch effort to see if he knew of anyone on his side of the family who might've taken you in, but... He said you haven't sent so much as a letter in years, so how would you know anything about his case? Hell, his case was closed the day he was sentenced and that's the end of it."

Cree laments the mistake of letting her self dip her into a filthy creek on the basis of lies; lies about her father's case; lies about dating Russ, and very likely, lies about meeting up again to trade places.

Cree, doubting she'll ever return to her own life, feels the prison come down around her, in the form of a replica that is just as wide open as the world she calls home, but claustrophobic with uncertainty. She breathes deeply and slowly; she's getting lightheaded. "Give me a minute please," Cree says. She raises a hand. "I just need a minute."

"I'll actually give you five days, as the nurse said. I'll see you on Monday." The detective half-turns toward the door, imparting, "I don't know what's the matter with you, or with Malik or Nathaniel – or whatever his name is – but y'all better start remembering *real* fast, ya hear? You don't get a celebrity pass, with me. Think of all the taxpayer money and man hours, scouring the city for the likes of you... And the best you can do is, 'I forgot'?" Detective Ryan's head shakes. "You gone have to come better than that, Miss Hughes."

She sits stark-still until the moment the detective clears the doorway. Cree scoots to the edge of the bed, reaches over and snatches up the hospital bag containing her clothes. She digs into the pockets of the damp cargo pants. She's in a tantrum; her breathing getting shallower by the moment, flirting with hyperventilation. "She was lying," Cree pouts. "Everything was a lie." She smooths the paper with directions on her lap, hoping to find some clue to get back to her world.

Cree's mother, Beth, enters with a gait of tentative jubilance. "How are you, Lulu," she says.

Cree nearly topples off the bed. "Who are you?" It is so vividly her mother, who, four years ago had her cancer secret outed only when she was admitted into hospice with days to live. She's here now, not opaque like a ghost, but in flesh – not lying in her casket, cold as clay, but standing, breathing, and looking at Cree as if she's plum crazy. Cree says, "It's really you, ma."

Beth side-eyes her. "You high?" Internally, Beth thanks the detective for extending the grace of not arresting Lulu, who is obviously too stoned to recognize her own mother.

Cree says, as faint and hollow as the second pass of an echo, "It is you, momma." Beth's voice, her cadence, this flippant way about her, is unmistakable. Cree comes forward slow, heavy-footed, and bowed under the weight of gratitude, like entering the surprise reveal of a newly renovated home; she can't believe her eyes. She squeezes her mother and bawls on her shoulder, smelling that same old department store perfume. "I thought I lost you forever."

"Baby, we thought we lost *you* forever. To God be the Glory."

Cree pulls back to examine her mother from arm's length, the walnut complexion, the skin pulled tight over shiny cheeks, the specks of aging around eyes that never relinquished its sparkle of youth.

In this world, Beth either defeated, or never had the bout with the cancer that took her life in the parallel world. Cree reckons if she be stuck in this world, that having her mother here, dwelling among the living, is a considerable consolation.

After the embrace, Beth tells her, "The buzzards are outside. As usual. I'll bring the car around. And you: you put on a smile for them."

Cree frowns. "Buzzards?"

"Reporters," says Beth. "Hurry."

There're cameras at the emergency room bay – photojournalists and reporters, like bees to a hive. Cree's taken aback by the microphones thrust under her chin, the volley of questions and the relentless shutter of long nosed cameras. This is not fanfare; this is the digital media, celebrity gossip thugs. Within the hour, these images will be posted on blogs under scathing bold-font headlines.

Each question is more searing then the last. *Is it true that you faked your disappearance as a publicity stunt for your upcoming concert? Was this a desperate attempt to resuscitate a dead career?* As she tries angling her body to cut through them, a question stops her. In fact, Cree only hears the tail end of the question wherein lie the word *has-been*. She smirks at the reporter. Having no pressure to represent the Rutledge name, Cree shoots from the hip. "Funny… me being called a has-been by a bitch who has *never* been."

Her mother comes around with the car, roaring into the emergency room bay, causing a scatter, which gives Cree a pathway to the passenger door. She stands inside the open door holding up double peace signs as she answers the last question. "Heck *yeah*, the concert's still on!"

Chapter 7

After Happily Ever

Lulu enters the Rutledge mansion for her first time and can't even take it all in. She's got the phone to her ear, and so does Russ. Word spread of the car accident, so phone calls had been rolling in from concerned family, friends, and company executives, from both Rutledge Enterprises and Cree's non-profit, The Icarus Foundation. Lulu is so bedazzled just to be here that it doesn't even dawn on her that her mother, Beth, hasn't called.

The moment Lulu hangs up, she moves her thumb to the side of her phone to power it down so she could just be... in paradise with her husband, but another call beats her to the power button. The name says Staysha. "Impossible." There's no way that Lulu's best friend is still best friends with that uptight Cree, Lulu thinks, as she answers. "Hello?"

"Thank God you're okay."

It's the voice alright, Lulu thinks, but... "Staysha?" After just a few minutes of conversation, Lulu determines that her new beginning in this world would have to be a lonely one – not because this Staysha lives away in New Jersey, but because somehow Lulu's "ride or die," here, is tea and crumpets, just like Cree.

This Staysha ended up marrying her rebound, Sean, instead of waiting on her true love, Jermaine, to be released from prison. Staysha talks nonstop, with Lulu *mm-hm-ing* and *uh-huh-ing* with the phone clamped between her ear and shoulder, as she enters the nearby study where there is an open laptop. Lulu researches Staysha's social media, following the breadcrumbs to her multiple websites.

Staysha's nonstop chatter is everything that her digital footprint professes her to be, this fashionista, soccer mom, and card-carrying Christian. There's a link to a vlog where she and her husband call themselves Christian relationship coaches. In the marquee photo they're at the beach, walking away hand in hand, a trail of wet footprints in their wake. Lulu scowls at the photo, seeing it as evidence that Staysha has undergone a thorough brainwashing that has made her obedient to the wishes of others, and it seems she's now coaching other women to force love with docile men that the church props up as ideal.

Staysha could be a valuable source of information for Lulu if Lulu could stomach chatting ever so often with this goody-two-shoe version of her best friend. She seems quite capable of filling Lulu in on the ten-year gap of experience she lacks in this world. Staysha speaks at length about Cree and Russ's issues, and how this near-death incident can be the catalyst to reviving the romance in their marriage.

Lulu rolls her eyes and sighs at the fact that Staysha is *still* talking. The moment Lulu thinks, *If this trick, cites one more scripture* – Staysha does it, "As it says in Ecclesiastes chapter four verse twelve, Cree, 'A cord of three strands is not easily broken.'"

Lulu has had enough. "Let me tell you something, Stace. Men are easy. When you're with your true love, you don't have to overthink it nor work up to it, okay… You see, Stace, your situation and mine are not the same." As Lulu takes the phone from her ear to power it off, she can hear Staysha, saying, *Cree… Cree* as the screen goes dark.

Lulu stands in the doorway of the study, eyeing Russ across the room, couched and on the phone.

Russ ends his phone call with a heavy sigh. He looks over and says, "Tia died."

"Tia?"

Russ's expression is as stupid as he believes the question to be. "Antron's Tia." He looks down at his phone again. "Guess I better call him and give my condolences."

Lulu remembers the name Antron, the man Cree kissed, who is now blackmailing her. With his wife dead, there's nothing left for the man to hide. If Russ makes the call, Antron, clouded by grief, might disclose the bribe prematurely.

Lulu strides toward Russ in the dress and stilettos that she'd traded off with Cree. She stops in front of Russ who scrolls down his contact list for Antron's name. Lulu throws a diversion. She steps a leg through the split of the dress. Russ takes his eyes off his phone, confused. "You a'ight, Cree," he asks.

Without a response, Lulu quietly bends forward over him, loosens his belt buckle, and then teases him out of his zipper. Russ frisbees his phone across the couch and takes a fistful of Lulu's hair as his eyes roll to the back of his head.

Halfway into it, they hear the deadbolt grinding. Russ's eyes unroll and blips back to focus. As the door opens, he and Lulu scramble, like musical chairs, to assume natural sitting positions on the couch.

Lena, the part time nanny, enters with Meryl in tow. Lulu and Russ are so quiet, Lena doesn't even notice them on the couch until she's deep into the house. Lena turns to greet them, but pauses. Something's obviously off with her employers. Mr. Russ has a magazine spread faced down across his lap, and Cree wipes drool with the back of her hand as she gets up to greet Meryl.

Cree's Meryl is nothing like Lulu's, who would've had that private school uniform tricked out with spiked collars, combat boots, fingernails colored with magic markers. This Plain Jane Meryl hugs her mother and then asks to see under her bandage. "Dad said there wasn't a concussion or anything," Meryl says.

"Because it's not, baby," Lulu says, but completes her answer in thought. *Because this mommy wasn't the one who wrecked.*

"I saw a picture of the car, on TV," Meryl says. "Either the doctors are wrong about the concussion, or you should donate your brain to science."

Lulu beams at Russ with pride. "You hear our daughter? She's a little scientist already, ain't it?"

Instead of smiling proudly at his daughter, Russ raises a brow at her mother. Young Meryl speaks for both. "The *ain't* police just said ain't."

Lulu doubles down with, "Who finna correcting me, small-fry?"

Meryl lights up at her mother's *finna*. Russ's head shakes.

With hands on hips, Lulu eyeballs the mutiny. "Oh, y'all comin' for me?" Her head twitches between husband and daughter. She jumps into action, heading toward Russ, where she stops and puts a hand out. "Mind if I see that magazine, dear?"

Russ, the stern leader of a multi-million-dollar corporation, giggles and begs, "Hey, Cree, quit playing." He clamps down on the magazine that covers his boner, laughing with all of his teeth.

The nanny cuts an eye from the kitchen and clears out, safely.

Lulu's hand is still out for the magazine. "I was reading that, Russ. No, seriously," Lulu insists, while struggling to contain her laughter. "Inside that magazine issue, Russ, is a thought-provoking article on what happens to people who try to come for me." Lulu flops on the couch next to her husband and withers on his shoulder with laughter. She leaves him with a kiss and takes Meryl safely down the hall.

Russ sits alone smiling, just so – trying to make sense of how that car accident could have changed his wife, but it has. In the last ten minutes, he's felt more alive than he has in the last ten months. Just this morning he'd been emotionally preparing himself for life without Cree and now, as he watches her walk down the hallway, obviously switching her hips as a display for him, he is utterly smitten with her.

Once out of Russ's sight, Lulu finds Antron's contact on Cree's phone and sends him a text of her condolences and a promise to get him the money soon, which is nothing more than a stall tactic.

Tron replies in one word: *Bet.*

Once Lulu settles into the home for a couple hours, she changes clothes and invents some errand to leave the house – not to pay Tron the money, but to locate her dopeman in this world, but not for dope; he also has the skill to hack Tron's computer to delete the video. For a simple errand, Lulu walks herself tired through the large mansion, just to find Russ and kiss him goodbye. She asks, "Want anything, while I'm out?"

Russ smirks. "You."

Lulu drives off in Russ's Bentley. Soon she's rolling slowly through an apartment complex in North Charleston. Desmond's phone number is in the phone she'd traded with Cree, but what are the chances that he has the same phone number anyway, she thinks. Lulu hopes chances are better that he has the same address. She waits in a parking spot and eventually sees one of the usual goons come out on the balcony, holding a stacked cup, no doubt sipping on lean.

She gets out of the car in a cowl neck blouse, ripped jeans, heels, and oversized gradient shades that covers much of her face.

The man she's looking for, is the one who answers the door, looking her up and down while rubbing his hands. "Whassup ma?" Lulu rolls her eyes. Desmond licks his lips. "You might got the wrong place, but you damn sho got the right dude." Lulu is a stranger to him in this world.

"I gotta get back home in a hurry, so I'll get right to it," Lulu says. "I got somebody tryna run a lick on me. I need the video they're trying to use against me to go missing."

Desmond asks, "Do you know me? What makes you think you can get that here?"

"You gonna invite me in? I told you, I don't have much time."

"I mean, you fine as a mug, but often that's the trap." He sticks his head out the door to look down the apartment stairs on both sides. "Who sent you here?"

A frustrated Lulu shoves him inside and slams the door behind her. "Do I look like I'm playin' with you, Desmond?"

One guy comes in from the balcony toward the commotion: another guy peeks from the kitchen. Desmond frowns, "Hold up, ma… First off, that ain't eem my name." A blatant lie. "Where you get that name from?"

"I got that name from state, when you was a software engineer major, but then yo dumbass dropped out and chose the streets. Acting like you all hard. Boy, you ain't nothing but a nerd in thug's clothing," Lulu says, and chuckles. "I always wanted to say that to your face, but you was my dopeman so…"

"Your *dopeman*, I ain't never seen you in my life," Desmond frowns. He veers that frown over to his comrades, saying. "Dis broad fool, innit?"

Lulu waves a finger across the whole crew, saying, "This *broad*, can pull each and every one of your cards, Desmond, Percy…" Lulu then points to the heavyset one. "And *yo* fat ass… I don't know your real name, but they call you Bean."

Bean looks at her, as he would a snake. He taps Desmond's arm with the back of his hand. "Dis chick po-po, cuz."

Lulu sighs. "I'm not no cop."

"How do we know," says Desmond. With a smirk, he adds, "For our own safety, we gotta check you for wires."

At the sight of lust in his eyes, Lulu digs the revolver out of her purse and waves it, yelling, "Check *who* for wires! Huh? Who gone check me boo?! You? *You?*" Her aim toggles between them, Desmond, Percy, then Bean. "Watch me air this bitch out!" The men sway out of the way of the gun, their palms up and eyes wide with terror.

"Now that I've got your attention," sighs Lulu. "Maybe now we can discuss why I'm here."

Chapter 8

Denial

For her safe return, they have a gathering at Beth's home. Her house is so packed with family, friends and neighbors, they spill out the back door. Cree tries to speak as little as possible to hide her gaps of experience here in this world and it seems to work; no one questions whether she's really their beloved Lulu.

All the love and concern they heap upon Cree, however, is meant for Lulu and it makes Cree sick to her stomach because in her own world, these same folks have given her nothing but venom. Her elder cousin Miss Shannon who leads a prayer, is the same woman who called Cree an uppity bitch when Cree paid her son's funeral expenses directly to the funeral home instead of putting the money in Miss Shannon's hand.

Because Cree dropped the nickname that this community gave her and insisted on being referred to as Cree, they created the narrative that she'd changed, but in Cree's estimation, *they* changed. After becoming Mrs. Rutledge, she couldn't so much as have a conversation that didn't always somehow lead to them expressing a need for money, which Cree gave freely, until she started noticing the disrespect, how money given for rent turned into a Gucci bag; money for truck driving classes became a Vegas trip so blatantly chronicled on social media. So, two years in as Mrs. Rutledge, Cree thought it wise to distance herself, like a lottery winner. Only at funerals and weddings, Cree felt the collective shade of those who were denied a turn at taking advantage of her, as if she should give solely on the strength of having it to give.

Cree is no stranger to the ideology of one man's overflow falling to the village, so she turned Russ's defunct Icarus Foundation into her way to give back, with education supplies, school clothes, tutoring programs, and healthier school lunch options, all funded through her nonprofit organization. Even this was met with ridicule, for help so indiscriminate, being resources versus cash-in-hand. However, the folks who pack Beth's home don't live in the world where they hate Cree, despite her pouring millions in aid, over the years, into this community. This is the world where they adore Lulu who had done nothing but earn fame and riches that she squandered solely on herself; she never even bought a new home for Beth, as Cree had done.

Naturally Cree wants to leave, when surround by a love for Lulu denied to her, coupled by the fact that her living mother, the one person she wants to spend all of her time with, is busy entertaining guests.

She needs to get herself to the home address on Lulu's driver's license, to study the material Lulu left her to prepare for the upcoming concert, but she has no car. Police had impounded her car to search it for evidence of her disappearance.

Russ is blowing up her phone. Cree doesn't answer. She's tempted to see him up close – this Russ who is free of the contempt that husband Russ holds against her, but Cree remembers the detective saying that Russ and Charlene's wedding is being rescheduled, so Cree figures the call holds no possibilities, that it's merely obligatory, since Russ feels responsible for her disappearance. Cree remembers the transcript of text messages between Russ and Lulu – one in particular, where Russ says it was a mistake reconnecting with her, and that, ultimately, his commitment to Charlene was sealed one summer night last year when he got down on bended knee before her.

Russ, Cree's husband in her home world, is here marrying the woman that he denies having an affair with early on in their marriage. Maybe here, the truth is out; maybe Charlene is the real reason behind their divorce in this world, and maybe in the other world, she's the underlying reason Russ heaps so much blame on Cree; he's projecting his own private indiscretion.

Cree sits in the shadowy den, half-listening to her chatty best friend Staysha who never moved to New Jersey, but is still bound to her hometown. This Staysha made the mistake of never marrying Sean, but waiting on her "true love," Jermaine, to be released from prison, only to find herself with him in this dead-end relationship, supporting an infidel who can't hold down a basic job.

Cree's phone buzzes again. It's Russ. This text reads: *I'm outside.* Cree has spent the evening hearing everyone plead with her to stay clear of Russ – not that Russ is bad, but that Lulu's love for the man is toxic. No one dare say, but Cree senses, that they suspect Lulu of staging her own disappearance to thwart Russ's wedding; therefore, Cree sneaks out of the house – not to be with another woman's fiancé, but for a ride to Lulu's apartment so she can start preparing for the concert. In this world, with her mother alive and a readymade singing career, Cree believes she could make a life here, if she can't return to life she knew.

They spot Cree outside getting into Russ's car and begin to call out to her. She and Russ drive off with Beth hurrying down the front steps as the car pulls away.

This Russ is different, Cree notices. He looks like a bad boy twin, with his low-cut, bristly beard. His car isn't the smooth luxury model husband Russ prefers, but a McLaren sports car that looks like a fighter jet, with more muscle under the hood. Likewise, Russ the bachelor has more muscle under his shirt, Cree notices. She keeps peeping at the veiny forearms that handles the steering wheel.

Russ asks, "Have you eaten yet?"

She doesn't catch that the question is an invitation to dinner. "I just really need to go home," says Cree.

"Are you okay, though?"

His glances are cunning, Cree observes. "I'm pretty good, considering, but that's probably because I'm not haunted by memory."

"What do you mean?"

"I can't remember. It's because I'm concussed; it happens."

"Why you talk like that?"

"Like what?"

"Different. Proper."

"I don't know." Cree's hands flop in her lap. "Does Charlene know you're here? I heard you're rescheduling the wedding – as you should," she says. "Be with Charlene. Marry her, Russ. I really don't care."

Russ gives a long blink and glitchy head shake, in the precise image of her husband Russ when he's frustrated with her. "So, you don't give a damn?"

Cree sighs. "I'm not saying that."

Russ glares. "You *literally* just said that."

"I meant romantically. You'll always be Meryl's father."

Russ's head turns like a dial. "Say what?" His *say what* doesn't mean he didn't hear, but what he heard, he couldn't believe.

Cree says, "Surprised I don't put my life on hold while waiting on you to decide?"

Russ's brow wrinkles. "Girl..." he sighs and tremors, not even knowing where to begin. "My mind has always been made up, Lu. I didn't send those texts – the ones that say, it's over between us. Charlene did and then broke my phone so I couldn't reply back. I *just* got a new phone."

The plot twists. Cree's heart pounds, but she keeps a casual face. "So, you come all the way to my mom's house for something you could've said in a text?"

"A text would basically put in writing that Charlene lied to the police. I don't want to get her in trouble, I just want her to move on."

Cree says, "So, you're helping the prime suspect when I could've been somewhere dead?"

"Her being the prime suspect was dictated by the cancelled wedding and our affair – not actual evidence of some doggone kidnapping plot, Lu." Russ has his eyes on the rearview mirror more than the road. Cree looks back. Russ grips her thigh. "Don't look. We're being followed."

Cree's heart leaps. "Like *followed*, followed?"

"I suspected it since I was on the way to your mother's." Russ keeps driving like normal, but when he approaches a red light is when it gets crazy.

He comes to a full stop, squinting in the rearview, waiting for the car behind them to stop. That's when Russ hits the accelerator, running the red light. Cree screams and stiff-arms the dashboard, fully expecting to T-bone a sedan and *be* T-boned by an extra-cab pickup truck. Russ somehow weaves through it, to the sound of squealing tires, blaring horns, and a fit of road-rage in their wake, *Are you blind!*

Russ punches it on the straightaway, his eyes searching the rearview mirror, his mouth speaking to it. "Either come out and show yourself, or take this L."

Cree has a hand over her heart, heaving as if gassed. "And if you kill us both in the process, *then* what?"

He swivels to her, one devilish brow raised. He shifts gears and Cree whips back in her seat. Cree digs her fingernails in the seat cushions; nothing moving but her eyes, stretching and rolling over to the driver. "Russ… Russ…"

He blazes up the entrance onto the Mark Clark expressway, the car growling like a leopard. Russ doesn't decelerate until he reaches the I-26 exit, the exhaust popping like popcorn. Cree's breathing levels off.

Russ asks, "Did you get a look at the car? Is it the same one they used when they kidnapped you?"

"I was blindfolded."

Russ sighs. He massages his bearded chin, identical to how Cree's husband does when has something difficult to say. "How much of your memory is missing," Russ asks, but foregoes her response. "Because earlier, it seems like you forgot that Meryl's not my biological child."

The skin crawls on Cree's face, although she plays it cool. In all their years, she's never let the sentence form in her mind, but now hearing it so casually from the man she feared it might destroy, makes her lightheaded, makes her hearing go liquid as Russ asks *You alright? Lulu?* Meryl's paternity is common knowledge here. Obviously Lulu knows, and since Cree is now Lulu, she can't let on that she didn't know, so Cree keeps calm; her stomach does not. She's getting sicker by the second.

"Babe, are you alright?" Russ assumes its motion sickness from the fast driving.

Cree bends forward and cups her mouth. Vomit spurts through her fingers like milk, as if purging the bile of all those years of denial and deceit.

Chapter 9

Mystery Man

Antron enters Russ's home, apologizing for calling him so urgently. It's the day after Tia's death, so Russ figures maybe Tron needs help paying for the funeral. Antron says, "Sorry, man, I know you got things to do, and all that, but um…"

Russ paws the air. "C'mon Ant. This *you*, brotha. I'll make time." Russ's head tosses in the direction of the bar. "Follow me."

Antron follows, humbly, hat in hand.

Russ pours. "You drink whiskey?"

Antron lowers his head to scratch the back of his neck. "Looks like I'm about to. Actually, I could use a drink right about now," Antron says, and then with lazy eyes, he mumbles, "*You* gone need a drink, for what I'm about to tell you."

"Huh?" Russ looks up from pouring. "You said something?"

"Huh?" Antron stiffens. "Naw, I was saying, I could use a drink right about now."

"I'm talking about what you said after that."

"Naw, naw, but what'd *you* say before that though? Right before asking if I drink whiskey? I didn't catch it." Antron is willing to shuffle the scenarios like three-card molly, for as long as it takes Russ to give up and move on with the discussion.

It works. Russ wiggles a stiff hand. "Never mind, man." Russ slides Antron his drink. Before they touch glasses, Russ offers some words, "Healing from something like this is like healing a broken bone; it's gotta be reset correctly, so it can heal correctly. That being said: for you to heal correctly, you need to understand that God does makes mistakes." Russ sees Antron's confusion, as expected. "You got three children. Don't let nobody fool you into accepting that this was *supposed* to happen or that your wife's death is of some fairness beyond our understanding, because the other side of that coin says, 'therefore you deserved it.' And if you can see yourself as deserving of this, how can you also see yourself as deserving of living your best life going forward."

Antron huffs, "Damn... Never thought about it like that before, Mr. Russ." They take their swigs. Antron's expression displays a glowing review. "This is smooth as hell Mr. Russ. What's the brand?"

"Uncle Nearest... It's black owned," Russ says, as he holds his glass up to the light, examining the tint.

"I lied a minute ago. I'm a cognac man, I actually don't like whiskey – but I like this." Antron, smirking at the glass in his hand, says, "So, this is what rich-people-whiskey tastes like, huh?"

"The best ain't always the most expensive. I still buy my drawers by the pack."

Antron waves a hand, clearing the unwelcomed imagery, "Don't nobody wanna hear about your draws, Mr. Russ." They chuckle together, not like employer and employee, but as if they'd been boys for years, but Russ is a man who used Antron's need to leverage a deal with the mayor, and Antron has kissed Russ's wife and is using it to blackmail them. Now that the small talk has run its course, it's time to confront the issue.

Russ asks, "So what's this thing you wanted to talk to me about?"

Antron stares downward at the table. "Let's see... How do I begin..." Antron shoves his glass forward. "If you don't mind..." He waits until after his glass is refilled and he takes a sip. With his face embittered with the sting of the whiskey, Antron says, "What I'm about to tell you, man, you not gone like it. And by the time we done talking, you not gone like me either."

"Don't tell me you didn't pay off the mortgage – fucked up the money on something else?"

"Naw, Mr. Russ. It's about your wife. She did you dirty, man."

Russ stands and then sits back down.

"Worst thing about it, is that it was with someone you know."

"Who!" Russ stands again. "I'll kill 'em!"

"Kill 'em?" Antron nervously hooks a finger inside of his shirt collar, as he sees Russ texting. Antron asks, "Dang Mr. Russ. You got shooters on speed dial, like that and stuff?"

Russ squints. "I ain't textin' no shooters. I'm texting Cree."

"Why? She ain't gone do nothing but lie. I got it on camera, though."

Russ clenches his jaw and fists. "What, nigga! You was the camera man!"

Antron waves his hand. "Naw, naw, Russ, you got it all wrong. It was captured on the doggie cam."

Russ pounds the table. "Doggie *what!*"

Antron rushes to clarify, "Look, it sounds much worse than it is, ok? Your wife isn't having an affair with anybody, as far as I know, but... What had happened was, while she was over at my place helping me pay off the mortgage, she started talking about y'alls marriage – what's left of it." Antron sighs. "And that's when Cree tried to get me to do sexual favors for that mortgage check–"

"–Bullshit!"

"Yes sir," Antron nods. "And in the process, Cree and I kinda kissed – and umm... yeah... as I said, I kinda have it on camera." A devilish smirk cuts into his cheek. "Also, I kinda want one hundred thousand dollars in order to keep – not only that video private, but also to keep quiet about you using my wife's illness to corner a deal with Mayor Childress."

Russ beams from the corners of his eyes. He downs a shot. He wipes his mouth with the back of his wrist, his eyes never leaving Antron, as if Russ is ready to bullrush him.

Antron starts backing away with his hands up. "Russ? Hey. Don't judge me, brotha. You don't know what it's like to be most people, man. We about the same age, yet I call you *Mister* Russ, huh… You were handed a thousand times more than everything I had to bust my tail for. And because of my wife's illness, which, by no fault of hers or mine, I damn near lost everything because you choose not to pay me what I'm worth. You pay me what you think I'm worth to you."

"Ungrateful bastard! I pay you more than you'd make for any other company! You want more?"

"The money you handed me for the mortgage, and the measly hundred grand I'm asking for, ain't even your money, Russ. Look at it as back pay. That's *my* fuckin' money!"

Russ snatches Antron by his collars. "Boy who the hell you think you're talking to!" Russ is ready to pound on him, but Antron's lack of resistance, and the smile spread clear across his face makes Russ think again.

Antron says, "That's what I want you to do. Steal on me. Give me a damage settlement as a bonus."

Russ unhands him. "Don't tempt me. It might be worth the fee." Russ views a text then looks up from the phone in his hand and says, "You're telling me you have it on video. Cree's saying there is no video, so which is it?"

Antron studders. "Well – I mean… I *had* it on video is what I meant to say."

Russ shakes a finger. "That's the sound of Cree pulling up, right now. We don't have nothing else to talk about until Cree walks in. Then I'll decide what will come of this."

"What is there to decide, though," Antron protests.

"You say the video is missing, right?" Russ claps his hands vertically as if beating off dirt. "So, you have nothing. I can tell you to kindly go straight to hell."

"The video is missing because Miss Cree got someone to hack my computer. I've got evidence of the spyware. I can easily find some tech guy to pull up the I.P. address of the hacking computer – find out who he is and begin connecting the dots. I'll do it if I have to, but it'll be too late for you. Our deal would then be off the table. That's when I take my findings right to Hal Sweeny, where he can present proof that you really are the crook that he says you are."

"I should slap the hell outta you. We pay off your mortgage and this is how you repay us?"

"Don't act like I'm doing you dirty. You did *me* dirty. For years!"

"I could've simply caught up your mortgage. I paid off the whole damn thing, but *that's* doing you dirty?"

Lulu comes through the door but she's not alone. There's a square faced blonde man with blonde eyebrows behind her, carrying a briefcase, and walking with no swing in his arms.

Lulu strides through the living room in elegant fashion. "Sorry to keep you waiting," she smiles, as if back from powdering her nose. "I see Antron's still here. Even better."

Antron looks around, feeling outnumbered. "Wait a minute, now. Who's this guy? Who is he?"

Russ is just as confused as Antron.

The man with the briefcase nods and smiles, "Gentlemen." He's been ordered to not introduce himself until Lulu queues him.

Antron, asks, "This your lawyer, Russ?"

"No lawyer of mine," Russ responds. "Cree?" He gives an animated shrug with empty palms for her to see.

Cree looks at Russ but keeps smiling and walking on the bounce of her hip. The CIA-looking man with the briefcase scans briefly and then points to the ideal space to execute.

Antron, gazing at the mystery man, tells Russ, out of the side of his mouth, "Just so you know, I ain't signing no non-disclosures until that money hits my account."

Russ goes a few paces toward the kitchen. "Cree! I asked, who the hell is this man. Hey! Bro!"

"Darling, relax," says Lulu. "This is going to fix everything." She floats a palm to the man to queue him, "Mr. Whitlock?"

Antron watches closely as the man set the briefcase upright on the kitchen counter, preparing to lay it open, so Antron nervously shuffles over, as if preparing to use Russ as a shield.

In front of the open briefcase, the man faces Antron and Russ, his fingers interlocked in front of him. "I'm Art Whitlock polygraph examiner, and I'll be conducting an examination with the subject, Mrs. Lucretia Antoinette Rutledge. Prior to the examination, I'll be giving you a bit of background on myself and a few mandated disclosures, and then a series of test questions, to demonstrate accuracy..."

The man is so monotone, words lose out to the garble of his own voice. Eventually, the time comes for Art to strap Cree in with the blood pressure sleeve and finger clip.

Antron laughs and shakes his head at the irony, "Aw man... If digging your own grave was a person..."

Cree is poised. Russ is the only nervous person in the room. "You don't have to do this babe. It was only a kiss," he says, thinking perhaps the blissful turn-around of their marriage must've been due to her regret. Russ can deal with suspicion, but if this lie detector test turns suspicion into fact, it will be the end of a marriage that has just reignited the same passion that gave him so much life early on in their relationship. If Cree could be tempted by the likes of an Antron, any man is a threat, in Russ's mind, and that's a level of paranoia he could not live with. "You don't have to prove anything to me, babe."

Cree calmly pets Russ's hand. "But I want to. For me."

Antron giggles in his fist. "Look at em. Lying to the last. Ya can't make this stuff up."

Lulu cuts her eye. "Shut up, Tron... There's not a disloyal bone in my body. My lips will never touch those of another man."

Tron's eyes stretch. "Well, it did, so..."

The examiner begins with a few lead-in questions. The needle goes haywire, scratching ink onto the spooling paper like a seismograph. Mr. Whitlock eventually asks the money question, if she kissed Antron. The examiner couldn't even fathom asking Cree if she's swapped worlds with the version of herself that did.

When the time comes for Mr. Whitlock to render the results, Russ covers his heart in preparation to gather the shards after it shatters to pieces. Antron, who remembers wiping Cree's lipsticks from his lips that day, now rubs his hands together in anticipation of his sure windfall. Neither man gets what they expect. Her responses were truthful.

Russ's heart doesn't shatter. He and Lulu celebrate with a lively embrace. Antron's jaw hits the floor. "What the... Hold on, now, Mr. Whitlock – or whatever your name is, man! There's gotta be some sort of mistake! You gotta run that back one mo 'gain."

Cree releases her lip-lock with Russ to turn to Antron and say, "You? Put your lips on me? Boy, you could never!"

Antron ignores her and crowds the examiner who's now gathering his things. "Hey, yo. Strap *me* in, dawg. Test me!"

Russ and Cree kiss and laugh.

"*Russ*," Antron screams. "What yall laughin' for?" He points from the hip, "You think we're done?" A smile spreads clear across Antron's face. "I still want my money. It don't matter *what* that faulty lie detector test says. You still can't deny that you used my situation to get in good with the mayor. Yeah," Antron's head goes nodding. "I still want my fuckin' money."

The examiner snaps his briefcase closed and adds, "But what you're doing is called extortion. That's a crime. And I'm now a witness. They could turn you in, even for the attempt."

The examiner gets a handshake from Russ who says, "*My* man!" Russ turns to Antron, and says, "Get outta my house!"

In haste Antron storms out, ranting how the exam must've been rigged and how he knows what really happened. Russ shows Mr. Whitlock the door and then returns to the kitchen and resumes a more private celebration with his wife, kissing her and holding her.

Lulu flirts, "Don't start something you can't finish."

Russ says, "Two days in a row?"

Lulu turns in his arms and looks back, "Let me know if you can't hang."

"Try me," says Russ.

Lulu pulls her hair aside to expose the back of her neck. She pulls his hands up from her waist to her breasts, but just when things get steamy, she thinks better of it. "Let me stop. I actually can't right now, as tempting as it is," she says between kisses. "Since the accident yesterday, it's like I've been so busy I haven't had time for momma." Lulu comes out of their embrace and looks for her keys and purse.

Russ stands stock-still, confused, thinking he must've heard her wrong, but talk of her mother reminds Russ to apologize. "Speaking of you mother, Cree... I wanna apologize for what I said, the other day. I spoke out of anger." Russ raises a finger to her lips to shush her. "I just want you to hear it from my mouth. I apologize, babe. That was uncalled for."

Lulu glitches momentarily. She's learned not to ask about things she should know, for fear of raising suspicion, but this one is about her mother; she must know. "Maybe it slips my memory, Russ, but what did you say about my momma?"

With his head hung in shame, Russ says, "How could you forget? You was mad as hell. I had called her a clown."

Lulu huffs. "It's not like you was lying."

Russ watches her, in disbelief, as she swipes her keys and purse off the counter. "Where you headed to?"

"Like I said, I'm gonna go check on momma. Her phone number somehow got erased from my contact list..."

Sorrowfully, Russ replies, "Cree, darling... That's because there ain't no cell phones in heaven, babe."

The news staggers Lulu. Her legs give and she withers down on the tiled floor, panting and repeating, "No, no, no."

Russ goes down to the floor as well and consoles her, in his utter confusion about how the car accident has made Cree forget.

Chapter 10

The Kidnappers

Bachelor Russ is in rare form, confronting gangbangers as if he himself is one. Russ glares at their leader. "So, you're following me now?"

The accusation appears to catch Hook off guard. Slowly, as if not in the least bit pressed by Russ's tone, Hook turns to face him. Between Hook's lazy eyes hangs a stray braid from the spaghetti bun on top of his head. He clears the braid away; there's an old ringworm scar on the back of his hand. "I wasn't fixin' to call you on that burner phone after you gave a statement to po-po, bruh." Still, Hook doesn't outright claim responsibility for tailing Russ, but leaves it up to reason. "Would it been better had I come to your house instead?"

Russ is sure to show strength by not looking away. It is inconceivable that they're the same age, looking at Hook's gold grill, the face tattoos of his old jersey number, 81, on a cheek, and the Arabic font scrawled along his sideburn in blue ink. Hook has the self-regard of a crime boss, but Russ observes a pack leader of lawless teens who follow Hook to fill the void of their missing fathers. Russ says, "You don't put no fear in my heart, bro."

Hook strokes his goat's beard; his smirk holds the suspense of violent intentions. "I ain't concerned about fear in your heart, bruh. I'm concerned about money in my hand. You got the money?"

"What I got is questions. You said you wouldn't harm a hair on Lulu's head. She's got a cut *on* her head and amnesia. Everybody was supposed to think she was in danger, except for her, so why was she running? Why did she have to be fished out of a creek?!"

"Bruh, you dumb to pull up without the money, but pull up *in* something worth ten times the money. Don't think just because me and you played football together back in the day, that we won't stomp you out until you sign over a bill of sale."

"Innit," one young man cosigns; his gun hand slips under his shirt.

The other young man, with too many teeth to close his mouth over, mumbles rap lyrics, a gunplay bar, like a prophecy that he's psyching himself up to fulfill.

Hook calls to someone in another room, "Nisha! You and Man-man go chill next door until I come get you."

A pecan-colored woman with smokers' lips comes walking through. Her split housecoat reveals a belly wrinkled to the texture of dried fig. "Baby need shoes," she teases and sticks out her tongue, her smile bearing gold side-teeth. Waddling after her, is a toddler with fists clenched at his sides like a little brawler. Hook and the two young men eye each other like three sly foxes, as if signaling the next course of action.

Before the situation gets out of hand, Russ says, "I got the money, jackass. But it's not that simple. Lulu was supposed to get the royal treatment; y'all were supposed to make sure she felt safe, so who was she running from, if not from y'all? Make it make sense."

Hook sighs heavily. "Bruh… I ain't about to make sense until I make dollars. Let me see the munny."

They escort Russ to his car, marveling at the burnt orange McClaren. The young men sound off with a local Geechee expression; the elongated second syllable of the word incredible *Creeeed!*

Russ pulls, from the trunk, a dry-cleaned suit still in its plastic. When they return to the apartment, Russ reaches under the plastic and unloads packs of cash to the sound of, *Creeeed!*

Hook hushes them. "Don't act grateful. Y'all work for dis."

While counting the money, Hook begins telling the story, how they gave Lulu the royal treatment. "She ain't been tied to no chair, sittin' in feces, bro. She been comfortable, in a room by 'e self wit' TV, bed... master bath and all." Hook pauses to ask his goons, "Lulu been comfortable, innit?"

They confirm. "Skraight up, bruh. *Too* comfortable.

Hook continues. "We been crackin' jokes. Lulu been laughin' wit' us. Laughin' *at* us... She thought 'e been a game. One time, when you called the burner phone, she talk 'bout: 'Give Russ my love.'"

Russ asks, "So what changed?"

"What changed is when she find out about Nathaniel."

Russ says, "That's the man they found near the scene?"

According to Hook, Nathaniel didn't get the royal treatment like Lulu received. Nathaniel was locked away in the basement, chained to the wall, a bucket for a toilet.

"It been Nathaniel who wanted to escape, and figured he needed Lulu's help to do it. I didn't think they'd be able to hear each other because between them there's a foot-thick concrete layer that prevents the basement from flooding out. Obviously, they was talking anyhow, because when Lulu got out, she knew to go down into the basement to get him."

Russ, nodding as if taking mental notes, turns those notes against them. "So, you're telling me I damn near lost Lulu because you took on a side job? You should've focused only on what I was *paying* you to do."

Hook's head shakes in denial. "You're only saying that because you think Nathaniel is just another man."

"That's all we really are, Hook; you included."

"But Nathaniel ain't one of us." Hook smirks and strokes his beard. "Say Russ, is you familiar with the fable of the golden goose?"

Hook narrates how they met Nathaniel on a casino boat. Since gambling is illegal in South Carolina, casinos exist only on boats that venture outside the state's territorial sea, beyond the reach of the gambling ban.

Nathaniel hit jackpot on two different slot machines, which is unheard of. He requested the payouts in cash. When the ship docked, Nathaniel drove away with twelve thousand dollars and a tail: followed by Hook, his baby-momma, Nisha, and two of his goons.

They later stick Nathaniel up at a rest area, where Nathaniel handed over the twelve thousand dollars without a fuss, but when Hook took Nathaniel's cane, the man fought for it like his life depended on it.

Hook says, "That cane is a relic, he said. He offered to pay me another five thousand dollars to buy the cane back from me, but said he needed to go to another casino to win it." Hook smiles at Russ. "So, we drove all the way to a casino in Tennessee – spur of the moment, just to see how he does it. Once we were there, in less than twenty minutes, Nathaniel hit a jackpot for over five thousand dollars, but it was a setup. That casino had already banned him for winning so much previously, so they not only deny him the winnings but sic their bouncers on us, which created an opportunity for Nathaniel to escape – bastard damn near did. That's why we lock him in the basement. That antique cane is charmed." Hook adds, "The night Lulu escaped, she was able to, because we had only one man on duty. We been on the gamblin' boat busy winning three bands."

"Coincidence," says Russ. "You is a fool to believe in magic."

"As if *you* got room to talk. You believe in boo-hags." Hook turns to his boys. "One day after football practice, Russ let them boys boost him up to stick a pin in Miss Tiller's footprint. Nigga couldn't sleep for days," Hook laughs. "Come gameday this fool threw three picks."

"Root lady, boo-hag… They're not out in the world, they're in our minds."

"We ain't win all that money in our heads, bro. We was on a gambling boat. And we had this cane." Hook picks it up from the floor and holds the scepter up for Russ to see. It's the color of polished copper and adorned with an Egyptian ankh. "I don't know quite if it's magic, but I was assembling a toy for my lil man, had the parts scattered out over the coffee table right over there. But the moment I set this staff down on the table, all the parts slid into alignment. It's all about alignment."

"Enough about that, man," says Russ. "My question to you is, how are you guys not in jail for kidnapping? Police questioned the guy yall chained in the basement. He could've given them information about the stickup at the rest area, the incident at the casino, and police could use that to I.D. you within hours. So, why would the man you all chained in the basement let you off the hook?"

Hook says, "Nathaniel got bigger problems, man. With Lulu being somewhat of a celebrity, this thing was all over the news, exposing Nathaniel's location to all the people looking to gut him over debt."

Russ points. "That's the hole in the story, right there. If Nathaniel can win all the money he wants, how does he end up in debt?"

"He damn sure ain't spending it on himself. He's up to something real big. He's slave to something higher than the men looking to kill him." Hook rubs his hands. "He said his money problems started when casinos started banning him left and right, so he had to travel more; that's how he ended up on a casino boat in a non-gambling state."

Russ dismisses with a lazy hand. "If you believe that, you crazy."

"*I'm* crazy!" Hook looks Russ up and down as if he's short. "You the man paying me to kidnap *one* chick, to justify breaking off the engagement to *another*? Fuck outta here, man."

Russ hides his embarrassment behind a grin that is so teethy, it outs him. "I have a deal with her father, the mayor. *He's* the one who needed things to look a certain way, so that when he delivers on his end of the bargain, he doesn't seem insensitive for helping the man who broke his daughter's heart."

"A lie is a lie, bro."

Russ holds a blank faced stare. "I don't expect you to understand the importance of a man's word, Hook. I bet it's easy for you to go back on your word when it ain't worth a damn. When I give *my* word, it's law. Back in '09, during the recession I promised no layoffs. I was just twenty-two years old, new at the helm of the company. The real estate market was so dead, even *birds* stopped building nests, yet I kept the company at full staff because no matter how foolish a promise it turned out to be, it was my word. So, I kept us at full staff, even though Rutledge Enterprises suffered."

"*Suffered*," says a wide-eyed Hook. "Don't make me slap the shit outchyou dawg." With that threat, even in jest, the energy in the room changes. "I can't hear your talk about suffering, because of that big ole silver spoon in your mouth–"

"–I wasn't talking about suffering. You picked that one word and made it everything. I was speaking on the value of a man's word." Russ notices how Hook's young and fatherless soldiers pique at the sound of man wisdom; they hunger for it. It is the source of Hook's power over them, which explains why Hook's anger deepens; he's insecure in the influence he has over them.

"Bruh, if your so-called 'word' was so valuable, you would've kept it, instead of handing thousands of dollars over to me, so who's the dumbass?"

"Not me," says Russ. "Since, all I'm doing, is giving you back a small portion of the money you surrendered to me."

Hook says "You sound stupid as fuck. What money I gave you?"

Hook's goons try to calm him. Hook protests, "Naw, lemme hear what this fool tryin' to say."

Russ, with a dare in his eyes, explains, "You used to live in Park Circle – helped turn it into the wild west, driving the crime rate up, but the property value down, which prompted builders like myself come in and buy up properties at cents on the dollar.

We enjoyed three hundred percent profit margins, all thanks to you. *Now* who's the dumbass?"

Hook stands, in outrage.

Russ stands, fearless.

Hook punches Russ in the mouth. Russ stumbles but he doesn't fall. Russ eyes Hook, who seems ready to launch another attack at the next sign of insolence. Russ smears a trickle of blood from the corner of his mouth and walks off laughing, triumphantly, for how Hook's act of violence demonstrates how Hook is still slave to the same violence has crippled and up-rooted his community.

Not long after Russ leaves, and Nisha and the toddler returns, there's another knock at the door. Buck looks at the peep-hole and sees a man in a white oxford shirt and a body holster, a badge by his belt buckle. Buck backs away slowly.

Hook asks, "What the hell is your problem, man. Who at the doh?"

Buck puts his finger to his lips to signal quiet, and then whispers, "Russ set us up."

From the other side of the door, the officer yells. "I just wanna talk!"

"Shiiiid," Hook drones. They jump into action, tiptoeing, hurriedly, in an attempt to hide money and flush dope. The door's deadbolt grinds and clicks.

When the door swings open, they freeze. The detective's hands are up, the skeleton key pinched between two fingers. Hook is as still as a statue, bronzed with a foot raised mid-step, and lips scrunched to a small o. Even the toddler freezes. Nisha is a statue of Greek classical antiquity, her lose robe revealing a boob as she stoops to tend her child, only she's stuffing the diaper with marijuana. Buck's mouth is packed with more than just teeth; a cough ejects a dime-bag, which brings this wax museum to life.

The lawman says, "I'm not with the county. Jett Johnson, P.I. At present, I'm simply an escort." The man steps aside.

Charlene enters, in somewhat of a disguise. Her bang meets the top of her dark shades; she wears a white scarf around her head and neck like a hijab, and she's covered up to the elbows with long gloves.

Nisha points at Charlene but looks at Hook, asking, "Who dis chick?"

Charlene completely ignores Nisha. She waves for the P.I. to leave.

Investigator Jett Johnson announces, "Don't say anything incriminating until this door closes or I'll be forced to act on it. I'll just assume that's the legal, non-THC cannabis you're stuffing in that baby's diaper," he says, and bids adieu.

The moment the door closes, Charlene says, "Russell Rutledge was just here, am I right?"

Hook replies before anyone else can. "I don't know nobody by that name, miss."

Charlene adds, "He came in and out of this very apartment. I have pictures that I can turn into the police. Ask yourselves, how would you fair against a felony kidnapping charge?"

"And Russ gets conspiracy," says Hook. "You gone have a jail cell wedding, must be."

"Then, so be it," says Charlene, without so much as a chink in her resolve. "I have all the leverage I need, yet I'll even pay you, to sweeten the deal. You work for me now."

Hook nods in thought, searching for a strategic out, but finding none. Hook's eyes lift, and he says, "What you got in mind?"

Chapter 11

The Train Wreck

The rainbow-colored clown wig sits on the kitchen table on a placemat that Beth had woven herself, in the traditional Gullah style of palmetto basket weaving. Beth's teeth and eyes seem stained against the yogurt white face paint. Her high-arching eyebrows and red, fabricated smile makes a mockery of her anger. "Damnit Lucretia, it's only an hour! I may have custody, but Meryl is still *your* daughter. I shouldn't even have to ask!"

Cree's eyes go lazy, but dare not roll at her mother. "I don't need you to remind me whose daughter Meryl is. I have an obligation. The concert's today, and this is the last and final promo."

"*And,*" says Beth.

Cree drops a hand on the table. "It's not just me and the band due at the radio station. The headliner, Darius Rucker, will be there too. I can't be late and risk looking like the train-wreck everybody already thinks I am." Cree throws her hands up in surrender. "You know what: I'll just take Meryl with me down to the radio station."

"Absolutely not! Going missing set you back enough already. Now, you wanna break the Child Protective Services arrangement? Get caught and you'll never get custody again."

"Momma? Momma. Hear me: I. Cannot. Be. Late."

"You won't be," Beth says, smugly, through her candy red lips. "I'll be back in time."

"In a perfect world, yeah, but what if something happens? What if there's a traffic incident? You can't call out, this once, ma? You act as if that hospital cuts you a paycheck."

"And *you* act like money is the only reward in life, Lulu. I'll tell you what…" Beth slides her cell phone across the kitchen table. "Call out *for* me. There's the contact, right there," the entry under her tapping fingernail. "Have them put Zack on the phone. He's nine… leukemia…You tell that boy he doesn't get a happy escort to his bone marrow transplant today." The hanging silence vindicates Beth. "Don't ever ask me to do something you won't do yourself."

"Okay, you win, ma," Cree pouts, although a smile blossoms as she studies her mother. "You…" Her head shakes. "You always have something to give. That's where I get *my* charitable spirit."

"Charitable!"

Cree laughs. "I have this silly idea of starting a nonprofit foundation in your honor." She already has, and can't even tell Beth.

The clown cuts her eye, snatches up her purse, and gets up to go. Cree stands in the way, not letting her mother by without a tight hug. "I love you, love you, love you, momma."

"I love you too, hon," Beth says with this nervous, shifty-eyed grin, as if agreeing just to get by this crazy person. Beth, with her chin over her daughter's shoulder, cuts her eye and says, "You crying Lulu?" Beth pulls back and thumbs her daughter's tears. "I swear, Lulu. How you get so tender-hearted all of a sudden?"

Cree's mother is who she has always been, but Meryl is a different story. She's been raised by Cree's counterpart, Lulu, a drug addict divorcee who failed to shelter Meryl from her music industry lifestyle in the Big Apple where Lulu lived up until a year ago, and now this Meryl seems headed in Lulu's footsteps.

Meryl, that little neck swerving sassy mouthed child, has been locked in her room all morning, per usual, on the phone either with boys, or with girlfriends talking about boys. Cree suspects that Meryl has been vaping, beginning a life of chasing the high. Cree decides she'll be casual with Meryl, for now, since Cree will only be here another day if Lulu shows up to swap worlds.

LATER, when Beth returns from volunteering at the hospital, Cree has just enough time. She speeds the whole way to the station, handling both the steering wheel and her cell phone, to call ahead. She nearly hit a crossing pedestrian in the process, but Cree just makes it to the Z93 station, flopping into her seat just as the radio personality, the lovely Kris Kaylin hit the On Air button.

As Kris makes the rounds for the introductions, all eyes are on her. Since Kris is the only one looking at them, she's the only one who notices the white stain on the nose of Lulu McQueen. Kris tries to signal her nonverbally so not to alert the listeners, but Cree misinterprets the gesture as shade, or as if she's being singled out for some sort of lowkey rivalry, since she's the only other woman in the room. It's the drummer, Bam-Bam, who clarifies, over an unmuted mic, "Lulu. Your nose. It's stained."

Kris smacks her own forehead. "Now the listeners know. I was trying to be discrete, y'all."

Lulu wipes her nose and studies her hand. "It's not what you think. It's face paint, I swear." She explains how she must've gotten a smudge from hugging her mother, who happens to be clown.

No matter how true, it sounds like the most outlandish lie ever told. The interview crashes, off top, and never really recovers. Lulu becomes the focus, even overshadowing Darius Rucker. When callers dial in with questions and comments, mostly of a heckling nature, they're all about Lulu McQueen, who nearly ran over a pedestrian to make it on time, but still ends up looking like the train wreck the media makes her out to be.

CHARLENE backs into her park, her driver's side door facing Detective Ryan's, so they can have a conversation without leaving their cars. "Detective," is her greeting.

"Miss Hamilton." Tension mounts.

Charlene sighs deeply and says, "I'm sure that, by now, word has made it down the chain of command to you. I *do* hope you were able to read between the lines."

"Superiors will say this or that," Ryan says, as he squiggles a finger by his head. "But my training, my conscience, and going by the book has never steered me wrong."

"They want to make an example out of Lulu."

"That's not the mood I'm sensing, internally. They who?"

"The attorney general of this great state. Do you know who funded Wells' campaign?"

"Here we go," gasps Ryan.

"The same folks who used to fund my daddy's campaign: big pharma. It's why this state has such a resounding legislative resistance to both medicinal and recreational marijuana. Mind you, our current governor is also the *former* attorney general – also bought and paid for by big pharma – which is why that bong incident with that Olympic swimmer resulted in the indictment of eight friggin' college students. So, Detective Ryan, I submit, that it is of the utmost importance to make an example of any celebrity traipsing around, promoting self-medication, cutting into big pharma's half a trillion dollars annually."

Ryan's face falls slack. "Frankly, I don't get into all that politics. All I can say is that being an addict ain't a crime, the crime is possession of the drug itself."

"Having it in your system counts as possession. Lulu had coke up her nose just this morning. Child Protective Services sees fit to open an investigation, and you don't?"

"You called CPS?" Ryan fumes with grit teeth and a slow shaking head. "If CPS wanna follow up your nonsense, let 'em."

"Nonsense?" Charlene is aghast at how cavalier the detective is. "You didn't tune into the radio this morning? My private investigator did. It came out, on air, that Lulu had a powdered nose. What more do you need to make an arrest?"

"*My* investigation pertains to her disappearance. Did your private investigator turn up anything on that?"

"Yes, actually. He's narrowed down the locations of her hideout."

"By what means? We had trained men looking for her – dogs who couldn't pick up her scent due to the rain. Inform your private investigator that if he's withholding intel on an active investigation, he's not only in violation of his license, but also giving the perception that he's tampering."

Charlene rolls her eyes. "Careful of that tongue, detective – or do I assume correctly that you're implying I'm paying someone to obstruct an investigation?"

Detective Ryan asks, "Gimme a name on your private I."

Charlene hesitates then relents. "Jett... Jett Johnson."

"Telling *me* be careful," Ryan grumbles. "*You* be careful this case isn't the thing that shows you the limits of your money and access."

"You'd love to see that. If you'd put teaching me a lesson over solving the case, you have no business even working this case."

Detective Ryan leans out of his driver's side window to give her a good look at his face. "Are you a Godfearing woman, Charlene? Sure, you go to church every Sunday, but do you actually believe that Jonah lived in a whale three days, or that Elijah struck the river with his cloak and the waters opened up?"

Charlene looks at him grotesquely. "You're insane–"

"–So, you *don't* believe it."

"What I don't believe is your comparison of God appointed men to a coke addicted woman."

"All addictions are attached to a substance – even your addiction to vengeance, Miss Hamilton, comes from a *lack* of substance. It takes but an ounce of grace to see that the vengeance you seek doesn't change Russ's heart," says Ryan. "But you say

I'm insane? If so, tell me how there're Lulu's footprints through the marsh leading up *to* the creek, but none coming out – and then hours later and miles downstream, there're Lulu's footprints coming out of the creek, but none going in… no sign of any boat. If I'm insane, tell me how one of the volunteer searchers said he looked Lulu dead in the face when the creek swallowed her. That volunteer is retired Coast Guard, been on countless rescue missions, said he never seen nothing like it in all his life – right hand to God. And that ain't all either," Ryan says, quaking with conviction. "I also caught up with the man who helped Lulu out of the creek but fled the scene – said Lulu suddenly come bubbling up out of nowhere, miles downstream and hours later. Are we *all* insane? Huh?" Ryan swats the air, "Ah, what the hell am I doing explaining myself to you. Go crawl into your big ole brass bed and cry it out like everybody else. It's a broken heart, Charlene. *Your* problem. Not the state's."

"Detective," Charlene says. "Do not take me lightly. You will make an arrest by today, understand? You've got Lulu dead to rights with the drugs. She snorted up just this morning; it's in her system."

"*Today*," Detective Ryan huffs. "I told Lulu; I'd question her on Monday."

"Monday!"

"Take it up with the doctors who recommended it." Ryan points at his head, "Concussion, remember?"

"So, Lulu gets to have her little farewell concert?"

Ryan's brow goes askew. "Are you forgettin' it's a charity concert for the flood relief? There are people in need, yet you wanna walk right up to the front of the line in your Louis Vuitton shoes and be served before them? That's not how it works."

"Russ doesn't get to back out of a wedding with the woman whose been beside him for all these years. *That's* not how it works. Since you're so dead set on Monday, you be ready to receive a call in about a half hour that's gonna change your plans," Charlene threatens.

Detective Ryan takes a deep breath, his head lops forward, teeth grinding. "Since you're obviously fixin' to tell on me, you can also tell 'em I called you a bitch!" Ryan squeals out of the parking lot.

Before Charlene makes the aforementioned phone call, she calls Hook. "What all do you have," she asks and then listens. "My God, man, you're gonna need more than just the bedsheets. Gather anything you can, like items from the bathroom, hair strands, things Lulu may have handled, like the toilet paper roll, soap... Go through trash cans for to-go boxes and plasticware, put it all in a big trash bag and move it to the new location. I don't know what association Russ could have with that house, but I don't want anything being traced back to him, you got me?"

Charlene hangs up and goes down her contact list for her next call, but suddenly there's an ambush of emotions. Tears well up and she can't seem to stop sighing. "It's not fair," Charlene cries.

Not fair that she must pull so many strings just to make things go as they should; not fair that she must fight for the heart she's already won; not fair that she's made to contend with a low life like Lulu; even the name, Charlene thinks, is a badge of ignorance.

If Charlene knew this would be the outcome, she wouldn't have bat an eye at Russ at that frat party long ago, as he leaned against the wall with his shirt open, looking like a cologne model. And when Russ touched Charlene's hand and asked, *Do you smoke*, she would've lied and said no; instead of clarifying, *you mean reefer?* So, hours later, the party diminished and littered, she and Russ were in the back, breaking the box spring on some poor chap's twin sized bed.

Russ always supplied the weed; it got him into circles that his charm couldn't. Charlene assumed Russ was some underprivileged brainiac. Charlene never asked Russ how he was able to afford the tuition, figuring she'd save him the embarrassment of confessing that he was a charity case, perhaps granted some rigged up scholarship that schools use to fill their diversity quota.

After a while of linking up with Russ, Charlene discovered, to her surprise, that Russ wasn't a charity case, after all; his family was more well-off than hers. The next time they crossed paths on campus, they didn't just speak in passing. Charlene stopped Russ and kissed him, as way to lay claim in the presence of friends of which she'd hidden their relationship.

That public kiss prompted Russ to pull Charlene aside and inform her that he'd gotten some chick pregnant. 'Some chick' was Lulu. Although Charlene and Russ's relationship was casual, Charlene felt like yanking out her hair, however, she calmly asked Russ if he had feelings for her, and Russ denied it.

Charlene monitored the situation by rumor. It became apparent that the woman that Russ doubted his parents would even approve of, was keeping the baby, and Russ was committing to Lulu as a way to commit to fatherhood. The child was a dealbreaker for Charlene and she moved on without an issue.

Two years after the shotgun wedding, and after college, Charlene heard that Lulu was leaving Russ, so Charlene reached out to him. Charlene became his listening ear; they talked more than they had back in college, when they were sexual. They talked often over the phone, but they ran into each other quite often as well. Since Russ was the heir apparent to run his father's company, he attended many of the same events alongside his father, who was showing him the networking ropes. Many of those events Charlene also attended, as a show for her father. At those events, Charlene felt no qualms about flirting with the technically married man. She admired how Russ resisted her advances; his loyalty only made him more irresistible.

Russ was still technically married, when Lulu was on a flight to New York to sign a recording contract, and when Charlene spotted Russ alone at the hotel ballroom wedding reception of a mutual friend, posted up at the open bar, drunk. Russ confided that the child was not his.

Charlene later cornered Russ in the hotel stairwell and they had a brief and aggressive romp, clothed and standing upright, her bridesmaid dress lifted.

Russ, out of guilt, vowed to steer clear of Charlene, and he did, until a year later when the divorce was final. By that time, Charlene had moved on to a relationship with J.D. Sumter who owned a medical billing company and seemed to be a fine prospect to marry, but eventually went to federal prison for Medicare fraud.

Charlene sighs, thinking, what people don't understand is that Russ did not string her along. She initiated half of their four breakups over the years, but when Charlene eclipsed age thirty, with no option more logical than Russ, she began pushing the issue of marriage and starting a family. Russ, also thirty with no children, and no option more logical than Charlene, made *going along willingly* look like everything he'd ever wanted.

Charlene and Russ had their wedding planned and deposits made with the vendors; their honeymoon flight paid for. To start a family as swift as possible, Charlene wanted to schedule their wedding and honeymoon in concert with ovulation, but months prior to the wedding, Charlene, newly off of birth control and after a series of gyno visits learned that there was no ovulation to schedule around. Hypothyroidism was the diagnosis; this is the detail in Charlene's text history that she wanted her lawyer to protect from evidence.

Charlene believes that her infertility is the reason Russ suddenly can't live without Lulu. Charlene also believes that Russ, in his haste to start a family, simply sought out the only other logical option, his ex-wife – regardless that she's prone to squandering anything worth having in life – the calamity would be worth it, to Russ, if it produces a legitimate heir.

Charlene considers her infertility and her being stood up at the altar, and wonders if she's somehow victim to her own karma, for the stairwell nookie with a man who was still technically married, but if karma would be so petty to steal Russ from a woman such as herself, only to give him to such a thing as

Lulu, on such a small offense, it is time that karma meets its match.

Chapter 12

In Concert

The Coliseum security seems awfully stacked; Cree thinks. There are many county squad cars, in addition to the coliseum staff. Cree wants to ask if this is normal, but she can't ask what the real Lulu should know. The V.V.S. band members, with whom Cree has rehearsed for three days, has already made a game of pointing out how different Lulu has become since her disappearance, so Cree doesn't give them yet another reason.

Together, they sit behind the dark tint of a limo, provided by the company that manages them. Dimples notices the security as well. "See that, y'all? All those squad cars?"

Bam-Bam, the drummer, looks up, tickled. "I swear to you, I've never met a saxist that doesn't worry like a mother hen. It's the escort, Dimps. It's nothing."

"Actually, it *is* something." Cree raises her phone, showing a text that just came through. "They're here to arrest me."

Bam-Bam tosses his hair out of his face. "Says *who?*"

"Says the lead detective." Cree holds her phone up, advertising the text message she cites.

Skeet, the bass player, asks, "Why warn you? Isn't that working against himself?"

Bam-Bam orders the limo driver to cruise past the Coliseum and go to the Convention Center. "We'll take the sky walk over to the coliseum and figure the rest out from there."

Dimps says, "With no security escort?"

Skeet, the bass player, yells, "We're has-beens, alright! Nobody fixin to mob us." A thick and sobering silence fills the limousine. Skeet shrugs, "It needed to be said."

Skeet's prediction proves accurate. As they trot down the green tinted skywalk, no one mobs them. Fans tap each other and point, they take cell phone pictures, but do not impede them.

The band files into the dressing room's common area like stowaways down in the belly of a ship. Faintly, they hear the sea of fans outside, cheering the current act on stage, Grammy Award Winning jazz-Gullah infusion group, Ranky Tanky.

Cree sees a locker tagged with her name. Her costumes hang inside. "Looks like the equipment manager's been here already."

In storms the man they call Fly Guy who is anything but fly, with deep wrinkles across his forehead like tire tread. He's called Fly Guy not for his looks, but for his sharp suits, matching down to the pocket hanky and socks. Guy who possesses the dramatic flair of a circus ringleader, announces, "There you are." He laughs. "I was out front with the police, watching yall snoop across the goddamn skywalk. It was unnecessary, folks. I worked it out."

A wowed Cree exclaims, "Really!?"

"They're gonna let you perform," says Guy. "But right after, it's…" He lays one wrist over the other and makes a click in his cheek.

"Me… Arrested…" Cree shudders at the thought of being in a concrete box room with addicts and gum-popping night walkers.

"Won't be the first," heckles Skeet.

The news of being arrested and booked after the concert, is a dagger in Cree's heart. It's a Saturday, so if Cree gets arrested, she can't post bond until Monday, and would miss her rendezvous with Lulu. Cree doesn't say anything to the band, but to avoid being trapped in this world forever, she'll risk it all to prevent going away in cuffs tonight. Cree gets dressed and tells them, "Guys, I'll be right back."

Cree hurries to the door, but pauses with the door open because she can feel their eyes on her back. She turns and says, "Chill. I'm not about to run, alright. I said I'll be right back." She closes the door behind her. No one follows her.

By the time, they're queued to the stage, there's no sign of Lulu McQueen. The band gets in position. On the other side of the thick curtain is an antsy crowd. "She cut and run," says Bam. "I knew it."

Skeet, with the bass standing as tall him says, "Guy is on it. All we can do is wait." The crowd grows restless.

Meanwhile Cree runs. She runs out of the engineering room and down the hallway to the elevator, which takes her down. She sprints down another hallway and goes into the door that leads backstage, where she runs onto the stage, to the band and backup singers' collective sigh of relief.

She stops front and center, the conservative Cree wearing Lulu's rhinestone encrusted choker and two-piece bikini over a near sheer body suit. Cree is just about naked with only a curtain and ten seconds between herself and thirteen thousand fans.

At least her backside is covered by a red cape that she'll helicopter above her head and toss by the second stanza of the first song, and then it's cheeks out for the regal Mrs. Rutledge, corporation head, and philanthropist.

While awaiting the inevitable, in a victory stance, with the unholstered microphone held over her head, Cree relaxes her breathing, so not to puke on her first note.

The lights go down. The spotlight swings to the curtain, beaming at Cree's silhouette. The crowd goes wild, which sounds like the heaviest rainfall imaginable.

Stage fog rises like dragon breath as the curtains come away. The bands strikes up the looming intro. Cree quivers with anticipation. This isn't open mic at some tapas bar. The deafening sound system, and the energy of thirteen thousand rabid fans is something that no number of band rehearsals could prepare her for.

Cree's future rides on this performance, whether that future be in this world or the next. Her head rears back to speak up into the raised microphone, where she yells. "Charleston are you ready!" They roar in response. Cree feels their energy reverberating through her, which she in turn gives back to them. "I said Charleston are y'all ready, out there!"

They're so loud, she must concentrate to hear Bam-Bam, the drummer, the timekeeper, who gives that signaling drum roll and smash, queueing a three seconds' pause, where even breathing isn't allowed. Cree's closed eyes open and scans from within her thick costume eyelashes, a snarl on her upper lip. She remembers that she was born for this, that – as Lulu said – every version of herself, but her, is doing this very thing, and so Cree now comes forward, singing, in a leggy catwalk, stride over stride, like Lulu does every performance of this up-tempo crowd pleaser. As she's studied in Lulu's concert DVDs Cree stops at the lip of the stage, microphone pointed to the crowd, giving the second bar over to her fans: *I had to be me, cause everybody else was taken!*

LULU

Lulu, the author of that line, doesn't need a reminder to be herself. For example, she'd learned that the family attends church every Sunday. Church isn't Lulu's style, but if she must, she'll do it with her own flair. She searches through Cree's wardrobe and although her church outfits are elegant, it's a bit conservative. Lulu wants Russ's interest piqued at all times, even at church, so she goes shopping for a new outfit. Since she and Meryl has struggled bonding, Lulu brings Meryl along, hoping some girl time might help the little uptight, overthinker to loosen up, and maybe laugh at a joke without having to dissect its logic.

Meryl picks up everything off the rack that Cree doesn't allow; ripped jeans, high tops. She holds up a hanger with a halter top. Lulu cuts her eye, "You runnin' out, now."

They take an armload to the dressing room. Meryl comes out twirling like a ballerina in the three-way mirror. Lulu gives a thumbs down, but then she examines from another angle, with a new critique, "I know what it is, baby. It's that hair. Your momma won't let you get no perm?"

"What do you mean my momma," Meryl asks. "So, who are *you?*"

Lulu tries to play it off. "Silly," she laughs. "I'm pretending to be one of your little friends, Meryl. You need to learn to just roll with it sometimes, or you're gonna always be on the outside looking in. Remember that." When Meryl returns to the dressing room, Lulu gasps with a hand on her chest, relieved at how well her excuse went over.

Ahead, in the three-way mirror, a woman catches Lulu's eye, which means she's behind. Lulu swivels in the woman's direction and verifies that it is, in fact, Charlene Hamilton over in the boys section with a teenager who is too old to be her own. Lulu spots a wedding ring on Charlene's hand and figures maybe the boy is a stepson from her husband's previous relationship. Lulu takes to the walkway to position herself to get a better look. The boy splits off from Charlene and goes his own way.

Lulu takes off, speed-walking to catch Charlene from behind, which isn't hard to do with this lumbering Charlene, who is about sixty pounds heavier, with lamb legs, looking a hot mess, Lulu thinks. This Charlene is no rival in this world, nor is she fit to be, but this is the only Charlene available to which Lulu can gloat about winning out in the end. Lulu taps her on the shoulder. "You tried it," Lulu gloats.

Charlene spins, confused. "Excuse me? Tried what?"

Lulu grins. "You had the right idea, but the wrong chick."

"If it isn't Lulu, or it's Cree, nowadays isn't it," Charlene says, with a facetious smile. "I see Russ lets you out in public now that you've learned to walk upright on your on your hind legs."

This Charlene, with that same sharp tongue, almost makes Lulu laugh at herself. "Keep running that mouth," warns Lulu.

Charlene peers into Lulu's eyes and says, "I could've destroyed you a long time ago. Careful not to wake a sleeping dragon."

Lulu slides one foot back in a ready stance. "Wake, then, hoe, so I can put you right back to sleep."

Meryl comes to a running stop, saying, "Ma! What're you *doing?*"

Charlene nods to Meryl. "Even the pup has more sense than you."

Deciding that Meryl has seen too much already, Lulu ignores Charlene's comment and puts her arm around Meryl to usher her away.

Charlene throws her voice behind them. "Jacoby Brooks," she says and stares, as if waiting for Lulu's head to topple off.

Lulu, walking briskly away, wobbles at the mere mention of the name.

Lulu hurries across the parking lot and to the car. Meryl, trotting to keep up with her mother, protests all the way, that she wasn't done shopping.

"*Get* in the damn car, little girl," Lulu yells, finally.

Meryl gets in and sits with her hands in her lap, spooked by an outrage that she's never seen from her mother.

Lulu rests her head on the steering wheel, beating herself up internally, while externally, dropping a litany of four-letter words. There's no way Lulu could know that the Charlene, in this world, knew that Meryl isn't Russ's child, but with that unnecessary confrontation, Lulu may have triggered Charlene to expose Meryl's paternity, the thing that ended their marriage in the other world; it may now do the same in this world, just three days into Lulu's happily ever after.

Lulu wants to be mad at Charlene, but can't – not with the voice of her mother playing in her head, *Lulu, you' your own worst enemy.*

Spontaneous, open-air confrontation is classic Leonard Hughes, with that short fuse and the abandoning of judgement, magnified by addiction. Like her father, Lulu knows well the depravity of addiction. Even now, in her mounting anxiety, her jittering hands, she fiends for a fix. In a world where she doesn't have her mother nor Staysha's presence to pull her together, she considers going back to Desmond – this time for dope, but no. Her head actually shakes no from her internal refusal; it's Meryl. Lulu remembers being the in the position of the daughter riding shotgun as her father would take her to the most poisoned pockets of the neighborhood, where dope is more available than candy, where women's blouses droop off of their shoulders and where men have never learned that it's rude to stare. Lulu would rather eat her own tongue than repeat that cycle in the presence of Meryl, so she heads home instead.

When Lulu returns home, Russ observes how Meryl marches straight to her room, with no word of their shopping adventures, and Lulu, herself, is melancholy. Russ asks, "Everything alright, Cree?"

Lulu offers some excuse and continues to mope around the kitchen as she sets the table for another crockpot dinner. When the meal brings all three members of the family to the table, it's apparent, to Russ, that Lulu and Meryl are not speaking, as he finds himself rotating between two separate conversations, one with his wife and one with his daughter. Russ asks, "Either of you planning on telling me what happened?"

Meryl frowns but keeps quiet. Lulu follows suit, hoping to avoid any discussion because it will likely lead to Lulu having to explain her confrontation with Charlene. Lulu does, however, give Russ eye signals to just let it go.

"What…" Russ half smiles. He suspects Meryl's first menstrual cycle. "It's some type of girl thing?" His grin, along with his question falls dead like a shot duck.

The scrape and clank of silverware sounds like fencing swords. With this Meryl, Lulu can sense this thing that she often observes in her own Meryl, the stillness of her head, the activity in her eyes; she's working herself up to an outburst. Meryl, with a sharp cut of her eyes, says, "You know I don't like oxtails."

Lulu stammers for an excuse. Her own Meryl likes them, but Lulu now remembers the years of coercion it took to train her Meryl's palate. Lulu explains, "I just thought that with the savory curry sauce and the coconut rice you might like it this way."

Russ looks away and rubs his forehead. Meryl calls his attention with a sharp, "Daddy? You need to take this woman back to the hospital and get her head checked."

"*Meryl*," chides Russ.

Lulu sizes her daughter up like an opponent. "'This woman'… You better duck, next time you come outta your mouth like that."

Meryl points at the threat. "See, daddy!"

Russ sighs. "She's just talking honey, ain't nobody raising a hand at nobody in this house."

Lulu warms her hand for a slap, breathing on her palm as she would, to fog a mirror. "Don't fall for that setup, Meryl," Lulu warns. "Try me again with that disrespect."

"As for you, Meryl," Russ warns. "You *will* respect your mother."

Meryl stiffens and her eyes widen. "Oh, I have no problem respecting my mother – only this person is not my mother." Meryl pushes back from the table and stamps off to her room.

"She's twelve," Lulu excuses. "On top of that, she's a girl. She invents her own problems." And that's the end of it, for Lulu, as she drops her napkin in her plate and gets up.

Russ, with a tickled brow, sums up the entire ordeal with one punchline. "Savory curry sauce, babe?" In more serious thoughts Russ acknowledges that, of at least one thing, Meryl is right; Cree has changed since the car accident. It seems as if Cree has reverted to a less evolved version of herself, where they're now allowed the simplicity of living in the moment, which is good for their marriage, but maybe a disservice to motherhood.

Chapter 13

Too Good In Bed

The end of Cree's performance reveals why she had vanished in the beginning.

On the final song, Cree's final note fills the rafters and slowly descends, her diaphragm deflating until the note, and herself, is spent. The crowd goes wild as Cree stands there panting. Lulu, was right; the stadium of fans helps Cree realize that she was born for this. The fingertips of both hands meet over her lips, then open outward to spread kisses over them; Cree can't express just how much life this audience has given her.

Cree goes off script and calls the band forward to the front of the stage to bow with her, which queues the engineer that Cree had convinced to help her, during the time she'd went missing and the band thought she'd ditched them. The untimely stage smoke appears to be some malfunction to everyone but Cree, who backs into it, disappearing under its cover, where she finds the centerstage platform that lowers her beneath the stage.

The officers waiting backstage to arrest Lulu, come out to the stage, scandalous and bumbling, in the glare of the spotlight. They squat for better vision in the rising stage fog. They find Lulu's boots on the centerstage platform elevator – a red herring, for the smoke clears to reveal that there's no Lulu standing in the boots.

Cree sprints down a series of hallways, stopping and spying at each corner. She takes a service elevator up to ground level and she exits an unmanned side door, wearing a backpack of her things, and speed-walking on a b-line for Russ's idling car.

Russ isn't alone. Charlene has found him and she is stooped at his drivers' side window, oblivious to the fact that Russ is Cree's getaway car. As Cree marches up from behind, she hears Charlene pleading for reconciliation, "Stop being dramatic, Russ. You do *not* love her."

Cree looks to avoid conflict by simply rounding the car to the passenger door, but seeing Charlene plead for Russ's love strikes some territorial nerve. There's a flipped switch – a switch she'd forgotten ever having – a rage, like voltage sizzling in her bones, unloading with each determined step steering her in Charlene's direction. Cree comes down on Charlene's head with both hands clamping fistfuls of hair, which Cree yanks like wagon reigns. Charlene rears back so horse-like, that the neigh seems oddly missing. Charlene drops, rump first. Cree has a knee raised like a flamboyant drum major, ready to stomp Charlene into a puddle.

Russ yells, "No!"

Cree comes out of the blood-thirsty trance, head down, eyes darting, as if looking for a visual of the demon exiting her chest.

Cree hurries around to the passenger seat.

Charlene hops up and runs at the car, screaming as Russ drives off. The skirmish goes unnoticed. They were shielded, both sight and sound, by the long line of idling concert busses.

Russ and Cree head on to their romantic plans for the night, discussing the incident along the way. Cree gazes into nothing, saying, "I don't know what came over me, Russ. I felt like I was capable of... of anything; that's not me. Is it?"

"Let's talk about something else," Russ says. The attack has disappointed him, deeply, it seems. He uses the remainder of the trip to their hotel to praise her concert performance, for which this night they'd set aside to celebrate together.

Russ had booked the resort while having no inclination that Cree would be a fugitive, so their destination is dangerously in the center of tourism downtown at Marion Square. If police were searching hotel resorts befitting the uber-rich Russ Rutledge, they would look no further than the uber-luxurious resort, Hotel Bennett, for which BET's cofounder, Sheila C. Johnson is a partner. The lure of such exquisite digs compels them to keep the reservation, despite its central location. They talk themselves into believing that police have bigger concerns than hunting down the likes of Lulu McQueen.

While Cree soaks in a hot bath, Russ makes a few calls, taking measures to avoid being seen. He cancels their rooftop dinner reservations, opting for room service. He then cancels the morning Swedish massage appointment, opting to take the job of her body massage into his own hands.

Dinner in their in-suite dining room dubs as foreplay. They're in bath robes feeding each other crispy duck confit and tiger prawns.

"Try the wine," Cree encourages, with such zeal that Russ suspects a prank.

It's the bottle of wine Russ ordered only because Cree was so adamant. Russ examines the label. "Abbey Creek Vineyard," he reads. The brand is foreign to him. He swirls the glass before the sip. He livens up as the full-bodied cabernet washes over his palate. Cree comes around and stands behind his chair while Russ examines the glass with wonder, but quickly tries another swig, not quite believing the thrill of the first. Russ lowers the glass and finds Cree through the corner of his eyes, "No joke, Lulu, this is my new favorite."

It's actually an old favorite, Cree thinks. The wine has been Russ's favorite for years in the parallel world, and therein lies Cree's edge: she knows Russ better than any woman that this bachelor version of her husband has ever encountered, which Russ learns quickly, as Cree kneels before him and unties his robe like a ribbon to a gift. It's been so long for Cree; the rush of inevitability overwhelms her as she begins.

Russ, with eyes clenched in pleasure, still turns away, as if the glare radiates through flesh rather than sight, but then his eyes pop open to examine how Cree makes such pleasure even possible.

Cree straddles him in his chair. He grips her bottom. He buries his face in her robe. She moves like a nautical ride, rising and dipping as if by the crests and troughs of ocean waves; Russ syncs with her rhythm, a tit in his mouth.

Eventually, Cree feels him staving off ejaculation, believing it to be some rush to an end, but Cree welcomes it. Russ traps her to his lap, stopping her in order to give himself reprieve, but Cree defiantly grinds there. As Russ jolts like a stroke victim, Cree raises up and covers him with a towel, feeling him throb in a burrito of linen while sucking his earlobe until his spasms cease.

When the wild leaves out of Russ's eyes, he stands with Cree, her bottom cradled in his hands. He takes Cree to the bed. They're two brown bodies on a canvas of milk white bedding. Cree is curious as to what Russ has learned out in the dating field for the better part of a decade.

This Russ is more intense, and muscular; he pins her arms to the bed. Every turn of Cree's head, he chases her eyes with his; he owns her. He licks his way down to her inner thighs where Cree learns that no one has had the heart to inform the man that he's going about it all wrong, with his stiff and flicking tongue.

She cradles Russ's face and brings him up – brings his mouth to her mouth where she kisses him ever so succulently, then gazes in his eyes and says, "Like that." She then guides his head down to kiss her below, as above.

Russ sees the immediate impact, with Cree's squealy moans over her gathered breasts. In time, Russ feels her peaking, but oddly, Cree stops him. "Not yet," she utters, as if there's something possibly more pressing than orgasm. The interruption confuses Russ; he forms an expression as if he doesn't know anything anymore.

What Russ doesn't know, is that Cree is showing him one, out of a few, pre-scripted sexual episodes that they've perfected over their years of marriage in the other world. Russ, now having earned a sparkling beard, has had time to recover.

He's behind Cree, who backs into him while looking back, her lip tucked in anticipation of what's coming. With Cree having been deprived for so long, this Russ, with the ramrod stroke of a bachelor, is perfect for the moment. Soon Russ realizes why Cree had previously passed on one orgasm: for the two she gets back-to-back – no three, or seemingly, however many he can drum out of her. For Russ, the visual of such carnality and pleasure plugged to himself, feeds his ego, which makes everything about her, all the more blessed and sacred.

When they're done, Russ drops on his side with a deep exhale. "Wow," he says, but is otherwise speechless. Cree backs into him, gathering his arms around her and braiding their legs below in a tight and loving spoon, a thing so sorely missing from the world that Cree is so adamant to return to, when in this world she has her mother, her singing career, and a Russ who is so in love with her that he's risked his freedom just to share this night with her. Why would she want to return? Although Cree lets the question form in her mind, she already knows the answer: it's Meryl. This world's Meryl will never feel like her daughter, and Cree's relationship with her own Meryl is cherished above all things.

Cree takes her phone from the nightstand. Although it's uncharacteristic of Cree to capture such a moment in a place other than her heart, she uses her phone to record their embrace, still shining in the gloss of intimacy, Russ with his sly smile, kisses her neck and cheek for the camera, unwittingly giving Cree evidence to present Lulu if she, in fact, shows up to their meeting the next day. Cree, instead of asking herself how she can possibly leave this world, the better question is, how could Lulu who thought Russ ended their relationship, not return, in light of video evidence to the contrary.

Cree's only interest in the little time she has left here, is learning the truth denied by her husband in her home world.

Cree sets the phone on the nightstand. "Russ?" Cree brings their interlocked fingers to her mouth, where she kisses the back of his hand. "Why did we divorce?"

"Is that a trick question," Russ asks, softly.

"No. I honestly don't remember. I kinda downplayed how much my memory was affected by that accident."

With alarm, Russ says, "You can't downplay stuff like that, Lulu; that's your brain."

Cree explains, "I didn't want them to keep me at the hospital, Russ. I had the concert to think about."

"Well, the concert's done now. The first chance we get I'm taking you to a specialist. I wanna make sure you're good, babe."

"Yes, Russ." Cree rolls on her back, looking up at the ceiling, her arms folded over her belly. "Did you have an affair with Charlene?"

Russ raises up on his elbow, his cheek mashed against a fist, "I guess you can't remember that even you, yourself agreed that it didn't rise to the level of an affair."

"But there was something, though…"

Russ sighs. "Let's not spoil this night, Lulu."

Cree says, "Well… that just answered my question. So, *when* did the affair take place?" Knowing when the affair took place, would help Cree determine if *her* Russ also had the affair. Obviously, Cree and Lulu were still one person one at the time of Meryl's conception, and their worlds split off prior to Lulu's divorce.

Russ now sits up in the bed, his back against the headboard. "So, you really don't recall jumping on a plane, and leaving me behind while you and the band went out to make a name for yourselves?"

Cree says, "All I remember is that from day one it seems like Charlene was an issue. Your dad kept dragging you to those political events, showing you the ropes. Charlene would be there, avoiding me, but time I leave your side, she's cheesing in your face. One thing I do remember: the day I got into your phone, wondering what in the world was Charlene doing texting you to see if you were attending some Spoleto Luncheon."

"Not together."

"You two shouldn't have been texting at all."

"Your memory seems to be working mighty fine to me," says Russ. "Plus, nothing was going on then. It was later, when I started confiding in Charlene. She would actually listen to me, when you wouldn't."

"You wouldn't have ended up confiding in her if you didn't keep the door open for her."

"Lulu, I'm not about to argue with you just because you've forgotten that we worked through all this already. When it finally became physical between Charlene and me, I could tell you the exact date. Why? Because the date is on the wedding invitations."

"Wait. Wedding invitations? I'm lost."

"You were in New York signing a record deal. We argued over the phone. I threatened to take custody of my daughter. And you was like, 'Your daughter? You can't take custody of a child that ain't yours. You ain't *got* no kids, Russ!'"

"Maybe I said that out of anger. Did we ever have her tested?"

"Yes, but that was later. At that time, though, you telling me over the phone..." Russ tremors. "It hit me like a brick. So, with *that* on my mind, I ended up at Jeb and Meredith's wedding reception posted up at the open bar drinking my sorrows away. Charlene was there. We did it standing up in a stairwell, by the way – if that makes you feel any better."

Cree does feel better, having learned that it was only this Russ – not her husband – that had sex with Charlene. It happened after Russ found out that Meryl wasn't his child, which never happened in Cree's world, so neither did the affair. All these years, Cree thinks, her husband has been innocent.

Cree, however, isn't so innocent. She churns in the covers to face Russ. "I apologize, Russ. I am so sorry for misleading you – lying to you. I wanted so bad for Meryl to be yours, I made myself believe it."

"You've apologized a hundred times, Lulu. It's all good."

Cree nods in silence.

Russ says, "Honestly, babe, I kinda knew – not at first because when Meryl was just a hand-baby, it was hard to tell, but at around eighteen months is when the doubts began, but…"

"But you wouldn't have had to be tortured by doubt had I been completely honest with you." Cree shrinks from her own words, thinking, blinking. They cuddle in silence until Russ falls asleep. Cree lay awake, unable to sleep because tomorrow is the big day; the day she reunites with Lulu.

Cree lay there in the dark, reliving the past, back when Russ was just a fling. Their colleges had fifty miles between them so they would date between semesters with little communication during, which is how Cree preferred it because she was focused on her studies, a full-time job, and music. She let Russ assume that she was entertaining other guys when he was the only one. He was the only one she had time for, and the only one she wanted.

The semester had just resumed and they were fifty miles apart again. A somewhat lovesick Cree went out with her girlfriends for some club therapy. She bumped into a classmate; a high school friend named Jacoby Brooks. He said he was enlisted and was being deployed to Afghanistan in a few days. Cree and her friends were ready to hop on to the next bar, but Cree, noting Jacoby's distress about being deployed, decided to sit at the bar with the man for a while. Cree told her friends to go ahead, that she'd catch up soon enough.

Cree bought Jacoby a drink, and they talked a while over a few more. Cree didn't realize how drunk she was until it was time to part ways. Jacoby had to shoulder her outside like a wounded soldier. Cree was no longer interested in catching up with her friends. She just wanted to go home, so she bummed a ride from Jacoby, who helped her inside her apartment, and further into the apartment to Cree's bedroom. He even went a step further to lay on the bed beside her, observing her in silence, despite a drowsy Cree asking him what he was doing. That's when Cree realized that she had been drugged.

Cree was in and out of consciousness. Each time she opened her eyes, Jacoby was there, studying her, petting and shushing her. She remembers only a moment of the weight of him mounting her. He lay a hand across her eyes so she wouldn't have to see. Cree was too out of it to fight him; her limbs were noodles. Cree never reported it. She was a full-time waitress, full time student and working on her music career, and in Cree's mind, she couldn't let either of those three plates stop spinning, figuring she'd hold off healing for some time later when life slows down and affords her the chance to face it.

Just days prior, she'd had unprotected sex with Russ for the first time; it was her idea, being tipsy from one too many glasses of wine and a shared blunt. It was their last evening together before they part ways for the semester. Cree remembers mounting Russ between rounds and folding him into her. Young Russ looked down the length of his body with panic in his eyes; the condom is off. Cree says, in an airy whisper, *I just wanna feel you.*

She wanted a night to remember, a keepsake to last her until the next interval when they return home to Charleston, where such evenings happen more frequently. Having unprotected sex with Russ just before she was raped, Cree had found herself a couple months and a couple missed periods later, staring at a positive home pregnancy test, with the knowledge that her rapist was killed in action, in Afghanistan.

LULU

They're getting ready for bed, which has been a flirty time for them of late, but tonight Russ observes, for the first time since the car accident, Cree doesn't seem up for it. She sits at the large vanity mirror, going down the assembly line of beauty products, circling toner into her cheeks, and smearing cold cream under her eyes with the finesse of her pinky fingers.

Russ comes up behind her, his chin over her shoulder; he tries to make eye contact with her reflection. He kisses her cheek, betting that his wife would see his cheek kiss and raise it, by offering her lips, but Lulu instead, gets up and wanders away, pretending to have lost something; rejection riding under the cloak of distraction.

Since the altercation with Charlene, Lulu has been wondering what would Beth do, and although she doesn't have her mother there to confirm, she figures Beth would prescribe honesty, and to let the chips fall where they may. But Lulu already knows where the chips would fall; she has the benefit of a whole nother world showing her that the chips fall to divorce. At least this time – according to South Carolina law – having a twelve-year marriage gets her six years of alimony instead of the one year she previously got.

"Cree," says Russ. "I know you hear me calling you."

Lulu refocuses and spots a frustrated Russ tossing his silk lounge coat on the back of the armchair. "Yes, darling? I'm sorry, I…"

Russ waves it off. "Never mind."

Lulu thinks, *I should tell him. I should tell him now. Okay. Here goes nothing.* She sips air to speak, but her courage fails.

Russ notices how Cree shrinks from something she wanted to say, but he doesn't chase it; he lets the moment pass. Something is wrong. Something has been wrong since the car accident, Russ thinks; the way she speaks, her sense of humor, her sex drive, has been like the woman he fell in love with back when she caught his eye as a bar waitress who went by the nickname Lulu – not Cree, the benevolent leader of the Icarus foundation, that she has become. Russ hasn't even asked when she's returning to work.

Russ figures maybe Cree's new outlook on life, owed to her near fatal accident, is finally wearing off – or just maybe, Russ figures, she's disappointed that he hasn't reciprocated the love she's giving him. Admittedly, Cree has been the whole vibe, as to why things have been so good. Perhaps now, it's Russ who must rise to the occasion and show his appreciation in a big way. Russ says, "What do you think about a vacation? Isn't it about time? Acapulco… Dubai… Just us."

"That would be nice," is Lulu's uninspired response. More than a vacation, Lulu needs an AA meeting.

Russ gently probes, "Maybe it's time to tell me what happened between you and Meryl. Ever since we got up from the dinner table you've been acting upset."

"C'mon, Russ, there's nothing for me to be upset about."

"If not that, it's something. Are you upset that I doubted you – that I needed a polygraph to tell me you were true?"

True is precisely what she is not, Lulu thinks, and Charlene will soon make that clear to Russ. Just three days in, Lulu is already awaiting the inevitable demise of the life she wanted. There's no way out, other than telling Russ about Meryl's paternity before Charlene gets the chance.

"Russ," Lulu says. "Actually, there *is* something I have to tell you. I don't know what this could mean for us, but... it's something I should have told you a long time ago."

"I'm all ears," he says.

Lulu lay across the bed, unable to stand up to her own truth. Russ lay bed behind her and tugs her to his body. Lulu clears her throat. "As you said, something *is* wrong..."

Russ kisses her shoulder and says, "Whatever it is, baby, it will not change my love for you."

Lulu pets the hand that embraces her. Her mind crowds with whispers of disaster, as she comes out with it. "I want a baby," Lulu says, to her own surprise.

Russ lights up like a pet dog. "A baby? Are you serious! No, wait," he dims. "Are you still on that surrogacy or nothing crap – knowing my folks is Catholic?"

"What're you talking about?"

Though Lulu is turned from Russ, he spies her scowl in the vanity mirror against the wall. Russ asks her mirror reflection, "So, you really want another kid..."

Lulu, from a sly grin, says, "Did I stutter?"

"Cree..." Russ shakes his head. "Why would you hold out on something like that when you *know* I want another child. Heck, if truth be told, the problems in our marriage started when I began pushing the issue. Have you thought about the foundation," Russ says. "I know how Icarus is your heart and... that's a lot: running the show at Icarus *and* a kid tugging at your skirt..." Russ rambles on, his mouth transcribing his thoughts as they come to him. "I mean, Tamara's doing it: bank president, infant twins... Look at Meredith, forty years old with that lil bad ass boy – she and Jeb, together running two long term care facilities. I'll see to it that we have 'round the clock childcare," Russ vows. "And your singing... Tell me how I can do more to support that dream much better than I have in the–"

"–Russ?" Lulu grips Russ's chin, causing his lips to shroom. "Won't you hush, and put a baby in me."

Russ, cross-eyed with eagerness, asks, "Like, now?"

"Now, my love." Lulu smiles and kisses him.

A tickled Russ shimmies out of his jammies. "Babe, you ain't said nothin' but a word."

A baby! It's ingenious, actually, Lulu thinks, as Russ kneels at her base, so unwittingly crazed with excitement and yet there is this solemn gratitude coming over him, as he enters her. "Oh Russ," Lulu moans, her legs together, flush up the front of his body, her feet flanking his face as if Russ has painted toenails for ears. Lulu breathes deeply and massages her belly. "Deeper, baby." She tenses at the plunge. If Charlene does expose Lulu, a positive pregnancy test should sway Russ to keep their marriage despite Meryl's paternity. If not, Lulu can take this pregnancy back to the other world and entice Russ with the heir that he so desperately wants.

Lulu gazes over at their sideview in the vanity mirror against the wall, at how Russ rolls his hips into her, like a seasoned dance partner whose movements are so second nature to him that he has the freedom to focus fully on the connection. In blessed appreciation he leans forward, smoothing his palms up and over Lulu's belly and ribs to cup her breasts, without one wayward thrust or even a glitch in his rhythm. It's not until he's glossed with sweat that his ebb and flow begins escalating to fitful jerking. Russ quakes, his mouth locked open for a yawn that won't come, as if his spirit is being pulled out of him. Lulu clamps him with a leglock, trapping him inside of her. She grinds into him while holding him flush. "Ooh, daddy," Lulu moans. Daddy has new meaning now that they're trying to conceive. Russ hovers, panting, spent, vulnerable. As the orgasmic spell lifts away, he becomes aware of the strength and dexterity of the leglock he's in. Lulu, with her hair scattered about the satin pillow, a curved strand stuck to her damp cheek, she appraises him from below, his sweat glistened gratitude to which Lulu professes her undying love; she coddles Russ until he fades to sleep.

Lulu sneaks out from under Russ and tiptoes out of the bedroom. She has learned, by being in the music industry around famous men and their harems, a trick groupies use to trigger ovulation to secure a financial lifeline. For Lulu, however, it's not about money; it's about love.

Lulu rummages through the medicine cabinet and comes up empty. She hurries to the kitchen and goes through its cabinets. She locates a bottle of vitamin C, takes a handful and chugs a glass of water behind it.

"What're you doing?"

Lulu leaps like a startled cat. It's Meryl. Lulu, in an irate whisper, says, "Girl, what's the matter witchyou – sneaking up on people like that." Lulu's nerves fizz like shaken soda.

"Is it a crime to get myself a drink of water," Meryl asks, while eyeing some scandal she's perhaps not yet old enough to understand, but what Meryl does understand, is her mother pinching her robe closed and scurrying out of the kitchen like she stole something.

Chapter 14

Confirmation

Cree slowly blinks out of an odd dream, where she was like a ghost in her own bedroom, watching Lulu and Russ make love. They were trying to conceive, but there was something wrong with Russ. He seemed weakened and helpless, with Lulu's legs clamped around his waist like pliers, squeezing the life out of him.

Cree rolls over and feels the chill of empty sheets next to her. Russ is gone, probably out fetching breakfast. His laptop is open at the foot of the bed. Apparently, this Russ is also an early-rising workaholic.

Cree crawls over to the laptop and examines the files spread out on the desktop screen. She checks the Profit & Loss form, and a debt to asset sheet, all of which is familiar to Cree, because she'd served as an assistant to the accountant for Rutledge Enterprises before turning her attention to the Icarus Foundation and making it a formidable nonprofit that has fostered relationships with wealthy donors, that has led to valuable connections for her husband. The Icarus foundation, under bachelor Russ, is still that same defunct tax haven with a non-working phone number. In the debt to asset ratio spreadsheet, Cree sees, right there in black and white, and with mathematical certainty, the value that she, as a wife, has brought to the table; the number is staggering.

Cree can see how those tough conversations, during times when Russ has brought his frustrations to her; those times when he's lost his bearings and she's had to remind him of the man she fell in love with, which translates to him also remembering his guiding principles as a businessman. Many a day, she's sent her husband into boardroom negotiations with his head on straight before closing multimillion dollar deals. Cree has always had some vague sense of her worth to the company, but seeing Rutledge Enterprises *with* her, in the other world – and *without* her in this world, the variance amounts to about fifteen million dollars; half the corporation's total value.

Cree notices the time at the bottom corner of the laptop and can't believe how long they've slept.

Russ returns with a breakfast that they lack the time to eat.

"Do you even know what time it is," Cree asks.

Russ's head is down, focused on the phone in his hand.

Cree hurries to get dressed. She hops in place to get her jeans over her hips. "I was being nosey a minute ago. I see you're drawing up plans for Phillips Community," she says. So is Husband Russ, she doesn't say.

Russ keeps gazing down at his phone. Distractedly, he responds, "The first meeting didn't go so well. Maybe it'll help if I get a megastar like you to accompany me at the next meeting."

"If you say..." She doubletakes at Russ who is still lost in his phone instead of getting dressed. "What're you doing," Cree demands.

Russ asks, "Have you looked at your Deepr app?"

"I just woke up."

"Well, one of your songs was playing in the lobby, right... So, you know how it automatically detects the music and brings it up on the screen? Well, it also gives suggestions by the producers and song writers and it indicates which titles are trending. Your song *Boss Lady* is getting streamed like crazy. A lot of your other songs are showing up and it looks like they're being streamed like crazy too."

"What are you talking about?" Cree approaches Russ while fastening her bra and drawing her blouse down over her body. She takes the phone and wanders away in astonishment at what she's seeing on the screen. She goes to the browser and checks the streaming charts, narrating the results, "*Skin Deep*, number four? *Let Em Hate*, number nine? What!" She runs a hand back through her hair, her jaw hung. "Another one: *Ratchet Chick*, number nine…"

Russ says, "You skipped one. *Eurostep* by Shawt Thug. You featured in that song, and it's up there too."

Cree lowers the phone on a dead arm. She seems ready to collapse, if not for the smile glazed across her face. "What does this mean?"

Russ shrugs. "That any press is good press? Maybe when you'd gone missing, people thought you were gone for good."

Cree blinks hard, looks left and right, then she gets back to getting ready. She begins stuffing her backpack. "I have to get back to my apartment."

"I understand that," says Russ. "But what I don't understand is why the hurry? What do you have going on that's so pressing on a Sunday?"

Cree slings her backpack over her shoulder. "I'm turning myself in tomorrow. I have to prepare, okay?"

"What time are you going to be done?"

"Why?"

"Because I'm available, that's why. You've been spending all your time with the band and with your mother. To hell with me, huh?"

Cree is tickled by a Russ that would argue for time with her versus time away. "Give me a couple hours, that's all," Cree says, not that it makes a difference; she'll be back in her home world by then, God willing.

Russ checks out at the desk while Cree takes a side exit; she's the one they're looking for. Thankfully, the place isn't surrounded by police.

The ride begins quietly. Cree asks, "Are you okay?"

"I helped you escape. They're probably looking for me too."

"Charlene was the only witness. If she reports you, she ruins whatever chance she thinks she has with you."

Russ sighs. "We'll see." He rubs his chin with the web between his thumb and forefinger, a gesture that husband Russ does when something's on his mind.

"If you've got something to say, Russ, say it."

He smirks and says, "Now, I don't know how much money all those streams and downloads amounts to, but I just hope it doesn't change your mind about us."

Cree's head doesn't turn; her whole torso does. "I should hit you, for saying that," Cree says with a half-smile; she's only half kidding. "If it was about money, I wouldn't have left you the first time."

"The first time you left for more money – at least what seemed to be more money."

"You smile as if you're joking, Russ, but you're serious. I know you. Look at me." Cree reaches for his face, but he evades her.

"Can't you see I'm driving?"

"Money can't make anyone happy. The only people who think it will, never had money. I've been rich and miserable before," Cree says, as if she's Lulu, who mishandled millions, but she's referring to herself, having all the wealth she could ever wish for, but unfulfilled in her dead marriage and for not doing the thing she loves. "You shouldn't have any questions, Russ. Did last night not feel real to you?"

Russ looks away; he's shy of his own feelings. "Hell, last night was... whew!" He reaches over, holds her hand, and doesn't let go until the car comes to a stop near Cree's apartment.

Russ parks not too close, just in case there are eyes on the building. They scan the surroundings. The coast is clear. Lulu's car is now out of impound and parked out front, courtesy of Beth, so Cree can drive herself to her true destination; at a storage unit where she and Lulu are scheduled to meet.

Cree leans for the perfunctory goodbye kiss, but she's caught off guard by an upswell of emotions. Cree sheds tears she cannot explain. It's likely the last kiss of this affair *with* her husband, or rather this passionate lover who is still buried somewhere inside of him. Upon her return to the next world, Cree vows to do everything in her power to exhume this man out of the grave of a man that she is married to.

She sees a bit of emotion break over Russ, who comes way from the kiss with a hand on his heart. "You don't know what you're doing to me, Lulu."

That name Lulu sends Cree's heart retreating deep in her chest like a cuckoo back in its clock. It is the *other* her that this Russ loves. "See you soon," says Cree. She kisses two fingers then touches his lips.

Cree trots up to the apartment for one thing: since she'll have to swap phones with Lulu again, she doesn't want to lose her pictures. Cree connects the phone to the laptop and transfers the pictures to a removable storage drive. Cree plans, upon her return, to tell her husband everything. If Russ thinks she's insane, she'll offer picture proof of Beth still alive, and selfies she'd taken with the band in rehearsal, and of herself in full costume before going on stage.

Cree exits her apartment with ample time yet she hurries as if she's running late. She hurries on the pride of the compelling case she has prepared to convince Lulu that life on this side is worth trading for.

Cree scrambles down the steps and hits the ground level in a trot. Cree gets into her car. Just as she adjusts the rearview mirror, she finds something alarming in it – a police squad car pulling into a park about two blocks back. Cree sinks in her seat and watches her side mirror. Exiting the squad car is Detective Ryan with a pair of cuffs dangling from a belt loop. Marching alongside him is red-bearded partner in wireframe sunglasses. The pair seems all business as they walk towards the entrance to her apartment – no, actually – they bypass the entrance; they're coming toward her car! Ryan slips between two parked cars to flank her on the driver's side. Red Beard stays on the sidewalk, coming for her passenger door.

Cree, knowing that the cost of leaving in their custody equals never again see her real daughter, it outweighs whatever cost might come of a highspeed chase. Cree cranks up and darts out into traffic. Detective Ryan and his partner have a long run to their car, which is parked two linear blocks back; Cree has a substantial head start. Cree believes that with the aid of downtown Charleston's grid of one-way streets, and some luck, she can lose them.

Her heart thumps in her chest. Cree is surprised that she's not bugged out by the sheer disbelief that she's evading the cops.

She drives fast, but not wild. She doesn't want to stick out in the flow of traffic. The storage facility isn't far. A red light stops her. Cree looks in her rearview; just sunbeaten cars, no spinning blue lights. Sirens, however, scream in the distance, getting louder, closer. In a panic, she's ready to jump the light. A squad car streaks by on the cross street. They don't see her.

The light changes green. Cree stomps the accelerator. The cop car that had streaked by, suddenly brakes, sliding into the next turn, to head her off.

Since Cree has been spotted, and her location no doubt radioed to other squad cars, she can no longer hide in the flow of traffic. She speeds towards another red light on a prayer that fails. She stomps the brakes for an oncoming car, the two squealing and fishtailing towards each other, their bumpers stopping just inches from a kiss of death. The abrupt stop throws the drivers back against their seats; their levitating ghosts returning to their bodies after the false alarm. They're still alive. Cree, with no time to even sigh, backs out and stomps the accelerator.

Ahead, the cop that was trying to head her off – has, but because Cree's setback of the near accident, his one-car roadblock has overshot, so Cree is able to turn off one block shy of him.

She's speeding again down the corridor of buildings. As she passes one intersection, clearing the wall of buildings, she realizes that one block across, she's neck and neck with another screaming, strobing cop car. Police have the advantage in numbers and they swarm with the aid of radio. Cree's advantage is being the only person who knows where she's headed.

By the next intersection, the cop car speeding one block over finds himself in a one-car race. Cree had already slidden into a narrow alley just wide enough for her to have opened her car door and squeeze out of her car.

She now goes out on foot with her backpack, her trotting feet crunching over the crumbly asphalt between the corridor of mossy brick buildings, a thin belt of a slow moving sky above. She stops at the other end of the alley, which opens up across the street from a service station-slash as-is car lot. Next to that lot is the storage facility where there is a unit that Cree and Beth has shared ever since her wedding.

Cree crosses the street with her head down like an indifferent college backpacker. She stops at the facility's iron gate and enters the code. Cree trots up the columns of storage units and then down the row to her unit. With sirens screaming all around, what stands between Cree and home is a pumpkin orange, steel roll-up door.

Chapter 15

Two-Faced Mirror

The room is dark and waiting. There's furniture stacked on the sides, giving an aisle straight to the back wall where there is a full-length mirror mounted. In front of the mirror there's a sitting pillow in the center of the floor where Cree kneels, where she waits, where she tries not to think about spiders. The only light is behind her, dashed in under the door. This storage room – this waystation between universes sorely disappoints. There's no neon rip in the space-time continuum; just the mirror, now wearing the smudge of the hand that Cree had just tried to reach through it. It is just glass – cold, hard glass.

Cree feels like she's been had – that this meeting was never real, but merely for the sake of making the ruse convincing. Gazing at her dark silhouette in the mirror, she's hit with an epiphany. *But why would Lulu go through the trouble of setting up the mirror and the sitting pillow?*

Sirens wail; they increase coming up the street and wane going away, like screaming pterodactyls circling he sky. It's only a matter of time before they descend upon her. Cree weeps. "I can't..." Can't spend any portion of her life on the inside of a jail cell. Can't fathom never again seeing her Meryl, with whom she shares so many growing pains and cherished mother-daughter moments that never happened in this world. Cree remembers the conversations they'd have in absence of Russ, things shared in confidence while braiding Meryl's hair. Cree feels the pierce of an arrow through her heart. Cree's mental state is deteriorating as she remembers the themed birthday parties for the kid who comprehends the responsibility and the legacy she stands to inherit and the greatness for which she is being groomed. Cree's sweet little empath who senses the growing rift between her parents, makes it her mission to build bridges between them. "I just can't," Cree says.

"Well, hoe if you can't, *I* can't," says Lulu, whose image fogs in over Cree's reflection like breath on cold glass, and then defrosts with Lulu's image sharpening focus, adorned with Cree's favorite church hat.

Cree bends with curiosity. "So, you're in this same storage room in the other world then?"

"Yeah," says Lulu. "But why you crying, girl? Walking a mile in my shoes got you messed up *that* bad?" Lulu sits in a chair and crosses her legs.

Cree raises one shrewd eyebrow. "You didn't wear that to church, did you? Pushup bra? Strapless dress?"

"I also had a shawl thank you," Lulu says. "*Russ* likes it."

Cree asks, "Did you get the video situation taken care of?"

"It was easy," replies Lulu. "I had my friend Dez hack Tron's computer. All traces of that video is gone, but yeah, uh... actually, um..." Lulu takes a deep breath, as if ready to break the bad news. "Ok Cree, it's like this—"

"—Before you say anything, Lulu?" Cree thinks best to interrupt just in case Lulu was about to deny Cree her life back, because once the words release, it thickens the commitment. Cree raises her phone for Lulu to see the bedroom video of herself and Russ. "See? Russ never sent those texts calling it quits," Cree says. "Charlene sent those messages then broke Russ's phone so he couldn't reply."

Lulu seems hypnotized by the selfie video Cree recorded at the hotel with herself and Russ cozy in the sheets. Basking in post-lovemaking glow, a charmed Russ plants kisses along the length of her neck. Lulu tilts, like a plant's tropism to light, she tilts ever so slightly into the kisses she imagines plotting up along the side of her own throat.

A passing siren startles Lulu out of the trance. Her eyes fall closed for the duration of an exhale, as if to recover from either being startled, or from the tantalizing video. Lulu then puts on a casual act, as if a moment ago she wasn't just stirred like a drink. "That sure is a lot of sirens, girl. Something happened?"

"It's nothing," Cree says. "A car accident a couple blocks over."

Lulu glances down. There's a briefcase at her feet, as if she'd come prepared to leave. "So, what about Charlene?"

Cree replies, "The wedding is cancelled—"

Lulu claps in celebration. "I just wish I could've seen Charlene's face. That's what she gets!"

Noting how Lulu takes such pleasure in Charlene's agony, Cree adds, "In fact, when Russ and I ditched the cops after the concert, Charlene was at his car door, pleading with him. I drug that hoe down by her hair, then Russ and me sped off together."

This time Lulu's head lowers and a hand raises as if she's still in church, worshipping. "Ooh, I wish I could've seen it," Lulu praises.

"Now," says Cree. "Does that sound like a man who wants to be with Charlene? Do not doubt Russ's love, Lulu. He loves you more than my husband loves me."

Hearing this, there's a change in Lulu. She's thinking and un-thinking, shuffling the facts like a deck, from which she pulls a curious card. "So, you ditched cops after the concert, huh... Are you sure those sirens ain't for you?"

"They're not, Lulu. You gotta believe me."

"I believe you're sweating like someone who's been running."

"I was running *late* – not running from the cops. Everything in your life is now falling into place for you. You have Russ, you have momma. And the concert! It was a success." Cree swipes her phone screen and stops. "Your songs are streaming to the tune of millions. How much money is that, huh? You have your career back, Lulu. Congratulations."

Lulu looks down and away. "That's all well and good, Cree, but…"

"But *what*," asks Cree. "You have a briefcase at your feet, Lulu. Aside from hearing that you have Russ, your career, and money, what else could you have possibly been waiting to hear to make you walk through that glass?"

Lulu shrugs. "I don't know. I just didn't know how I would feel standing face to face with… *me*. So, I brought this briefcase, full of some of your expensive shit — jewelry and cash, just in case. But now that I think about it," Lulu sighs. "Walk through that mirror for what? To have to work for what I already have *here*? Risk having Russ string me along for ten years then change his mind like he did Charlene?"

Cree unloads, "You'll trade the life of your own mother for a man?"

"Me and Russ are happy, Cree. We're trying to have a baby – something your bougie ass wasn't willing to do."

"Only because we needed to fix our marriage first."

"I did that, in just a matter of days, Cree. The problem was you. Men are easy; it's *you* who was being difficult."

A gut-punched Cree struggles to give wind to her words. She cries, "You lied about everything… Russ… Daddy… How could you do this? I shouldn't have to *ask* for my life back!"

Lulu's head shakes in slow and adamant denial. "You should've thought about that before you walked out on your life."

"Lulu, listen–"

"–No, *you* listen, Cree. My life is at stake."

"Is it, really? Or are you just evil and selfish?"

Silence drops. They've reached a stalemate. Lulu resets with a deep breath and asks, "How did you deal with it?"

Cree snaps, "Deal with what!"

"Jacoby."

The question throws Cree off balance. "I… well… you never stop dealing with it. Prayer, mainly."

"I'll tell you how I dealt with it: cocaine."

Cree shakes. "While knowing what it did to daddy?"

"Don't compare me to him! He was on crack, okay?"

"There's hardly any difference between the two."

"I could never do crack! Let's get that straight. Crack is wack," Lulu yells, loud enough to silence Cree. Lulu then adds, somberly, "Something was taken from me that night. I didn't feel how big of a hole was in me until *after* I left Russ."

"But did you do hard drugs before the record deal? No. Why am *I* not on drugs, huh? You got sucked into an industry where coke is culture, and you folded! That's facts! You're just reaching for a more honorable sounding reason. No, sis. No."

Lulu's head lowers and shakes. "Just because you're not on drugs doesn't mean you're free. There ain't no empathy in you, and that ain't normal."

"Empathy? For the person who stole my life?"

With a pair of lazy eyes, Lulu says, "I swear, the other day, I should've just shot you in the head and been done with it."

"In effect, that's what you're doing now, Lulu, if you don't walk through that mirror!"

Lulu raises one brow. "Be that as it may…"

Cree notices how Lulu keeps studying the back of her hand, the hand opposite of her wedding ring, where there is another ring that looks ancient, like it has somehow survived the ages. There are twin stones, one so black it eats light, while the adjacent stone dances with light, as if it's activated by its proximity to the mirror. "That ring," Cree says. "Is that what lets you cross over?"

Lulu drops the hand out of view. The other hand raises a number one. "I have one more time – one – to pass over, and then I'm stuck forever, so I can't cross over on a maybe," Lulu says. "If I were to come through there, what then? You go back to your marriage and run it in the ground again. Single Russ strings me along… Make it make sense. The only time my life has been stable, is with Russ. I need drugs only in absence of him. I have him now, until death do us part. Why cross over and trade guarantee for chance?"

Cree breaks down crying.

A sympathetic but resolute Lulu watches her. "Just take care of my baby. Take care of Meryl better than I could."

A piercing sound stiffens them both. It's the police calling over megaphone. They're near. Witnesses must've pointed them in this direction. They're lurking the rows of storage units.

"They're calling my name," says Lulu. "I guess that would be your name, now."

"Please, Lulu!"

Lulu sneers, "Emphatically, no."

"I need your help."

Lulu picks up the briefcase and stands. "Russ is waiting for me."

"Police want to charge me with faking my disappearance, because my story doesn't add up. I need to know what happened, so I can give them an account of events that sounds believable."

Lulu gives an emotionless, "Sorry hon," and turns to walk.

"Lulu, give me something. What if I go to jail? Do you want Meryl without a mother?"

Lulu stops. She abouts face. "Ok," she sighs. "Ok." Lulu returns to her seat and crosses her legs. Police can be heard going down the line and knocking at the steel doors.

Cree listens intently while Lulu recites every detail, such as where she was held prisoner, when she escaped and to where; how she got the scrape by her sideburn, what happened after leaving the doorcam's view – all of which Lulu fully explains by the time police arrive at their unit.

One officer calls to the others, "I got voices over here! It's this one!"

Lulu then gets up to leave, but she pivots again to offer one last detail, but struggles to say it.

"What is it," Cree urges, knowing police would bust in any second.

Lulu opens her mouth to speak, but she's cut off by the voice of Detective Ryan outside the door. "They're fetching a bolt cutter as we speak, but this'll go a lot nicer if you just come on out!"

Lulu, who is tensed to bolt, sighs and says, "As much as I hate to put a damper on this little romance you have with Russ... He's the one who hired those thugs to kidnap me. Don't ask me why."

"What?" Cree cements with disbelief. "No way. He would never do anything to hurt me – you."

"I'm pretty sure one of them was an old friend of his, named Hook." The steel door begins to roll up. Lulu scurries out of view. The mirror goes dark; along with Cree's chance to return to her life.

Behind her, the steel door rolls up and light comes in. Detective Ryan waives to the officers to keep their guns holstered. He stands at the entrance, eyes darting. "You alone?" He's sure he'd heard two voices. Cree doesn't reply. She's embalmed with disbelief and sadness; Russ... kidnap... The two words can't occupy the same square in her mind.

All Detective Ryan sees is Lulu with her back turned, sitting on a pillow like a turned Buddha statue, in front of a mirror in an empty storage room. He figures, perhaps Lulu needs a psyche ward instead of a holding cell.

Chapter 16

Filling Holes

In cuffs, they take an indifferent Cree downtown to the precinct. Her face is still frozen in that same shellshocked reaction to Lulu saying Russ was her kidnapper. Cree's expression hardly changes during the swabbing of her mouth to test for cocaine in her system. She remains wooden and bled of hope while they escort her to interrogation where she sits in a plain room, waiting to be questioned.

Her singular hope for sanity in this world was to fall in love with Russ all over again; this time, armed with the lessons she'd learned from their failures in the other life. But if Russ was, in fact, Lulu's kidnapper, Cree's hope was fool's gold. Cree looks around the interrogation room in the blank space between four angled walls, the perfect microcosm of her life, the emptiness and the pending questions.

Detective Ryan comes in and hits the button on a handheld recorder. From his shirt pocket, he pulls a stack of photos like a deck of cards. "So the plot thickens," he says, while dealing the pictures to Cree. There are pictures of tagged evidence: to-go boxes, bedding, toothbrush. "Familiar?"

Cree quivers. "It's just that nothing stands out, really."

"Your DNA's all over the stuff, especially the housecoat with the *door key* in the pocket – I mean, how are you prisoner when you're in possession of the front door key?"

"I wasn't."

"My sentiments exactly."

"No! Not that I *wasn't* a prisoner. I'm saying I *wasn't* in possession of any key – at any point in time."

Detective Ryan peels another picture from the stack and lays it on the table. It's a photo of the house exterior, its siding tongue pink.

"*This* is where you found those items? I was never in that house. This is definitely not the house," Cree says confidently, because it's nothing like the house Lulu described. "The house was beige with olive-colored shutters. It had a huge basement–"

"–Basement? In the Lowcountry? Who's dumb enough to build a basement to get all flooded and rotted out. But you're saying the house where you were held has a basement…"

"I swear to you. The basement is where they held Nathaniel. It even had outside entry." Cree drops a hand on the table. "In fact, where's Nathaniel, now? I need to talk to him." Cree requests nonchalantly, as if Nathaniel isn't her only ticket out of Lulu's godforsaken life.

Detective Ryan turns sly-eyed. "We're trying to locate him. He must've bolted as soon as he was released, but even if he were here, I'd have to make sure your two stories match up independently before we let you two start refreshing each other's memory." Detective Ryan leans forward with gathered hands. "So, you're sure this isn't the house?"

Cree shakes. "I'm sure."

Detective Ryan tilts back in his chair, hands clasped behind his head and his eyes roll upward, thinking and mumbling to himself. "Figures… why your DNA wadn't on near doorknob nor faucet," he frowns. "But why haul items to another house when ya could've burned them…" Detective Ryan comes out of the trance. He asks, "Take me through the events from the time you got kidnapped, to the time that that fisherman found you."

Straight from the memory of Lulu's telling in the storage room, Cree narrates for the detective.

They came to my home–

"–They?"

A man dressed like a limo driver and a woman in a gown. Wrong place, I told them. The woman called me by name, then said Russ requests my presence at an undisclosed location. How romantic, I thought. I was ecstatic. I played right into their hands. I was the most-giddy kidnapping victim you'll ever see.

At the same time, I thought something didn't look right about the woman. Her side teeth were gold. You don't see that every day. The limo wasn't a limo; it was a black SUV. I gave them permission to blindfold me. Knowing I wouldn't be able to use my phone blind, I put it away in my purse, but I was also blind to the fact that the woman had slipped my cell phone out of my purse and removed the battery.

Detective Ryan interjects. "They remove your battery so we couldn't triangulate your location by cell tower."

They told me there was a hitch in the plan. Russ was thrown off schedule, so they had to make a stop and wait for him. The blindfold wasn't taken off again until after I had arrived at the place. They then took me to the master bedroom. Even then, it seemed legit. They had fruit, cheese, wine chilling... a big pretty bed. They said I was just waiting at the house temporarily, for Russ, who was running late. I went to text Russ and that's when I realized my phone was missing. When the woman had went out to the car, supposedly, to go searching for my phone, she closed the bedroom door behind her, and that's when I discovered that the door was locked from the outside.

They treated me so good, I thought me being locked in the room was some sort of prank – a prank that was a bit romantic and kinky maybe. I never saw the woman or the driver again. The next time – and every other time that someone entered the room – they wore masks. They were all men, young men, bringing me food, spring water, they even brought in some fresh cut flowers. They kept me fed and comfortable.

I kept hearing these faint noises. I thought I was going crazy, the isolation... A whole day had passed before I realized that there was someone in the basement trying to get my attention. I had to get down in the dry tub and put my ear to the drain in order to hear him, then speak into the drain for him to hear me; that's how we communicated. He said his name was Nathaniel. He said they were holding him because of some money issue and that they were going to kill him. That's how I learned, for certain, that this was no joke. They used my association to Russ to lure me into that place.

Of course, Cree doesn't mention how Nathaniel promised to make all of Lulu's dreams come true, if she could free him.

I could hear the men out front, talking, playing cards. I waited until there was a time that the house sounded really quiet. I unscrewed one of the posts off the canopy bed and waited behind the door for one of the young men to bring dinner. As soon as he opened that door, I came down on his head with the post. He was out cold, Cree says, *omitting the part where Lulu takes the young man's gun.*

I tiptoed through the house to the basement where I tried to help Nathaniel, but there was no key to his chains, nor tools in the basement or the shed outside to cut them, so I left, promising to return. In that house the basement actually has a door to the outside, to steps that go up to ground level, so I exited out the basement door, leaving it unlocked.

I ran into the woods. I was running and looking back, running and looking back. Guess I looked back for too long one time – ran smack into a tree. So, that's how I got the bruise. I was out cold for – I don't know how long, but I got up and wandered through the forest in pitch-black. That's when I came upon that house. Since no one was home, I went around back and into their shed where I grabbed a bolt cutter, just in case I wound up back at the house where I was held hostage – because it was so dark, I really couldn't see where I was going.

Lo and behold, I did stumble upon the house again; it's like those were the only two houses for miles. I found the house totally empty. I didn't know if the kidnappers were out in the woods searching for me, or if they abandoned the place, fearing I'd already called police.

Cree omits the part where Lulu said she and Nathaniel had searched the empty house – Nathaniel for magical cane and Lulu for her cell phone, which she found and attempted to call the police but Nathaniel slapped the phone out her hand. "No police," he demanded. "That would do nothing but expose my location to people that're trying to kill me. As Lulu's reward for saving his life, Nathaniel gave Lulu the magic ring and the instructions on how to use it, in order to make all of her dreams come true.

Instead, Cree says, "So, Nathaniel and I left the house and ended up running visible along this long, dirt road that leads to the highway; that's when we saw headlights. Nathaniel ran, so I ran. We went in opposite directions through the woods. Cree pauses because of Detective Ryan's Grin. Cree asks, "What?"

Slowly, he adjusts in his seat and says, "So you and Nathaniel are both out of the house at this point. Did you two return to the house later?"

"Why would we? No."

"You see, the deeper truth is in the details one omits. At this point in your story, if you had left the house for the last time, you had to have been in possession of your cell phone."

"I was getting to that–"

"–Getting to *what* – to what could possibly be more important than using your cell phone to call the police, at this point in time?"

Cree pounds the table. "You act like you don't understand what it means to be chased in the woods at night? Ya can't just have a phone conversation – you can't even turn the phone on, or that lit screen stands out, in darkness, like the North Star."

Detective Ryan squints. "Didn't your screen light up at 4:47 a.m. when you texted Charlene?" Before Cree could reply, the detective shushes her with a finger to his lips. He stops the recorder. "Lemme turn this off before you mess up and say something you can't take back," he captions. "I'll tell them it was a malfunction," he says, with a wink. "I just got the text that your swab came back clean; furthermore, your testimony satisfies this sheriff's office. I'm certain enough that your disappearance was honest. Obviously the kidnappers knew about your relationship with Russ and used it to lure you into their custody. I'm sure we can overlook the highspeed chase in exchange for your cooperation."

Cree collapses over the desk in relief. "Thank God. Thank you, Detective."

"Much obliged, Miss Hughes, but we're not done. We've gotta bring the kidnappers to justice, right?"

"Certainly," Cree straightens up and nods, although her heart sinks. Bringing the kidnappers to justice could mean sending Russ to prison.

"I've got a few more questions. I'm not trying to hold you all day, but if you and I were to go out riding around that area, do you think you'd be able direct me to that house?"

Cree's head shakes slowly with her response, "My blindfold wasn't taken off until I'd arrived. I was able to see the outside of the house, but not how I got there. All I know is that it's really remote; no neighbor close by in any direction." Cree squints, pretending to strain her memory. "When I escaped it was so dark. All I remember is this ink-black labyrinth of trees."

Detective Ryan sips from his coffee mug. "So, the items with your DNA on it was moved to another house. It was discovered by a realtor who showed up to her open house and found their staged home looking a mess. That house didn't have a basement. Nathaniel's statement didn't mention a basement. The only person talking about a basement is you. Now, if there is, in fact, a basement, a livable basement, it shouldn't be so hard to find."

Cree, a dutiful helper, adds, "The basement was quite liveable too. Maybe it's an investment property. There could be a rental listing..." She stops because she sees Ryan eyeing her in a peculiar way. "What is it," Cree asks.

His hand slaps the desk. "I just find it amazing how you're sitting here talking to me, like normal, as if you *didn't* vanish underwater. I need to know why the change from Lulu in the door-cam, desperate for help–to the Lulu who gains possession of her phone but doesn't use it to call for help, but instead texts Charlene, but *not* to ask for help, nor out of any form of distress. Your predicament hadn't changed other than the fact that you helped Nathaniel escape. *I'm* thinking because of all the debt hanging over Nathaniel's head, it's reasonable he wanted to avoid the police. So, I'm betting he convinced you *not* to call us. Maybe he made you an offer you couldn't refuse. Just *maybe*, he somehow made it to where you really *could* – as you said in that text – be with Russ 'in another life.'"

"Detective… Are you alright?"

"I wouldn't have believed it one bit until I've seen, with my own eyes, how the doorcam video shows that cut by your side-burn and now it's moved to your forehead." Detective Ryan tilts and stares. "No one heals that fast, nor so completely that there idn't even a scar in the spot."

"You can't be serious, detective." Cree pushes away from the table. "My God, you *are* serious."

"When you first came out of that water, you seemed like you didn't even know your own name, Lulu. Standing outside that storage unit, there's no question I heard two people talking." Ryan jabs the table with a rigid finger. "Don't *look* at me like I'm crazy, mam. Both voices were yours, but different, like multiple personalities. Problem is, you only got one mouth, so how the hell were you talking over yourself? Your call history proves you weren't talking to someone over speakerphone."

Cree stands up, praying hands at her chin. "Please, let's take a break, okay? You're making me uncomfortable."

"I'm really in need of a friggin' lifeline, right now," says, Detective Ryan. "And I think you, or Malik, or Nathaniel – whatever his name – can help me."

The door flies open and bats the wall. It's Charlene busting in, yelling, "What the hell are you doing?"

Detective Ryan doubles her outrage. "Are you out of your ever-loving mind?! Who the hell let you in here?!"

Charlene points at Cree, but yells at Detective Ryan, "Test her again! Just yesterday morning, she had a mess of coke on the tip of her nose. There's no way it's out of her system already."

Detective Ryan, fists on hips, examines Charlene like a delinquent minor. "You shouldn't even be in here. You think just because your father's the mayor you can—"

The thrust of a finger in Ryan's face stops him. Charlene berates. "—I warned you not to take me lightly!"

Cree, despite the altercation is still in awe of the fact that the mayor, in this world is not Childress, but Charlene's father, Wade Hamilton.

Marching in through the open door, is a furry-browed black-haired detective. "There he is," announces Charlene. "Detective Ryan? Meet Detective Dean. He's taking over Lulu's case."

Dean cosigns with a wink and cheek click.

Ryan thumbs back over his shoulder to point at Dean, "This foot-loose looking sum-bitch ain't taking over *jack!* What kind of shit-show do you think we're running here! I could care less who your daddy is. No one elected *you.* No one appointed *you!*" His pointed finger actually taps Charlene's chest. Ryan stalks forward and she retreats back.

Dean cuts in, shielding Charlene. Dean says, "Real tough, putting your hand on a woman. Try me."

On that word, Detective Ryan loses it. He snatches Dean by the collars and drives him all the way back into the wall. Officers storm in to separate the men. Dean calms down rather easily, but Detective Ryan keeps unraveling.

Chapter 17

A Troubled Detective

Detective Ryan is a heartbroken man. His heart is as dark and empty as the interior of his car. In the passenger seat sits a stuffed bear with button eyes and a cloth red tongue that Ryan cannot deliver, due to a restraining order. He parks fifty feet away, binoculars pointed at the tavern on the corner of East Bay and the historic Market Street. Through the glass storefront, he watches the brown-haired bartender, backed by neon beer logos that gives her this golden aura. Her top exposes a few inches of midriff. She's in impeccable shape for forty-four. She's a Zumba instructor during the week, bartending on weekends, today working on her birthday. Her bar customers, all men, at present, have no reason to suspect that their sexy little bartender once identified as a man, all the way up through college.

Or maybe the bar customer with in the tweed Shelby hat, who gazes at her mouth every time she speaks, knows – like Ryan knew – but feigns ignorance, like Ryan did, hiding shame behind an affront of ignorance.

Detective Ryan raises the binoculars again, stargazing. She has this intense way about her, eyes ever so slightly close together; her lips naturally pursed, commas at the corners of her mouth that gives this boasting energy, like a runway model hitting her stride. Her stature is tiny, and rather feminine, and her shoulders, thin, which are prized features to a man like Detective Ryan who wishes to pass, in public, albeit at a distance, as a heterosexual couple. Tina once shared, as a fun fact, that she has more estrogen running through her body than most women, but still testosterone has its imprint on her knuckly hands and the hard jawline, although hedged by her flowy brown hair. Her collar bones are pronounced as crowbars where they join with her small but muscularly defined deltoids. Her brow is somewhat bony, but softened by thick lashes and the high arch of her drawn eyebrows. There are no areas where masculinity glares so bright that Ryan must shade his eyes. In Ryan's eyes, she does not possess the look of a costumed man, or he could never bring his lips to hers, and yet if she were born a woman, he could never feel so alive with her. The problem lie in the fact that eventually they must go out in public, where any pair of eyes has the chance to look long enough, starts thinning in judgement, and every family member or long-time friend or members of his church would seem ready to discard their entire relationship on the basis of who he loves; moreover, Detective Ryan, being a religious man, is always under the beam of God's eyes.

Detective Ryan peels back the paper bag on his bottle of whiskey, takes a long swig and wedges it back between his thighs. He looks down into the neck of the bottle where the stirred brown liquid begins to bear the images of his regret, where he'd made Tina furious on a dinner date by requesting a table at the back of a restaurant, and then on another day, seeing an old friend in the movie theatre lobby and releasing Tina's hand, and then there was another event that proved to be the last straw. Ryan looks down at the back of his hand and momentarily sees the bloody knuckles from the day he punched a wall right beside Tina's head.

A thump against the window startles the life out of Ryan, like a bird flying into the glass. It's Tina at the driver's side window, bent forward, peering into his car.

"Tina!" Ryan lowers the window.

"You're not supposed to be here," Tina says.

"Wrong. I'm not supposed to be *there*," he says with a nod in the direction of the bar. "Outside of fifty feet, it's a free country."

"Free country to sit in your car with an open container? *Go*, before I call the police!"

"Showing off in front of your bar customers? Is that what you're doing? You wanna turn them on by showing off the fact that you got a bough that just can't get you out of his mind?"

"The *one* time you're face to face with me and you choose to be an ass? Real smart."

"You have a standing offer, need I remind you? Be with me. I messed up."

"Some mess-ups don't deserve second chances, plus I'm not about to be anyone's best kept secret."

"I left God for you."

Tina replies, "Then you should have no problem leaving this parking spot and going home. If you're *not* gone in five minutes, I'm calling the police. I'm giving you an out, today, only because I don't want that kind of scene on my birthday."

"I got you a gift." A drunken, Detective Ryan fumbles the teddy bear and it falls on the floor. By the time he retrieves it and turns, Tina's going away with a leggy walk, middle fingers raised by her shoulders.

Detective Ryan doesn't realize, until after he'd ruined the chance, that his love for Tina is bigger than his shame, and that the shame itself is of his own making. He's made a mistake that cannot be undone. His head wobbles in misery as he recites Lulu's text, but instead inserts himself, "If I can't be with Tina in this life, I'll have her in the next."

Flirting with the parameters of his restraining order isn't the last ill-advised stop that Detective Ryan makes on this night.

CREE is at her apartment, sitting in a bar stool, her elbows on the island kitchen counter, her head in her hands as she comes to grips with Russ admitting that he had her kidnapped.

"We were going to get married again," Russ explains. "We were going to elope."

"I don't recall that discussion," Cree says, meaning Lulu did not inform her of any such discussion.

"We didn't talk about actually doing it, but we discussed it on a few occasions. I wanted it to be a surprise."

"I was a prisoner in that house!"

"Day one, I was coming to get you, but then I realized I was being followed. Turns out, Charlene had hired a private detective and he was tailing me, so I had to lead him away. I asked the guys to keep you calm and entertained. I was coming by the next day. So, one moment the guys are telling me you were in good spirits. Next thing you know, they're telling me you escaped. I meant to go to the police but then that video of you appeared on the news. You were bloody. If something had happened to you, no one would've believed me." Russ paces away from her. "Why did you run, Lulu? Why?"

"Don't put this on me! Those men were killers. Nathaniel said they were going to kill him. They had a real hostage, so I had every reason to believe that I was a real hostage too!"

"Nathaniel wasn't part of the plan. I would've never cosigned it, had I known they were holding him."

"So, you had everything with my DNA moved to another house? Trying to cover your ass?"

"That wasn't me. The guys said *they* didn't do it either."

"Guys? Or murderers?" She watches Russ shrink in shame, a shell of the man she believed him to be just this morning at the hotel. "Here's the problem I have with all of this, Russ. You said a minute ago that when you saw me bloody in the video and it didn't occur to you that withholding the truth could've cost me my life?" Her eyes fill with tears.

"It's not like that, Lu. You know I love you. It's just that I knew for sure that no one was trying to hurt you." He tries to comfort her.

"Don't!" Cree backs away, pointing. The reality slips over her shoulders like a chill. "You thought only about yourself." Cree's face goes slack with disgust.

Russ, on the brink of tears himself, leans into his explanation, his mouth open for seconds before his voice arrives. "I froze, Lu. I froze."

"Don't hand me that, Russ. Freezing is momentary; you had hours. The police questioned you. And you answered them with a straight face. Let's be real."

"I don't know if anything I can say will make you understand, but I am an only child. Everything my grandfather and father worked for goes up in smoke if I go to prison. You may think I have it good, but you'll never know what it's like to have to carry that burden, Lu. It weighs a ton. It broke me."

"We made love," she says as if she's now soiled by it. "...for the last time. There is no *us*, because when it came down to it, you were all for yourself." Russ tries to speak but she cuts him off. "No, Russ. No. For all I care, you and Charlene can go ahead and reschedule your wedding. I'm done."

"That's what your mouth says," counters Russ. "I'm looking at the math: you now have money coming in, so you no longer need me. Let's call a thing, a thing."

Cree points to the door. "Get out."

Russ, in dismay, tosses his hands up, but it freezes, suspended at the sound of a knock at the door. They look at each other in shock, then look to the door in silent confusion. Cree runs quietly to the door and peers into the peephole. She turns, in fright, and then hurries quietly toward Russ, her hands waving to shush him. She spins him around and guides him toward the bedroom, Russ protesting in whispers. "What're you doing? Who is it?"

A wide-eyed Cree whispers. "The police."

There's another knock. Detective Ryan, from the other side of the door, yells, "Lulu! I just wanna talk."

Cree closes Russ in the bedroom and runs back to the door, seeing a wobbly Detective Ryan, convex to the roundness of the peephole. Cree asks, "What are you doing here this late? Are you drunk?"

"Somewhat," Ryan says with a hiccup. "I had a few."

"Good bye, Detective Ryan. It can wait 'til morning."

"Ok, I'll go," he says. "But first do me one favor."

"Not if that favor has anything to do with opening this door."

"After you see what I'm about to reveal to you, I won't even have to ask you to open the door."

"Out with it, then. You're wasting time."

"Call it a freak coincidence, but get this: the time you sent the text was 4:47 a.m. If you turn to the New Testament–"

"–The New what?"

"Go get a bible, I'll wait. You *do* have a bible don't you?"

Cree gasps and marches away from the door, mumbling profanities until she puts her hand on the bible. She returns. "I got the bible – if this is what it takes to get you outta here."

"Your text was marked at 4:47 a.m. Go to The New Testament, the fourth book. Should be the book of John. Now find the 47th verse, and tell me what you find."

A minute, or so passes and Cree's apartment door opens in silence. She's standing there just looking at Detective Ryan, holding the open bible like a plate of food. She's too at a loss of words to even demand an explanation, or invite the detective in.

Ryan staggers in, a righteous finger wagging beside his head. "Numbers don't lie."

Cree offers a stool at the kitchen counter, the seat furthest from the bedroom where Russ hides, but Ryan waves it off. "Couch is fine." Ryan, heading to the living room, gives a moment's pause, for the decorum, which is a microcosm for Lulu's financial decline, the juxtaposition of her impressive penthouse furniture against this unimpressive, low ceiling apartment.

Cree sits in the loveseat opposite of him. "What does this mean?"

"What did you *see?*"

"Right off the bat, I saw the name Nathanael." Cree, spying a smile growing on the detective's face, says, "…As if you're onto something. This is ludicrous."

With a hard swallow, Detective Ryan begins, "A friend of Jesus, named Phillip, introduces them. It's the first time Jesus ever laid eyes on Nathanael, but Jesus claims to know him already. Jesus describes Nathanael in a way that is reserved only for the divine – as having *no deceit* in him. Out of both this description and Jesus knowing Nathanael in advance of meeting him, is born a hotly contested debate about Nathanael. I'm on the side of those who say he was an angel in flesh. The Hebrew meaning of his name even hints at it: *given by God.*"

Cree apes disbelief, because to confirm that Nathaniel is not of this world would only complicate her chances of returning home. "So, this is why you came here this time of night," Cree asks, irreverently, but leaving no window for a reply, she follows, "You're crazy."

Earnestly he replies, "I don't deny that. But I'm not crazy in my head; I'm crazy in my heart. Big difference."

"If you came here with questions about Nathaniel," says Cree. "I can't help you, but when you find him, do give me a call."

"Why? You already got what you wanted from him. Ya got Russ." Ryan gets up and paces. "I read the texts where Russ doubled down on his commitment to Charlene. Now, all of a sudden, after your encounter with Nathaniel, Charlene is complaining to the police department that you and Russ are back together, thinking it's our fault for not arresting you sooner. But I know the real reason." Ryan flops back into the couch. "As was the case for you and Russ, it's over between me and someone that *I* just can't live without. All I want is the chance that you got, whether it be – as you put it – in this world or in the next."

"Here's the thing, Detective Ryan. It was never over between me and Russ. Russ wasn't the person who sent those texts."

"Who did, then? Charlene?"

Cree, respecting Russ's wish to protect Charlene, evades the question. "If you think Nathaniel somehow magically got me and Russ back together then maybe your time is better spent trying to find him."

"Oh, I'm a stickler for finding folk who don't want to be found. I caught up to him 'bout an hour ago. Talked to em by phone."

"So, you found him?! Where… What's his phone number?" Cree scoots to the edge of her seat, as if to spring a for a pen.

Ryan halts her. "Not happening. Any communication between you two's gonna come through me." Ryan's chin tucks and he belches. "Nathaniel already admitted right out of his mouth that he indeed can help me, but before he helps me, he needs help himself."

Cree fears for Russ. "Did he identify the kidnappers?"

"I sense that he knows who they are, but won't tell me. But I'm no longer on the case, so that's neither here nor there. I want his help, and you want to get face to face with him, so let's you and me work together on us both getting what we want. In order to do that, we have to get Nathaniel what *he* wants—"

"—Which is?"

Detective Ryan gets up on wobbly legs. He walks over and sits next to Cree and speaks in a low voice. "Nathaniel says he needs to acquire this one thing, that will help him get his hands on another thing. It's something the kidnappers took from him, something of great sentimental value – family heirloom sort of thing. Anyway, he seems to need it back like he needs air to breathe. To do that, he needs money – money I don't have, which is why I'm coming to you."

Cree lights up. "I actually have some streaming revenue coming up. It's gonna be big, but it doesn't hit my account for another sixty days, I'm told."

"He ain't got no sixty days. He needs it now."

"I don't have it now."

"I beg to differ. You know how the old saying goes: there ain't no such thing as broke to a woman."

Cree folds her arms and fixes her eyes on the detective. "No, I don't know that saying, and I don't like the sound of it."

"I'm talking about Russ." Detective Ryan whispers even lower. "When I go out this door, you go on back there in the back and have a talk with Russ about this money. That man loves you; he'll give you anything if you ask hard enough." With that advice, Ryan gets up to go. As Cree escorts him to the door, Ryan, no longer whispering, says, "We haven't even touched on how you had that cut heal in a matter of hours. I'm starting to think you're not the same person that disappeared into thin air. That explains why you were slow to answer to your own name and couldn't remember a thing. Case in point, yesterday after you gave us the slip at the concert, I questioned your mother and even *she* says it's like you came back a totally different person."

"Bye, detective," Cree says, and closes the door in his face.

Russ sneaks out, asking, "I heard mostly everything. Why the whispering if you're supposedly alone?"

"He knew you were here, all along."

Russ says, "Lulu, that detective may sound crazy, but he's not the only one. The thing Nathaniel wants back must be that staff."

"A staff?"

"They say it's magic. He uses it to hit jackpot on slot machines."

Cree rotates with wide eyes. "You too?"

"Doesn't matter if I believe it. It only matters that *they* believe it, but what I want to get to the bottom of, is why you need to talk to Nathaniel so bad. What're you hiding?"

Cree fabricates a snide half smile, as if humored by this apparent nonsense. "Hiding?"

Russ stiffens and looks from the corner of his eye. "I heard that detective. *Are* you a different person? Is that why you're so damn different?" Russ paces away and grabs his head. "Can't be. Can't be…"

Cree rolls her eyes. "Russ, stop this."

He pivots just inside the kitchen and squints. "A concussion doesn't make a person talk different. You done lost ya humor, seems like…" His arms flop at his sides. "The Lulu *I* know would understand me not giving myself up to the police, putting my freedom on the line while knowing – good and hell, well – that no one was trying to harm you, but you want to end our relationship over it?"

Cree gasps. "I'm that same Lulu, fool. I wasn't putting an end to anything. Was I in my feelings? Yeah, but had you taken one step towards that door, I would've been on you like white on rice."

"So, it's not over between us?"

Cree approaches with a charmed grace, saying, "It might be, if you keep talking this craziness. You didn't think I was a different person last night when we were fucking."

"Earlier you called it lovemaking," he says, pointing back to the kitchen where she'd said it. A smile lets into his cheek. "Speaking of last night, it was so damn good that even the *sex* is suspect. After all this time apart, how do you suddenly know me better than I know myself?"

Cree leans into his body, a lower leg raised like the finishing pose to a dance. "I can say the same for you." She tries to be convincing; she tries to embody Lulu, her identity before being shaped by marriage and before becoming the face of an organization. She remembers a love for small talk and quiet kisses. She kisses Russ and asks, "What am I going to do with you, Russ."

"Marry me." He pulls a jewelry box from his pocket and lifts the lid on a sparkling engagement ring. While Cree tears up and fans her face, Russ lowers to one knee. "This is the ring I was going to surprise you with that day, if I wasn't followed. So, I'm asking you now, will you be my wife, again?"

Cree breaks down. She's getting the bended-knee proposal that their first shotgun wedding didn't allow. Too choked up to speak, Cree shakes her head yes.

They kiss and embrace, Cree, with an angled gaze, looks up at Russ like he is her wish come true. She leads Russ to the bedroom, remembering the detective's old saying: there ain't no such thing as broke to a woman. While the engagement seems to secure a lifetime in this world, it secures the help she'll need from Russ to get face to face with Nathaniel – her Wizard of Oz, with the power make her real wish come true: to go home.

Chapter 18

Nathaniel

Charlene is parked on the littered highway shoulder under a graffiti-tatted overpass in Valdosta, Georgia. She leans against the rental car, checking her makeup in the clamshell mirror, wondering what magical powers await her. The more she ponders it, the more her reflection seems to favor that of a sorceress, with her cheek mole, the oxblood blend in her dark brown hair, draped softly at the sides her smug beauty. Charlene lowers the mirror to reveal Jett Johnson helping Nathaniel out of the other rental car and removing handcuffs from the man Hook referred to as a real-life wizard; he looks nothing of the sort.

"So, this is the great Nathaniel," Charlene says, while appraising this bald-faced, racially ambiguous man with dreadlocks spilling over his shoulders.

Nathaniel glances at Jett, as he replies, "I asked him about my staff. He told me to ask you. Do you have it?"

Charlene approaches in four long strides, each step kicking the hem of her long dress; the angled shadow of the overpass slips over her. "I don't. Hook and his boys got it," Charlene says.

"I heard about what it can do, which is why I'm really keen on learning what other charms you might have."

Massaging his freed wrists, Nathaniel says, "Relics aren't for everybody. They can poison you with their power."

"What power, though," Charlene asks. "What do you have?"

"What do you *need*," returns Nathaniel.

Jett kids, "Gimme a love potion, if you got one."

Charlene feints as if her first mind was to slap him. "Do you hear how dumb you sound? Why would I need a love potion for a man that's already crazy about me?"

"I said, *I* need one," Jett grins. "…To use on you."

Charlene browbeats until Jett's smirk dies. "Don't play with me, Jett. In fact, leave us for a second. Let me and Nathaniel speak in private will ya?" Jett retreats to the car and closes himself inside. Charlene, still looking on in disgust, steers that disgust over to Nathaniel, and says, "So, you're just gonna stand there like a deaf mute, or tell me what you got?"

Nathaniel sighs and says, "Since you won't tell me your problem, I'll tell you what I know, Charlene. I know that you've been visiting hospital nurseries and gazing at the glass."

Charlene is stunned for three full beats. "If you know, why ask?"

"Out of respect," says Nathaniel. He then says, "If it's fertility, modern medicine is about as good as any relic."

"Modern medicine wants me to take a bunch of pills every day for about a year and then maybe… while Russ is out here so desperate to start a family *now* he'll resort to an addict to make it happen."

"Have you ever thought about–"

"–I didn't come to you, Nathaniel, to hear you talk about what other people can do for me. What can *you* do for me?"

"Nothing," says Nathaniel. "The relic you need, like most relics, are on the other side of the world; therefore, out of reach."

"No, it's not out of reach. How do you think we got here in Valdosta in a half hour? I've got a very rich gentleman friend that can put me on a private plane any time I ask."

Nathaniel responds, "Yeah, I've heard of Russ."

"I'm wasn't talking about Russ," Charlene glowers. "This man's old enough to be my deddy."

"Sounds like you've already got a relic then," Nathaniel's chuckle is so lonesome, he coughs it away. "To answer your question, the basin is rumored to be in Qatar—"

"—Kay what?"

Nathaniel's hand wipes down his dumfounded face. "The relic is the closest thing to a fountain of youth. It's not mentioned in the bible, but it's rumored to have helped Sarah give birth to Isaac at the age of ninety. Did you know that at the time of Sarah's death, she appeared to be only thirty years old, when she was more like *a hundred* and thirty years old? Anyway, the story behind this relic is that there was this hot spring pool located on the fault-line along the Mediterranean, in the land of Canaan, modern day Lebanon. The water itself was deadly — possibly high concentrations of hydrogen sulfide. You benefited only if you lived nearby and breathed the very low concentration that mixes in the air, like the biblical Levantine giants. Slowed aging also meant prolonged adolescent growth spurts. Anyway, the pool was destroyed in an ancient earthquake, but prior to its collapse, someone thought to chisel away some of the rock that holds the millions-of-years-old mineral deposits, and crafted it into a small basin. You pour hot kettle water into the bowl and inhale it's fumes a few times a week. It makes you younger inside and out."

Charlene, tapping an impatient foot, says, "Levantine giants?"

"Do you doubt? King Og of Bashan's thirteen-foot bed is on display in Rabbah, to this very day."

Charlene waves Jett out of the car to join them. "Come on back, Jett," she says, and then turns back to Nathaniel. "So, let's talk about this basin thing. How do we get it?"

"Well, the problem with that — as I was saying — is it's believed to be in the possession of the Queen of Qatar, Sheikha Moza, who, in her lifetime, has bore seven children, is well over sixty years old but still as vivacious as a college girl. To get the basin, we must steal from a royal family and pray we don't get caught and have to face a firing squad."

Charlene's arms flop at her sides. She looks over at Jett, who rejoins them. "Well, if he'd *led* with that, it would've saved all that yapping, am I right?" She turns to Nathaniel. "What do you have right now that can help me?"

"I have something," says Nathaniel. "But first I need your help in getting my staff back."

Charlene swivels, as if looking to see who Nathaniel must've been talking to. "Didn't you hear me say Hook and his boys got it? Can't buy it from him when it's just as good as money. Or do you suppose we go in and try to snatch it out of the hands of killers?"

Nathaniel looks over at the man with the gun belt.

Jett returns a look of pure amusement. "I'm a detective, brother; not a bounty hunter."

Nathaniel looks back at Charlene and says, "The reason I'm here in Valdosta, is for another relic."

"Well, can it make Lulu disappear, or turn Russ against her?"

Nathaniel blinks slowly. "It's an old handcrafted pair of specs. The frame is made of ivory; that alone, should tell you how old it is. The lens is even older. It's at an antique shop not far from here. If they knew what they had in their possession they'd ask a lot more for it."

Impatiently, Charlene asks, "What does this thing do, again?"

"It lets you see seconds into the future."

"I fail to see how that would do anybody any good."

"If I may," says Nathaniel. Although Charlene rolls her eyes, Nathaniel continues anyway. "It belonged to a doctor – a dentist – during the wild west, but this dentist had a set of proclivities that often got him into gunfights. It was odd, being a busy dentist without the time to practice his draw like other legendary gunslingers but there he was, among them. He was never pictured or depicted wearing glasses, which is part of the reason why the piece can't be authenticated."

"Wait a minute," Jett frowns, with the sum of the story's clues gathered in his brow. "Doc Holliday? This fool pulling our leg, Charl."

Nathaniel protests, "I promise, I'm not pulling your leg. Those specs are the reason he survived that deadly shoot out at the O.K. Corral, or any other gunfight he's been in. He did not die by the gun; he died of tuberculosis in Glenwood Springs, Colorado. Fast forward to the nineties when the film Tombstone made him a household name again, there was an effort to cash in on tourism, to restore the old Valdosta home where he grew up, turn it into a museum filled with his belongings, but since his Derringer was never recovered, they scrapped the idea—"

"—Can you get to the point, already," urges Charlene. "We're standing under a dang bridge, for Pete's sake."

"My apologies. Where I come from, we're all history buffs." Nathaniel shrugs. "So... with the project scrapped, the belongings were sold to various collectors, but many of his items couldn't be authenticated because his last living relative, author of one of the all-time best-selling books, had died fifty years prior. The material and craftsmanship on the glasses were still so convincing that a collector purchased them on pure rumor."

With tossed hands, Charlene blasts, "A got damn pair of glasses?"

Jett, with a cautious smirk, says, "It's a piece of history, Charlene. I, for one, would like to see if the thing actually works."

Nathaniel appeals, "Charlene, if I simply give you what you seek now, what would be your incentive to help me get what I seek? But as a token of my commitment to you, I can retrieve, for you, a relic in advance. It's a bottle of perfume, but it's like truth serum."

Charlene yells, "I already know the dang truth – that Russ is reeling right now, and he's about to make the biggest mistake of his life. If you can't help me, Nathaniel, just say that. That way, I can go on about my affairs and not waste another minute standing here, listening to your drivel!"

"But Charlene," Nathaniel pleads. "You may think you know the truth, but too often we create our own truth."

"Aw, you are quite the bastard, ya know… I shouldn't have come here," Charlene leans in with one final squint of her eyes, and then she pivots and marches for the car, leaving Nathaniel and Jett with puzzled looks.

Nathaniel pulls a necklace from under his shirt, opens the locket and takes a silver coin from inside. He calls Charlene, who is at her car door. When Charlene looks back, it seems as if she's stunned. Nathaniel submits, "Give it a chance, Charlene. What better option does walking away present you?"

Jett watches Charlene, who isn't looking at Nathaniel, perse, but she seems somewhat hypnotized by his twirling coin.

The usually stubborn Charlene is suddenly agreeable. "Alright, I'll go along. But you'd better make it worth my while."

"Follow us," Nathaniel says.

As soon as the men get in their car, the detective says, "From here on out, you keep that damn coin in your pocket, here me?"

Nathaniel straps on his seatbelt. "It's not as bad as you think. It's the power of suggestion. It only helps someone make a decision. Within minutes, they're free to rethink that decision, but that rarely occurs. Why? Because whenever man makes a decision, human nature compels him to see it through."

Jett nods. Refusing to look over at his passenger, he focuses solely on driving.

To disrupt silence, Nathaniel says, "So, you're a fan of Doc Holliday?"

Jett replies, "His best friend had a higher body count, that being Wyatt Earp, plus Earp was a lawman."

Nathaniel says, "Lawman like you, huh?"

Jett Johnson smirks and carelessly looks over. And there it is: the coin, rolling between Nathaniel's fingers.

Chapter 19

Dreams Upon Dreams

Cree materializes on an overpass in a city she doesn't recognize. This could be any overpass, any city's observatory of downtown's digression of industry. Skyscrapers and the piping chimneys of factories fade into the horizon's accumulation of smog. Cree figures she must be jogging, and then it is so. She's treated to a few clues; the sneakers on her feet, spandex, and the sudden pressure of earbuds in the conch of her ear. This is all real to her.

There's the sound of an argument, a woman yelling below. The woman is Charlene. Within her tirade, is something Cree should never hear in this world: her real name, *Cree*. Cree claws the chain linked suicide fence as she watches below. The man is someone Cree can't quite see because he's blanketed by the shadow beneath the bridge. The sun, warming the side of Cree's face feels absolutely real; however, Cree's eyes blink open and she's in her bed, where it's her pillow, not the sun, warming the side of her face.

Her dreams have been odd since entering this world. Each time, she's been a bystander, no longer the protagonist in dreams of her own making.

Cree sits up in bed. The morning is still dark, but she's as alert as she would be at midday. Cree decides to follow her dream and go for a run, since she's got over an hour to burn before it's time to leave for her mother's house, to see Meryl off to school.

Cree usually runs on a treadmill in the gym in their home. Here, her only option is to hit the pavement, where she expects to tire quicker than on a motorized treadmill, but the opposite happens. Even more perplexing is how two miles is a challenge on a much easier treadmill, but in this world, running on pavement and on a slight incline up Church street, Cree clears two miles feeling fresh enough to clear another.

Upon returning from the run, Cree sees a missed call. While toweling her sweat, she listens to the voicemail on speaker. It's Detective Ryan, reporting that he has suddenly lost contact with Nathaniel. Ryan goes on to say that he checked arrest records for the city of Valdosta and Lowndes county, and every hospital within range of Nathaniel's last known location, but to no avail. Ryan goes on to say that he believes that Charlene and her private detective, a man named Jett Johnson, must have gotten to him. Cree's dream now looks like prophecy; the man under the bridge with Charlene must've been Nathaniel. After a hot shower, while Cree gets dressed in her bedroom, the TV plays the news.

By the time Cree arrives at her mother's house, she can't recall any part of the news – not even the day's weather report, nor can she ever, in this world. If respiratory endurance is some augmentation of living in a world other than the one in which she was born, then a quirky handicap is being incapable of retaining anything she sees on the television set.

When Cree arrives at Beth's home, she goes straight to Beth's stove to make breakfast because her mother is tired, complaining that she couldn't sleep last night. As if Beth's fatigue doesn't worry Cree enough, a dry cough shows up. "Ma," Cree says, as she dumps eggs out of the pan into three plates. "Have you been keeping up with your doctor's appointments?"

Beth comes to the breakfast table, her face wearing the disdain of being questioned. "Yes, I've been keeping up with my appointments. I done beat cancer more times than you know of," Beth grumbles, as she scoots her chair forward.

Cree can't resist worrying because in the other world, Beth kept her second diagnosis secret, and was outed only by a hospital stay, from which Beth never returned, but Cree lets go of the subject, turning her attention to Meryl. Cree yells, "Meryl! You better not miss that bus this morning!"

"Keep playing, with me Lulu," Beth protests. "Don't nobody yell in this house but me." Beth frowns, although she's kidding. She's proud, seeing Lulu make every effort possible to reestablish herself as an authority in Meryl's life. Before the kidnapping, she would never get out of bed this early to see Meryl off to school, and if Beth could even picture it, she'd imagine that Lulu would be dragging her feet, still in a robe and bonnet, and sitting at the table waiting on breakfast – not cooking it in full dress and make up, talking about how good of a run she had this morning.

Meryl marches up from the hallway, leaning to offset the weight of the heavy backpack she totes in one hand. She eyes Cree at the stove, and comments. "Ew... Look at you, tryna cook."

In passing, Cree dots Meryl's forehead with a kiss. In response, Meryl thumbs over her shoulder and raises a brow at Beth.

The breakfast table becomes Meryl's performance stage; her mother and grandmother is her audience. Cree just can't get over how her own Meryl is a brainy introvert, yet *this* Meryl – the same girl, literally – bursts with personality. While Meryl goes on and on in a sassy rendition of middle school current affairs, that little right hand of hers is like an emotional lightning rod, how it hangs when she sidebars, or wiggles stiff to deny a thing, and how, with her playful disses, the hand draws upright into a slack fist that pops open with her punchlines.

After breakfast, Cree follows Meryl out on the porch. Meryl stops and spins to side-eye her mother, as if Cree is cramping her style in front of the kids on the idling bus. "Walking me out to the bust stop ma? Is *that* what we're doing now?"

Cree sees through the act. She sees the validation in her daughter's eyes, to know that she matters as much.

After the bus grumbles onward and Cree returns from the porch, Beth is in her recliner, turned to the legendary news anchorman, Bill Sharpe, who she's had a crush on for as long as Cree can remember. Cree cherishes the time spent with Beth, how fulfilling it is just to sit with her mother after being taught, by grief, just how precious days like this should have always been. Cree questions Beth about the distant relatives from Maryland that Cree had met, for the first time, in the other world at Beth's funeral. Cree mines Beth for stories and for forgotten branches of their family tree, as if compiling a family archive.

As far as Cree is concerned, this world is home, since Lulu reneged on her promise, and since Detective Ryan has lost track of Nathaniel. Cree isn't worried about Charlene finding him because she's probably trying to build a case that Cree orchestrated her own disappearance, but Cree rests assured that no substantial amount of evidence can be attained for something that never happened. Cree figures best to sow seeds in the world she's in, rather than wasting energy on a most improbable return to her own world, and missing out on mornings with her mother, along with the sweet distraction of affectionate morning texts from Russ.

After replying to Russ with a long text, Cree looks up to continue her conversation with Beth and finds her head hung.

Cree gets this odd worry. Maybe it's because of the dry cough Beth had this morning and now with her head down and sleeping so peacefully – too peacefully. Cree gets up to check her mother's breathing, but before Cree brings a finger under Beth's nose, she begins to snore. The feeling isn't about Beth, but the vague urge is still there, and growing. Inexplicably, Cree pulls out her phone and watches it in her hand. Lo and behold, it rings. It's Guy. Cree is numb throughout the conversation, where Guy convinces her to forego a lunch date with Russ in order to meet him for what he calls an amazing opportunity.

Cree sets the phone down slowly, afraid to do anything quick, as if the device is a bomb. She looks around. She feels her face. She studies the lines of her palms. There has been too many coincidences for either one of them to have been merely coincidence. Even before Detective Ryan's voicemail confirmed her dream, there was the eerie feeling about the coliseum security that turned out to be accurate, and now having felt a phone call seconds before it arrives, there's no shaking the feeling that maybe she's… Cree refuses to think the word psychic. Cree takes a deep breath and shakes the nervous energy out of her hands. She was never one to dream of fish and have a friend or relative turn up later with a swollen belly. Cree has always been envious of the likes of Beth, her uncle Vernon on her father's side, and her cousin Mimi, who never needed a cemetery to visit relatives that have transitioned, for they manifest in her dreams, as tranquil and wise as they are well-dressed. Cree wonders, now, for how long she's been this way without noticing; how many of these worries she's dismissed. Cree wonders how many dreams she's written off as just dreams. She initially thought nothing of the lucid dream of Russ suspended in Lulu's leglock, like a female spider overtakes it's mate and eats him alive. Even the next day, at the portal, Cree had made no correlation between the dream and Lulu mentioning that she and Russ were trying to conceive.

Cree gets up, for no reason other than to climb up out of her thoughts. She pulls the throw from the couch and takes it over to Beth, who sleeps in the recliner. While adjusting the blanket, Cree's hand lands on her mother's bosom where she feels a prosthetic under her blouse; Beth has had a mastectomy.

AT NOON, Cree finds herself parked in her car at an old, worn shopping center where half the businesses are closed except for a pool hall, an Asian food store, and the bail bondsman office that Guy setup after leaving the music industry.

Guy appears in the frame of the glass door, decked out, as usual, in a suit and wearing a money smile. He guides Cree down the hallway along a line of various framed musical accolades, all of them belonging to Lulu and the band, Guy's only group to make it to the big time. In Guy's office, he pulls out a chair for Cree. He comes around the desk, banging the top twice, and then bumping it with his hip, and a secret drawer pops open, from which Guy pulls out a fifth of brown liquor and shot glasses. He offers Cree a drink as he pours his own.

Cree politely declines, as she crosses her legs, looking around in confusion. "It's just me, then? The band's not coming?"

Guy leans back in his chair, his head shaking. "*First* thing out of your mouth…" He takes a sip, sets down the glass and looks Cree over with a chink in his smile. "I admire your loyalty to the band, Lulu. I understand how you say, without them there wouldn't be no you. After that first album hit, we tried to get you to go solo, remember? You took a lesser deal just to keep the band on board–"

"–I have things to do, Guy. Can you get to the part about this 'amazing opportunity'?"

He raises two hands, as if backing off the speech. "Basically, here we are again; the opportunity in your lap. They want you."

"Who is they?"

"They, is everybody," he says, as he gathers his hands on the desk. "That press number on your website goes to me. I've gotten calls and emails from magazines: Nuovo, Scale, and Vinyl, to name a few."

Cree is speechless.

Guy tries to make sense of her. He finally asks, "Don't you think this is good news?"

Cree's phone goes off; it's her mother. She ignores it for now and returns to the discussion. "Interviews are good, Guy, but I must admit, I was hoping for another record deal."

The man nods like a woodpecker. "Yes, yes, but the music is nothing without momentum behind it. I'll be doing a press wire – see what hits, but I need for that press wire to say that you're working on a comeback album, so that every platform you appear on – every radio show, morning show or podcast – you'll be promoting this album." Guy's arms spread in grand fashion. "Who doesn't love a comeback story?"

"So, the album is without the band, though..."

Guy deflates behind the desk. "You've done all you can for the band, Lulu. You bombed two albums by holding onto them. With those failures attached to your name, nobody wanted to touch you after that. Now that your name is in people's mouths again, it's bringing the hitmakers back to the table. We're in talks with a couple of brothas that simply don't miss: Brian Knox on the song writing and Dante 'The Matrix' Bates on the production." Fly Guy puts a hand out to pause Cree's amazement. "But wait. There's more. None of this really comes together without some major artists featured on the album. For one, how about John Legend?"

Cree's jaw drops. She's so giddy inside; it traps her words. The thing she's dreamed about in the other world is here, now, staring her in the face. Cree notices that down in her lap, her phone, now on silent, lights up again with a call from her mother.

Guy taps the desk. "What is there to think about?"

"Yes," Cree says. "It's a deal." No sooner than agreeing to the deal, Cree is overcome with this odd feeling again that makes her frown and apologize. "I'm sorry I... I'm just getting this feeling that something's wrong."

"The band will be alright."

"No, not the band–"

"–Something's wrong with who *me?*" His voice squeaks on the word me; Guy's brow raises, causing his already wrinkled forehead to sandwich. "I personally am guaranteeing that you get a fair split."

Cree wipes the air with both hands, saying, "No, it's not you, Guy. It's not even *this*... Call me crazy, but I've been getting these visions–"

"–Visions?" Guy looks at her sideways in comedic appraisal. "Or is it *hallucinations*," he says with a pinky finger at the corner of his mouth.

"Child please. I'll never touch that stuff again in my life, but... It's like an intuition, and it's not the first time it's..." Cree's phone buzzes again. "The feeling I'm getting is about this call. I gotta take it."

Guy sets an open hand in the middle of the desk's, his eyes stern as an eagle's. "By all means take the call, but I *do* have your verbal commitment, right?" He waits for her nod, then continues, "So, now we'll get all the lawyers together – see if we can get a lucrative deal in ink. If it all works out, we'll be signing to the Aurora label, a two-album deal. Meanwhile you, Lulu, pack your bags because you'll be on a plane in three days."

"Three days?" Cree's phone has stopped ringing.

"If not sooner," Guy says, with a grimace and a slow shaking head. "I'll get there a day ahead of you, make sure everything's setup how you like it. We'll be meeting up at Matrix's home studio in Manhattan for one week, putting in sixteen-hour days if we have to. It'll be just a five-track album, so we can get some material out there quick-fast and in a hurry – but still quality."

It's Cree's phone again. "Sorry, Fly, I have got to take this." Cree answers. She has the phone to her ear for only a few seconds before she covers the mouthpiece and says, "I gotta go."

Guy hurries behind her, preaching down the hallway. "I understand emergencies come up, Lulu. But you got to put the drama on pause for a little while. They won't tolerate you canceling dates, going missing, like you've been known to do."

Cree pivots and explodes. "This is about my daughter, okay!" Guy flinches as Cree's hand flies up – not to hit him, but to point at the framed accolades on the wall. "Before all of this, I'm a mother first," Cree yells, her maternal instincts fully engaged over a child she thought she could never see as her own.

CREE picks up Beth and they ride to Meryl's school together. Beth was called, saying Meryl had gotten into a fight and that she was so uncontrollable, she had to be detained by the school's resource officer, a man with deep set eyes who, upon Cree's arrival, hands over Meryl's backpack, his face fixed in the judgement he withholds from the child. Gingerly, Cree takes the backpack. "Thank you," she says.

In the place of *you're welcome*, the peace officer imparts, "Next year she's thirteen. Won't be no more call for pickups. It's straight to DJJ."

Cree and Beth meet with the teacher and principal and hear their account of the incident. They gasp at the week-long suspension. They're guided to the room where Meryl sits behind a locked door because they say she'd been spitting at staff. As the door opens, Beth yells, "*Bring* your behind on here, girl!" On the way back to the car,

Beth let her have it. "I'm 'bout sick of you, young lady! And if you think you got yourself a week off from school to do whatever you please, that's a damn lie! We gone have that house spick and span. We gone be moving furniture, cleaning the oven. The works! There ain't gone be no rest for you!"

Beth puts the car in gear next to an empty passenger seat. Cree rides in the back, her neck so stiff with disappointment, she can't look over at Meryl. Cree looks to the front seat, seeing the side of Beth's face as she continues to berate the child.

Cree, a tentative bystander, decides to cut in and take a stab at diplomacy. "Meryl? Hon, won't you tell me your side of what happened?"

It's the moment Meryl had been waiting for. Her head turns on a swivel, her eyes astounded with both anger and opportunity. "I know *you* ain't talkin'!"

Cree feels the loss of a daughter. Eyes cannot hold such hatred while bearing silhouettes of the mother. This is Lulu's Meryl. Cree says, "Whose side do you think I'm on? I'm your mother."

Meryl yells, "My *mother* is driving this car!"

Beth says, "Watch it, Meryl. That's how it started last time?"

Cree asks, "How what started?"

"You jumped on that little girl like she was a grown-ass woman."

Meryl goes off again. "You remember for the police, but when it comes to me you're confused? I'm not about to sit here and listen to you tell me how this is all my fault. These hoes always coming for me because I'm the center of attention." Counting off on her fingers, Meryl lists, "They betray me. They gossip about me, because they can't *be* me. They try to outshine me, but they can't. I'm gonna keep on handling them bitches like you handle me!"

"–Little *girl*," yell's Beth. "Don't make me pull this car over!"

Cree can't believe the scene she's in. Cree's past repeats with such accuracy that it mocks her. She's seeing her family dynamics now with such clarity that it exposes the selectiveness of her memory – things she's made herself forget in honor of her deceased mother. Cree says, "Momma? Momma."

"What," says an irritated Beth.

"I'm asking you nicely to never threaten my daughter again."

Beth's eyes target Cree in the rearview mirror. "Lucretia! Who the hell you talking to? You got me so hot, I done 'bout slapped your reflection in this rearview mirror. You can start telling me how to be a parent as soon you stop putting that powder up your nose."

"I used to be so afraid of you that I would never backtalk."

"Afraid of what? I hardly laid a hand on you, growing up."

"That's not the only fear there is ma. Being on your bad side was not a good place. I responded to it by being really well-behaved, up until I went off to college. I remember being too afraid to backtalk you, so what I'd do, is go off on daddy – but for you to hear. Now the positions are the same but the people have changed: I'm daddy and Meryl is me. Can't you see that? Everything she just said to me was for you to hear – that she feels targeted at school and all this yelling and intimidation and threatening we're doing in response to her behavior, is giving her the playbook on how to respond to the behavior of others. We have to stop pointing at her. We have to see the us in this."

"Us!" Beth's head clicks right, side-eyeing her adult daughter in the back seat. "Us? How about you, Lulu! If you was half a mother, she wouldn't be living with me, in the first place."

"You're right," says Cree, unfazed. "But your need to be right is bigger than your need to right wrongs. That's what allowed you to stay married to a toxic, dopehead husband – at the expense of his influence on your kid, me. He's in prison but you now have me to constantly judge, in his place, and Meryl, instead of me, to put fear into."

Meryl, who'd been uncontrollably angry moments ago, sits as quiet as a mouse now that there's someone speaking on her behalf.

Beth fights tears. "I'd be a damn fool to listen to what comes out of your mouth. There ain't nothing you can tell me about being a mother."

Clearly, Cree has benefited from being in what's been a good marriage, for the most part. Their two stints of marriage counseling forced she and Russ to peel back their layers and see themselves through the eyes of the other, which prompts the type of self-evaluation that being right would never make room for. This moment shows Cree just how valuable their marriage is, and how foolish she and her husband were to lose sight of it.

Speaking on behalf of Lulu, Cree turns to Meryl and says, "This may not be worth much to you right now, but I am sorry. I don't know what I was thinking, to put my hands on you."

But there's more that Meryl wants her mother to answer for. She looks at Cree with tears sparkling in her eyes, her mouth trembling as she whimpers, "You called me a heifer. And you said that when you were pregnant with me, you prayed for a miscarriage." Tears race down Meryl's face.

Cree frowns and says, under her breath, "Damn you, Lulu." She looks at her daughter. "You know I didn't mean that, Meryl. I love you, baby. I love you so much, that nothing makes me more depressed than failing you. You have such a fool for a mother, I'm often mad at you for not finding it in your own self to be better than the example I'm setting. I see the work that building a good relationship with you requires, and I'm intimidated by it. I'm going to have to come face to face with my own demons and they scare me. But I've got to change that if I want the path you're on to change." As Cree speaks, her wisdom surprises even herself. "All this, being the center of attention... I was the center of attention, many times on a concert stage before a stadium packed with fans." Cree nods with a near smile. "You learned from the best." Meryl responds by throwing herself into her mother's arms, where she weeps. Cree rubs her daughter's back and says, "I may not remember everything from that day, but I promise to make it up to you."

They haven't made it home yet, but Beth slows down to pull over.

Cree looks to the front seat. Before she can ask why they've stopped, she sees Beth wipe her nose with her hand and there's red blood smeared across her palm.

Rod Palmer   165

Chapter 20

Torn

As Charlene walks through the open door, Russ silently prays that Lulu never finds out. Lulu has just accepted his proposal of marriage and already Russ is meeting his ex-fiancé in secret. Russ asks, "So where's this video you were talking about?"

Charlene heads straight to the window sill, picks up the remote and retracts the eight-foot-tall blinds. "Let some light in man... sittin' here in the dark like damn bat." She turns and says, "I'm gonna show you the video like I promised, but first let's talk."

Russ closes the door and follows the trail of Charlene's perfume, which smells like no fragrance Charlene would ever wear. It's Roses with a back-kick of sassafras. The odor makes Russ woozy.

Charlene, with an expectant glare, asks, "Like my new perfume?"

Russ opens his mouth to lie, but truth leaps out. "Smells like you reached for the perfume, but picked up the bug spray by mistake."

Charlene smiles. "That's the kind of answer I was hoping for."

Already, Russ can't even recall the 'answer' she speaks of.

Charlene goes on to the next question, "Am I beautiful?"

"C'mon with the silly shit, Charlene. 'Course, you're beautiful. I damn near married you, didn't I?"

"Prettier than Lulu?"

"You have your days – this sort of charm about you, that, when it's clicking, there ain't too many women can stand next to you."

"Simple yes or no. Prettier or not."

"Than Lulu?"

"You heard me."

"No. But it's a slim margin. And, being completely honest with you, when the clothes come off, that margin increases." Russ twitches and flicks out a pointer finger. "You got the titties, though. Gotta hand it to ya, but…" He goes dim with confusion. "What're we talking about again?"

"Oh nothing," Charlene shrugs. Slowly she approaches. "You were just explaining how, for years, you would tell me I'm the most beautiful woman you ever held in your arms." She stops face to face. Quietly, she says, "Now you're saying Lulu is prettier. You bastard."

Russ torques slightly. "But why would I tell you that?"

Charlene sees precisely what Nathaniel meant when he handed her the charmed perfume bottle. He'd warned her to beware the questions she asks, as the truth can cut like a knife. Charlene shuffles right up to Russ's chest and asks. "Did you cheat on me with her? I know you did, emotionally, but I'm talking about physically."

"I'm no cheater. The night of the concert was the first time. And what Lulu put on me, that night, in that hotel? Let's just say, that margin widened some more."

Charlene slaps his face.

Russ's head snaps back. He chastises himself through clenched teeth, "Why can't I answer you the way I want to?"

"You may not have cheated, but Lulu knew exactly what she was doing," Charlene says. "Lulu was dangling that fanny in front of you like a carrot to a horse."

"Obviously, you've gotten to Nathaniel. He must've given you something that's got me talking crazy right now. I mean... I can't sugar-coat shit," says Russ. "And yet you're using this opportunity to focus all your questions on Lulu? Look, I love you, Charlene, but I swear you got your ways about you. Instead of looking at yourself, you're trying to confirm that Lulu did you wrong, in order to justify trying destroy her with that video. Stop trying to fix the situation and fix yourself! You're so damned angry all the time, and it's tiring... tiring."

"I don't need to justify a thing to put Lulu away. You're the one who needs to justify how you left a good, Godfearing woman for a product of the ghetto."

Russ replies, "How can you, of all people, stand in judgement of the ghetto – when your family and the people your family endorses, are the architects of the systems that keeps people in ghettos."

"How convenient to grow a conscience after using those very systems to line your own pockets."

"No. I did what my daddy taught me, until I learned the industry for myself. Now, I'm my own man."

"So, now you wanna be some sort of valiant leader of the buhlack community, huh?" Charlene laughs initially, but then she stiffens, alert with the realization. "My God, you do... And you left me standing at the altar because you don't think you can lead them with someone by your side who looks like me? Is that it?" Russ's shameful silence has him dead to rights. Charlene adds, "Lulu, on the other hand – why, she's a celebrity. She is beloved in your community... perfect for what you're trying to do, but I've got news for ya. I overheard my deddy talking about how them plans you drew up is absolutely ridiculous. The same people you're trying to help is gonna be the same ones to spit in your face."

"I'm not shallow, Charlene. Look at me. Look at me. You know I'm incapable of lying, right now. So, believe me when I say this: I love Lulu more than I have ever loved any woman. Race… it was only the icing – not the cake."

"Well that'll be also my icing for turning this video in to the police." Charlene pulls out her phone with the display turned to Russ as she narrates. "This is Lulu, on camera the night she was supposed to be missing. Not lost in the woods, but hauling a mirror into that storage unit. She played everyone. She's given false statements and obstructed an investigation. Best case scenario, she serves two years imprisonment. You left me for an inmate!"

Russ shuffles closer, towering over her. "Charlene. Don't do this."

"After what you did to me?" She looks up at him with an odd mix of both anger and wonder. "How dare you fix your mouth. This is your own karma. Deal with it. You and Lulu decide if you wanna start a family after she gets out of jail or do you put a baby in her now and let her give birth in prison. Or… come back to your senses and try your damnedest to win me back."

Russ rubs his chin and says, "How would that be possible when I'd be in jail too. I set up the damn kidnapping – and it wasn't even a kidnapping, it was more like a prank."

Charlene shrugs. "Didn't think I knew, did you? Hook told me."

Russ's eyes round like an owl's; he mocks its call. "Who? What you know about Hook?"

"Didn't need to know him. Followed you right to Hook's doorstep. So, I paid Hook to clean up the scene to steer the investigation away from you; therefore, this video only gets one person convicted and that person is Lulu. All the embarrassment and shame you caused me, and here I am, protecting you. Can you now see the forest for the trees?"

Russ looks troubled, conflicted and yet out of his mixture of emotions arises a smirk of madness. The smirk grows into a grin and then a chuckle. "You got me bound to the truth, and you don't even know which questions to ask."

Charlene responds, "Here's a question for ya, then: Was I the chess move, as Detective Ryan put it? Do you love me, at all?"

"Yes, I love you, Charlene. After my divorce, it was you who was hesitant to commit, remember?"

"Not hesitant; afraid. Time I fell in love with you, Russ, you told me you had some chick pregnant, and for nearly three years we all thought you were that girl's father. By the time of your divorce, I had gotten used to holding back when it came to you."

"Charlene?"

"Yes, Russ."

Russ takes her hands in his. "Charlene... I'm asking. Is there anything I can do – anything – that would make you forget about turning in that video?"

Her head shakes slowly, her eyes teary. "There's one thing and one thing only. You keep your proposal to me."

"Under the pressure of threat?"

"Even so, you'll later look back on this and realize that I'm saving you from yourself. Even your folks can't stand her and they love me. Lulu is going to ruin you just like she's ruined her own life, twice."

"You talk about commitment... I made that same commitment to Lulu years ago and I feel like we didn't even have a chance to see it through. We were torn apart by obligation. The family business kept me rooted here in the south while music pulled her north and the rest was history."

"History – ya big dumb oaf – is fixin' to repeat itself. Lulu will be in New York, directly, working on a new album."

Russ stiffens as if struck by lightning. It makes sense. Cree had cancelled their lunch date for a meeting with Fly Guy. Russ's head tremors no. "Wait, what did you hear?"

Charlene adds, "Her manager just posted on social media that there's a new album in the making. She's about to be pulled north again, jumping on the first thing smoking and leaving your dumb butt down here all heartbroken. So, now what?"

Russ is woozy. He stumbles back into the couch and falls seated.

"You should see the look on your face, right now. It's as if you'd seen it coming a mile away."

Russ remembers after seeing Lulu's surge in downloads, asking her if her success was going to change things between them. He sighs twice back to back.

Charlene sits on the couch arm and hugs Russ, whispering. "It's okay, love. It's going to be okay; I promise."

Slowly, Russ realizes that Charlene's arms are around him and his head on her bosom, albeit in a gesture that is caring and not romantic, but Russ thinks from Lulu's perspective, how she would feel if she were to walk in on them, so Russ slowly works his way out of Charlene's arms, and just so that he's clear on where he stands, Russ says, "Let me make one thing clear to you, Charlene. You already know I can't lie, so believe it with your whole heart when I say, if you turn in that video. I'd sooner marry a dog than marry you."

Charlene rushes him, with claws trying to gouge Russ's eyes out. She screams, You son of a bitch!"

Russ collects her hands and renders her powerless. "Charlene!"

There's a beat of silence. Charlene twists lose. "You think I need some video? All I have to do is sit back and watch." Charlene, with a pointed finger marches Russ back toward the door in a tirade, "All those years, Russ! And you do me like this! You'll be sorry. I swear you're gonna be sorry! This is my last time trying to appeal to your better senses. I'm gonna sit back... and I'm gonna watch you fall on your fucking dumb face!" Charlene, still coming forward with her pointed finger has marched Russ's back to the front door, where Charlene yells, "Get out of my way!"

The moment the door closes behind her, Russ takes out his phone, selects a contact and waits for the answer. "Yeah, Mayor Hamilton? Hey, look man, we got a problem. Your daughter knows."

While Russ informs Mayor Hamilton over the phone, Charlene is out at the nearest gas station approaching Jett, who stands outside his car looking into the backend of a camera that's about as big as a coffee maker. Charlene joins him shoulder to shoulder, saying, "He didn't have a clue. As soon as I stepped inside, I retracted the blinds, still I was worried about the sun glare on the windows."

"No, they're good, actually." Jett scrolls through the photos he took while hiding in the bushes on the grounds of Russ's estate. "See that one? You're embraced with his head angled up to you, it looks like you two are about to kiss."

Charlene laughs. "Lulu's gonna piss herself when she sees it."

Chapter 21

Blackmail

Beth is weary. Months ago, she had refused treatment. Realizing she's had more cancer diagnoses than common colds, in the past few years, and then staring down another round of grueling treatment, she had closed her eyes and shook her head no in silence; she'd endured enough. She continues to volunteer at a hospital across town, inspiring hope when there is no hope for herself. When the commitment to living comes with perpetual suffering, death becomes the highest form of self-love. But death hasn't claimed her yet.

Beth's nosebleed was the result of a spike in blood pressure, from the bickering – from Beth, the steadfast matriarch, being put down by her very own daughter.

For the moment, Beth is doing better than Cree, who cries and pleads with doctors to let her in the room. "I'm trying to apologize to her," Cree pleads. "If anything, it's going to help bring her blood pressure *down*. You see, I had said some things that…" Everything Cree says makes them more opposed to the idea. Three white coats come in tight and march forward, forcing Cree to plead while retreating backward out of the hallway.

Cree's best friend in both worlds, Staysha, sits with her god-daughter, Meryl. Staysha, the lazy-eyed eccentric with a storm cloud of hair, puts a hand over her mouth when she sees Cree returning to the waiting room on slow legs and a hung head.

Cree says, however, "She's ok." Staysha and Meryl sigh as one. "But she's not okay."

Staysha and Meryl look at each other and back to Cree.

"Momma has terminal cancer; she's known for a while now."

"Terminal," exclaims Staysha.

Meryl, although knowing the meaning of the word, can't wrap her head around the idea of death. "There's something they can do, momma," Meryl says. "They haven't tried everything."

They're interrupted by a nurse or counselor of sorts, whose nose looks as rigid as a book spine. The woman holds a pamphlet open and outward-facing as her fingernail moves down the bullet points on what to expect. Doctors expect Beth to return to normal activity for a time, but no one knows the hour when Beth would find herself too weak to get out of bed. The nurse hands over the pamphlet she just summarized and gives Cree a contact card for a hospice care facility for when homecare becomes too great of a burden. The nurse then leaves them with her blessings. Cree takes a seat, her heels resting on the chair spoke, a jittery leg pumping.

Staysha says, "I guess Miss Beth say she ain't done yet, girl. Beth gone hold on until you get back custody of Meryl, watch."

Cree pretends not to notice, but Meryl, after hearing this, rotates forward and stares blankly, as if it just now dawns on her that she is not the afterthought she believed herself to be. She's at the forefront of both her mother's fight to stay clean to regain custody, and her grandmother fighting off death to keep her out of the foster care system in the meantime. Meryl recoils her legs under her, sitting Indian style. She bites her nails while coming to realize how her behavior at school desecrates the labors of the two women who loves her more than anything. Meryl leans on her mother, in silence, listening interestedly while Cree and Staysha tell stories about the Beth they knew when they were

Meryl's age – how Beth would feed Staysha and braid her hair like a child of her own. They reminisce over the sleepovers Beth has blessed with her famous peaches and biscuits. They rehash memories that took place right in front of Beth's house because her yard was the bus stop for the entire street; therefore, Beth was like a guardian and counselor to them all. She was there to break up every fight and even march kids home to lecture their parents. Beth was – is – fearless. She'd even confront neighborhood drug dealers, in the same manner in which she now confronts death; with a straight face. The only thing Beth ever feared in life was lightning. During thunderstorms she'd have them sit quietly in the hallway, forbidding them to move or speak until the storm subsides.

While reviewing the past, Cree is wondrously distracted by the present – not from Meryl leaning on her and playing with Cree's ring hand, matching the length of their fingers – but Cree is distracted by the differences between the Staysha sitting next to her versus the Staysha of the other world.

Staysha, in Cree's world, is a serial entrepreneur, a legit big city fashionista, Instagram brand ambassador, relationship ministry podcaster, independent author, motivational speaker, wife and soccer mom. Cree pities the Staysha sitting next to her, who is a grown man's meal ticket. She's no big city fashionista; she frequents consignment shops and redesigns the pieces into something new; she handmakes beaded necklaces and bracelets in her spare time and sells them downtown at the old stone markets that used to sell humans. Cree finds herself staring at Staysha's shoes, a retro ruby red slipper, indicative of the jewels that Staysha is able to find with regularity; fashion is still very much a part of who she is. Cree wishes she could fill Staysha in on the life she's missing out on, without mentioning the parallel universe and having hospital staff haul Cree three floors up, to the psyche ward.

Cree asks, "Do you have any idea what Sean is up to nowadays? I always had a feeling he'd go on to do great things." Like the NBC Network producer, he is in the other world.

"Great *things*..." Staysha's brow drops like a broken shelf. "If you call a floor supervisor at a call center, 'great things,' but he swear he's somethin' though."

Cree asks, "Is he married?"

Staysha leans away, her mouth twisted. "To a broad from Honduras that he found online. Pretty girl, but you ought to see how he flaunts her – as if she is everything that black women ain't."

"Oh, so he's one of them," says Cree.

Staysha confirms with a drowsy look-away. "She seems to not know when he's using her as a prop, so I don't fault her, but I must say that upon closer inspection... I found an old profile of hers. Come to find out, she used to be a prostitute. Sean did what a lot of brothas are doing now. They might be broke to us, but to women in third world countries, they're rich. So, these prostitutes sucker they weak behind into marriage, with the hopes of rescuing their families back home. And this is who Sean touts as his queen."

Cree sizzles air between her teeth as if to the sting of a papercut. "Sorry I asked."

Staysha lights up gleefully. "Oh, don't be sorry, baby. Be happy for me that I didn't fall for it."

Cree is confused because even this Sean who Staysha describes sounds like a better option than the man Staysha is with. Cree can't resist asking for clarification. "What do you mean almost fell for it?"

Staysha says, "What I mean is, her highness can have Sean, with his stank feet and ten pumps."

Cree goes dead with laughter and slinks in her chair. Meryl's brow wrinkles at her mother and godmother. "A ten-pump? Is that a gun?"

Staysha's hand falls limp. "Not a gun, child. A pea-shooter."

They have a good laugh but clean it up quickly, as this is a hospital waiting room where laughter feels out of place. Cree and Staysha clear their throats and changes the conversation to the new record deal.

Meryl is the most optimistic of the three because it would mean returning to New York, which is more home to her than here. She has more friends she'd left behind than friends she's gained here in the year since their return to Charleston, a city that Meryl has grown only somewhat familiar with, on her four short visits annually and her extended visits during Lulu's concert tours.

Staysha offers, "You can't be two places at once, Lulu. I'll check on Beth and Meryl every day while you're gone. But what you *don't* do, is pass up a once-in-a-lifetime opportunity that finds you a second time."

The offer has little effect on Cree. "That's my mother. I can't."

Staysha argues, "It's not like she's gonna just go, at the snap of a finger. The lady said she'll become very fatigued and disoriented. That's when you call hospice, where she could spend days or even weeks. I'm sure those big-time producers can put you on a straight flight and get you home in no time, Lulu."

Cree replies with both hands pinched in front of her as if holding up a t-shirt inscribed, "So momma suddenly collapses, and Meryl goes through that experience without me?" Her head tremors to shake out the thought. "It's a no, for me."

Staysha doubles down. "My offer still stands if you change your mind, Lulu, but... Can I be real with you for a second?"

Cree sighs. "If you're not real, you're fake, so go on and say it."

Staysha doesn't even look at Cree while speaking. "I know Beth is mostly why you're staying; I'm not discounting that. But that ring on your finger got a lot to do with it too. You don't see that record deal as an opportunity, when you know you'll be rich either way."

"Staysha," Cree looks over at her friend, appalled. "If that came from anyone else, it would sound like shade."

Staysha pats Cree's hand. "But it came from me, so you know it ain't. You made the right decision ten years ago, and it would be the right decision now, but you're afraid because you think you might mess up the money again? You're wiser now, Lulu."

Cree gazes in thought. Meryl examines her mother's gaudy engagement ring. Almost thinking to herself, Meryl says, "So, daddy may have slid back into your life, momma, but he won't win me over so easily."

Cree and Staysha steal glances. Meryl still thinks that Russ is an absent father. Cree responds, "First of all, Meryl, I wasn't easy."

Staysha interrupts, "The lord saw fit to bless you with a second opportunity. Most people don't get one. That's favor."

"Truth be told, Staysha, the opportunity is Russ's." Cree has seen her impact to the company's bottom line, and as far as the man himself, the only facet in which bachelor Russ exceeds the husband, is romantically. Cree finds Staysha's side stare. "What," says Cree.

"The opportunity I was talking about, Lulu, is your music career, not Russ. Let's not get it twisted."

Cree blinks hard as if hit with smelling salt. "'Get it twisted?' Are you kidding me, right now?"

Staysha looks down at her hands and sighs. "I just think you should wait until all the facts of this case comes together. You don't know what he is capable of."

"And what's *Jermaine* capable of, Staysha? Should we go there? We know he's capable of selling drugs, DUIs, not holding down a job."

"You act as if those things are not behind him. He had a hard life growing up. He's doing really good, now, to say he came from nothing."

"It's not what happens to a man, it's what a man makes happen for himself. What he came from shouldn't factor into what you accept."

"That man loves me, and I'm sure of that."

"Russ loves me enough to marry me. Twice. When's *your* wedding date?"

"When Russ divorced you, was that love too? Jermaine and me may have our ups and downs but we have 'em together. When things get tough, it never even occurs to him to leave."

"Struggle love," Cree's eyes roll. "If Jermaine leaves, he's homeless. Take the struggle out of it, then see if it's love that keeps him."

"You mean like Russ? When he saw that you no longer needed him, he became too insecure to bear a relationship with you. This time around, what you really need to worry about, is losing him just like you got him."

"It was over with Charlene. She was in denial."

"You slept with him on the day that would've been their wedding day. You and Russ can count your days – that's all I'm gone say."

Although Cree doesn't look, she feels Meryl's evaluation of her, which will outweigh anything Cree can teach her with words. "Look, Staysha," Cree drops a hand on Staysha's knee and says, "The one thing constant through all the mess, is us. We can have our differences without saying hurtful things, amen?"

"Nuff said, then. Let's kill that."

Cree sighs and says, "Well, they'll be monitoring momma for a while so… In the meantime, are you guys hungry?"

Staysha and Meryl exchange glances.

Cree wants in on the joke. "What?"

Meryl obliges, "You guys? No, ma. The proper way is *y'all*. Got it?"

Their laugher is somewhat forced, to lighten the mood. Cree and Meryl hold hands as they walk beside Staysha down the hospital hallway. Reality hits Cree, like walking under soft, cool air from a ceiling vent. This is her life now. Walking the hallway with her daughter and her best friend, shouldering a crisis; it's her first sense, in this world, of not feeling displaced like an Alice in Wonderland.

Staysha may not have been right about Cree's reason for not going to New York, but she wasn't wrong either. The record deal, however, is still a maybe. It could fall through and take one option away, so Cree isn't in any rush to call Guy and inform him of her decision to stay at the side of her mother.

It was never lost on Cree that she agreed to Russ's proposal as part of her plan to cut a deal for Detective Ryan to give her access to Nathaniel. The engagement is much more tentative than anyone knows, but how can she not be open to marrying her husband. She looks forward to building a relationship with this Russ, armed with the wisdom from mistakes she doesn't have to make here.

This is Cree's plan for the foreseeable future – for all of ten seconds – until the *un*foreseeable emerges from an intersecting hallway to the left, approaching with a toss of her hair, saying, "Funny running into you here, Lulu."

It's the woman Cree pulled down by the hair at the concert and drove off with the man who was technically her fiancé just days prior; the woman Cree suspected to have had an affair with Russ in the other world. Judging by the wide smirk on Charlene's face, she'll insist on being a problem in this world too. "Charlene," Cree nods, with a plain expression like a mask over her utter shock.

Charlene stops in front of her, holding a manila folder. She looks back over her shoulder at the hallway from which she came, saying, "I was just seeing a friend. We thought it was major, but turns out it's only an anxiety attack."

"Good. I wish her well," Cree says. "Now, if you'll excuse me." Cree attempts to shoulder past Charlene. Charlene stops her with a strong hand pressing the folder to Cree's belly. Cree's eyes pop wide with pure bottled rage. "Charlene?" Her tone alone is warning enough.

The two are locked, with Cree's vicelike grip on the hand pressing her abdomen. Charlene says, "Different, when you don't get to sucker me from behind, idn't it?"

Cree feels herself on the verge of snapping again; she bites down to cage that rage inside of her. "You'll *see* how different this time, when I actually finish you off."

Staysha is infuriated, pulling off her earrings already. "Oh, she wanna pull up?"

Meryl, with her chest puffed out, says, "Lady, you 'bout to get these hands!"

Charlene and Cree remain in standoff, Charlene, a forehead taller, whispers, "Call off your dogs – unless you want them finding out you're not actually Lulu... Cree."

Cree twitches away as if that name went across her face. They back away in truce. Cree asks Meryl and Staysha to cool it. Meryl complains, "But she put her hands on you, momma. You always told me–"

"–Wrong, baby! Momma told you wrong," Cree says, with a glare fixed in the utmost conviction. Although moments ago, Cree herself nearly released the kraken, she says, "Charlene and I, we're going to find a place where we can sit down and talk it out."

Staysha and Meryl return to the waiting room. Cree and Charlene take the elevator. With the sinking feeling of the plummeting elevator, Cree asks, "So you're dealing with Nathaniel. Where is he?"

"As if I'd tell you," Charlene says. "Back there in the hallway, Lulu would've taken a swipe at me, for sure. I knew you were acting different; never would've thought to consider you actually *being* different."

Cree says, "We didn't meet here by chance, did we? You're stalking me just like you're stalking Russ."

A fast-walking Charlene spits out of the elevator. "I thought you were crazy when police found you in that storage room, sitting in front of a goddamn mirror. Now it makes perfect sense."

"What's in that folder," Cree asks.

They sit in the back corner of the cafeteria. Charlene puts away the folder and pulls out her phone instead. The video is grainy. Cree leans in, straining her eyes. Charlene narrates. "This is you pulling into the storage facility." Charlene swipes to another video. "And here's where the second camera picks you up unloading the mirror, while the whole damn police force is out searching the woods for ya."

Cree remembers Lulu saying she took Nathaniel's car, which was parked in the driveway, to carry out Nathaniel's instructions while he stayed back in the empty house searching for stashed money, but Lulu didn't return because, in order to avoid a roadblock, she had to ditch the car and go on foot.

Cree, looking at the video, the object of her demise, feels like her heart is pounding its way out of her chest, yet she suppresses her worry and responds brazenly. "So, why are you wasting time showing me something you should be showing the police?"

Charlene perks up. "Alrighty, then." She shifts her feet under and gets up. "Say no more."

"*Wait,*" Cree says with such force that patrons look up from their cafeteria trays. Quietly this time, Cree says, "What do you want?"

Pleased by Cree's desperation, Charlene lowers back into her seat, upright as ever with her hands stacked on the table. "I figured you'd have more sense than the real Lulu. Even your posture is somewhat respectable. You're less intense. You don't talk like some around-the-way girl; you're actually quite articulate."

Cree sighs. "I'll say it again. What do you want?"

Charlene, savoring the moment, stays the scenic route to her point. "It never even occurred to the police who found you in that storage unit to check surveillance to see if you'd been there before. Anything funded with public dollars is second rate, including detectives on city payroll. My private investigator runs circles around them – just like the public schools and state funded university you went to, versus my private college. You can't outthink me, Lulu. I see your little mind working behind those eyes, trying to think of a way out of this, but I've got you trapped like the rat you are."

"Rat?" Cree leans forward, menacing. "For your information, Char-*lene*... The nameplate on my door says chief executive – of a company that moves millions annually. I have touched down on nearly every continent on the face of this earth. I sup with senators. I break bread with the likes of Rod Gilmore and Vandy Meyers. Blanch Barr – whose behind you love to kiss – *I* appointed *her* to *my* board of directors." Cree looks her up and down in one swath. "You think you're something, just because you're allowed in the room at fancy galas and exclusive parties, but when it's time to talk business and politics, you and the other armpieces are dismissed, while *I* am still at the table. And by the way, I just built a new building, a state of the art office, heifer. You cannot hold a light to me."

Surprisingly, Charlene smiles and begins clapping slowly, heartily, with gleamy-eyes, as if to an encore-worthy performance. Again, their table draws stares, though Charlene doesn't seem to mind. "After all that, the fact remains that you fucked my fiancé, which makes you nothing more than a slut in anybody's opinion."

Cree counters, "Your fiancé is my husband. Where I come from, Russ and I never divorced—"

"—Only because the dumb schmuck doesn't know the child isn't his. That marriage you speak of, is counterfeit," Charlene says, smugly, but then in an odd twist, she lights up with wonder, as if asking in on a secret. "What about *me* though? What am I like, over there in that other world?"

"You married your sugar daddy who's old enough to be your—"

"—Ha!" Charlene claps a hand over her mouth to trap her laughter. Tears of mirth fill her eyes. "*Ed?*" Her hands wave to wipe her thought-cloud clean of the image. "And *me?*" Her laughter trips up into a cough.

Cree adds, "Yes, you and Ed. You're raising the children from his previous marriage to a woman not much older than you; she's in and out of mental institutions."

"Hannah… No different than in this world… Wrist looks like a tick-tac toe board," Charlene sneers.

"You might laugh," says Cree. "But those children have actually made a good mother and a good person out of you."

"Question." Slyly Charlene asks, "Any children of my own?" Cree's head shakes no.

Charlene sighs happily and says, "Well, it's been fun, but I've got to get going, so let me go ahead and give you the terms of engagement. If you don't want me turning this video over to police, where my father will make sure you get consecutive maximum sentences on all counts for faking your disappearance, here's what you do: you take your fanny on up to New York—"

"—Charlene," says Cree. "There's no way I can do that. My mother is dying. She has terminal cancer, and she doesn't have long."

"So, you decide accordingly. It's up to you whether you want her to croak while you're in the Big Apple or while you're in jail. If it's New York, you go there as if it is your heart's desire. You mention a word of our deal to Russ or anyone, I put you away. And you can't simply end it with Russ. You have to end it in convincing fashion, because let me tell you, sweety…" Charlene leans in. "If I get the sense that he's distracted by some hope of you two one day getting back together, hell, you can get on that plane and I'd *still* put your ass away, ok? So, you'd better cut him deep, ya hear? Do that, and I'll call in a favor to the head of Child Protective Services who happens to be dear friend of my mother. Miss Debbie will see to it that you regain custody of Meryl and you can move her with you to New York or wherever your career takes you, outside of here."

Cree rocks back and forth in her chair, as if she's on the verge of a breakdown. "Have some decency, Charlene. My mother's dying. I just told them I was staying."

"*Un*-tell them!"

A pokerfaced Cree, says, "I find it rather interesting that you didn't just turn that video into the police, but instead you're here talking to me. Why? Because you know Russ will never forgive you, and you will have no chance with him, after that."

"Force my hand, and you'll be in prison. Maybe I will lose Russ and that will be the end of it. I'll take that, actually – losing him to no one, rather than losing him to the likes of you." Charlene pulls out the folder and opens it. "And another thing. You act as if you have that man's heart outright. Russ is torn; he's torn between us. As you can see, while you were out, today, tending to your singing career, Russ and I was together." Charlene slides the photo across the table.

The photo of Charlene and Russ embracing nearly spurs Cree to go with one of a few initial reactions to slap Charlene, or flip the table over; it's a miracle that she doesn't. Cree steadies her emotions, and proposes, "I've got a better idea. I know you've been talking to Nathaniel, because you know who I really am. Let me meet with him and I swear, I can be out of your hair for good."

Charlene shrinks back, frowning. "Why would I do that?"

"So, I can go back to my life. I never wanted to be here. I was tricked, and I, personally, have never done anything to you."

"If you go back, then I have to deal with the other you – that ole irrational, loudmouth? No thank you. You have no leverage to warrant any concessions. You know my number. Text me when you board the plane. Now, if you'll excuse me." Charlene tucks her folder under her arm and leaves.

Cree's head becomes as heavy as a bear's; it drops in the cradle of her forearms over the table. Face down, she can't see the picture on the table, but she can't stop seeing the image of Charlene sitting on the chair arm next to Russ whose face, (possibly crying) is held to Charlene's bosom, as if he's regretful of ever leaving her. Cree stays head down at the table for minutes, until Meryl and Staysha locate her.

Charlene leaves the building. She's out, walking across the parking lot and making a phone call. "Hook," Charlene says. "Thank God you're still alive. I thought maybe Jett had gotten to you already. I think Jett's under some kinda spell. He's fixin' to kill you."

Chapter 22

Riddles

Russ is determined to protect Lulu at all cost, even if means risking himself. He stuns police by showing up, voluntarily and unannounced, to give a statement, after he'd already given one the day Lulu's search went underway. As Russ awaits legal counsel, he sits there looking just as stunned as the police.

Russ did not call his own lawyer, who, just a week ago, sat with him during his first statement. This lawyer, now entering with slick hair and a handlebar mustache, is Frank Tivola, the right-hand man of Mayor Hamilton; Charlene's father. The hard squinter, throws the door open with one hand and before it closes behind him, he has, in one fell swoop, removed his jacket and slung it to the opposite shoulder by the hook of his finger, his briefcase seamlessly switching hands in the process.

He follows an officer to Russ, who Tivola greets without a handshake, but with a slight head bow, "Mr. Rutledge." The officer escorts them to a room where they can talk in private. Russ doesn't even sit. He asks, "Have you talked to the mayor?"

Tivola meticulously lays his jacket across the back of the chair and brushes the hair shed from the shoulder. As if nothing can proceed before one thing is understood, Tivola asks, "Are we sitting, or are we standing?" On that note, both men take a seat.

Russ says, "Hamilton hung up in my face, then refused all my calls after that. Got his attention, now, huh."

Tivola squints harder. "First off, let me state that I'm under a retainer agreement with the mayor, so if this… *matter* presents a conflict of interest, the retainer activates my service to the mayor, which means, I cannot dually represent the conflicting party – the conflicting party being yourself – thus attorney-client privilege cannot hold up beyond the moment that such conflict becomes apparent–"

"–Bro, you have *got* to loosen up," says Russ. "I need those building permits, man. They were escalated to the Chief Building Officer, then forwarded all the way up to the mayor himself. Wade said he wasn't signing jack, as long as I'm engaged to his daughter, but that I had to break it off in such a way that he could justify signing off on the building permits for the man responsible for breaking his daughter's heart. So, it was Wade's idea for me and Lulu to take a little trip without telling anyone, drop a few clues to where it looks like something's happened to her. Then I could pretend to be emotionally distraught and end the engagement seemingly in some morbid sense of guilt. I couldn't get Lulu to take a trip with me if we were not involved, so that's how the affair happened. Although I had already broken it off with Charlene, she ended up finding out that I was seeing Lulu, right as we were executing the plan."

"Attorney client privilege, Mr. Rutledge was voided the moment you mentioned the building permit being forwarded to the mayor; therefore, I cannot advise you legally–"

"–I'm not asking you to advise me – never was. I just want you to get the sumbitch on the phone, because there's a couple things I'm asking him to do: one, to do whatever he has to do to make his daughter get off of Lulu's back; she's the *one* person faultless in all of this. I'll go to prison if it means keeping her free, but there's no way for me to go down without Wade going down too. The house where Lulu and Nathaniel were kept, is actually the mayor's place that he bought for a mistress of his. So, you tell him, give me my damn permits. Holding that land hostage is holding my people hostage." Russ jabs the table with a rigid finger. "You tell Wade that if I don't get a PDF copy of the signed documents sent to my email in a half hour, *both* of us going to jail this evenin'!'"

Tivola seems distracted. He gazes through the blinds. Policemen yell into their radios and at each other, holding their hats to their heads in the scramble. Tivola says, "Appears something awful has happened."

DETECTIVE Ryan's dilemma sounds like a thing of riddles. How do you have a conversation with someone from over fifty feet away without yelling or speaking by phone? It's a riddle he solved by stapling a series of messages on telephone poles, like lost dog posters, along Tina's jogging route. Ryan remains parked in his car beyond the limit of the restraining order.

He checks his watch and then his rearview mirror, where he spies Tina stretching in her driveway, until she starts jogging. Tina stops at the first poster. She stops long enough to have read the message and then resumes running. Detective Ryan comes out of his park and cruises slowly down the street, advancing to keep his legal distance, and checking the rearview mirror, where he sees Tina rip the second poster off the next pole.

Small in his rearview, Ryan sees her scanning her surroundings and spotting his car. Ryan parks again, idling, waiting.

The second poster gives Tina two options: the first option is to continue jogging along her usual path as a signal for Ryan to leave. Tina takes the second option and crosses the street, consenting that Ryan can stay put while she encroaches the restraining order.

Tina walks over, gesturing as if she was talking to herself along the way. "You're crazy," she says and gets in. Poster in hand, she adds, "As much as I'd like to think that this is somewhat adorable, this gives off some creepy, creepy vibes, man."

Ryan's head is bowed as if undeserving. "Thank you. Thank you."

"So passionate," she says. "Had I known that same passion translates to anger too…"

Ryan, being reminded of his error, pinches the corners of his eyes. "First, let me formerly apologize." There's no confusion as to why. Tina remembers sobbing behind forearms shielding her face as a lobbed chair crashed against the wall behind her while Ryan tried to destroy his home like Samson did the temple. Detective Ryan remembers his drunken, slur-filled tirade, where he pulled a gun from his ankle holster with no intention of using it. The other hand punched the wall inches from Tina's face. He buckled and wept over his bleeding knuckles as Tina ran out the door.

With a frog in his throat, Ryan looks over to the passenger seat and says, "Looking back, I wasn't even sore at you. I was mad at myself for being… what I am."

"As if it's some curse," Tina gasps. "Had you told me up front that you were a friggin youth pastor, I would've ran the other direction."

"I beg to differ," says Ryan with a wagging finger. "Time we locked eyes, we couldn't go nowhere but to each other."

"Maybe." Tina says. "But some of that was due to assumptions. I saw that grey streaking back along the sides of your head and assumed you were not new to this. Then we talked, and, come to find out, you'd been divorced for quite some time, your kids, grown. I assumed you must've come-out *years* ago. I'm too old to be the source of someone's shame. I did that in my twenties; no way am I going back to that."

"All I'm asking for is another chance. I can get past this. I *am* past it. And if you're worried about the time I went off on you, just know that that's the only time in my life I'd ever lost it like that, and still I had the presence of mind not to lay a finger on you."

"You can't 'get past' that level of disgust without fixing what fuels it. You say you left God, but no. You left the church, yet you still fail to realize that God is greater than what's written in that manmade bible."

"The Word is what it is. The one thing I won't attempt to do is change it for my sake. The only thing I can change is my choices."

"And go on believing that you barter your soul to be with me?" Tina, gazing blankly, adds, "All the lovin' in the world can't cover that."

"You're being dramatic–" Ryan stops because of the call coming in on his radio. "Shit! I gotta go."

"Do you?"

"It's a four, forty-four, officer involved shooting. I'm sorry."

Tina slips a hand over his hand, which has the gear in its grasp. "Ok, I know you gotta go – which makes this even harder for me because there's no time to beat around the bush, but…" Tina licks her lips and shoots, "The whole reason I'm sitting in this car with you right now is to let you know that I'm seeing someone."

Ryan swivels, his mouth ajar. "'Someone' ain't me. Tina, I've watched you in my arms, unable to even fathom what's come over you."

"I know where you and me ends, Ryan. I want something that goes beyond that."

"You know what…" Ryan looks away, out the window, canceling what he wants to say, but changing his mind, he darts back. "If you can move on that quickly–"

"–Oh please! How long were we together – two months, if that?"

"It's not how long, it's how deeply we fell."

"Get. Over. It," Tina says, behind a pointed red fingernail. "Everyone's first is like this, Ryan. The quicker you let the next one in, the faster you'll learn that I'm not the only one who seems to be everything that your past girlfriends, or wife, was not." She slips out of the car. Ryan calls her. She holds the door open for a last word.

Ryan says, "Who is he? One of your bar customers, or co-worker?"

Tina's answer is a door slam. Ryan's fist slams the steering wheel. He sets his strobe light on the dashboard and speeds off, heading to the scene of the officer involved shooting.

Chapter 23

The Witness

There is a parade of strobing cop cars near the dilapidated apartment buildings. Ambulances park onto the courtyard. Police converse more with each other than with the potential eye witnesses among the crowd of residents bunched together in protest of the deadly shooting, of which they're sure the officer would be acquitted, if trial is even explored. Jett Johnson, now in custody, attests that he only came to ask questions, but found himself in a shootout leaving four dead, one just fourteen years old. Jett says he fled the scene, fearing retaliation from the neighborhood. Just a few blocks away, Jett was pulled over by officers who happened to be patrolling the area.

Detective Ryan approaches the traumatized crowd of residents who cry out and wail as if funeral processions are underway; the paramedics loading the bodies onto the gurneys look more like pall-bearers.

There's a vengeful element along the fringes and across the street, young men glaring, pacing, possibly eyeing a chance at revenge by opening fire on the crowd of officers.

Detective Ryan speaks to the crowd, he sides with them; he mingles with them. They yell and scream, venting to Detective

Ryan for incidents going back years. Detective Ryan's twenty plus years on the force has taught him that the loudest ones know the least. Those who have information are quiet. Contrary to popular belief, those who have information *want* to aid the investigation, just not openly. They don't want their brethren knowing that they are, in anyway, aiding a system that daily patrols, apparently, for the sole purpose of rounding up their loved ones. Although their conscience quiets them, they extend their olive branch via telepathy.

Ryan locates a pair of eyes that glances back at him even when she looks away. Detective Ryan shuts out the noise of the crowd and focuses on the woman with long braids, raised cheekbones, her fox eyes giving a subtle distress signal. Ryan tries to approach with his contact card, but her eyes flair wide, stopping him. Her head flicks up, her eyes aimed at an upstairs apartment window, the silhouette of a sitting woman behind sheer drapes.

Detective Ryan goes for the stairwell under the window, passing by an ambulance gurney, the sheet pulled over the young man's face. When he knocks on the apartment door of the silhouette woman, she cracks it; her eyes are raw with tears. Detective Ryan reassures, "No one saw me come up."

She pulls him inside and backs against the door.

He hands her a card. "Detective Ryan."

"They call me Nisha." She folds her arms as if to contain her emotions. To speak, she must fight through crying. "Hook got a call, warning him that that private detective was coming to kill him."

Detective Ryan means to ask who called, but he's thrown off by a glimpse of Nisha's gold incisors, something you don't see every day – as Lulu had put it – when describing the woman who helped kidnap her. Ryan asks, "You were close to him, Hook?"

Her face clenches. "Our son is just two."

"Aw man, I'm sorry this happened. You saw it?"

Her eyes say she can't unsee it. "I got it on video." She hands over her phone. "He told me to record it, so we'd have evidence that the detective was the aggressor."

Detective Ryan begins watching. Already, he's saying. "I don't know if they can get a conviction out of this. It looks like these young men were waiting in ambush – their guns already drawn."

"What was they supposed to do, after getting that call?"

In the video, Jett Johnson gets out of his parked car and walks onto the courtyard across unkempt grass, riddled with dirt patches and dry puddle basins. The sun glares off the lenses of his antique-looking glasses. Jet's thumbs are tucked in his pockets; a toothpick rolls between his lips. He stops in the middle of the inner court by the birdbath centerpiece that was once considered decorative during segregation when this complex was constructed for white workers of the Navy yard nearby. Now the cherub birdbath is mossy and blotched with bird droppings, like poached eggs.

Judging by the camera's perspective, Nisha, all the while, records from upstairs through the window, too far to capture clean audio, so it's a silent film.

Jett speaks from by the fountain; he doesn't come any closer. Hook perches on the bottom steps of the stairwell where there's a few salvaged dinette chairs, and a bucket to accommodate the crew where they hang out daily, so dope fiends always know where to get their fix. The bucket and chairs are empty. Hook seems to be by himself, but he is far from alone. His soldiers are getting in their positions, one flanked to the right on the second-floor balcony; another to the far left in the shadow of another stairwell, and then there is another on the move, snooping around the side of the building towards Jett Johnson's rear.

Hook stands. At his side is a staff that looks to be made of copper. Detective Ryan knows it's the staff that Nathaniel wants back. Hook raises the staff in premature victory. With Jett surrounded, Hook is confident that he has checkmate.

Slowly, Jett Johnson lowers to one knee. He puts one hand in the dirt and picks up a pebble the size of a chestnut. He stands with the rock in hand, and begins tossing it and catching it from the same palm, all along words are being spoken.

By sleight of hand, Jett makes a mighty toss of the rock towards the shooter on the second story balcony, which distracts Buck's aim. Jett's offhand has already drawn and fires a shot across his body into Buck's sternum, a blood vapor at his upper back shows where the bullet exits his body. Buck gets off an errant shot which splashes dirt right in front of Jett, who spins counterclockwise in an open stance using the birdbath to shield against the man to his left, giving him time to fire a shot into Hook's chest that throws him back onto the stairs. Nisha, who is filming, screams, "No!" She's hysterical. Everything goes out of view momentarily.

In that moment, three shots ring out. By the time the camera steadies to sound of Nisha's sobbing, the young man from the left comes into view, staggering out from under the stairwell with blood spurting through the clenched fingers of the hand pressed to his throat. With the other hand, he raises an unsteady gun and shoots. The birdbath cherub's ear explodes. The young man collapses and there's a slight swirl of dust in front of his nostrils, giving a visual of his final breath. Jett Johnson advances on the young man who'd setup to his rear. His back is against the wall as he fights with a jammed gun. By the time the young man uncovers to locate Jett, Jett has located him. The shot hits the young man in the face, snapping his head back violently, as if from the force of a punt.

Detective Ryan watches in awe. The shootout couldn't have been choreographed better in an action movie. Ryan wipes a hand down the side of his face, "It's like Jett saved this guy for last, as if he *knew* his gun would jam." He looks up and finds Nisha with her eyes closed and hands clapped over her ears to avoid reliving the video through sight or sound. Detective Ryan touches her shoulder and asks. "You do notice that Jett went over to Hook's body and ran off with that staff he was holding."

Nisha says, "Let him keep it; it's evil. Hook used it to make money. He wouldn't part with it. He'd clutch it in his sleep. Now he done lost his life because of it."

Detective Ryan grasps Nisha's upper arms and looks her in the eyes. "I gotta go. Guard that video with your life, and keep in touch, ya hear."

Ryan hurries out to his car. He drives a couple of blocks down to where Jett was detained. Jett's car is still there, tagged and awaiting a tow. The responding officers must've left this scene to congregate among the crowd of officers at the scene of the shooting. Ryan peeks in and spots the staff laying across the backseat, not tagged for evidence. No one has seen the video to know that the staff is the reason four men are dead. Detective Ryan takes the staff, slides it down the leg of his pants and tightens his belt to hold it in place, then walks back to his car with a limp, as if he has a peg leg.

Just prior to arriving on the scene, Detective Ryan was finally convinced that he was out of chances with Tina, but now he's recovered the one thing he could use as leverage with the man who can get him another chance.

Chapter 24

A Way Out

Cree gets the call that the record deal is inked. Fly Guy sends her a QR code for her travel pass. Cree texts Charlene the flight's departure time and begins packing, not only her suitcase, but Cree is also packing away her thoughts in such a way that she can live with this outcome.

She can have her career as a singer. She'll have wealth that she will have amassed on her own; she will grace the covers of magazines. It's a dream come true, that spoils if Beth dies while she is away and Meryl goes into foster care. Cree can only hope for the best. She has no choice in the matter; the choice is Charlene's.

This sense of powerlessness seeps from Cree's mind and into her body. She hoists the suitcase onto the bed and it feels three times its normal weight. Every hanging garment pulled from her closet drops her arm down by her side.

Suddenly Cree gets a spark of energy, from an idea. She wonders how it hadn't occurred to her the moment Charlene showed her the incriminating video. Cree needs a video to disappear – just like Lulu who hired someone named Desmond to make Tron's video disappear.

Cree finds the contact in the phone listed as Dez, and calls it. He greets her as if it's been a while. "Whassup Lu! Thought you was going clean, baby girl," he laughs. "What you want, eight-ball?"

A desperate Cree launches, "Hey Desmond, listen. I'm in a bind right now, and I could really use your expertise–"

"–Hold up, ma. Hold up," says Desmond through the phone. "I don't know who you is, or how you got Lulu's phone, but you have a blessed day, ya hear?"

Cree remembers to switch on her inner Lulu. "Boy who is you playin' wit? This me, Lulu, nigga. Fuck you think this is?"

Desmond nearly collapses with relief. "Damn girl, don't be scarin' me like that," he says. "Hell, I thought I was being spoofed by my parole officer, or somethin'. *My* dumbass comin' on the phone, talking about a damn eight-ball," Desmond laughs.

Cree says, "You right about one thing. My nose is clean and it's gonna stay that way, but I still need you, bro. This chick is comin' for me. She got me on video doing some shit–"

"–And you need the video to go away?"

"–Like asap!"

Desmond says, "I hope you ain't talking about Charlene."

"Yes, Charlene."

"Ain't no way," says Desmond. "I got one foot in the jailhouse as it is, and you askin' me to hack the mayor's daughter? I ain't foolin' with them people."

"Ten thousand dollars!"

After a brief silence, Dez says, "I want the money up front, nonrefundable."

"I'll get Russ to front the money."

"A'ight, bet. But I got a couple questions, where's the video?"

"On her phone."

"Did she *record* it with her phone?"

"No, it came from a surveillance camera at a storage facility."

"So, you been out here stealing," Desmond kids, but switches back to being serious. "How'd she get the video from the storage facility, though? It couldn't have been subpoenaed by the police or you'd be behind bars by now, innit?"

"Must've been her private investigator."

"Private investigator! What if he has a copy on his hard drive or something. So, I'm supposed to hack him too?"

"*Fifteen* thousand dollars," Cree says, hoping Detective Ryan's saying is right, that there ain't no such thing as broke to a woman.

"Who's the P.I.? You got a name?"

"Um... I know the name is different," Cree says, as she strains her memory. "Oh, yeah, it's Jett Johnson."

"*Get* outta here," Desmond spats. "Jett Johnson! I'm lookin' at buddy on the news, right now. That man shot four niggas dead down there by The Waylyn."

"What!"

"Straight up. I kinda know one of the dudes, go by the name Hook. Hey Lulu, you on your own with this one."

Cree says, "How about if you just do Charlene and the storage facility and take Jett totally out of the equation."

"Oh, he *in* the equation, baby girl, whether we like it or not. He's been in contact with both Charlene and the storage facility. That man is under investigation. I don't care what number you throw at me, fifteen thousand, or *fifty* thousand," Desmond concludes.

"No Dez. Don't do me like this Dez," Cree pleads. "My mother is dying."

"I know you going through it, right now – and I feel for you sis, but I can't risk my freedom like dat."

Cree pleads harder. "I'm about to lose custody of my daughter, Dez."

Desmond sighs deeply and says, "Ok, I'll tell you what I *can* do."

"Please anything." Cree listens intently.

"If you need a lil somethin-somethin' for the stress, I'll spot you an eight-ball till next week–"

Cree hangs up in Desmond's face. She stops herself from throwing her phone against a wall, and instead, rakes her suitcase off the bed. She plops on the bed and buries her face in her hands. Her phone buzzes. Cree splits the fingers covering her eyes to peek. It's Charlene. Cree takes a deep breath and answers.

Charlene says, "Have you talked to Russ?"

Cree responds, "No. I've been busy packing."

"What are you waiting for?"

"I know what I gotta do, Charlene."

"Don't wait until the last minute. This isn't going to take just one conversation, it may take four, between now and the time of your departure. But however many conversations it may take, I want nothing left unsaid by time you hop on that plane."

"Got it," says Cree.

"If it wasn't for you, I'd be Mrs. Rutledge, honeymooning at a lagoon in Bora Bora, right now. I'm not on your time, Lulu; you're on my time, hear me? And remember: make it convincing!"

Charlene hangs up.

Cree lays out on the bed, studying the ceiling, wishing for normal problems like a dead-end job, or asshole neighbors. Come to think of it, after breaking it off with Russ, Cree will become a single mother with no prospects or even exes to entertain, and only a couple of years remaining before pregnancy becomes a stunt.

Cree has no idea what to say to Russ, or how to even begin. She already has a growing cache of text messages from Russ that she has yet to respond to.

RUSS looks to the phone laying on the passenger seat, hoping the text that just came through was a reply from Lulu, but it's not. It's one of the organizers of the emergency community meeting that he's enroute to. Lulu, once again, is set to fly New York, a record deal in the works, and just like a decade ago, she's suddenly seems detached, emotionally. If Russ didn't know any better, he'd swear he was in some sort of time loop.

Russ, now with the mayor-approved building permits in hand, arrives at the community center and is getting out of his car, with one foot on the ground, when he stops and thinks better to call Lulu, but one of the organizers stands in the doorway of the venue, waving for Russ to hurry.

This isn't the first meeting. Russ has already bombed with the elders, so this time the meeting will include the elders' more educated fifty-something-year-old sons and daughters who could easily digest the numbers and concepts.

They give Russ the floor, an easel board, and a faded dry erase marker to explain his grand relocation scheme – how the land, for which he'd just received building permits, puts them right on the edge of a good school district while avoiding the heavy annual tax burden.

Without any visible indication, Russ still feels his townhall style audience cringe at the idea of uprooting the community. They get antsy when Russ mentions putting their current property up for sale as soon as possible, to avoid getting caught by imminent domain where forced sales will go for less than half the price. They cringe again when Russ suggest they *not* use the sales proceeds to outright purchase the newly built homes, but to shift the sales proceeds to interest-bearing family trusts and then mortgaging the new homes against the family trusts, as a way to avoid banks and to instead, pay loan interest back to themselves, so the family trusts become a mechanism for generational wealth.

One man rises to his feet, bracing on a cane and wearing a cap, the brim embroidered with a military veteran laurel. Before he speaks, he wants to ensure he has everyone's attention, so he looks around at those still chattering and calls them out by nickname, starting with the dwarf. "Bubba Clutch... Puddin'... Grip... Sanny..."

Russ vaguely remembers them from his childhood visits with his mother. Nodding at the veteran, Russ hopes he recalls the correct name when he says, "Mr. Bub-Daddy, you have the floor."

"Young man, I'm gone say this as nicely as I can, out of respect for your momma. You not the only person comin' 'round thinking they can tell us what to do with our land. But you is the *only* one thinking you some damn Marcus Garvey – gone pick us up and set us down at the place and time of your choosing..." The chatter rises and drowns Bub-Daddy out.

"Let the man talk," booms a voice coming from the back wall. It's a tall thin man with deep set eyes who goes by his initials.

L.P. says, "The man ain't talk five minutes good and y'all already tryin' to get ya own word in? Listenin' won't hurt a dern thing. *Not* listening is what got us here. Remember me telling y'all, over thirty-sum years ago, to band together and refuse the city water and sewage. Y'all thought I was crazy. Next, they run the cable TV wire. Ya took it like candy to a baby. Y'all da same folks who swore the city been spendin' millions in infrastructure for *us?*" L.P. gazes around the room. "Do you *now* see that they been really laying the infrastructure for big developers to come in and take what our great grandparents bled for! Let's not repeat the same mistake. Listen to what the man got to say." In closing, L.P. raises both mitts. "That's all I got to say."

A seated elder, Miss Bea, says, "We sho do 'preciate yo two cents, Lawrence, but listenin' go both ways." Miss Bea then swivels to Russ and says, "Ween interested, Mr. Rutledge, in sellin' our land. As Bub-Daddy say, we talkin' to a numba of folks about this matter, namely a group of three lawyers who ain't tryin' to rush us to sell, like you doing. They trying to help us hold onto our land by submitting our bid to be declared a historic community. Now, I'm sure, Mr. Rutledge, that on the way to this meeting, you saw all the sweet grass basket stands along the highway. This Phillips Community is the last community of its kind in this zip code."

Gently, Russ replies, "With all due respect, Miss Bea, those lawyers play golf with the same developers who want to take your land. That historic landmark bit, they use as a tactic to feed you hope. Hope keeps you from taking action. They'll *keep* feeding you false hope until it's too late. Those lawyers advising you, will be the same lawyers transacting the wholesale seizure of this community. That's exactly what happened to McDaniel Island."

Mr. Marion, also known as Coyote, stands and yells, "Mc-Daniel Island! You sure you wanna talk about McDaniel Island? I used to commute through dey, back when all dat construction been goin' on. Who sign I see all up-and-through dey? Rutledge Enterprises, Rutledge Enterprises… Every corner I turn, Rutledge Enterprises."

The air lets out of the room. The attendees are appalled. Russ, feeling hot under the collar, replies, "But this isn't McDaniel Island. My mother still owns land here. Think I'm trying to pull one over on my own momma?"

Reverend Herbert, in his pulpit voice, reams, "Well, *show* us… We know you in good wit' da mayor. Why don't you use dem big ole britches you got to defend our right to *not* be driven off land we own."

Russ looks the attendees over in disbelief. "This is not about rights. Nobody's serving you from the back door, nor telling you which fountain to drink from. Some of you got property tax liens right now as we speak. You're sitting on waterfront property, asking for the right to live here when you can no longer afford to – and while failing to exercise the right you *do* have: to cash-in its value and use the trusts to provide financial security for years to come, so your grandchildren will be in a position to always be able to determine their *own* fate. Us black folk got to stop seeing everything through the lens of Civil Rights. That movement has taken us as far as it can go. Social equality is impossible without *economic* equality. It is time for the pastors to now get behind the business men and developers such as myself, who'll lead the way in strategic economic engagement. We can't keep letting developers run circles around us and we end up begging legislators to step in at the stroke of the final hour to stop the bulldozers."

Dawn Habersham gets up, using her right hand to rub the opposite side of her face in confusion. "Is it just me, or dis man talkin' down to us?"

Sweet Roll yells, "Economic engagement! Sound like double-talk for using us to make yourself richer!"

Russ frowns and shrugs, "Do you expect me to build homes for free?"

With that, the meeting falls off the rails rather swiftly. Bubba Clutch yells, "'E a crook just like 'e damn daddy!"

The one comment that sends Russ storming out, clutching his documents, is delivered by Phillip's very own Deebo, a hulking wide-faced bully called Stuffy, who yells, "Y'ole black cracker!"

Russ storms out with dropped papers swirling in his wake. He gets in his car and speeds off. Once Russ has had a minute to cool down, he checks his phone and learns that Lulu had left a voicemail. The voicemail says that Hook has been shot dead by a cop. Russ's heart stops. He remembers Charlene admitting to conspiring with Hook and wonders if she had anything to do with it. Russ tosses the phone on the passenger seat, and heads straight for Lulu.

Hook is an old high school football teammate and one-time best friend, and Russ can't even mourn him. Russ's head pounds with frustration. He's upset at himself for failing to connect with the community. He's upset at his father for earning a reputation as an exploiter, which seems impossible for Russ to overcome. He's upset at his people for letting the reputation blind them to the fact that Russ's plan gives the best possible outcome and that every other option keeps them in the predicament they're in, or worse. Russ bites down and mumbles, *black cracker*, as if it's the most ridiculous thing he's ever heard, and yet Russ can't bear to look at the white of his palms.

Chapter 25

In Convincing Fashion

Russ arrives unannounced. Cree's apartment door opens with the unwelcoming chill of a refrigerator. The chill is emotional, how Cree unlocks the door and pulls it gently, so that by the time the door swing passes to reveal her, she's deep in the apartment and returned to her chores. "I'm packing," she explains while digging through a hallway closet. Cree still hasn't decided what angle she'll use to end their relationship, 'in convincing fashion,' per Charlene, but she figures she'd set the tone at the door.

Russ closes the door behind him and stands there like an exchange student, hesitant for fear of violating a custom. Observing how Cree either pretends he doesn't exist, or that the neck pillow she pulls from the closet is more pressing than a welcoming kiss, Russ isn't so sure this is the same woman who, days ago in this very apartment, tearfully accepted his proposal of marriage.

Cree doubletakes at Russ who's still standing by the door, like a pizza delivery man. "Did you think I'd leave without coming to see you?" Her question is sauced with rancor.

Russ tempers his inclination to go off on Cree, although he's still brooding for being run out of his mother's hometown. Russ says, calmly, "You haven't replied to any of my texts. I had asked you a question. When are you coming back?"

The nerve of him, Cree thinks. He was in Charlene's arms earlier today. Cree is not allowed to mention the picture, but she repeats his question to accentuate its audacity. "When am I coming *back?* Is a date and time what you really want? Just so you can read into it and judge where I have you situated among my other priorities, like my career, or my sobriety? Do I disappoint you for not putting your desires ahead of me getting my life together with a home and stability, to show Child Protective Services that I'm capable of raising my own daughter?"

Russ puts out a stiff hand. "First of all, Lulu. You need to calm that tone *all* the way down. Second: cut the shit. You talk as if I'm the obstacle, when a home and stability comes automatic with me, so what are you even talking about? My name is still on Meryl's birth certificate. As far as the *state* knows, I'm her father, so your chances of getting back custody is way better *with* me."

The logic behind Cree's attempted breakup now so thoroughly destroyed, she's forced to reach for a new reason. "Better with *you*," Cree says with a tight smile. "The kidnapper?"

Russ nearly loses it. He shuffles in one spot as if stuck in a phone booth. "The same kidnapper you agreed to marry – because you knew that if I wasn't forced to turn around that day because I was being followed, we would've been at a private wedding, with me putting that same ring on your finger."

"I don't *know* anything, Russ. I only *know* what you told me."

"And you believed it because you were in the car with me the very next time I was followed."

Again, the case Cree makes for leaving him is destroyed; she's getting desperate. Her arms flap at her sides. "Why elope, though? huh?"

"Where the hell is all this coming from?" Russ looks at Cree as if she's possessed. "Are you a'ight, Lulu? You back on that shit?"

"Wanna know what I think? I think you wanted to elope, so you can rush us into a decision that couldn't easily be undone. Seeing me behind Charlene's back was a mistake. You got caught. And then you chose me because you figured that being with me was easier than dealing with damage you caused to your relationship with Charlene. You, sir, are more torn between us than you'd like to admit."

Russ eyes her sideways, nodding, with some new discovery. "*Now*, I know where all this is coming from. Call it self-sabotage, if you wish, but it's your own insecurity telling you that you're an addict and a screw up who is undeserving of the love I have for you–"

"–Bingo! So, that's how you really feel about me."

"Don't act like I was speaking for myself just now. What the hell is wrong with you? That was me reading *your* mind. But I'm telling you, Lulu. Stop trying to psyche yourself out, okay? You need to believe me when I tell you that my love for you is real. And you are *so* worth it!"

"Well," says Cree. "I guess I have nothing else to say, other than, you suck at reading minds." If he could read minds, he would know about Charlene's threat to use the incriminating video to cage Cree in a population of cornrowed Tomboys looking to turn her out.

Russ may be unable to read minds, but he is able to sense that there's something Cree isn't telling him. "You say Hook was shot by a cop. What made you call to tell me that? What do you know about Hook?"

Cree realizes, now, that calling Russ about Hook's death was a mistake. She doesn't recall Hook ever being named in their discussions about the kidnapping nor in police reports. It was Lulu who named him from the other side of the mirror. "I don't recall ever meeting Hook," Cree says, "But I think I remember the name from your old football stories, I guess."

Now confident that Cree is oblivious to Hook's involvement, Russ pushes the conversation onward. "I was down at the police station when they must've called it in, because suddenly cops started running out the building like nine-eleven." Russ's hands come together in front of him as if nervously bending an imaginary hat. "Hook and me was close for the couple of years we played together. I knew Hook was in a gang, so I tried to keep his head on straight. My family even took him under our wing, tried to show him a better way."

"And you wonder why it didn't work."

An unoffended Russ looks on, curiously. "What do you mean?"

Cree answers, "Showing someone better, doesn't address the reasons they might still run towards worse." Cree can't believe how far off topic they've gotten.

"Reasons?" Russ frowns. "What reasons?"

Cree looks down as if searching the floor for the right word. "Honor, or something *like* honor," she says. "When you come from a poor, crime ridden community, you're often on the edge of survival; therefore, you are surrounded by people who have literally kept you alive, sat you at their dinner table and made four plates from a pot for three. They've thrown rent parties to rescue each other out of homelessness. People would hold on to things they don't need, waiting to come across someone who does need it. In the fifth grade, I was given a winter coat by girl who couldn't stand me."

"If there's so much love there, why'd you leave? Why go to college while busting your butt working through college, waiting tables just to get outta there."

"Because, with the people around me, they made it clear that I would disappoint them by staying. The only way to honor them and the sacrifices they'd made, was to leave. Did you ever go with Hook to where he lives? Ever hang out on the block with him and risk falling victim to a drive-by?"

Russ's head rattles no. "Ain't no way, Lulu. You're telling me ya can't pull somebody up without risking your own life? Is that what you' saying?"

"What I'm saying is that your bond with Hook couldn't compare to the bond he had with the gang members who were with him in the trenches–" Russ tries to interrupt, but Cree stops him with a raised finger. "–*Therefore*, Russ, you were the wrong person for the assignment. You could never be the one to pull someone like him out of a situation like that; they have to be pushed out from within. But that doesn't – in any way – diminish what you did. Bless you, Russ, for trying. Do *not* hang your head over this." Cree looks off, distracted by her own thoughts, internally kicking herself for mending the heart she should be breaking.

Russ bites his lip and then says, "Thank you, Lulu. You know how hard I get on myself and you..." Russ huffs and shakes his head. "You know how to get me out of my head and into my heart. You know how to be my peace, Lulu. Don't you know how valuable that is to me?"

She's seen definitive numbers, and yet they're less telling than now, with the man himself, bearing his heart and smoldering with emotion; Cree finds herself caught up in it. Russ floats toward Cree. She nearly panics as Russ lifts her chin and slips his lips into the grooves of hers. Cree finds herself irrevocably kissing back, thinking there's no possible way, now, to convince her fiancé that she doesn't want to be with him. He wouldn't accept it. Cree pulls away from the kiss.

Simultaneously, they attempt to speak then stop. "Me first," says Russ. "I promise you're gone love this."

Cree nods in acquiesce.

Russ says, "Okay, the reason I was wanting specifics on your return, is... Well, it's not what you think. I wasn't trying to control the situation, babe. I was looking to get our schedules in line. I have my eyes on a house."

"A house?"

"It's been on the market for a while – due to the price tag, no doubt – but I wanna get it under contract, keep potential buyers out, and I was wondering, Lulu, if, within that thirty-day timeframe if you–"

"–We can get a house anytime Russ. You can *build* one, any time."

"Yeah, but I can't build it in the perfect location, babe, because this house is already there... You should see it," Russ gleams. "It's a freakin' castle. It sits off by itself, on a couple of acres, the backyard has a pier and boat dock. It's set a quarter-mile back off the road with this stunning yellow cobblestone road leading right up to the front steps."

"My God..." Cree steps back, slipping out of Russ's grasp. "Sixteen O-one, Emerald?"

"You know about it? What... Heard it on the news? Something evil happened there?"

Cree is at a loss for words. She's devastated after realizing that for her freedom, she's sacrificing the entire reconstructed life that she's been trying to return to. If not for Charlene, Cree could have Russ, Meryl, and herself under one roof in the same Mediterranean style mansion on Emerald Cove where they've lived for the last seven years, and yet she must tell this man that she's choosing a record deal and make it make sense. She must choose the path of freedom until she gathers some kind of leverage against Charlene. "Forget about the house, Russ," says Cree. "I can't."

"'Can't' what?"

"Can't be with you."

"What is wrong with you," pleads Russ. He gently squeezes her arms. "Is it your mother? It's gotta be."

"I am messed up inside, Russ. I am one, messed up, individual," she says, now going with some private torment as the excuse.

Russ presses his temple. "I'll tell ya what: I'm gonna leave right now, let you sleep this off – whatever this is – and maybe tomorrow you'll wake up with some sense."

Cree's hands come together, as if praying. "I honestly was never truly in love with you, Russ."

Russ bites down and torques against her words. "As I said," says Russ. "We'll talk tomorrow." He turns promptly to leave. Russ gets as far as putting his hand on the doorknob.

Cree takes a page from Staysha's argument. "Your problem is, you need to be needed. And me: when I do need you, I have this way of making myself love you. I now got this record deal, Russ and... well, I don't need you financially, so I'm really not up for pretending."

Russ does not turn from the door; he looks back over his shoulder and says, "Look, Lulu. If you wanna put your career first, you do that, but don't try to make up some bullshit excuse to run me off, because I'm gonna believe this moment over anything you try to tell me later."

"Is it so hard to believe? Ten years ago, I bailed on you the moment I got the record deal and here I am, doing it again."

Russ turns. "No, you're not... You're not."

"I'm from the same situation Hook is from. No matter how close you think you are, we'll always see your kind from a distance."

"My kind?" Russ points to the very spot where they just kissed. "You're telling me, *that* wasn't real?"

"If you think *that's* convincing... Did your momma ever put a box cutter in your hand when sending you to the store – and you, an eleven-year-old have to convince two grown men threatening to rob you, that you have every intention of slitting their throats and bathing in their blood? You don't know the limits we're pushed to, the darkness we endure, and how it makes us capable of almost anything. There I was, just days after being raped, coming to see you." In reality, Cree was raped after; not before; nevertheless, Cree's hands move to her hips and her shoulders roll in a seductive impromptu. "There I was, purring up against you, pretending to be so... turned on by you, doing everything I can to convince you to go in me raw, as if I was so desperate to feeeel you," Cree says and almost giggles. "Sucker."

Russ can't even look at her. "Lucretia! Stop this *right* now!"

"So, you divorced me because I lied about it... but don't think, for one second, that I felt the least bit of guilt." Cree's head shakes. "My conscience has always been clear. Why? Because I knew that you were no better. You think you're *down* just because your daddy let you go to a public high school. The day I met you, I had you pegged as an out-of-touch-rich-boy sniffing around the HBCU campuses because rich white girls at your private university don't wanna be seen in public with your *buh-lack* ass. I figured you believed the same racist stereotypes *they* believe, that black chicks are easy, and yet it never crossed my mind to trap you. As you said, I was busting my tail to get through college and it often got overwhelming. With you, I was just looking to enjoy a casual relationship with someone who could also take some of the weight off of life. And here I am, now, doing the same thing. I'm telling you Russ, you deserve someone who can love you, because I can't. You're a mark, Russ. And I can't see you any other way."

Russ's head shakes. He wipes his thumb across his lip and says, "The day you met my parents. Pops pulled me aside and said, 'I prayed the lord to take away that taste you got for the slums. She gone be your lesson, watch.'" Russ says, "Everything that man has said about you over the years, is true. But where was I at today? *My* fool ass was down at the police station, fixing to send myself to prison in order to protect *you?*" Russ chokes up, as the reality hits him, his throat fat with built up emotion.

"Protect me how?" Cree struggles to think of a way to inquire about the video without mentioning it. "I'm in the clear, they said. Unless some new evidence surfaced."

"Charlene's got something and it's pretty damning, so I went down to the station threatening to give up her father, the mayor."

Cree frowns, "The mayor?"

"Wade withheld my building permits unless I broke off the engagement with Charlene."

"So, I *am* second choice."

Russ's head rattles no. "A year ago, when you moved back to Charleston, I was wishing you had returned a month sooner or I would've never proposed to Charlene. But since I did, I was gonna suck it up and marry Charlene on my word, regardless of my feelings for you, but then I needed the building permits, which changed everything because her father demanded I break off the engagement, which is what I wanted in the first place."

Cree backs off in abhorrence. Russ's truth is worse than the fiction she created to push him away. Her arms fold. "Building permits..." Her foot taps the floor. "I'm relieved, actually – to know that you had your own set of ulterior motives."

"For myself? Or for my people?"

"Whatever, Moses."

"Whatever, *yourself*," Russ says. "I'm just glad you revealed who you really are." Russ watches the tears dripping off of Cree's chin and it has no effect on him. "You are dead to me. Hear me? Dead!"

Cree swallows his words as if they're rocks.

Russ looks at the tears in Cree's eyes and says, "It's over. You can stop acting, now. Dirt bitch!"

The door slams. Cree stands there weeping long after Russ leaves.

Chapter 26

Finding Nathaniel

Detective Ryan doesn't hand over the staff right away. What he wants in return, he now struggles to ask. Ryan approaches the window and scans through the blinds. "So, this is where they're keeping you?"

Nathaniel nods. "For the time being. I go and come as I please, still got my cell phone. A lot better than being chained in the basement."

Detective Ryan turns from the waist. "This is the house where you and Lulu were kept?"

"It is." Nathaniel looks up. "Different experience though. Charlene has been gracious." Nathaniel folds his arms and raises on tiptoe.

Since it's obvious, now, that they're beating around the bush, Detective Ryan says, "Surely, you didn't think I risked my career, removing evidence just to hand this cane over to you for nothing in return, right?"

"I am anything but naïve. I know what to expect from man."

"So, you're *not*, man," asks Ryan. "Are you Nathanael of Galilee?"

"There are things I cannot confirm or deny."

Ryan points up. "But you are from, up there?"

Nathaniel says, "Heaven is more complex than you know. I belong to an order. Our goals are very much in line with God's, but we have more freedom in our dwellings with man."

"Hell," Ryan chuckles. "When you were in custody, at first, you acted like you couldn't talk. Then you told us the truth to make us think you were nutso."

"My problem is, I'm incapable of lying. Gets me into a lot of trouble." Nathaniel asks, "Anyway, what deal do you have in mind?"

"I'm getting to that," says Ryan. "It's just that… I'm now realizing *what* I'm asking and *who* I'm asking it of. This played out a lot easier in my mind."

"You should not hesitate to say things that I already know."

Ryan dips a little and says, "Well, there's this gal, you see…"

Nathaniel says, "And you're worried about how God looks at you for being with, *her* – but not how God looks at your divorce? Or your drinking?"

Bashfully, Ryan mumbles, "One sin was sort of a symptom of the other, so…"

"Look, Detective. I can help you."

Ryan twitches. "Help me what?"

"Magically swoon Tina into your arms."

"Even if I end up roasting in hell? Would I?"

Nathanial waves a hand and says, "I'm not going to answer that question right now. When I get what I want, I will offer you an answer to that question, and help you in regards to Tina. It's your free will."

Detective Ryan hands over the staff.

Nathaniel strokes it like a returned pet. He then looks at Detective Ryan with a smirk and says, "Thank you, but this isn't all that I need. Now, all I require is a car."

"I brought you the cane."

"I'm not a genie, you know."

"A car?" Ryan arms drop to his sides. "I don't have a car to spare nor money to buy one."

"But you have family, man. Be creative. For example, Charlene said she didn't have it either, but now she's blackmailing her father, since she's found out that he bought this place as an investment property for his mistress, but halted the renovations the very day that the mistress's live-in boyfriend asked her hand in marriage. You can get the money, Detective Ryan. I just need a dependable car, or fifteen thousand dollars to purchase one."

"Fifteen thousand! My family ain't Charlene's family. My folks can't afford to let go of that kind of money. Can't squeeze blood out of a turnip."

"Remember when you located me, and we talked initially over the phone? You said Lulu would get the money from her lover? Call him."

Detective gives a backhanded wave. "I can't call him. I have to call her, then she calls him, but something isn't adding up. If my memory serves me correctly, Nisha said this thing *makes* money, so why do you need money from me?"

"It doesn't create money out of thin air. This once belonged to the disciple Bartholomew, who is associated with miracles of manipulating the weight of things. It just so happens to have an effect on slot machines."

"A gambling angel?"

"I've told you, I'm not the type of angel you think I am. The reason I need a car is because we're in a non-gambling state. The casino cruise in Myrtle Beach is an hour and a half drive from here. I can't Uber that."

Detective Ryan snatches the staff. "I'll just keep this cane then."

"It's ok, Detective Ryan. Keep the staff. We can forget this conversation ever happened."

"But then you won't have your staff."

"I will, eventually. Jett is being released, and when he learns that it is you who has it, he'll get it for me. With his glasses, he can see everything you do before you do it, so it would not be wise to resist him."

Detective Ryan stares Nathaniel down. "Is that a threat?"

Nathaniel's palms go up as if robbed. "I am incapable of harming anyone. Appreciate the information. Think what might've happen had I not told you."

"So, if through Charlene and Jett, you were going to get the money and your staff back anyhow, why'd you even answer the phone when I called?"

"While things maybe amicable between Charlene and I, right now. I fear this situation we have, might soon spin out of control. Charlene, you see, is deteriorating from a mental condition spurred by infertility. She'll do anything to become a mother, like that baron lioness that adopted a baby antelope, instead of eating it."

Detective Ryan gives in. "A'ight. I hate to do this, but I'll give Lulu a call and see if she can convince Russ to hand over the money. She wants to talk to you just as bad as I did. And you, come with me. Let's go before somebody returns."

Together, Detective Ryan and Nathaniel exit the house. Ryan feels the splash of sunlight like never before. He'd just been crushed by news of Tina seeing someone else, thinking perhaps he'd lost the only person with whom love is possible. Now, as his gravel steps soften to grass as they cut across a field where his car is parked in hiding, he feels like a lottery winner, heading downtown to collect his happily ever after.

Chapter 27

Window Seat

Cree texts Charlene a picture from her window seat, the glass bearing Cree's ghost reflection. Cree switches her phone to airplane mode early, knowing any reply from Charlene would make her feel even worse.

Cree is reminded that she's a celebrity when a pair of women seem to recognize Cree as they walk past. They end up sitting in the seats just behind the first-class curtain, where they discuss the shooting; the injustice of a white cop killing four young black men and being released from custody with no criminal charges.

Cree suspects the ladies are speaking loud enough to be heard, hoping to strike up a conversation with a celebrity. Autographs and selfies may soon follow, which might invite requests from other passengers and turn preflight into a media event, everyone wanting their piece of her, oblivious of the loss she's suffering by leaving her dying mother and being forced to walk away from the love of her life, all for the sake of avoiding prison.

Cree sighs and lays her head back into her neck pillow, and puts on the same disguise of dark shades and a ball cap pulled tight that she wore through the airport terminal. This is how Cree plans to ride out her flight.

The last passenger boards and there are about ten people still standing in the aisle, sliding between each other and jamming their carry-ons into the overhead compartments. The captain and crew are readying for the flight, the next dismal course of her life, now inevitable.

Suddenly, Cree gets a feeling, much like the feeling she had in Guy's office when her mother was calling, which turned out to be accurate. Some knowing is forming in her mind and she fears it has something to do with her mother or Meryl. She tries to shake the feeling, thinking maybe it's jitters. Just to be certain, she takes her phone out of airplane mode. The moment the device is back online, a call comes through. It's Detective Ryan.

RUSS doesn't want to go, but Charlene won't let up. Russ says, "I thought we weren't going to try to force things."

Charlene replies, "This isn't about us. It's about that little girl."

She takes Russ's hand from his lap and leans back with all her weight to get him up from the couch.

Russ goes with her reluctantly. Soon they're in the car, halfway to Beth's house, Charlene driving. "Hopefully the officer isn't there yet," Charlene says, as she spools the steering wheel through her hands.

Russ protests. "Just because you're forcing me to go doesn't mean I'm signing any papers, Charlene. I told you. I don't want nothing to do with Lulu ever again, you hear me?"

"Oh shush, Russ. You get so stubborn when you're upset. Once you're stuck in that big ole head of yours, can't nobody get you out of there and into your heart."

Russ nearly says, *wanna bet?* He only gives the look that would've accompanied those words.

"I'm keeping you from doing something you'll regret," says Charlene. "This is a child. A child you once loved and cared for as your own. You're gonna let her fall into the foster care system? I don't know what Lulu has done to turn you so cold, Russ, but it's not this little girl's fault." The car goes quiet as Charlene waits for Russ's reply. She looks over at the man and sees him quite satisfied with silence, so Charlene continues, "Good thing the CPS director happens to be an acquaintance. She tipped me off. Hopefully we get there before the officer arrives..." A text comes in on Charlene's phone. She checks it. It's a text from Cree containing a picture from aboard the flight, as evidence that she's leaving. Charlene turns the phone face down in her lap to hide it from Russ.

"...Said when the social worker got there, they discovered that her guardian, the grandmother, isn't fit to watch after Meryl or hardly her own self, and of course you know Lulu is not only on a plane right now, but her visitations have to be supervised, so it's not like she can take a flight back and take custody of her child." Charlene reaches over, jabbing Russ's thigh with her fingernail. "*Your* name is on the birth certificate. *You're* the only one who could take her in without the red tape."

Russ asks, "What's a social worker doing there in the first place?"

"Following up on a complaint—"

"—Probably made by you," pouts Russ.

Charlene cuts her eyes at him. "Keep on. Keep right on, Russ. You're in enough hot water with me as it is. I'm not putting up with attitude from you, buster. I'm telling you. Your job, over the next few months is showing the whole damn city just how remorseful you are for treating me the way that you did and how grateful you are to be given a second chance. You will kowtow, you will make yourself the fool you made of me, and you will ask me, again, to marry you, and then *maybe* I'll say yes," Charlene says, as she pulls into Beth's driveway. The squad car is already there, the officer just getting out.

Charlene puts the car in park and looks over at Russ. She takes his chin with an underhand grip and says, "I don't mean to be hard on you, Russ, but... It's not too much to ask when you think about the shame and embarrassment you put me through." She takes his silence as acquiescence and kisses his lips once and again, and again, until she feels the slight pinch of his lips kissing back. "Now go on, and talk to the officer, tell him you're here to get Meryl," Charlene says.

"Who me?"

"You're the parent."

"I'm still a black man and that's still a cop."

"Ugh!" Charlene gets out of the car. The officer stands on the porch. The social worker backs out of the open front door, pointing back into the house and telling the officer, "She's in there. She's hiding her." She, meaning Staysha, who blocks the hallway with her head down trying to call Lulu, and then cursing for another call going directly to voicemail.

Staysha says to the social worker and the officer. "She's okay. She was up this morning, making breakfast… she's just having a little spell, right now; they come and go."

The social worker turns to the officer and explains, "The report says she has terminal cancer." Information Charlene amended to her previous report after speaking with Cree in the hospital cafeteria. The social worker then turns to Staysha and says, "That is not the description of someone fit to have a child in their care. Look at Miss Beth." Beth lay on the couch, unable to turn her head at the sound of her name. Even swallowing is labor.

Staysha, admittedly, is disheartened by how suddenly Beth has declined; she cannot justify Meryl staying in Beth's care without sounding reckless.

Charlene joins them on the porch, announcing, "All this isn't necessary, mister officer. I have the biological father right here."

Staysha spots Charlene and loses it. "You called them! Huh?!" Staysha lunges to squeeze between the officer and the doorframe to get a piece of Charlene, but the officer blocks Staysha and orders her back in the house.

The officer, the social worker and Charlene go to the car to question Russ for a while.

Staysha figures best not to disclose that Russ is not the biological father, that way Meryl avoids foster care. She disappears down the hallway then returns holding hands with a weeping Meryl, Staysha giving a pep talk. "It's either Russ or strangers, ya hear? Soon as I get in touch with your momma, we gone work things out, okay?"

Staysha ushers Meryl into their hands. Staysha, having given up on calling Cree, begins to use her phone to record, otherwise Cree would never believe how Russ and Charlene conspired to steal her daughter. Aiming the phone, Staysha yells, "You ain't nothin', Russ, hear me? You weak. You' a weak ass man." Staysha turns the camera to Charlene. "And *you*: you the devil. I don't know who sewed your forked tongue together, but they did one hell of a job."

Charlene leaves the circle where the officer, Russ and the social worker discuss Meryl's handling. "Is that thing recording," Charlene asks as she approaches Staysha. Charlene points to her chin and says, "Come and get me square." Charlene comes close to the recording phone and lowers her voice so the others wouldn't hear. "Like I said, Lulu, you can't outthink me. You can't out hustle me." Charlene, impish with pride, flashes the engagement ring Russ never took back. "Russ and I are going to live happily ever after, raising your daughter." Charlene points at the house behind her, saying, "And when I show her better than this fuckin' dog life you've given her, it'll be nobody's fault but yours if she grows up hating your got damn guts. She'll be calling *me* momma."

The last insult sets Staysha off. Staysha swings. Charlene ducks and backpedals off balance, sprawling toward the officer, who catches her and gets between them, saying to Staysha. "Hey! You! Chill out, alright!"

Charlene yells, "Chill out? That's *all*? How about you arrest her, right now! She assaulted me!"

The officer tugs up his belt and appraises Charlene. "She couldn't swing at you, if you didn't go to her first."

Charlene's eyes pop wide and her head cocks to the side. "Oh really? Well, what it looks like to me, is that my father is Mayor Wade Thomas Hamilton and if you don't arrest her right now you'll be out of a job. Now, *do* it!"

The officer contemplates momentarily and then approaches Staysha with his palm out, fingers tickling for her to come on quietly. Staysha pedals away, "You gonna let her tell you what to do?"

"I was trying to show you leniency, mam, but technically you did assault her. I saw you swing. C'mon, now. Don't make this hard on you, or me." He reaches for Staysha's arm. Staysha reels away. The officer escalates with a tackle. Staysha ends up face down, her arms pinned behind her back under the officer's knee. The officer says, "I'm not arresting you. I'm only detaining you until our business here is done."

Staysha has skid on her elbow and a bloody nose. She screams out over and over, "What did I do?! What did I do?!"

Charlene yells, "Ya took a swipe at me, that's what ya did!"

Russ stops short of rolling the officer off Staysha. Russ is right up on them, pleading with the officer to take it easy but also pleading with Staysha, to relax.

Behind them, an astonished Meryl comes out of her paralyzing shock, and screams.

CREE now face to face with Nathaniel, feels Meryl's scream in her gut. "Something isn't right," Cree says.

"What is it," says Nathaniel.

"Nothing, really. It's just that I've been getting these feelings and… Never mind," Cree relents. She's puzzled as to why her intuition won't go away when she's answered the call, ran out of the airport and is now poised to get instructions from Nathaniel on how to get her life back. Her mother's health and CPS at Beth's door is the real reason this feeling reverberates in her gut, like a struck tuning fork.

"As I was saying," says Nathaniel. "You could ask your fiancé, the wealthy Mr. Rutledge, to purchase a car for me, or better yet, lend me one of the cars he no longer—"

"—Russ and I had a falling out." Cree offers her own keys. "Take my car. The tanks is full."

Quietly and reluctantly, Nathaniel takes the keys to Cree's car. "Now that that's taken care of," he sighs. "I will tell you exactly what you need to do in order to get back to your world."

Cree smirks with confusion. "What do you mean tell me what I need to do? Give me a ring like you gave Lulu."

"That ring is the only one of its kind."

"Well, why am I giving you my car then!"

"Calm down, Lulu—"

"I'm not Lulu, I'm Cree," she yells.

Detective Ryan interrupts, "I *knew* you weren't the same person."

Nathaniel rolls his eyes and says, "He is beginning to sicken me." Nathaniel looks sternly at Cree and says, "It's not going to be easy, but you do have a chance. A real chance. Listen to my instructions carefully. Here's the first thing you must do…"

Chapter 28

A Far Cry

After hearing Nathaniel's instructions, Cree is outraged. "I gave you my car for *this?*"

"What do you mean," says a confused Nathaniel.

"You did nothing but tell me what I already knew – to meet Lulu at a portal between worlds and convince her to cross over first. I already tried that."

Nathaniel replies, "It's the only way."

"What if she never returns to that storage room ever again, and even if she does, how am I to know *when* so I could show up on my end?" It's beginning to look like a lover's quarrel at a public park; Cree is as furious as anyone who'd just been conned out of their automobile.

Nathaniel shakes his head. "Why are you stuck on that storage place Cree? You, having lived your entire life in the other world, should be able to locate mirrors, here, in the same location. Any one of them can be a portal."

Cree caves in. "Really…"

"Yes," Replies Nathaniel. "Weren't you listening? Besides, convincing Lulu to trade back again is not as hard as you think."

Nathaniel adds, "She is you. You – better than anyone – would know how to push your own buttons."

Cree shakes her head in misery. "My God... If Russ and I were married..." Being married to Russ is all Lulu seems to care about. Now Cree wanders away, woozy with regret; she's now made it impossible for Russ to ever agree to marry her, so she'll have to think of something else.

Detective Ryan now takes Cree's place in front of Nathaniel. Ryan nods at the keys in Nathaniel's hand and says, "You got your car. Now, what you got for me?"

Cree walks away for privacy and calls Staysha, who has just been released by the police officer. What Cree hears on the other end of the phone nearly kills her where she stands. Cree listens with her mouth open, unable to say a word. Her intuition wasn't about this meeting with Nathaniel; it was about Meryl.

Cree pockets her phone and hurries over to Nathaniel, who is now twirling the key in his hand and advising Detective Ryan, who listens intently, like a tin man with an empty chest, wanting a heart.

Cree taps Nathaniel on the shoulder. "I need to borrow the car. My mother's health just took a turn for the worst, and my daughter's in trouble right now."

Nathaniel frowns. "You pull this, *after* I advise you?"

Cree says, "How is it that you, of all people, *not* know that I'm telling the truth?"

Detective Ryan sides with her, "It's her child, man."

The slight distraction of Nathaniel glancing at Ryan's comment affords Cree the split second to snatch the keys and take-off running.

Detective Ryan takes off as well, calling after her. He runs Cree down by the time she gets to her car door. Cree turns around to defend herself, her fists up by her face like a boxer. Detective Ryan says, "I'm trying to help. Is she in danger? What's happening?"

Cree lowers her guard and says, "It's something I can handle it on my own."

"Take this just in case."

Cree looks down and sees Detective Ryan's offering of a taser. "Thanks. I'll call you to meet so I can hand over the car," Cree says, as she takes the taser.

Ryan bids adieu with a soft salute. Nathaniel finally catches up. He bends forward hands on knees, blowing hard. "This is the thing I like least about being in a body... Getting winded."

Ryan says, "So where were we?"

"Oh no you don't," Nathaniel frowns. "I'm not telling you anything until I get the car."

CREE speeds through the city to her mother's home. Turning into the driveway, the prow of her car swings to Staysha sitting on the front steps, still coming to grips over hugged knees, a few sympathetic neighbors leaning on the porch rails, offering support at a home from which the system has taken, though thankfully not a life. The pains in Staysha's body shows in how gingerly she stands and in the grimace on a face that yet registers confusion for Cree's impossibly quick arrival.

Cree hurries to Staysha, hugging her.

Staysha asks, "How'd you get here so fast?" She also wonders why Cree wasn't already thirty thousand feet in the air by the time she finally answered her phone, but her curiosity is overridden by guilt, thinking her advice is what prompted Cree to change her plans for Manhattan, which led to Meryl being ripped away in Cree's absence.

Cree bypasses Staysha's question for a more pressing one, "Are you okay?"

"Yeah," says Staysha although her head shakes no, as she begins to relive the event she must explain. Staysha offers the long version of the harrowing tale while handing over the video she'd captured. Cree gets an up-close view of Charlene taunting about stealing Meryl. Cree boils. She couldn't fathom Charlene taking vengeance to such an extreme, even now in hindsight.

Meryl, however, is safe in Russ's custody, so Cree doesn't let herself stew over the outcome. "How did Meryl take it?"

Staysha says, "She was freaked out when cop threw me down, but she strong though. When I was sitting in the back of the squad car, she came by the window and blew a kiss. She's a trooper."

"That damn Charlene," Cree says and takes a deep breath, her cheeks ballooning on the exhale. "She's messing with my family. Lord, please keep me from killing that chick." Cree goes hesitantly up the steps to check on her mother, fearing the very thing she sees. Beth lay motionless on the couch, already with this wooden, postmortem look about her. Every slow blink flaunts with death.

Cree grips her mouth to muffle her cry. Staysha hugs her from the side, whispering comforting words. Cree shudders and fights through the hiccups of crying, this expert vocalist having no control of the grief blurting up from her lower register. "She was fine just this morning," Cree whines. "When I came over to say goodbye..." Cree gives up on words and mews in Staysha's embrace.

Staysha whispers, "It's alright, Lulu. It's alright."

It takes a coordinated effort from Cree and Staysha both just to tilt Beth forward to swallow a drink of water.

Beth wears a frown of concern, and her eyes keeps rolling to the corner in appraisal of Cree, as if she's a stranger. Finally, in the feeblest voice, Beth says, "I see you, now."

Cree, kneeling next to the couch where Beth lay, leans over her. "Yes momma. I'm right here. You're not alone."

Beth swallows laboriously, and whispers, "You did change."

Cree and Staysha look at each other and back at Beth. Cree wonders if Beth somehow recognizes that she's standing in for Lulu. Cree tries to smile the insecurity out of her own face. "I'm right here, momma. Don't you recognize me?"

Cree wonders if Beth defers to something beyond sight, beyond senses, because even a blind person could feel the ridges of Cree's face and recognize the mental mask forming through a sort of inward sight, where she would be physically identical to Lulu. Perhaps Beth, with one foot on the other side, is already projecting from outside of her own body. Perhaps Cree radiates differently than the daughter that this Beth is used to, her chakra not bound up in a defensive coil. Cree has become strange to

Beth, and Cree suspects that it's not due to any form of mental decline.

Cree realizes the time and effort it would take to care for Beth, and what she must do now to get back to her world. She decides to call the number for hospice care, given to her by the hospital on Beth's recent E.R. visit. While they wait for the transport to arrive, Cree walks Staysha out to the porch and tells Staysha about Charlene threatening to send her to jail with the video if she didn't end her relationship with Russ.

"So, that's why you changed your mind about staying, after talking to Charlene at the hospital?" Staysha looks away and back. "Call your manager Lulu," Staysha encourages. "He'll understand."

Cree puts a hand on Staysha's shoulder and says, "Call me Cree."

Staysha looks at the hand on her shoulder and then looks at Cree.

"Staysha," Cree says. "I have something to tell you. It's something I've been keeping secret because I knew you would think I'm crazy. But now I *have* to tell you. Because I have a plan to take my life back, and there's no way I can do it without you."

Staysha studies Cree from the corner of an eye, bracing for what she might hear from Lulu who now wants to go by a different name.

Chapter 29

What God Is Like

Detective Ryan and Nathaniel sit together under the carport of a diner style fast-food joint where brown-bagged burgers and fries are delivered on roller skates to patrons who wait in their cars. Detective Ryan can't get over the fact that he's shooting the breeze with somewhat of an angel. Ryan looks over and asks, "Tell me this, Nate. Were you, like, born? Did you evict the poor soul outta this man's body, or what?"

The question catches Nathaniel off guard. He pauses with a potato wedge next to his mouth. "This body I'm in... this person had attempted suicide. They were clinically dead for a half hour. Their soul had departed, so his body was as a mere vessel."

Detective Ryan looks on, chewing in awe. Realizing that after Cree delivers her car and Nathaniel drives off, he'll never again have the opportunity to sit with the likes of an angel, so Ryan thinks of more questions to ask. "What's He like?"

"*He?*" Nathaniel looks and blinks twice. "Do not insult God."

Ryan is dumbfounded. "Don't tell me, all along, He is a She."

"Gender is earthly. There is no pronoun for God. Did you not read the passage of Moses and the burning bush? Anything outside of God's many given names, you refer to God as I Am," Nathaniel says. "You ask what's God like? How is that even a question? You have the opportunity every day to increase God's presence inside of you."

Ryan gazes meditatively, "Sometimes I go out to the pier, looking at the water, the horizon, the beauty of all God's creation—"

Nathaniel chokes on his drink and then wipes his mouth on his sleeve to say, "You can't be this bad off, man. *You're* a pastor?"

"Was," clarifies Ryan. "Youth pastor, at that. I didn't go to no divinity school or nothing."

"You don't need a divinity degree, detective. The word is right there for anyone who can read. If vanity takes you further from God, then, surely humility draws you nearer, right? Do a selfless act and you'll feel the smile of God in your bosom."

Nathaniel seemed done one moment but the next he raises a finger. "Now, I'll add that there is this close relative of vanity – which you all refer to as romantic love – where the laws of attraction makes you *think* you're seeking someone who fits your identity, your values, your norms, but within that framework you're subconsciously seeking a shelter for your fears, insecurities, trauma and you're also seeking fertile emotional soil for you to grow and develop where you lack; nothing else can be more humbling. That's why when man falls in or out of love, it is never a conscious decision."

"Amen to that," says Detective Ryan.

The car goes quiet for a spell. Detective Ryan plucks a leaf of lettuce from the breast of his shirt and eats it. Nathaniel catches him, but neither comments. Unprompted, Nathaniel offers, "I'd been away from earth for about fifteen hundred years. This is my second return in the last ten years. That should tell you that times are about to change."

Ryan asks, "So, why'd you come down the time before this?"

"I came as a lawyer, to influence a broader interpretation, by the U.N., of one of the articles of Global Human Rights Laws." Nathaniel smirks. "I was a lawyer, but I was also a woman."

"A woman," Detective Ryan parrots, with a packed mouth. He's in such shock that Nathaniel has to point out his ringing phone. Detective Ryan fumbles the device initially. "It's Lulu. I told you she'd call," Ryan says, before answering. Quickly, Ryan and Cree arrange the meeting and end the call. Ryan reports, "We just sit here. Lulu and her friend is on her way to us."

As Detective Ryan is talking, Nathaniel notices the man's hand easing toward his side gun holster. "What're you doing," asks Nathaniel.

The response comes from another man's voice. "Don't try nothing fancy." It's Jett approaching the car, displaying a badge in one hand and a gun in the other, the sun glaring off his glasses. "Show me your hands."

"Excuse me," says Detective Ryan, with his hand still hidden and inching towards his gun. "If anything, I should be arresting you. Are you aware, sir, that I'm a cop?"

Nathaniel grabs Detective Ryan's hand and says, "He knows everything you do before you do it. It's the glasses."

Detective Ryan remembers how Jett anticipated every move from Hook and his gang, coupled with the fact of a magical cane, a parallel universe, and an angel of sorts sitting next to him, suspends any inkling of doubt, so Ryan gives in.

Jett hands Ryan a pair of handcuffs to put on. "You have a right to remain silent—"

"—You have got to be kidding me. For what?"

"Finding you two together tells me the staff is in this car, which translates to removing evidence from a crime scene and obstruction of justice, to name a few."

Jett removes Detective Ryan's side arm, and cuffs Nathaniel who asks, "What have *I* done?"

"Conspiracy… attempting to bribe an officer." Jett guides both men over to his car, reading them their rights as he helps them into the backseat. Jett takes the staff to the front seat with him.

Detective Ryan turns suspicious. "Why are you not on the radio, calling this in?"

"No need," Jett replies, as he straps on his seatbelt. "I'm taking you both in, myself."

Just minutes into the drive, Detective Ryan realizes what's happening. They are not in route to the precinct.

CHARLENE'S eyes can't get their fill of Meryl, from stolen glances at the sobbing girl in the rearview mirror to now standing under the chandelier at the home of her de facto grandparents. The welcome is lukewarm and short lived. Before anyone can sit, Russ's parents are setting the boundaries around Meryl's arrangements. She'll need to spend most of the day with Russ's parents during the weeklong suspension from school.

Meryl stands off to herself, but across from Charlene, whose head rotates a full ninety degrees, observing Meryl's inner turmoil; her silence as passive resistance, her lips scrunched in anger, her measured breathing, and flexing hands. Charlene is so honed-in on Meryl that the discussion between the adults reduces to murmurs, and when Meryl turns slowly from the feel of being watched, Charlene doesn't initially notice that the girl's eyes have set squarely on her, looking, not with the despair she's obviously feeling, but with a rivalry that burns in Meryl's eyes.

This moment, for Charlene, identifies Meryl as a fighter, even better than the hospital altercation. Charlene, a fighter herself, knows that there's no better way to win-over a fighter than to fight for them when they're in no position to fight for themselves.

Charlene cuts in on the conversation between Russ and her soon-to-be in-laws. "Mr. and Mrs. Rutledge? Forgive me, but I don't understand what all the hesitation is about. This is your granddaughter," Charlene says, with a wink-wink reminder that Meryl still doesn't know the truth. "You act as if you're taking in a stray. You don't think she can feel that? She didn't ask for this and there's probably a mess of other places she'd rather be, right now, than here," says Charlene, to the audience of three, staring down her little act as she tap dances near a cliff's edge. "You're gonna nitpick over week? Less maybe – once I pull some strings to get her back with her mother? Now," Charlene says, with a tug to the hem of her blouse and a newly minted smile. "I'd kindly appreciate it if you'd show us to her room, Miss April."

April decides against putting Charlene in her place, in the presence of the child. The contempt in April's brow settles and she beams a maternal smile at Meryl. April approaches with the posture of a ballerina, deliberately nudging past Charlene on the way to Meryl. "Come on Meryl. Let's see your room."

The two hold hands down the hallway, April saying, "Forgive me for not having time to prepare." April looks at Meryl more intently. "You are gorgeous just like your mother," a subtle dig at Charlene.

Charlene tails them to the only room with wall pictures of a married Russ and Lulu holding baby Meryl. April goes straight to spreading the drapes, her back to Meryl while sharing a few fond memories from the two years they thought Meryl was their grandchild.

Somehow, on the belief that the Rutledges are her grandparents, Meryl doesn't regard them as strangers. It's like going on prison visits to her grandfather who she also didn't know well, although she insists on a relationship to spite the system that keeps them apart.

Charlene stands by the doorway, her back to the wall near the light switch, as she tinkers with her phone. She glances up to say, "A bowl of ice cream would be nice right now, wouldn't it Meryl?"

A perturbed April rotates slowly, "If you would allow me the chance, Charlene, I was just about to ask *my* granddaughter, if I could get her anything."

April sits on the bed next to Meryl, smiling to her. "Would you like some ice cream, baby?"

So, Meryl's first words since leaving Beth's home is, "I'm not hungry."

April, who seems satisfied with the answer, is interrupted by Charlene. "She said she wasn't hungry – not that she didn't want any ice cream."

April looks back at Meryl and finds a shy smirk. April places a hand on Meryl's knee. "Child... You can never be a burden to me or your grandpa, understand?" As April heads out for ice cream, she stops at the doorway with a stiff finger to the tip of Charlene's nose, warning, "You'd better mind, Charlene."

With April gone, Charlene peels her back off the wall, giving up on whatever she was doing with her phone. "I can't seem to get in contact with your mother."

"I don't like you," says Meryl. "I will never like you."

Charlene replies, "Oh, well then, maybe I *shouldn't* be pulling strings to get you back with your mother, then." Meryl dims, realizing her error. Charlene adds, "Maybe I *shouldn't* contact a good friend of my father, Superintendent Davis to overturn your suspension because the same girl you sucker punched has a slew of bullying complaints on file from other students. You were provoked by a very problematic child. Your mother never questioned their telling of the events because she believes that *you* are the problem child. She taught you to fight with your fists. I can teach you to fight with your brain, and pretty soon you can have that bully standing in front of a family court judge and receiving a year of court-ordered reform school," says Charlene. "That's how *I* operate. Whether you like me, is your business. Whether you respect me, is *my* business." Charlene stops at the open drapes and surveys the estate. "It's a business that I tend to with an iron glove. Like me or not. It would behoove you to stay within my good graces."

"Yes mam," says Meryl.

Charlene sits on the bed next to Meryl. "*Like*, is a bonus. And whether or not you like me, I actually like you. Afterwhile, I'll bet money that we're gonna end up liking each other a whole lot."

By the time April returns, she nearly drops the bowl of ice cream at the sight of how comfortable they've become; Charlene combing her hand through Meryl's hair and commenting how fine it feels.

Chapter 30

Smoke And Mirrors

The Emerald Court mansion still has the original porcelain floors that Cree and Russ renovated out for Italian marble back when they purchased the home. Cree is led through its rooms and corridors by a realtor in a silk shirt, who is thrown off his game by Cree knowing more about the home than himself.

Although Cree has no intention of buying, she can't help thwarting the agent's attempts to bolster the price tag. This raspy, tall-toothed agent says the black tile incorporated into the master bathroom design, is authentic obsidian slate tiles, but Cree casually corrects him, "It's actually artificial quartz – not that it matters much."

"I beg to differ," he disagrees, although hedging his challenge with phlegmy laughter.

On the way out of the master bathroom, they reenter the bedroom. Cree stops at the wall, her arms spread, as if hugging the home. She says, "Here's where I would put my vanity mirror, in this precise location."

While following the realtor out, Cree sags back and ducks out of the hallway, stealthily slipping through a few adjoined interior rooms.

The realtor, hearing only one set of footsteps, looks back and sees nothing but hallway. He wanders through the home "Miss Hughes?" Cree stands with her back to a pillar opposite of the realtor.

Cree doesn't reappear until after running off to one of the back entries and leaving it unlocked.

Hours later – through that same unlocked entrance – Cree and Staysha haul a large mirror, secured to a hand truck with rope.

They wheel the large mirror Cree purchased, to the master bedroom where they wonder how they could possibly lift something so heavy.

In the other world when Cree and Russ purchased and renovated this home, Cree was so hands on with the interior decorator that she remembers the precise measurements. Cree and Staysha stand on each end of the tape measure, Cree moving along with a leveler and drawing the outline.

Staysha is still skeptical. "I'm really, really giving you the benefit of the doubt, Lulu – I mean Cree. If this turns out to be one big fantasy, I'm taking you to a shrink and you're not allowed to fight me on it."

"Deal," Cree says confidently. Cree moves the steel brackets in place over the drawn and leveled line and uses a cordless drill to fasten the brackets to the wall.

They take opposite sides and clasp their hands under the bottom corners of the large mirror and bend at the knees. It takes all their might to hoist the mirror up onto the steel brackets. Staysha stands in front of the mirror, her hands on hips, waiting for something to happen, but all she sees is her reflection against the bare painted wall behind her.

Cree makes another call to Detective Ryan. "It's still going straight to voicemail," Cree says. "I think something's happened to them. They told us to meet them at the diner and–"

"–And we did," says Staysha. "And the car was empty. I'm starting to think that was just some abandoned car you found earlier and incorporated it into your wild, skitzo fantasy."

Cree's head shakes. "I don't blame you for not believing me, but you will find out soon enough. Let's go."

"Go where?" Staysha is a tower of resistance. "I got a life, Lulu."

"Which means you gotta eat. We may as well get our food there – kill two birds with one stone. You drive behind me."

"No, *you* drive us. I'm not wasting my gas on this foolishness."

"If I'm giving away my car, how do you suggest we get back, then?"

"Whoever you give your car to, better drive us back."

On the drive there, Staysha asks a slew of questions, not so much out of curiosity but to catch possible inconsistencies. "…So, in the other world, you and Russ are married and y'all live in that house we just broke into, right? What about me?"

"Girl," Cree swats, as if she were waiting to be asked. Cree details the different outcomes between both worlds in convincing fashion.

Staysha, entertaining this theoretical, says, "That life sounds like everything I ever wanted *except* Sean."

Cree asks, "What if you knew, beforehand, the good life you would have with Sean? Would you have chosen him then?"

Staysha's eyes widen and blinks. "I don't know. He just didn't do it for me. He's such a cornball."

"He's what you call an introvert," Cree corrects. "Sean opened up eventually and now he keeps you in stitches."

Staysha sighs and says, "I don't know how some women do it, but I couldn't – with a man who can't last as long as I can hold my breath."

Cree draws back. "Oh, I forgot."

Staysha adds, "With me and Sean, that was our elephant in the room. We never discussed it. He acted as if he was confused as to why I didn't want to be with him. That day we broke up, he cursed me *all* the way out – talkin' about how a good man like him should never be made to compete against a felon for a good woman – which he said, was proof that I'm *not* one."

Cree says, "I remember while we were in the hospital waiting room and you talked about how Sean touts his ex-prostitute wife like a queen. *You're* the queen, Staysha, because in the world where you two stay together, is where he rose to the level of kingship. Some men need a queen to stoke his inner king."

"Exactly," says Staysha, although none of it is reality, it's still all a hypothetical that Cree has imagined in an elaborate and consistent network of details.

They arrive at the fast-food joint. The car is still there and still empty. While awaiting their orders, Cree walks over to the car and pulls on the handles; the doors are locked.

Cree cups her hands at the driver's side window, and she gets a vision beyond the inside of the car, a vision that leaves her visibly shaken.

When Cree returns to the driver's seat of her car, Staysha detects her uneasiness. "You alright?"

"I've been getting these feelings – now visions, I guess."

Staysha's brow flattens. "Visions…"

Cree sees, in Staysha's eyes, just how wild she must sound. Cree tries to explain, without sounding insane, "I saw a vision of Nathaniel and Detective Ryan chained in a dark room – and before you say anything, let me tell you this: the reason I got to momma's house so soon after you called is *because* of this intuition. I knew to jump off that flight, although we hadn't talked yet."

This is the first thing from Cree that sounds somewhat credible, to Staysha. Staysha says, "They're held hostage, so what're you gonna do, call the imaginary police for your imaginary friends?"

"I can't call *any* police if I don't know where they're located."

Their dinner is served by a roller-skating carhop and they're off again to return to the mansion at Emerald Court. Cree says, "My original plan was to see if I could convince Russ that our breakup was bogus, elope, like he originally wanted, and have him come with me to the mirror, to show Lulu that we're married because Lulu had this fear of being strung along. But when I saw that video on your phone, my plan changed."

"If this is all real," Staysha prefaces. "I think you should go with the first option, Lulu – I mean Cree. You show her that video, which shows her a life without Russ or Meryl, you're not giving her much of a reason to come back."

"The reason I'm showing Lulu the video, is because she is what I used to be: hypervigilant. Plus, she hates Charlene with such a passion, that it doesn't matter how good life is on the other side, it'll never sit right with her, knowing Charlene has won in this world. Also, if Lulu's experience is like mine, she's realizing that my Meryl can never replace her own Meryl and Lulu will be damned if she lets Charlene raise hers."

Chapter 31

Can I Get A Witness

Night is falling when Cree and Staysha return. As they enter the mansion, Staysha is on the phone explaining to Jermaine that she won't be coming home because she's spending the night with Lulu since her mother was admitted into hospice and her daughter, who is also Staysha's goddaughter, was taken. The excuse goes over well enough, but the charades is working Staysha's nerves, and sparking shady side comments right up to the moment of truth.

Staysha waits in the doorway of the master bathroom, waiting to admit Cree into a mental asylum once the fantasy is exposed.

Cree places a foldout chair in front of the mirror. They hold their positions and wait.

It's after ten pm when Lulu enters her bedroom and sits at the vanity for her nightly facial routine. The mirror's reflection begins to change. Lulu says, "What the...!" It's not her own reflection, Lulu begins to realize. "Cree?"

Staysha, standing in the doorway of the master bathroom is denied an angle of the reflection, but she sees that Cree's lips never moved, and that the glow of the track lighting from Lulu's side illuminates through and shines on the face of Cree. Staysha covers her mouth in shock. All the psychotic gibberish of parallel worlds and alternate realities, shifts from fantasy to reality.

Cree says, "I won't take up much of your time." Cree pretends to cry, wearily, as if she's done with life; the act seems quite convincing.

Lulu stops her. "Wait." Lulu leaves her seat and soon returns after locking the bedroom door. "So... you figured it out, huh," Lulu says. "Alright, make it quick before I break this damn mirror and tell Russ it was an accident."

"I just want to show you this." Cree holds up the phone, displaying the video with the policeman and social worker in the background, as Charlene boasts about raising Meryl as a child of her own.

"What in the entire hell!" Lulu trembles with the turmoil of anger and disbelief. "Where were *you* when all this was happening?"

As if every reply is burdensome, Cree sighs, and then she looks down and away as if in shame. "I was somewhere else," is the response she settles on.

Lulu pounds the vanity desktop. "Somewhere else! That's your answer? So, what are you doing to fix this!"

Cree's hand wipes slowly down her face, as if she's lost all interest in life itself. "I don't have the will to fix this. If you must know, while this was happening, I was somewhere else, trying to do what I was doing when we first crossed paths. I was about to take my own life, when I got the call."

Lulu, remembering the car wreck for which she suspected Cree of attempting suicide, believes her. "We *can't* be the same person. We just can't be," Lulu says, somberly. "You are one weak woman, you know that? You're gonna let Charlene do whatever the hell she wants, and you don't fight back?"

"Momma's in hospice," says Cree. "She doesn't have long. I'll hang around long enough to bury her. That's more than I have to give. So, the only reason I'm contacting you is to tell you that I will be gone soon, so you can't return. You can't have people thinking I've raised up from the dead, okay? That's really all I have to say."

Lulu crosses her legs and looks Cree up and down in a few head flicks. "Don't get it twisted, Cree. You don't ever have to worry about me crossing over. I don't care if the world's ending, if locusts swarms blot out the sky. I'll pray the lord my soul to take, and call it a life."

"I just came to tell you. That's all…" Cree says as she smears cold tears across her cheeks with the heel of her hand. "…What you do about it, doesn't affect my destiny at all. Good night, Lulu," Cree says, as she gets up and walks past the mirror's edge. The mirror fogs and clears into just a mirror, reflecting the naked back wall.

Cree goes to the master bathroom and finds Staysha sitting on the tiled floor, too shaken to stand.

Staysha looks up, helpless. "This mess is real, like…"

"So *now* you believe me."

Staysha gets a shot of energy. "Cree! Lulu was clearly frontin'. She wanted to come through. Why'd you stop? Why suddenly walk away?"

"She can't disappear at a time when Russ expects her in bed for the night. She's got the ring, so she doesn't need me. She's gonna come through alone, when she thinks I'm not here."

"But the ring gets her across, not back."

Cree huffs. "Do I have to explain this all over again? When we're both on the same side, either of us can pass through our *own* reflection – ring or no ring – that's how I got here in the first place. So," Cree sighs. "Because we have no idea when she's coming through, that's why we're spending the night."

They take their overnight bags up to the second floor where, in the morning, they would be able to look out the window and spot an unwitting Lulu exiting the house, and Cree could easily run to the mirror in the master bedroom and cross over back to her life; that is the plan.

The best friends lay on the hard floor and talk late into the night, both finding it difficult to sleep. Staysha asks, "Why so adamant about returning? Your other life is where you always regretted not singing, and always wondered *what if*. You've got your career back. You can still get Guy to delay the record production. You can find a way around Charlene, still have Russ and be living the life you always dreamed of."

Cree sighs. "Basically, this isn't home. As much as I'm grateful for you, Staysha, it would break my heart to never again see the *other* you. As bad as things got between Russ and me, I don't want to quit on my marriage. It's my marriage. I was too busy looking at his wrongs that I never really took the time out to look at my own."

"One thing I can say about you, Cree, is that you are way ahead of Lulu in this thing called life."

"Being in a good marriage, you have an accountability partner. If love is anything, it is honest, so it helps to see yourself through the loving eyes of someone else, yet it forces you to evolve before you're ready. It's like, even where there're problems in a good marriage, it makes you better. Knives sharpen against stone; not a sponge," says Cree. "Where you run into problems, like Russ and I did, is when you begin taking each other for granted, and then you start to work against each other for the sake of yourself. I let myself believe, on so little evidence, that Russ had an affair, as an attempt to justify my plan to step down from the Icarus Foundation to pursue music. Then just the other day, I learn, with absolute certainty, that there was no affair."

"Maybe you didn't need any justification," Staysha offers. "Maybe all you needed was to tell him how important music is to you."

"You're right, Staysha. It's just that, the marriage has to be in a good place, or me steeping down from Icarus would've been taken for spite."

Staysha doesn't say a word, but Cree is aware that silence from her talkative friend says something. "What," Cree says.

"I didn't say anything."

"I know; that's why I asked."

"Well..." Staysha raises up on an elbow to look at Cree. Staysha says, "I'm just glad to know that I'm actually using my gift to do some pretty big things. You don't know the level of confidence that gives me, to go ahead and do it here in this world; it's in me."

"You've done some *really* big things," Cree corrects. "You have a few big-name clients on your resume like B. Diddy. You designed the suit he wore to the Grammys back in, like, 2015? Your brand took off after you designed that wedding dress for actress Reagan Good. I personally feel like, if your attention wasn't split with your relationship podcast, you could take over the fashion world, but of course, I'm biased because I love you."

"I love you too, Lulu – I mean Cree," Staysha says, nodding. "For me, I'm starting to realize that I need to be with someone who motivates me to be my best self – not someone who attacks my self-esteem because he's afraid that I'd outgrow him." Coming right on the heels of realizing she must do better, Staysha rebuttals herself in a tone-change of unworthiness, "Who am I kidding. Most of the good men my age are probably already married. I feel like, for so long, I've been in the sunken place with Jermaine, like, where do I get off looking for someone to add to my life, when nothing about me says I can add to theirs?"

"Because, the more they love you, the less that matters. Do we throw out two hundred years of psychology, along with the fact that a person's exes all possess the one quality that's irresistible that person? Does it matter to Russ whether I'm the head of a corporation or an addict? If what someone can do for you materially, was so important, both versions of you would've chosen Sean. I fell in love with Russ not for his material power, but for his inner strength. He's in control of himself; he's even-keel. I fell in love with Russ because he's the polar-opposite of my father."

Staysha says, "What I liked about Jermaine is how he stay on point. Whether he got a job or not, he gone stay fresh to death. I guess it translates from him thinking highly of himself, and I'm attracted to that. I just need another version of him that doesn't come with the bullshit." Staysha yawns and stretches, which brings the discussion to a close. They lay on the cold, tiled floor, their pillowed faces awaiting sleep, their dreams and desires projecting on the blank walls.

Chapter 32

Gotta Run

Cree wakes to a grey morning just before the alarm on her phone goes off. She's roused early, but with an epiphany that maybe she's not early enough. "Dammit," she says. "Dammit, dammit!" She crawls on the hard tiled floor to Staysha and nudges her awake. "Staysha, Staysha." Staysha wakes confused, wondering where all her bedroom furniture has gone.

"Staysha."

"I'm up."

"I gotta make a run. I totally forgot about something."

Staysha rubs her eyes and says, "Forgot what?"

"The storage room." Cree explains. "Last night wasn't the first time Lulu and I met like that. There's a portal in my old storage unit."

Staysha sits upright. "What about if Lulu comes through *this* mirror while you're gone?"

"Text me. If I haven't smashed the mirror in the storage room by the time you text me, I can just walk through it," Cree says, while rummaging through her things. Cree slides Staysha the taser, and says, "Take this, just in case." Cree hurries on, disappearing down the stairs.

CHARLENE is coming up the stairs complaining the whole way as she enters the house. "I don't know what could be so important that I must get outta my bed this time of morning and drag my butt all the way here to meet you. It'd better be good, Jett. You could've told me over the phone or say it now, instead of grinnin' like a chess cat…"

"Go on," urges Jett. "It's in the basement."

"I let you get too comfortable with me. I have myself to blame for that," Charlene complains, as she goes down the staircase. "I'm supposed to go over to Russ's parents' house this morning and spend time with my daughter, not…" Charlene blanches the moment she descends enough to clear the basement ceiling and see Detective Ryan and Nathaniel chained to the walls. Charlene reverts one stairstep. "What have you done, Jett?"

Jett had hoped for at least a thank you. He eyes Charlene as if he's swallowed a few four-letter words. "If you're puttin' on for the detective, Charlene. Don't worry about him. He won't live to tell any of this."

"What?!" Charlene realizes that all along she'd been consorting with a madman. "I don't know who you think you're dealing with, Jett, but this is not my style. I do my fair share of dirt, my friend, but I wouldn't much kill a mouse." Charlene trots down the steps, thumbing back over her shoulder and pleading to Ryan. "As you can tell, Detective, this was all him. I had nothing to do with this."

Detective Ryan looks down at his chains and back to Charlene. "You're involved by knowing. Report it, or you become an accessory."

Jett marches over to Detective Ryan and punches him in the gut. Ryan lowers to one knee, his chained hands suspended above his head. Jett only needs to look at Nathaniel and the man trembles in fright.

Jett turns to Charlene and says, "Detective Ryan stole the staff from the crime scene and at the same time, Nathaniel went missing from this very house. I never removed the GPS tracker from Ryan's car, so I found the two together, trying to ruin everything we were trying to achieve. Now, Charlene, do you see that this had to be done?"

Charlene advances, her finger jabbing Jett's chest on each word. "You do, what I pay you to do! You don't haul off and do something like this!"

"What if I tell you that Lulu never left for New York and that they were fixing to meet up with her to help her get the best of you."

"Then I'd be calling you a damn lie. I have a picture." Charlene digs into her purse for her phone.

Jett counters, "I've have a GPS tracker on her. Her car left the airport."

"That only means someone dropped her off."

"Well, tell me how is it that when I reviewed her GPS history, twice her car been to the very spot where I took these two into custody? She was attempting to meet with these two numbnuts. That could've been pretty bad for you if I didn't stop it."

Blood seeps into Charlene's eyes as she abouts-face to study the men in chains.

Nathaniel raises a hand like a pupil. "Actually, I wasn't plotting against anyone; I only needed her car…"

A glare from Jett, silences Nathaniel. Jett sets a calming hand on Charlene's shoulder and says, "Let's talk out back." Jett then ushers her through the back door and up to the backyard where is an empty swimming pool and a deck with a built-in outdoor jacuzzi.

With Charlene and Jett gone, Detective Ryan says to Nathaniel, "We might not make it through this, old chum."

"I suggest you take this time to pray and ask for forgiveness."

"For what," asks Ryan. "Because of my relationship with Tina?"

Nathaniel frowns. "For any and everything."

"Tina included?"

"You, again." Nathaniel's head shakes. "Sure, the law says that man should not lay with man, but if you truly want to be enlightened, think not in terms of either or. More will be judged for how they treat those who fall within the grey area, than those who do."

Detective Ryan scratches his head with a chained hand. "You're gonna have to be a little more direct than that, bough."

"Do you think gender lies in genitals alone, or even in the presence or absence of a y chromosome? You had a boyhood crush on someone who has all the parts of a woman, but from on high she's viewed internally as more male than a lot of men – she even said in her memoir that's how she feels, and her feeling is correct."

"Boyhood crush," says Ryan. "Not Jamie Lee Curtis."

"A secret crush."

"Kim Christy? No." Ryan mumbles, "Can't be her, actually, she—"

"—It's Grace Jones," Nathaniel sighs.

"But Grace is a mother. She gave birth, as a man?"

Nathaniel rolls his eyes. "Didn't I just ask you not to think in terms of either or?"

Detective Ryan looks at the chains on his hands, as if they're quite new compared to the chains around his mind. "Question," says Ryan. "I know you don't have the car you had asked for, but just for kicks – since there's a good chance we won't make it out of this alive – how were you going to help me with my problem, some sorta love potion or spell?"

"You, like most people don't need relics. You only need to stop thinking about yourself. You keep asking for another chance without proving that you deserve it."

"So, basically, you couldn't help me, then."

"All you have to do is openly profess your love for Tina in the presence of all who you would hide it from, that way you *earn* a second chance instead of just asking without merit."

Detective Ryan turns skeptical suddenly, perhaps due to his distaste for the proposed solution. He glares at Nathaniel. "How do you see all this stuff and couldn't see that Jett was coming for us?"

"I can see a person's history. Not their intentions."

Detective Ryan bites down with renewed determination. "Tell me exactly how those glasses work. You say Jett can see everything I do before I do it? How far in advance?"

"Three seconds."

"So, if he's seeing me three seconds from now that means he can't see me in real time, then."

"He sees you real time through the glasses, but foresight displays in his mind."

Detective Ryan sinks into deep thought, then resurfaces with tears and with the words, "It's been a long time since I had more of a reason to live, than I do right now. I ain't dyin' today."

JETT and Charlene are out walking along the empty pool; it's black with sludge and has a large puddle of muck and rainwater sitting in the bottom. Jett can't believe Charlene's lack of appreciation for all he's done for her. "I get it, Charlene," he says, although he doesn't. "Since Lulu didn't get on that plane, you can turn in the video, but where does that get you, if you'll lose Russ because of it?"

Losing Russ means losing Meryl a day after Charlene saw hopes of growing a bond with the child. "If you're still keeping track of Lulu, I want you go get her. The only way I get what I want, is if she's found dead in her apartment with a needle in her arm."

Jett is taken aback by the suggestion. He'd logically backed Charlene into a solution he did not want. With a toss of his head, Jett says, "Come get a look at this." He leads Charlene around the back of the pool enroute to the shed, saying, "I honestly don't see what you desire in a man that messed around behind your back then left you standing at the altar like that."

"At first, it was plum over, but I got to thinking and I just knew something wasn't right about the whole thing. I just found out what it was. When Russ went down to that police station, my deddy was forced to come clean with me about something. The only reason Russ left me standing at the altar is because my father threatened to reject his building permits if he didn't. He was forced into being with Lulu, so how can I fault Russ for the affair?"

Jett smiles coyly. "Honestly, I had a mind to tip the police off about the video myself."

Charlene's mouth falls open. "Why?"

"Hoping Russ would blame you and it would be over for you two, then maybe I'd have a chance."

Charlene dips forward, aghast. "A chance with who?"

"Here we go," Jett looks away, smiling.

"No really," Charlene says. "Consider who I am, and who you are, and tell me how it makes sense."

"Look at me and tell me you don't find me attractive, Charlene."

"Looks can only go but so far. You do not have the pedigree, sir, to even entertain me as a catch."

"Pedigree? Or money. The staff is money."

"I prefer a man who has the qualities and the intellect to get his wealth out of the world, not from some magic wand." Jett grips her waist. "Don't," says Charlene. Jett grins as he pulls her into his body. Charlene feeling, from the force in his hands, how futile any fight would be, she sighs and tries to reason with the man who has two humans chained and ready for slaughter. "Jett, how can you expect me to choose anyone other than the man I love?"

As Charlene sways away to prevent a forced kiss. Jett sways with her, like a charmed cobra. "I'm making things happen for you right now that no man of your rank is capable of. The thing with you is, you wanna look like everybody else in your fancy little circle; dress like them; marry like them. You want a name next to yours that makes folks draw their breath. Well, if your father wanted to get between you and Russ so bad, there ain't no limit to what he would do to put me in Russ's place – to elevate me to be the kind of man you would approve of. I can start up a security firm and I'd bet you he'd hand me a lucrative city contract, or even back me if I were to run for Sherriff. Think, Charlene."

"Well, since you put it that way…" Charlene, for the firsts time looks into Jett's eyes, as if his spiel was convincing. "What do I even know about you, Jett? Handsome guy like you will probably have all kinds of women coming out the woodworks. Been married before? Any children?" Charlene's selling of hope, charms him into releasing her.

"Neither. Never married nor no children," he says proudly, unaware that no children, in Charlene's eyes, is a dealbreaker.

"A'ight big man," Charlene says. "Here's your chance to prove yourself. I want Lulu gone completely – and for it to look like an accident."

"Why would I do that? So, you can be with Russ, instead of me?"

"Me knowing all that Lulu has done to try to destroy me… I've come to realize that as long as Lulu is alive, she'll be coming for me." Charlene extends a hand that caresses Jett's cheek and she says, "I want you to get rid of her. That's what I want. And you will see, that there's nothing – I mean nothing – that turns me on more than a man who can give me what I want." Charlene detects that Jett isn't so convinced so she adds. "I'm not gone lie; this situation has made my feelings for Russ change for the worse. He let my father manipulate him. What would I be doing with a man who so easily folded, when I know there's another man as attractive as yourself who'd kill for me?"

Their eyes lock in. Just as the gravity of attraction begins to draw them inward, Charlene diverts, "You were showing me something in the shed?"

Jett comes out of the trance. "Yeah," he says. He turns, opens it and points to labeled jugs stacked on the shelves. "Know what this is?"

Charlene gives him lazy eyes. "You know I don't."

"Pool cleaner. Looks like they were about to clean this pool right before the renovation was stopped."

"You brought me out here about some pool cleaner?"

"Acid. Potent stuff."

"If it's so strong, why doesn't it eat the plastic jugs they're in?"

Jett, in the shadow of the shed, stuffing one hand in a rubber glove he'd found, explains, "It doesn't react with plastic, but it'll burn metal, it'll liquefy flesh just like that." That, being the snap of his fingers. "This is how the Latin cartels get rid of bodies. Teeth and bone... give it a few hours and it'll turn a body into this foamy, pinkish sludge. They call it pozole after a traditional Mexican stew. Just release it down the drain. No dead body, no murder charge."

Charlene points into the shed, saying, "There ain't near enough in there to fill that pool deep enough to submerge a body, Jett."

"Just because the acid is meant for the pool, don't mean we need to put it in the pool. Bet it'd fill up that jacuzzi over there. Nathaniel, Detective Ryan, and Lulu will live on forever in the federal database of missing persons."

Charlene wags a finger. "Not Lulu. I don't want her to be a missing person, to have Russ searching the face of the earth for her. Needle in the arm, remember?"

"Right. Right." Before Jett stuffs the next hand in a glove, he takes out his phone, explaining, "Texting this drug dealing informant I know, seeing if I can get a lethal amount of dope off of him." Jett continues to scroll through his phone and stops with a frown. "The GPS is telling me Lulu's on the move right now as we speak. Hey, keep an eye on the house, will ya? I'll go nab Lulu right quick."

Chapter 33

The Real Lulu

Staysha hears this gentle, ethereal ringing, like wet delicate fingers teasing over an armonica of wine glasses. If walking through a mirror in fact makes a sound, this would be it, but Staysha can't be sure. She mans the second story window above the front door, phone in hand, waiting to text Cree the moment she spots Lulu snooping out of the house.

Staysha waits, and she waits. And she waits. After a long while, there is still neither sight nor sound of Lulu, so Staysha gathers the rope they used to secure the mirror to the dolly and goes on the move, taser in hand, stealthy in her soft bottom sneakers. She tiptoes down the stairs and edges toward the hallway, the rope draped around her shoulders. Staysha listens. The house is rock quiet. She tiptoes down to the master bedroom. Staysha's heart skips when she sees a pair of high heel shoes placed neatly together in the middle of the floor.

"Stace?"

Staysha freezes. The voice behind her is Lulu's.

Lulu says, "I'm gonna need you to hand over the taser." Her resolve makes her sound as if she's armed.

Staysha looks back, then her body unwinds under her turned face; she's staring down the barrel of a gun.

Lulu's other hand is out for the taser. "Slow," Lulu warns. "You know I love you, Stace. But I will blow your got damn head off." Lulu has the gun she'd picked off of Buck the day she clocked him with the bedpost, the same gun she'd failed to use on Cree, but now her conviction, her coldness, is the result of the lesson learned. "Nice of you to bring your own rope," Lulu says.

Staysha's breathing rises from the cavity of her chest to the restricted pipe of her throat, threatening hyperventilation. "Lulu... Here me out, okay."

"Tuh," Lulu smiles. "Listen to you try to convince me to stay here, when you have no clue what I'd be leaving behind on the other side?"

"Things are going good for you, again," Staysha argues. "You got money coming in from all the streams. You got a new record deal, ten times better than the deal you got before."

"And Russ?"

"Yall had a little break, that's all. But it can be fixed," Staysha nods. "He proposed to you just the other day, no lie."

"Not good enough," shrugs Lulu. "Now, slowly, you walk yourself on out front and stand with your back against a pillar."

Staysha refuses. "You're not about to shoot me, Lulu. This *me*. Your best friend."

"Let me make something clear to you Stace. I can blow your brains out the back of your head and still have my best friend when I cross back over." Lulu, ensuring her aim, adds, "Give me a reason to take the easy route."

Lulu, with a flick of the gun, directs Staysha to lead them to the living room where she stands with her back against a pillar. Lulu takes the rope and walks circles around Staysha and the pillar, lapping the rope around her as many times as the rope has length. With each pass in front of Staysha, Lulu questions her. "Where is Cree?"

"I don't know."

"Don't lie to me," says Lulu.

"Cree's not worried about going back."

Lulu stops at the rear of the pillar to tie the knot, adding, "Meryl is with Russ, right now?"

"Russ's parents."

Lulu digs in Staysha's pocket, takes her cell phone and dials Mrs. April. "Grandma April should have the same number in both worlds." She does. "Hello Miss April," says Lulu. Sorry to wake you so early. I just wanna drop a few things off for Meryl. Oh, it's too early? Okay. I'll just stay put for right now, then. See ya later on, then, Miss April."

Lulu digs in Staysha's other pocket and takes her car keys. "This'll save me the trouble of calling a cab."

Staysha, made brutally honest by way of defeat, says, "Whatever it is you think you're chasing, Lulu, you can't fix it on the outside; you have to fix it inside of you."

Casually, Lulu says, "Oh really?"

"Cree has done it. Cree has made more out of your life, in days, than you have in years."

Lulu bites her bottom lip to calm the urge to slap her best friend. "How can you say that, when that hoe ain't walked about a mile in my shoes and already fixin' to kill herself?"

Staysha turns sullen, as if Lulu's point is proven. Sharing the truth that Cree was only pretending to be suicidal, might prompt Lulu to double back through the mirror.

"So, you're not gonna tell me where Cree is?"

Staysha concocts a story. "Hospice called. Beth is slipping away; Cree left to go be with her."

Lulu gets teary-eyed. "How is it that momma's suddenly dying?"

"It was sudden for everyone except Beth; she kept it secret."

Lulu wipes her tears. Her head shakes to rattle out any remorse that might hinder her from doing what she must do. She disappears down the hallway barefoot and returns in heels. She stops to kiss Staysha's forehead and say, "I won't be long."

On the way out, Lulu notices that the ring is now dead. The twin stones are now both dim like black ice, and no longer any good to her. She takes the ring off and let it hit the floor.

By the time Staysha can hear Lulu drive off with her car, she's wiggled her arms free, and begins tugging the rope, inching the knot around the stone pillar to the front where she unties it, freeing herself. Without a phone to warn Cree, nor a car to reach her in time, she doesn't see the need to hurry. On her way out, Staysha finds the ring and studies it; the stones are black like tiny blown light bulbs. Staysha slips the ring on her finger and the stones begin to sparkle. It must've never entered Lulu's mind that the stones re-energizes and the count resets, when placed upon a new hand.

CREE pulls up to the storage facility and shifts the car in park, frowning. She's getting another one of those feelings that something isn't right. This time, Cree takes a moment – hands on the steering wheel, head bowed – to sit with this feeling and attempt to decipher it. Cree remembers getting her signals switched, thinking the feeling was about Detective Ryan and Nathaniel trying to reach her, when it was really about Meryl being taken from Beth's care. Cree doesn't want to be wrong again with so much at stake, so Cree sits still in the driver's seat and meditates.

To Cree's surprise, her intuition is getting stronger, from urges to her vision of Ryan and Nathaniel being trapped in a basement, now it's even more than a vision; she's out of body. The same young, sepia sun that shines warm on Cree's face as she sits in the car meditating, also shines through the windows of the mansion on Emerald Court. She's floating through the rooms, from the third floor to the second floor, stopping to hover above the pillows and blankets that she and Staysha left there; there's no Staysha. Cree floats on through the mansion, down the stairs, and down the hallway into the living room where she sees rope coiled at the foot of a pillar.

Cree's eyes pop open. Lulu has come through, which means Cree can finally return home. She doesn't question it; she trusts her intuition.

The storage room portal is but a hundred feet away, and Cree knows that when she places a hand to that mirror, she will enter it.

Suddenly, Cree knows, also, that the car closing in, with its blinker signaling to turn into the storage facility, is none other than Jett Johnson hunting her down.

Hurriedly, Cree jumps out of the car and runs. Jett hops out, giving chase, yelling, "I just wanna talk!"

Cree pedals her feet as fast as she can, determined to make it to the rear of the building to the portal. Having no time to stop and enter her code in the gate, she attempts to scale it. Cree leaps and grasps the cross bar, her feet slipping against the wrought iron bars. Jett catches up, slamming into Cree, who screams from the impact of her ribs and sternum against the iron bars. From behind, Jett squeezes her waist and bears his weight down. Cree's grip starts to give.

Destiny lay right around the corner and Cree is smashed against a gate with a whole man hanging off of her. Cree's fingers slip. Cree screams as she falls back on top of Jett, who covers her mouth with a chloroform rag, and clamps his legs around Cree's to keep her from thrashing loose. Slowly, the struggle leaves her, the tears in the wells of her eyes, reflecting a picturesque dawn sky.

The morning is, by now, teeming with commuters but not on this littered one-way street that's just wider than an alley. No one sees the take down. Jett carries Cree to his car as if he's assisting someone who'd been out at a nightclub, drinking till morning.

Chapter 34

Nisha and Russ

Russ can't believe his eyes as he watches the video. At the sound of each gunshot, he blinks painfully. He lowers the phone and sighs. "Dammit, man I hate that ole Hook went out like that."

Nisha, holding back tears, says, "How do you think I feel?"

"So, what are you trying to do with this?"

Nisha says, "How about, for starters, let's gone and get some charges brought up on this Officer Johnson."

"Tragic as it is," says Russ. "They let Jett Johnson go because they say these young men waited in ambush; this video only proves it."

"There was no attempt to escape or deescalate, he just started shooting, plus there was a phone call from Charlene, warning them that Johnson was coming to kill them. That makes Jett Johnson the aggressor. Hook and his boys were playing defense."

Russ hands Nisha her phone back. "Turn in the video and report Charlene's call, then. Why include me?"

"Because you know the mayor. The mayor can pressure the sheriff's department to actually *do* something about this. Also, before I turn in this video, I want a lawyer to make a notarized copy, so if police try to doctor the footage, in any way, we can expose them."

Russ's head shakes. "I just wanna be done with *all* of it."

Nisha stares him down. "And I thought you were an ally."

"I am, but...," Russ stammers.

"No buts," Nisha says, as she gets in Russ's face, a finger pistol pointing at his dome. "What you don't understand, Russ, is that you are *going* to do this. I thought, since you and Hook go way back, that you would come on board voluntarily, but don't try me, Russ," Nisha warns. "I know too much. And I am not afraid of you!"

Nisha is on the brink of tears and Russ can't stand to see it, so he gives in. "Ok. Okay, Nisha. I'll do what I can. Promise." Russ hugs her, even. Nisha cries tears of relief on his chest. Russ steps back and appraises her. "Look at you," Russ says. "Out here fighting for your man... for justice... But don't be so resilient that you forget to grieve."

A bashful Nisha smiles through her tears, but then gathers herself. "There's one more thing. There's still some money stashed at that house, but I can't seem to find the copy of the key you gave Hook. Do you happen to have another key?"

"Only one," Russ says. "I'm not about to hand over the last copy, so I guess we have to go together," Russ says.

"When," asks Nisha.

Russ shrugs. "Well, you already here. Let's get it over with." Russ starts heading for the front door while still fastening his cuff links.

"Okay," Nisha says with a hard blink and look-around, as if things were moving too fast. "Russ? Slow up for a second, umm... Is Lulu up? I wanna be respectful. I don't want your fiancé thinking..." Nisha's hands roll around each other signaling what she doesn't want to say.

"Forget Lulu," replies Russ. "Me and Lulu done. For good."

Nisha's eyes stretch. Quietly wowed, she walks through the front door held open by Russ; she tiptoes down the front steps as Russ gentlemanly, offers his hand as her guiderail.

IT's the same house, different world. The Rutledge doorbell chimes like a church steeple. The moment Mrs. April Rutledge answers, it's obvious that she isn't the doting mother-in-law from the world Lulu just left. This April couldn't imagine ever calling Lulu the daughter she never had, as the other April refers to Cree.

Although Lulu is dressed in a regal beige, long sleeve, sheath dress, befitting the duchess of the Rutledge empire, this world's April sees nothing more than an exquisitely dressed trash can. April goads, "Back so soon from New York? Did something happen?"

"Everything happened how it was supposed to happen," says Lulu.

April finds the comment quite deplorable. "You're saying, none of this should have been prevented? You think it's our privilege to take on your responsibility?"

"You asked about New York – not Meryl. Don't be so eager to take a stab at me, that you venture off topic to do it; you only make yourself look simple." Lulu begins thinking after the comment and begins to regret it, and April is obliged to highlight why.

"Talk about simple," April says. "You don't have the self-control to *not* insult the one person who can deny you the very thing you came for?"

Just then Meryl runs up from behind, forcing her way between April and the doorframe and runs into her mother's embrace – with her smiling, almond face and curly puffs; she's nearly as tall as Lulu.

Lulu and Meryl embrace, both in tears. April backs off, disappearing out of the doorway and into the shadow of the home.

Meryl grips her mother's shoulders to say, "Momma, you look nice. Grandma says she's gone teach me the piano!"

"Wow. That's good, hon. And where's grandpa?"

"Golfing, I think. He left in plaid pants."

Lulu leans to make sure Miss April is out of range. "Listen to me." Lulu gathers Meryl's hands into hers and whispers, "I'm gonna bust you out of here, okay? Me and you are going to be together, mother and daughter and we won't have to worry anymore about outside people getting between us…" Lulu stops because she sees her daughter's head shaking no. Lulu asks, "What's wrong?"

"You want us to run like fugitives, ma? We'll end up in even more trouble. We gotta use our brain, *outsmart* the system, not fight it."

"Or…" Lulu raises a finger between them. "We can change systems altogether."

Meryl's brow wrinkles. "What?"

Lulu, fibbing on the fly, says, "I found a loophole." More like a wormhole. "If we beat the deadline, their rules won't apply to us."

"What're you talking about," asks Meryl.

"What is most important, right now, is that we get a head-start. Nobody can know, right away, that you're gone. First, you go back in there and act as if everything is normal. The first chance you get, go to your room, lock the door, hop out of the window and then cut across the field."

Meryl nods yes.

"Then you just take the trail by the pond and keep going. You'll see me waiting in the clearing."

Meryl nods again.

"Now go on in there. Do as I say. Trust me."

Meryl hugs her mother again and then she returns inside, alone, rubbing her sweaty palms on the front of her dress; doing her best to pretend like everything is normal.

Chapter 35

The Secret To Flying

Per Jett, injecting Lulu with all the heroine at once, would look like murder. To make the overdose look realistic and unintentional, he must inject Lulu in small doses, periodically, throughout the day, up until the wee hours of night when he can return Lulu to her apartment unseen. "…Then I sit and watch, and wait," Jett says, as he kneels in front of Cree, who is tied to a chair, pleading for mercy. Heartlessly, Charlene observes as Jett plucks Lulu's forearm to coax a vein. "Her heart rate and breathing will then begin to fade," Jett explains. "The brain, starved of oxygen will shoot one last surge through the nervous system to try to kickstart the heart. She'll tremble and quake a little bit, and then she'll slip away while staring open-eyed at her apartment ceiling."

Cree fights her ankle and wrists ties. Cree's eyes swell cattle wild as the needle sinks into her, filling her with narcotic. Her thrashing diminishes to tremors; her screams weaken to a feeble mewing. Her pupils dilate like ink drops in water, expanding, along with the expanding hallucination that changes the very color of her surroundings.

Behind those bloodshot eyes, Cree is thrashing in darkness, in what feels like a cocoon woven of fine black hair. Her squirming combs her downward until she flakes through the bottom, and the upwind of freefall helps Cree realize that she has wings growing out of her back, which she uses to beat upward through sheets of wind. Suddenly, darkness opens up like the release of cupped hands and Cree finds herself fluttering about in a sweetgrass field that she recognizes from her childhood. The euphoria of the heroine high is so pure, Cree would shun heaven to remain.

Beth waits expectantly, in the high grass, in her favorite floral print dress. Cree is unable to speak nor is Beth, but her mother exudes such peace and serenity, that she's obviously left her body in its hospice bed. A white bright light with a halo of prism colors descends, and Cree watches her mother walk into that light, going on to glory. Cree is lucky enough to have met Beth in this waystation between the here and yonder, while Cree is also *un*lucky enough that her own physical body is shackled in a basement, her head slumped, her jaw misaligned, out of which a web of drool strings clear to her lap.

Charlene looks at Cree in disgust. "Damn junkie," Charlene says. She and Jett return to the backyard, where she sits in a lawn chair, sunbathing with her blouse open. Jett, in elbow-length rubber gloves, treks between the shed and the deck, filling the jacuzzi with acid.

OUT FRONT, Russ notices Charlene's car parked in the driveway, so he orders Nisha to sit tight while he goes in. Russ remembers Charlene saying she worked with Hook to remove evidence from this house, so Charlene being here isn't such an odd thing, but it's a thing Russ feels he should sort out before letting Nisha come in. Russ walks through the house, calling out Charlene's name. "Charlene? Charlene. I know you're in here."

Russ goes down the basement steps. He sees Detective Ryan with his chained hand in front of his face, holding a finger to his lips.

Russ rubs his eyes and looks again. "What the…" He shuffles down the steps. He hurries to the square in the back access door where soft light enters the dark basement. His eyes follow the outside steps up to ground level where the angle allows a view that's just a slice above the blades of grass, where he can see Jett, small in the distance, coming out of the shed with jugs in his gloved hands.

Russ hurries off the door to ask the men if they knew the whereabouts of the keys to their handcuffs, but his eyes land on Cree who is slumped, sleepy-eyed and breathing heavily; the sight caves him in. Russ drops to his knees. "Lord no. Lulu." He finds ties on her hands and feet, an incoherent Cree, apparently inches from death.

"She's alright," assures, Ryan. "They drugged her is all."

Russ repeatedly pats Cree's cheek, "C'mon, Lulu. Wake up, Lu."

"Go," urges Detective Ryan, "Get the hell outta here! And call the police, while you're at it."

He pats Cree's face again. "Lulu." Russ seems on the verge of a meltdown, but first he looks back to clarify one thing. "So, where're they keeping Charlene?"

"They *is* Charlene," says Nathaniel.

Russ seizes up in disbelief. With no change in expression, Russ hops to his feet and scrambles up the steps, running to the kitchen where he comes to a sliding stop at the knife rack.

Detective Ryan spots Russ coming back down the steps just seconds after going up. "What are you *doing*," berates Ryan, through grit teeth. "If Jett catches you here, we're *all* dead."

Russ kneels in front of Cree with the kitchen knife in hand. "I'm not leaving without Lulu."

"Russ," Cree whines. "Charlene made me say mean things to you."

"I know babe," Russ coddles, while he cuts away her ties.

Detective Ryan has his own plan. To be ready for the hell that would break loose if Jett were to return and find Russ, Detective Ryan turns to face the wall, crossing his chains. Nathaniel looks over, frowning in confusion, but what Ryan is attempting becomes clear the moment he plants a foot on the wall, high enough for his chained hand to reach, which causes the hem of his pant leg to hike up and reveal a pistol in an ankle holster, which he pulls out. To Nathaniel's wide eyes, Detective Ryan says, "I sure hope you're right about them three seconds."

After cutting Cree's last tie, Russ tells her, "Stay right here." Cree doesn't listen. She gets up on Bambi legs and staggers after Russ as he hurries to the backdoor for another look. He places cupped hands on the glass to see if Jett's coming and freezes in fright. "He's here!" Russ backpedals as if there's not even time to turn and run.

An intoxicated Cree sees the door fly open and a shaft of sunlight burst through; she takes it for the afterlife that she'd just seen Beth walk into. Cree runs to Russ, in an attempt to save him, yelling "Don't go into the light!"

A startled Jett, on reflex, is pulling his gun, adrenaline slowing time; he observes Russ sprawling back, Cree sliding in front of Russ, and in the path of Jett's aim.

Cree's face is splashed with blood, which confuses Jett, because he did not pull the trigger, and there was no bang. Jett hears, from his right, Detective Ryan counting down: three... two...

The blood exists in a future Jett will never see with his own eyes, because the blood is his own. His life comes to an abrupt end when Ryan's three-count expires and his gun bangs. As Jett had witnessed in foresight, an aerosol of Jett's blood sprays Cree's face.

Cree screams well beyond the range of any note she's ever sang.

At the sound of the gunshot and the scream, Charlene runs across the yard and hurries down the steps, stopping in the doorway, panting, seeing Russ and Cree embraced and crying, and Jett face down in a pool of his own blood. "Thank God,"

Charlene yells. "Ya got the bastard. Jett was trying to kill me." No one buys this narrative. Charlene runs over to Detective Ryan and Nathaniel, pleading with them. "You heard me tell Jett I didn't want any part of this, remember!"

Nathaniel says, "You helped him tie up Lulu."

Detective Ryan cosigns, "You should've called the police."

Charlene stamps. "He took my phone. I *had* to make him think I was going along or I would've been in chains right alongside you two. You gotta believe me!"

"Russ," calls Ryan. "Check his pockets for the keys, will ya."

Russ, who comforts Cree while mopping her bloody face with his shirt, then jumps into action. He swipes the gun off the floor, fishes the keys out of Jett's pockets and runs over to Detective Ryan and Nathaniel. Russ struggles to unlock the cuffs, his hands trembling like a leaf.

With the men distracted, Charlene turns her attention to Cree, saying, "Lulu, you'd better side with me on this. You know what I have on you."

Cree, considerably sobered by the gunshot and the commotion, seems somewhat coherent.

"Come with me," urges Charlene. "You don't need to see this." Charlene helps Cree step over Jett's dead body and guides her outside.

Charlene ushers Cree outside to the deck to negotiate near the acid filled, built-in jacuzzi. "We're gonna get off Scot free, you and me, if we just stick together ok?"

Cree, in and out of her high, has a moment of clarity where she says, "You smell that?" It's the eggy smell of the acid-filled jacuzzi right next to them.

"Stay with me Lulu. Focus." Charlene grasps Cree's shoulders as if to petition for her cooperation, but is really using her grasp to reposition Cree's back to the jacuzzi of acid.

Russ peaks out of the back door and yells for Cree.

Cree takes her eyes off Charlene to look at Russ; Charlene takes advantage and shoves Cree. Cree, tips at her heels, sure to fall back into the jacuzzi. She's surprised when her fall stops with her back bent over the pool. On reflex, she'd snagged a fistful of Charlene's blouse. Charlene has to lean back with all her weight to teeter Cree upright or be pulled in behind her. Charlene pounds at Cree's hand. The hand slips, but Cree's other hand snatches the neck loop of Charlene's blouse.

Cree struggles up and gets her feet under her. Charlene tries to drive her back again, but Cree braces, and they tussle, Cree slowly losing ground, her back foot sliding to a stop where the steps lead down into the jacuzzi. Charlene offers a eulogy through grit teeth. "Your little fairy tale ends right here, you ole wench!" Charlene thrusts with all her might.

Cree pivots, letting Charlene's own force carry her into the hot tub while Cree, herself, isn't out of the clear, as she leans forward like ski jumper, smelling the singe of Charlene's hair and flesh and seeing the water clouding red, Cree realizes the boiling isn't from the jets. Cree desperately winds her arms backwards in circles to reel herself upright. Charlene, emerges from the water, smoking and with flesh running off of her like water, the sockets of her eyeballs already cooked away, her lips shed; flesh and skeleton exposed, and then she collapses again, lifeless in the soup, melting.

Russ comes up from behind and lays an arm over Cree's shoulder; the other hand covering his nose for the stench. "Damn," Russ says, while watching Charlene boil. "Police are on the way."

They go to the front lawn where Detective Ryan, Nathaniel, and Nisha congregate, Cree never letting go of Russ, as she explains how Charlene leveraged the video to force her to end their engagement. It is simply understood that they are back together, their engagement still on.

Nathaniel brings the staff to Russ, asking to stash it in his trunk to avoid it being taken into evidence.

Russ walks Nathaniel over to his car and places it in his trunk. With the trunk still open, Russ asks, "Why is this so important to you? What are you doing with the money?"

"Building a church, a church that will be a place of protection a long time from now, in the last days," Nathaniel answers.

Russ slams the trunk and pivots to go tend to Cree, but Nathaniel grabs his arm.

"Russ… I know what you're trying to do with the community, and I commend you, but I'd like to offer you some advice, if I may?"

Russ turns square with him.

"Like most people, you already know what you have to do, but you're trying everything but that, because it's difficult."

Russ folds his arms, skeptical. "What's this one thing, then?"

"You already know, Mr. Rutledge. Let me hear it from you."

Russ thinks hard and sighs. "I have to disassociate the company from my father," Russ says. "But that's my dad and my grandfather's legacy."

Nathaniel smirks. "The needs of many outweigh the desires of a few." Nathaniel pats Russ's shoulder and says, "And another thing: logic and numbers might work with the large companies you often negotiate with, but for everyday people you must sell the dream. Make this new development out to be some kind of promised land – and it won't hurt to name streets after elders and leaders of the community. Man loves seeing their names on things."

Russ takes the advice with earnest nods. "One question. Considering what you are and where you're from, that should mean that your advice is guarantee, right?"

Nathaniel replies, "I'm not supposed to say it, but the answer is yes. Just as sure as if Detective Ryan takes my advice he *will* be reunited with the woman he loves, the same with you and the community. You'll take a community that's about to be pounded back into poverty, to a community that will begin to build generational wealth, although, in the eyes of history, you won't get much credit for it."

Russ shakes Nathaniel's hand and thanks him sincerely.

Sirens are coming in the distance. Nathaniel joins Detective Ryan and Nisha, who is satisfied that justice, this time, doesn't need the involvement of courts. Jett, who lived by the gun, has died by the gun, his end delivered with biblical justice.

Russ finds Cree, oddly, standing with her eyes closed, and remembers that she's been drugged. "You ok Lulu? Lulu?"

Cree is not okay, and it's no heroine stupor; she's having a vision. She sees Lulu and Meryl in the car together closing in on the Emerald court mansion and she knows exactly what Lulu is doing. She never came to protect her Meryl; she came to take her.

Cree even sees into the other world, where her own Meryl stands at the vanity mirror, as directed by the note in her hand, oblivious that Lulu is luring her into a trap.

Cree's eyes pop open. "Meryl," she says. "Meryl's in trouble!"

"Calm down, Lulu," says Russ. "She's with mom and pops."

"No, she's not. I need your car – no!" Cree's head shakes. "There's not enough time!"

Nathaniel hurries to her. "Cree! You *do* have time! Try flying."

Cree, buckling under the stress, yells, "What the hell are you talking about?"

Nathaniel wrangles Cree's flailing hands and says, "Close your eyes, take a deep breath, and envision yourself floating away."

Cree, desperate for anything, tries it. She meditates for a spell, but feels nothing. She opens her eyes to glare at Nathaniel and curse him, but there's no Nathaniel; she's eye-level with treetops, hearing the shushing sound of breeze combing back as far as the eye can see. Russ, Detective Ryan and the others below are the size of toy action figures.

Cree extends her hands out front; her body teeters and levels parallel with the earth's surface. With a mere a thought, Cree bolts; the wind, in her wake, cards over the treetops. She is a missile shot over the suburbs; her speed fueled by her sense of urgency. The wind hardens and breaks over her face, spreading tears outward and into her pinned ears. A look down shows the city rushing under her like rapids.

Still, she sees, in her mind's eye, Lulu and Meryl now entering the mansion. Cree becomes more desperate to reach them, more furious. Thunder booms, suddenly, as if Cree's inner turmoil is the source of weather. The sky darkens. Black clouds and a wall of torrential rain gives chase, threatening to consume Cree.

Lulu and Meryl are in the master bedroom, approaching the mirror. Her own Meryl coming into view on the other side as Cree descends on the home, shattering through the bedroom window and tackling Lulu, both knocked silly by the impact; Meryl unconscious in the corner. The torrential rain and darkness envelops the mansion. The gun has slidden to a far corner of the room. If either attempts to go for it, they surrender the mirror.

Lulu gets to her feet first and tries heading for the mirror, but Cree brings her down by the ankle and mounts her back with a chokehold. Lulu bucks. The force loosens Cree's chokehold. Lulu forces two hands up through Cree's and begins prying her hands apart from around her neck, they grunt and bare teeth from the exertion. Lulu throws her head back, butting Cree in the face. Cree stumbles; a line of blood drips from her nostril. Lulu lunges for the mirror again but Cree catches her. They lock arms, wrestling for leverage, heaving and throwing one another off balance. They turn and turn, lighting flashing on determined twin faces. Their feet trip up and the two go hurling apart, Cree stopping with her back to the mirror and Lulu against the far wall – too far away from the mirror or the gun to stop Cree from entering. "It is over," an out of breath Cree says. "Have a nice life." Cree turns to go through the mirror.

Lulu yells, "I'm pregnant!"

Cree looks back, an eyebrow raised. "Congratulations."

"*Wait*," Lulu screams. "Think about what you're fighting for. Here, you'll have everything you ever wanted, your singing career *and* Russ."

Cree allows the exchange, knowing there's too much distance for Lulu to stop her from entering the mirror. Cree replies, "Since you think it's so great here, Lulu, why don't I just go on through, and leave you to it? And by the way, Charlene's dead. She won't be in the way."

Lulu yells, "You used me to fix your life! Tron would've ended your marriage if it wasn't for me." Lulu pats her chest. "Let me keep what I earned – the marriage *I* brought back to life, and the promise of Russ and me bringing another child into this world." Lulu gathers her hands. "Good for you, Cree, that you have, in so little time, jumpstarted my music career and gotten a commitment of marriage from Russ." Lulu extends a stiff arm. "You keep what *you* earned."

"Your world is not home to me, Lulu, nor will it ever be," Cree sighs. "I don't want a life where everyone looks at me and expects... you: an impulsive, hyper-vigilant, petty, diva. On the other side of this mirror is the life and the reputation that *I* built, brick by brick, and a marriage that I–"

Lulu yells, "Don't hand me that! You don't even believe yourself! You want to go through that mirror because you're more at-home in a life of lies. Russ doesn't even have a clue that he's fatherless!" Lulu steps forward. Cree steps back, preparing to flee. Lulu adds, "But that lie isn't only for Russ. That lie is also for all them *white* folks you rub elbows with, because God forbid, they find out that your little nuclear family is illegitimate and they label you as just another typical nigger!"

Expressionless, Cree shakes her head. "Have a good day, Lulu."

"Oh, that *bothers* you?" Lulu flips her hair and chuckles. "*Huh?* It would bother you, if everybody knew that you were a baby-momma?"

Cree spats, "*You're* a baby-momma!"

"Struck a nerve, didn't I?" Lulu then rears back laughing, flashes of lightning illuminating her mirth. Lulu knows she has lost, but in an attempt to gain at least a small win, she tries to infuriate Cree with a two-step and a taunting song, to the rhythm of the Dr. Pepper tune, "I's a baby-momma, you's a baby-momma, we's a baby-momma..." Lulu looks over at Meryl who reappears out of nowhere, as if for the sole purpose of finishing the song in chorus with Lulu. "Wouldn't you like to be a baby-momma too!" Meryl seems to love the tune as they run it back with a butterfly dance, knees dipping inward in sync with the roll of hips and winged elbows.

As Cree studies the minstrel show, she rages like a furnace. Her rage is so overwhelming, it consumes all logic and shifts her target from the mirror, to Lulu. Cree, charges, squandering her proximity to the mirror. They collide with the clap of thunder, Cree wild-eyed and screaming as she drives Lulu backpedaling clear across the room, but toward the window. They try to stop, but it's too late. Momentum carries them crashing through the window, plummeting to the earth with sheets of glass and rain.

Chapter 36

The Truth Shall Set You Free

It's quiet. There is no more booming thunder. No more dumping of rain. Cree is dry. Her eyes open and there is a bright white light. Oddly, the light is in the shape of a rectangle. There are voices. Ceiling panels blur into vision. She hears beeping sounds. Bedsheets. It's a hospital! Cree tries to sit up. "No, no," she says, feebly. A nurse takes her hand and asks her to lie still. "Everything is ok," the nurse reassures. "You were in a coma."

"But Meryl…" Cree looks around. "Where's Lulu?" She tries to get up but only has the strength to lift her head.

The doctor hurries in and comes to her bedside; there's some sort of tool in her hand. "You're at MUSC hospital, Intensive Care Unit. I am Dr. Omi." She has short hair and an accent, Nigerian, perhaps, how the consonants tap dance to singsong vowels.

Cree calms down, realizing it's too late to undo whatever has been done and that the quickest route out of this hospital is cooperation. Cree says, "I guess I'm lucky to survive a fall like that, huh?"

"Fall?" The doctor blinks rapidly. "Car accident. But you're fine." She takes the device from down by her side and presents it to Cree; it's a mirror. "See," says Dr. Omi. "You're still as pretty as ever, Mrs. Rutledge."

Cree, studying her reflection, notices that there's no trace of the healed cut on her forehead, but then she catches the salutation. "You said, Missus... Rutledge?" How can she be married to Russ, Cree wonders, when she never returned to the mirror. She thinks back to where her reality must've bled into fantasy. "I guess I was never really flying – must've been the heroine."

Dr. Omi seems quite interested, "You've been experiencing lucid dreams? That is quite rare." She looks as if she wants to dart for her clipboard, but decides not to squander their rather personable rapport. Dr. Omi sits sidesaddle on the edge of the bed and says, "Starting from the very beginning, can you remember when things started getting odd?"

"That's just the thing. I was driving by and saw another version of myself walking along the side of the road. This was *before* the car accident, so don't try to tell me the accident caused–"

"–How long before the accident?"

"Just before. Just before running off the road."

Dr. Omi takes a deep breath and says, "Let me explain something to you Mrs. Rutledge. It is medically impossible to remember anything before the accident up to fifteen minutes." Dr. Omi claps the heels of her hands together. "The *instant* of blunt force trauma, the brain switches priorities. It focuses on recovery, and everything held in the short-term memory bank gets dumped before ever being recorded into long-term memory. Your mind, Mrs. Rutledge, has fabricated its own backstory leading up to the accident."

Cree stares into space. "Fifteen minutes? I was... I was at Tron's house and..." Cree covers her mouth. "Maybe I never even kissed him."

A delighted Russ walks in on the tail end, saying, "Kissed who?"

Dr. Omi spins around, smiling as if hiding something behind her back. "She was talking about you, of course."

CREE'S accident is their clean slate and their marriage has become a safe space to be open, to confess, and to serve – how Russ leaps to assist Cree with the slightest thing. Lying for so long has her coordination off.

Cree regains her independence just in time for Tia's funeral, where Cree fills tissue after tissue with her tears, in that small, hot church, as the sweat-dabbing Baptist preacher growls, in petition, about being in good standing with God and with each other, about how precious life is, and to be good stewards of what little time we have here.

As if Russ couldn't possibly feel more fortunate for a second chance with Cree, Tia's open casket gives him a stark visual of their near fate, which buckles him. Men come to Russ's aid and shoulder him along, as if *he* is the surviving spouse.

Russ wouldn't leave the church grounds without personally offering his condolences. Russ and Cree wait at the outskirts of kin gathered around Tron and his children.

Cree attempts an escape by pretending to see someone she knows, but Russ squeezes Cree tight to his body, his emotional breakdown too fresh to let Cree leave his side. So, Cree is right there as Russ has a long talk with his grieving employee, Antron, who doesn't show any signs that anything inappropriate happened with Cree. Even after parting ways with Tron there's no distant glances gleaning inside knowledge of anything. Hand in hand with her husband, Cree leaves the funeral, confident that the kiss with Tron was nothing more than a part of the backstory that, Dr. Omi insists, was fashioned by her mind.

Cree still can't get over the dream itself. Often she finds herself staring in the mirror waiting for something to happen, maybe for Lulu to appear in the reflection. Cree's elaborate dream is the topic of most of she and Russ's discussions.

The first time they make love, it's bedtime, Russ listening intently as Cree narrates the adventures of her dream, like an ongoing miniseries, but then Cree frowns as a realization hits.

"That detective… Detective Ryan… I remember meeting him in real life a while back, come to think of it. This was before we met. I was at Staysha's house when he came asking questions about Jermaine. I noticed that he couldn't keep his eyes off of our trans friend Drea. Maybe nothing is ever really forgotten; the mind captures more than what we're aware of."

"And who is Jermaine," inquires Russ.

Cree looks at him with rounded eyes. "You've heard me talk about Jermaine. Staysha's first love."

"Never met him," says Russ. "I think he was already in prison by the time we met."

"Anyway, in the other world, she's shacking up with Jermaine – not married to Sean. I think the fact that you and I divorced after just two years turned her against marrying a man of ambition."

Russ's pillowed head turns to face Cree, offering a half smile. "You talk as if that other world is really out there."

"I can't make myself believe that it's not. It wasn't like a dream. My reality wasn't flighty, it was solid. I felt the days and hours expire off the clock just like it does here."

Russ answers, "It can't be all that real if I let our marriage come to an end because of your career in music. There's no way I'd fold that easily, or…? Is there something else you're not telling me?"

Cree suspects that Meryl's paternity – the part she left out – lay in the blindside of Russ's question. Since waking from the coma, Cree has vowed to tell Russ, when the time is right. Cree looks into her husband's eyes. "I'll tell you what was sadly unrealistic about the other world: how much better we utilized our time together in bed," she says. The mischief in her eyes is a dead giveaway.

The guilt of that secret is never more at the surface than now, as they kiss and stir in the covers. With each caress and the warm compress of bodies, Cree's willingness to confess is pressed deeper beneath the surface, and with each intense entry, Cree's truth is further internalized. Tears drain from the corners of her eyes.

Russ stops, on the support of his locked arms, frowning. "Babe. Are you ok," he whispers.

Cree whimpers, "I was afraid that you had stopped loving me."

"Never," Russ whispers. He lowers to kiss her, which, in effect, feeds him deeper into her body; they sigh. "Never," whispers Russ. "I will never stop loving you. You hear me?" Russ is as reassuring as he is tender. Cree isn't sure that his promise would hold up beyond her confession. There would be no righter time to confess than this, but Cree chokes up. A wheezy, "I love you too," is all.

Cree is set to return to the helm of Icarus in a few weeks, so she has time on her hands, although no time or place seems fitting to tell Russ the truth about Meryl. Besides, their relationship now flourishes; telling him would be like setting a brush fire in heaven. They've become quite flirtatious. Russ comes home now looking for her, looking to meet her at the stove and slip his hands around her waist. Cree would swing her hair to the side, exposing her neck for him to kiss. They're back to playing board games with Meryl and it seems as if family outings on Saturday afternoons is back on. No one is more pleased than Meryl, that the clouds of a bad marriage has cleared away, and her parents are now affectionate; her father is now back to doting on both his girls.

Cree cringes to think of what could happen to their family by exposing the truth, as she prepares the roasted chicken and root vegetable dinner that she plans to tell Russ over.

Russ comes home late from the office. He's on the phone having a heated conversation with Mayor Ted Childress as the candles on the dinner table burn. Cree had dropped Meryl off at her grandparents.

Russ tries to clear his head as he arrives at the table, apologizing for his mood. Cree asks, "Is everything okay?"

"Ole Ted," Russ says, as he slings his tie back over his shoulder. "We paid off Tron's mortgage, and this sumbitch turn around and renege on our deal."

Cree reaches across the table and pours his wine, saying, "Renege is a strong word isn't it? I remember Ted saying only that he'd would *see* what he could do."

Russ cuts his eye and says, "Dinner looks great, by the way. How was your day?"

"I didn't mean to upset you," says Cree.

"I'm not upset," says Russ. "Let's talk about something else."

Cree gathers that Russ's current mood doesn't lend itself to telling him that his daughter isn't his daughter, so they talk about other things. Cree sips her wine and says, "You were trying to do the same thing in the other world."

"In your dream?"

"There was some undeveloped land near the Charleston-Berkley County line near Hanahan."

Russ frowns. "That's actually true. I've looked at it before. I'm not the only developer who has."

"Really?" Cree is stunned. It reinforces her belief that the dream was more than a dream. "There's no way I could possibly know that. That dream was a lot more than make-believe."

Russ offers, "Ya think, maybe you heard me mention it before and it ended up in your dream somehow? But still, though, the problem with that area is the railroad tracks right there; property value suffers—"

"—But if property value suffers, property *taxes* will stay low, even though it falls, technically, within a good school district…" Cree second guesses. "Well, at least that's what *bachelor* Russ was saying."

Russ rolls his eyes, playfully jealousy. "There we go with this Bachelor Russ mess again," but then husband Russ pauses, contemplating the option. Russ scoots his chair back to get up, but stops for permission. "Do you mind?"

Cree joins him in walking out on dinner, following Russ to his study, where Cree stands behind his chair, massaging Russ's shoulders as he researches on the laptop. Cree begins filling him in on the rest of the plan; the tax write-off for low-cost construction, contingent upon the sales proceeds being transferred into trusts.

Russ adds, "That way they have a built-in mechanism for generational wealth." Russ swivels in his chair, eyeing Cree. "That's genius," says Russ.

"Well, maybe Bachelor Russ had that one stroke of genius, but he's really no comparison to you, my love."

Russ squints. "But Bachelor Russ doesn't exist. This is out of your mind – it's *your* genius. Sounds a lot like a self-sustaining trust to subsidize teacher pay doesn't it?" Russ marvels at his wife. "It's your idea, only applied to the dilemma in Phillips."

Cree tries not to seem too pleased with herself. "But none of it can happen if the mayor doesn't sign off on the building permits."

"Oh, he better," says Russ. "After that stuff he just pulled?" In short time, Russ verifies that the location checks out. With a slow shaking head, Russ says, "There's only one thing I worry about, though. It seems as if any plan you put before the community they don't want to act on it. It's as if they prefer letting imminent domain hit and be forced to sell their property at half the value – just to say they never willingly sold out."

Cree says, "But that's where Nathaniel's advice comes in."

"The angel," Russ says, with a ridiculous look, as if make-believe has now gone too far.

"He wasn't quite an angel, by the way. He said to let the elders and leaders know that you'll name all the streets after them. Nathaniel felt like you spent most of your time appealing to other businessmen like yourself, with numbers and logic, but to appeal to regular folk, you have to sell the dream. Make them believe they're moving to some sort of promised land. What you're selling, is community, self-determination, and the audacity of hope."

Russ half-turns. "Just like you did in your ribbon cutting speech – selling the audacity of subsidizing teacher pay."

Russ gets on the phone again, calling his surveyors, assessors, and his architects, offering them unlimited overtime to design the subdivision and make ready the sketches and miniature replica as soon as possible. Russ paces through the home from room to room, as happy as a clam, while setting plans in motion.

Cree returns to the kitchen and clears the plates, her secret still caged in her breast.

By the time Russ is done on the phone and sending out emails, Cree is in bed pretending to be asleep.

Chapter 37

Truth Be Told

Months go by. Cree still has yet to tell Russ; her guilt grows. Cree's fear of spoiling their renewed bliss is overcome only by this growing sense of injustice in their marriage. Russ seems to be getting everything he wants; intimacy, support, and peace in his home. To beat all, Russ gets to be Moses and lead a mass exodus of his people out of economical bondage and into the "promised land." While Cree is back at the office, running the Icarus foundation – instead of singing, and then Russ has the gall to ask for *more*, which triggers Cree to finally spill the truth about Meryl.

They're in their bedroom hurrying in and out of closets and drawers, getting dressed for the ground breaking ceremony of New Phillip's Community.

Cree comes out of the closet smoothing her dress, but then looks up and nearly hits the floor when she sees Russ now in a different colored suit than the one she'd dressed for. "*Honey*," Cree stamps in mach terror. "What happened to the grey? And the red tie?"

A smiling Russ raises the forearm of his blue suit to fasten a cuff link, saying, "Seemed a bit cliché, I thought."

Cree stands next to her husband in the mirror and floats a palm forward at the travesty of their reflection. "Look at us! That's a clash I can actually hear, Russ. Do ya hear it?" Russ laughs from his belly. Cree contains her giggles in order to stay in character. For a calm reset, Cree takes a deep breath and draws the five fingers of an open hand together to a point. "Is that what you're wearing, Russ? Are ya sure," she toys, and then marches back to the closet to change into an aggreable dress.

Russ practices for photo ops in the mirror, squaring his shoulders and turning his torso, even shaking an imaginary hand in the mirror. He hears more of Cree's playful banter coming from her closet. Russ adds some banter of his own. "You know what, you can go 'head on somewhere with that attitude, babe. In fact, go on and step through that mirror and send back Lulu." Russ chuckles and then starts counting off a list. "Hell, the way you talk about Lulu, she don't nary complain; we'd probably be getting in a quicky right about now," Russ kids. "O'girl was trying to give me another baby after just two days instead of ten years, shiiid." Cree shows up in Russ's periphery; he sees her standing in her closet doorway, but Russ misses the fact that she's fuming and staring him down; he notices the dress. "That dress, babe, whew!" Russ doesn't notice the silent treatment until Cree goes to the vanity and he hears nothing from her but the swishing of her dress and slip as she walks by.

Cree avoids Russ's reflection in the mirror while she replaces her earrings with a set that matches her new choice of dress.

"Cree," Russ says, fixing her in his eyes. "Don't tell me you're jealous of someone who isn't even real–"

"–And yet you accept that reality when it proves that you didn't have an affair with Charlene?"

Russ glitches noticeably. "Look, Cree, even if Lulu did exist, you'd be jealous of no one other than of yourself, babe," he says, with a grin of embarrassment. Russ adds, "Do *I* ever get offended, with all the wise-cracks you make about me versus Bachelor Russ?"

She's back to the silent treatment. Cree adorns her neck in pearls and fastens the bracket without a word, as if she sits in an empty house.

It's their first argument since the coma, and Russ seems all for it. "I know what it is," says Russ, as he adjusts the noose of his gold tie. "It's not about Lulu at all, is it? Our marriage has been a thing of beauty for a while now. We haven't had one argument. All of a sudden I mention children and now look at us. This is the thing that drove us apart in the first place, if we're being honest. You always say *sure* you want more children, but here you are, again – at the mere mention – engaging in sabotage, so you can blame not having more children on something other than your own selfishness."

Cree gets up from her vanity stool and pivots, showing Russ that her beautiful, calm face glistens with trails of tears. Emotionally, she's deteriorating fast. Her knees shake; a hand presses into her gut to steady her words. "The last time I was pregnant... I was carrying the child of my rapist."

"Say what...?" A gut-punched Russ stoops over and looks up with eyes wide but lifeless. "*What?* Cree... What're you saying," says Russ, as he rises to her and catches Cree in his arms because she can no longer stand on her own. Russ sits Cree on the bed, where she lay over on her side because she lacks the strength to sit upright. Her outpouring of sorrow won't let in a word of explanation. Russ lays facing her, his mouth quiet, his mind as loud as a packed auditorium with all the questions. He lays quietly in his navy-blue tailored suit, and Cree in a mint green marling wrap dress, their foreheads touching, Russ pets Cree's face and strokes her hair for what seems to linger on for an eternity.

Russ throws out guesses to save her from speaking. "Was it that personal trainer from a while back that made you uncomfortable? Was it Bruce? I've heard of this happening to other people, the wife and mother keeps a rape secret as some attempt to protect the emotional wellbeing of the family, or the reputation of her husband. I don't know what makes you think you couldn't come to me, or that I would put something like my reputation above you... So, what happened to it, was it a miscarry? Abortion?"

"She was born." Lying sideways on their marriage bed, Cree says, "Meryl is not your child." She cries audibly. "I'm sorry Russ. I'm sorry." Russ's eyes close as tight as fists. The man whimpers and pulses under Cree's embrace, but he does not try to get out from under it. Cree continues to explain the circumstances in whispers, asking herself the questions he would ask if he were capable. "Did I know, going in, that Meryl wasn't yours? No. Even after Meryl was born I still didn't know until she was about two years old and her features started coming in... I couldn't even lie to myself. Meryl is the spitting image of... him."

Russ rolls away and sits on the edge of the bed, his back to Cree as he says. "Around six years old, for me, is when I started having real doubts. I'd see parents out with their children, their mini versions of themselves. As hard as I tried, I could never see myself in her," Russ cries. Still sitting on the edge of the bed with his back to Cree, Russ says, "I'm sorry for what happened to you, Cree. It's not your fault, but keeping it from me, is."

"Russ," she cries. She pulls the bedsheets to wipe her eyes. "I'm so sorry, and although, I know that what I'm about to say doesn't make up for it at all, but not pursuing music was my private penance for misleading you..." Cree reaches a hand out. "Russ, please forgive me. I love you. I loved you from the beginning. We may have had a shotgun wedding, but it felt like a dream come true for me, trying on gowns, planning this big beautiful wedding with a groom that's tall, gorgeous and—"

"—and Rich..." Russ still sits on the edge of the bed, his back to Cree.

There's a moment of silence. "*Yes*, rich," Cree says. "I'm not going to lie about that. With you, everything I watched momma scrape and scratch for, would be a given for me and that little baby growing inside of me. I wouldn't *have* to work – I wouldn't *have* to run that hamster wheel. But I *did* work. I worked to prove my worth in this marriage."

"If you knew how I felt about you," says Russ. "And still do – even in this moment – you'd know that you don't have to prove a thing to me." Russ sighs. "Our relationship wasn't exclusive at the time Meryl was conceived, so don't you think it was odd how I never questioned whether the child was mine? This may come as a shock to you, Cree, but growing up was tough for me, being an only. Times are a little different now for Meryl, but for me, growing up black and well-off in the nineties, you were a loner. Going to private school, being one of few blacks – where the other black students didn't really care about being friends with each other; they were vying for their place among the white kids. That's why I really pushed the issue to get dad to send me to a public high school and even there, I was rejected by the black students because I wasn't *real* enough. I didn't even have a relationship with cousins my age. Because we had money and they were struggling, our extended family treated us like we were a different race, and of course, the feeling was mutual because my folks seem to think they're better than regular folk. I've always tried to prove them wrong with that. Our relationship did that. We may not have gotten together in the traditional way, but you won them over with your love and humility. You've been an asset to the company, and your help is really the thing that made daddy let me loose at the head of the company at such a young age; it's not so much what he saw in me, it's what he saw in us. But for me, also… becoming a fixture in your life made your friends my friends, your family became my family. It gave me the tribe I'd always been looking for. The acceptance from my own people that I'd been always seeking, came through you. We may have married for the wrong reason, Cree, but we eventually *made* it the right reason."

Cree feels the weight lift. Her heart swells to the size of a basketball in her chest, but she gives nothing more than a deep sigh. Her sad tears are now blessed tears running down her cheeks. She comes around to Russ and takes his hands in hers. Russ stands and lifts her chin with the crook of his finger, but does not kiss her. He says, "Alright," and sighs. "We've got a groundbreaking to go to."

Cree frowns, "Really, Russ? Table *this* discussion?"

Russ nods with an uneven brow. "It's been tabled our whole marriage, babe. One afternoon more, won't hurt."

"Ok," Cree relents. "But my makeup is a mess."

Russ turns to go bring the car around while Cree sits at the vanity one last time to retouch her makeup. Cree stops him, "Russ?" Their eyes meet in the mirror. "When do we tell Meryl?"

Russ's head dips with wide eyes, as if he can't believe the question, but he answers anyway. "She's only twelve," he says, and leaves.

Hurriedly, Cree pats witch hazel around her eyes to flatten the puffiness and then, to clear the redness, Cree uses eyedrops. She's blinking rapidly and her eyes are blurry, so what appears in the mirror, Cree believes it is but an aberration of her blurry vision.

It appears to be a blurry Lulu on the other side of the mirror, as if she's purchased this very home in the other world. She stands with her arms folded, studying, evaluating. She has a slight baby bump. As if addressing people beyond the mirror's edges, Lulu squints and shakes her head, as if disapproving of this location for her vanity. Lulu doesn't say a word, she points to relocate the mirror to the left wall. Bachelor Russ who now wears a wedding band, comes up and hugs Lulu from behind as the mirror is being moved, their image sliding out of view, as the blur from Cree's eyedrops drain out of her eyes, and the image is gone. Cree is left staring at herself, her heart thumping.

Epilogue

With Russ's blessing and wholehearted support, Cree steps down from the Icarus foundation and appoints a successor. She seeks out the V.V.S. Quartet, with the songs she'd memorized from the other world, which she now realizes were songs she'd written back in college. By the band's estimation, the lyrics, today, should still hold.

Cree adopts the stage name Lulu McQueen and helps them recreate the sound for which the other world coined the term Neo-Pop fusion. In Cree's imaginary world, the unique sound had produced a one-hit album, but proved to be nothing more than a passing fad – a fad they'll try passing here in this world.

Judging by Lulu's failures in the other world, there was never a better time than now, for Cree to pursue her dream. The wealth couldn't change her now, nor would she be as young and foolish to squander it. She is too solidly herself to let the industry influence her to put anything up her nose besides fresh air.

She and the band have regular rehearsals to refine their sound until they're performance ready. Next they test out their sound on live audiences at bars and taverns. Quickly, they gain popularity just as Cree starts developing her own baby bump.

One night, they're performing and Cree spots Detective Ryan sitting at a table by himself, checking his watch. He wears a wedding band. Perhaps, in this world, he never divorced his wife. Cree sings on, while trying not to stare.

Detective Ryan waves toward the entrance, signaling his location. It's the date he'd been waiting on. He slides out a chair for Tina. Before she takes the seat, Detective Ryan kisses her mouth in the middle of the packed tavern, just as Cree finishes the song. The audience applauds. Russ, not to be outdone by any fan, stands up on the seat of his chair, his thumb and forefinger forming a letter C, inserted between his lips, through which he blows a piercing whistle.

About The Author

Son of a carpenter and a nanny, Rod Palmer was born in a historic Gullah Geechie community in Charleston, SC. He received his degrees in creative writing and Afro studies at the University of South Carolina. Currently he resides in Europe where he is a dedicated husband and girl-dad, enjoys travel and writing the next novel.

His other works are:

A Pimp In The Pulpit
The Work-Husband Caper
The Harvest
Karma Wears Versace
KWV II: Man Eater
The Waymaker